# Amulet of Aria

## Jeffrey Poole

# Jeffrey Poole's Epic Fantasy Books
## Bakkian Chronicles:

*The Prophecy*
*Insurrection*
*Amulet of Aria*
*Disneyland Debacle (short story)*
*Winter Wonderland (short story)*

## Tales of Lentari
### (coming soon in newly edited editions)

*Lost City*
*Something Wyverian This Way Comes*
*A Portal for Your Thoughts*
*Thoughts for a Portal*
*Wizard in the Woods*
*Close Encounters of the Magical Kind*
*The Hunt for Red Oskorlisk (short story)*
*May the Fang be With You (Pirates trilogy #1)*
*The Hammer is Strong with This One (Pirates #2)*
*These are Not the Stones You're Looking For (Pirates #3)*
*Blast from the Past*

## Dragons of Andela
### (coming soon in newly edited editions)

*Harness the Fire*
*Strike the Spark*
*Clear the Water*

# Mysteries by J.M. Poole
## The Corgi Case Files Series

16 delightful cozy mystery novels featuring corgi
sleuths, Sherlock and Watson

# Amulet of Aria

Bakkian Chronicles, Book III

Jeffrey Poole

Secret Staircase Books

Amulet of Aria

Published by Secret Staircase Books, an imprint of
Columbine Publishing Group, LLC
PO Box 416, Angel Fire, NM 87710



Book layout and design by Secret Staircase Books
First Secret Staircase paperback edition: December, 2022
First Secret Staircase e-book edition: December, 2022

* * *

**Publisher's Cataloging-in-Publication Data**

Poole, J.M.
Amulet of Aria / by J.M. Poole.
p. cm.
ISBN 978-1649141187 (paperback)
ISBN 978-1649141194 (e-book)

1. Steve Miller (Fictitious character)—Fiction. 2. Lentari
(Fictitious location)—Fiction. 3. Epic fantasy fiction 4. Dragons and
mythical creatures—Fiction. I. Title

The Bakkian Chronicles Trilogy : Book III.
Poole, J.M., Bakkian Chronicles epic fantasy series.

BISAC : FICTION / Fantasy/Epic.

813/.54

*For Giliane —*

*Insert thoughtful quotation here …*

*:)*

# Acknowledgements

Once again, I need to take the time to thank a few people who were instrumental to the creation of this book.

I have to thank my beta readers: Scott (IndieBookBlogger), Jamie (my sister from another mother), and various family members (including my own mother) who sacrificed their personal time to read through it and tell me where I went horribly wrong. In addition, the beta readers from Secret Staircase Books: Susan Gross and Sandra Anderson—Thank you!

Finally, to my wife Giliane, who made (strongly encouraged) me to rewrite several chapters and completely scrap the last chapter to get it right. Yes, it's much better now, thank you. :) Love you always & forever, babe!

# Table of Contents

# Chapter 1 - Grand Canyon Railway

Clouds of fluffy white steam billowed up from the passing locomotive as it traveled deeper into the dense forest. The steam engine wound its way through a variety of evergreen trees, including ponderosa pines, aspens, Douglas-firs, and oak as it journeyed farther north. Most people were under the false impression that Arizona was comprised of nothing but cacti and arid deserts, but surprisingly, six national forests called the Grand Canyon State home. Kaibab National Forest, the one the train was presently traveling through, was located in the northern part of the state, and stretched across an area of nearly one and a half million acres.

The temperature was a very pleasant 65°F, and with the train traveling at a steady 40 mph, a cool refreshing breeze found its way through the cabin's interior. Enhancing the picturesque voyage was the fact that it was now the middle of fall, and many of the trees were turning various shades of red, orange, and gold. Not an empty seat could be found on the entire train; unusual since this particular day was a Tuesday. Tourists from all across the country were clutching their digital cameras and fancy cell phones, eagerly waiting for the train to arrive at one of the Seven Natural Wonders of the World: The Grand Canyon.

Three such visitors were aboard the train, their first trip together to see Arizona. Both adults had already witnessed the beauty the majestic canyons offered, but the young man sitting next to them had not. He was dressed in a light grey sweatshirt, khaki tee shirt, and blue jeans, as he sat with his face plastered against the window. The woman sitting next to him had her smart phone out and was carrying on a text conversation with her sister. Sitting next to her was a man who was deeply focused on the tablet device sitting on his lap. One of his favorite games, Ornery Ornithoids, had just recently undergone another update, opening up an additional fourteen levels of addictive porcine-bashing fun. He, and presumably millions of other worldwide fans, had been devoting huge chunks of time playing each new level while striving to get a score worthy of three stars.

Admitting the purple pigs had won this round for now, he turned to the boy sitting next to his wife. He grinned as he recalled the battle of wills they'd had earlier. It had taken them nearly thirty minutes to convince the teenager that the great metal beast was not some mutant form of land dragon and was perfectly safe to board. Once the train departed, however, all traces of nervousness vanished as multi-hued trees and various wildlife started passing by the windows.

"Look! What is that up there on the top of that tree?"

"Good eyes. That's a bald eagle."

"What is an eagle?"

"It's a bird," Sarah answered, looking up to smile at Mikal. "Umm, a kyte. A big one."

"Bald?" Mikal squinted at the large white-headed bird. "There are no feathers on its head?"

Steve suppressed a chuckle. "Actually, there are. In this case 'bald' refers to white."

"Why not just call it the big white-headed bird?"

"Doesn't really have the same ring to it, does it?"

Mikal turned from the window and grinned at Steve. "I guess not." He raised an eyebrow, a habit he had picked up from his honorary aunt, Annie. "Are we there yet?"

"Would you relax? I told you, this ain't no dragon."

"I still do not understand why Sarah could not simply teleport us there."

"Careful," Sarah cautioned. "Keep your voice down, Mikal."

"Sorry. Would it not have been easier for you to just, well, take us straight there?"

"Half the fun is getting there. Besides," Steve argued, "everyone loves train rides."

An hour later, the three of them were slowly making their way to the first observation point. However, the narrow ledge of rock was standing room only; there simply wasn't any space. Kids were yelling and shouting as their parents all jockeyed for the best vantage point to snap a picture.

"Come on," Sarah suggested. "Let's find someplace a little quieter."

Mikal turned to follow her. He and Sarah followed single file behind Steve as he forged a path through the bustling crowds, continuing to head east. Several minutes later they found what they were looking for: a small, relatively obscure lookout point. Mikal reached out and tapped Sarah on her shoulder.

"Could you please get her now?"

Sarah handed her camera to the boy. "Okay, this should be secluded enough. I'll be right back." Casting a quick look about to make sure no one was watching, she vanished.

"I still say they should have allowed her on that train thing," Mikal muttered.

Steve nodded his head in agreement. "Just between you and me, I was ready to try anyway. What were they going to do, kick us off?"

"Sarah would not have approved."

Steve sighed. "No, she most certainly wouldn't have. That's why Peanut was left in Phoenix."

Sarah appeared, holding a wriggling corgi in her arms.

"Hi Peanut!" Mikal walked over to the struggling dog and

gave her a friendly pat. Sarah gently lowered the dog to the ground and handed the leash over to him. She looked at her husband.

"Have you bought any water yet?"

Steve shook his head and twisted to look back at the distant tourist-infested gift shop. He let out a massive sigh. "No. Couldn't you just, you know, zip back here and pick up a few bottles if we need them?"

"That'd be a waste of jhorun and you know it."

Steve sighed. "Fine. Wait here. I'll go get us a few."

Two hours later, the three of them were carefully picking their way along Rim Trail, one of several day hikes available for exploration. Thankfully, the vast majority of tourists were more interested in taking pictures than going for a hike, so there weren't many people on the trails with them. In fact, they hadn't seen another person for nearly half an hour.

"There's nothing like this back home, that's for sure."

Steve clapped a hand on Mikal's shoulder. "It's breathtaking, isn't it? You want to know what still freaks me out?"

Mikal turned questioningly to his bodyguard. "What?"

Steve gestured to the sheer precipice a scant five feet away. "There are no freakin' hand rails!"

Mikal edged closer and leaned out to take a look. He whistled. The ground was hundreds of feet below. "I would not want to go over that edge."

"That's my point. There's nothing to prevent someone from falling over."

"Are you afraid someone will push you off the trail?"

"Well, no."

"Are you afraid you will lose your balance?"

"No."

"Maybe he's afraid a big gust of wind will whisk him over the edge," Sarah suggested, with a wry smile.

Mikal turned to his foster mother and grinned. It was a well-known fact in the Miller household that Steve was not a fan of heights. He looked back at Sarah and winked.

"Tristan was telling me there are some terrible storms in Arizona. They might have strong enough winds to push you over."

Steve glanced up at the sky. "Not likely. There aren't any clouds, so no storms today. And don't think I don't know what you're trying to do."

Mikal cleared his throat. "These storms, Tristan said, are very dangerous. There are no warnings. No one is able to see anything. You could walk right off the path and plummet to your death!"

Steve hesitated a moment, then much to Sarah's delight, he glanced over his shoulder and cautiously checked the area.

"What else can you tell us about these freak storms, Mikal?" Sarah asked him, winking back at the grinning teenager. "How did Tristan hear about them?"

"He always researches the places that we go, to make sure it is safe. He goggled it."

Sarah let out a laugh. "He did what?"

Mikal looked confused. "That is what he told me. He goggled it."

Steve chuckled. "By that I take it he Googled it?"

"Google. Aye. Google, goggle, same thing."

"Not quite, kiddo," Steve laughed and then he paused. "Er, is there anything else we need to know about these storms? You're totally making this up, right?"

"I am not. It's called a boob." Mikal couldn't stop the smile from spreading across his face.

"A *what?*"

Mikal's face flushed red. "He said these storms are called boobs."

"He had to have gotten that wrong," Steve insisted.

"He did not. I did not believe him, either."

Steve turned to his wife. "Is he serious? Why would someone call a storm a boob?" Now he couldn't stop the grin from forming.

Sarah sighed. "Boys. Hold still." She spun her husband around and unzipped the backpack's large interior compartment. She pushed aside the picnic lunch she had carefully packed and pulled out Steve's tablet. She tapped the Internet application and waited for the search engine homepage to appear. She typed in her search query and waited.

"There it is. It's actually spelled H-A-B-O-O-B. There's an 'h' in front of it."

Skeptical, Steve took the tablet from his wife and read aloud the entry for the unusually named storm. "A haboob is a thick dust storm commonly found in the deserts of Arabia and India." He handed the tablet back to his wife and rounded on Mikal. "Hear that, squirt? Nice try."

"Ummm, they have them in Arizona," Sarah corrected, reading a recent news story from a Phoenix news channel. "I never realized that's what they're called. Anyway, Tristan is right. Arizona does get these dangerous storms. However, only in desert areas."

Steve visibly relaxed. That was good to know. He had no desire to stumble blindly about the trails up here with the possibility of a dust storm appearing out of nowhere.

"I really do like that thing," Mikal said as he watched Sarah stow the tablet back into the backpack.

"My tablet? You think you want one now? Those are expensive little toys, you know."

"Like we have to worry about that, what with discovering all those accounts your grandparents had set up," Sarah chided.

"That's not an excuse to just throw money away."

"Did I say we were throwing money away when you bought yours? I told you then that I didn't think it was a practical device, but I relented. And I also told you, you may recall, that it would only be a matter of time before Mikal would want one, too. As long as we're talking about getting tablets, I think I might like —"

"Hey! You said you like your smart phone, and that the tablet was too big, remember?"

"I'm just teasing you, honey. I'm fine. I'm just saying that our checking account alone has two commas in it. Two commas! And that's just the checking account. We have accounts in—"

"Alright, alright, we'll talk about it when we get back."

Steve pretended to adjust the straps of his pack as he discreetly watched Mikal and his wife give each other a high five.

* * *

"What do you think would happen to us if we get lost out here?" Mikal wondered aloud, munching away on his salami and cheese sandwich.

Sarah turned to him as she nibbled on a pretzel. "Do you think we *could* get lost out here?"

The teen took another bite of his sandwich and slowly looked around the clearing where they were having their lunch. Three picnic tables, two trash cans, and a small barbecue, cemented in place, met his eyes. He turned to look out at the canyon, which stretched over twenty miles across at its widest point. Silently, Mikal turned his eyes skyward and he scanned the horizon. Several large black birds circled lazily, far overhead. Out here, it was easy to believe they were the only three people who existed on this world.

"Easily."

"That's not gonna happen, sport."

"I realize the chances are unlikely," Mikal began, taking a sip from his bottle of water, "but it is a possibility, right? Are you not worried?"

"Not in the slightest. Here's why. First," Steve ticked the points off on his fingers, "all you have to do is follow the trails. Eventually they'll lead you back to the main information center."

Mikal looked back at the trail behind them and grinned sheepishly. Why hadn't he thought of that?

"Second," Steve continued, "all of our phones, yours included, have built in GPS capabilities."

Mikal nodded. Having been only recently introduced to the mechanical magic of GPS, the thought hadn't occurred to him.

"And third, you're forgetting about our secret weapon which will guarantee we never, ever get lost."

"What secret weapon?" Mikal wanted to know, surprised he was not aware of what his bodyguard was referring to.

Steve pointed at Sarah. "Her."

Realization dawned. Sarah could teleport them to any

destination she had previously visited. The only thing she needed to perform a successful teleportation jump was an image of the destination; the starting point was irrelevant. Mikal sighed. If Tristan were here, he would have had to endure another lecture about how future Lentarian monarchs should really take the time to consider all options before speaking out. Depressed, he stared at the ground.

"Don't worry about it," Sarah offered, giving Mikal a pat on his shoulder as she stood up. "Why do you look so dejected?"

"Tristan is always telling me I need to think about what I should say before I actually say it."

"Don't sweat it," Steve said jovially, holding out a hand to pull Mikal to his feet. "We think you're doing great. Tristan is hard on you 'cause he wants what's best for you. You're a future king. Kings are supposed to be smarter than everyone else."

"Really? What happens if I am not?"

Steve grinned. "Fake it. They'll never know."

Both Mikal and Sarah laughed.

"Come on." Steve pulled out a padded disc from his pack. "Let's go back to that small glade we found. I'd like to see how well you're doing with Peanut. You two are definitely getting good. Besides, if you're serious about going to that canine agility competition in Sacramento next month, then you need to be certain both of you are at your best."

Mikal caught the disc one handed as Steve threw it his way. He expertly spun the disc around his index finger. Peanut, who was napping on her back in the warm sunshine, all four paws sticking straight up, was instantly on her feet. She barked enthusiastically as she ran circles around Mikal.

"Don't throw that thing until we're all well away from the rim of the canyon," Sarah cautioned.

Moving from the canyon's edge, Steve watched as Mikal skillfully spun the disc in multiple directions. Belying the nature of her short legs, Peanut zipped by him at breakneck speeds. Steve didn't know how she did it, but she always managed to catch the disc just before it made contact with the ground.

"Want to see some of the new throws we learned?" Mikal asked, picking up the disc that Peanut deposited at his feet.

"Absolutely! Show me what you got, kid."

Mikal placed Peanut in a sitting position, backed at least ten feet away from her, and flipped the disc end over end at Peanut. Without missing a beat, the corgi briefly rose up on her hind legs and effortlessly caught the disc.

"Whoa! How did you…? Do that again."

Mikal repeated the trick, this time from a distance of about fifteen feet. Peanut's paws didn't leave the ground. She arched her neck up and snagged the disc from the air. Mikal was ecstatic.

"That's my pretty girl! Good job, Peanut!"

The corgi's short stump of a tail wiggled happily back and forth, but she did not rise from her seated position; Mikal had yet to release her. The teenager looked back at Steve and grinned.

"What do you think? That was the butterfly throw."

"Very impressive! So how long did it take for you to teach that to her?"

"Not long. It is just a matter of timing."

"Do all those special throws and catches have unique names?" Sarah asked, sitting nearby on a flat rock.

"Aye, they do," Mikal confirmed.

"How many have you taught her?"

"Present count is ten."

Peanut was still holding the disc firmly in her mouth when both of her ears suddenly jumped straight up. The disc dropped, forgotten, to the ground. Her nose angled up as she sampled the air. Moments later her hackles rose and she softly growled a warning.

"What's the matter with her?" Sarah asked, rising to her feet. "Does she smell something?"

"What's the matter, girl? What do you smell?" Mikal asked the dog, briefly glancing down at her before swinging his gaze around the picnic area. Nothing appeared out of the ordinary to him either.

"I don't see anything." Steve stood up on his tiptoes to peer farther down the trail. "She has to smell something.

Probably some type of animal. I know there's lots of wildlife around here."

"Could be a serpent," Mikal suggested.

"If it's a serpent," Sarah began, "then this vacation is over and we are *so* out of here."

Peanut's soft growl suddenly switched to a menacing one. Whatever it was, it was coming closer.

"I don't know," Steve confessed, unable to spot anything dangerous in the area. "Maybe it's—"

All three humans clapped their hands over their ears as a loud shriek shattered the solitude. Even Peanut was whining as the earsplitting wail drove everyone to the ground.

Steve couldn't hear himself swear, let alone hear his wife scream in pain. He had his fingers jammed in his ears as far as they would go, noticing both his wife and Mikal had done the same thing. Using every ounce of strength he had, he forced his right eye to open a crack. A migraine had sprung up and all he wanted to do was to curl up into a ball and keep both eyes screwed shut. His eye cast about haphazardly as it searched for the source of the shriek. There! What was that? Even as he blinked through tears of pain, he was able to see something sitting on the branch of the closest tree. It was an ugly gray color and the size of a German shepherd, but had a pair of leathery bat-like wings. The body resembled that of a primate, while its head was vaguely humanoid in appearance.

Whatever it was, it had to go. Steve held out a hand and conjured a swirling ball of fire the size of a basketball. The chaser hesitated a moment before speeding off toward the creature. Intending to frighten away rather than kill, Steve directed the fireball over to the creature's right, figuring it should miss the thing by a few feet. However, the sight of the ball of fire streaking toward it caused the creature to leap off the branch and fly off to the right as well. It leapt directly into the path of the chaser.

The agonizing shriek tapered off as the creature became engulfed in flames and fell toward the ground. Faster than a burning meteor disintegrating in earth's atmosphere, the creature crumbled into ash and fluttered away on the wind before it could strike the ground.

Steve pushed himself to his knees and sat on his haunches. He gave himself a few seconds for the ringing in his ears to stop before he crawled over to his wife and pulled her upright.

"You okay?"

Sarah pressed both hands against her temples. "What *was* that thing? Where'd it go?"

"I, uh, hit it with a chaser."

"You did what? Honey, what if that was some endangered species?"

"I didn't mean to. I threw a chaser at it hoping it'd fly off. Instead, the damn thing flew right into it."

"It flew? What'd it look like?"

"Like an ugly gray monkey with wings."

"Monkeys don't have wings."

"Thanks, I'm aware."

Sarah turned to give Mikal a hand up. "Are you okay?"

The teen boy was still rubbing his ears. "I am fine. What was that noise? I could hear it even when my ears were covered." Suddenly remembering that he had been playing with Peanut, he jerked his head around looking for his furry companion. "Peanut? Where are you?"

"She's right over there. She's fine."

Mikal spotted the corgi sniffing all that remained of the strange creature, a small pile of black ash.

"Peanut, *off.* Leave that stuff alone."

Upon hearing the command, Peanut abandoned her investigation of the strange substance and came bounding toward them. However, another strange scent manifested, bringing the dog to a stop. Once again, she growled as she turned to face the opposite direction.

Off in the distance, and closing rapidly, three more of the strange flying creatures were seen soaring over the massive canyon, heading straight toward them. Screeching animatedly, all three of the gray creatures adjusted their flight paths as they were spotted. The flying monkey in the front of the group opened its mouth, ready to begin its paralysis-inducing shriek.

"What's the word?" Steve asked his wife, not taking his

eyes off the rapidly approaching creatures. "Still want me to treat them as though they are endangered species?"

"Absolutely not! I don't want to hear that noise again. Do something!"

Eyes hardening, Steve waved his right arm, generating three large chasers. He flung them straight at the flying monsters and watched as they sped unerringly toward their targets. The lead monkey screeched in anger and reversed its course.

The monsters took off in three different directions. Having been given the order to pursue and eliminate, the chasers parted ways and sped after their targets. One right after the other, the targets were hit. Within seconds, all three of the grey monsters were engulfed in flames and turned to ash.

Sarah stood up and brushed bits of leaves and twigs off her jeans. "That's it, it's time to go. We're leaving, right now."

Without saying a word, Mikal leaned down and picked up the end of Peanut's leash. Steve hastily packed up the rest of their belongings and stowed them in the pack.

"We need to talk to Tristan. I don't know what those monkey things are, but I do know they are not native to this area. I think they were Lentarian."

# Chapter 2 - Cookbook Nook

Lia Manning approached the heavy wooden door and scowled as she shuffled the large load she was carrying. Noticing that her mega ninety-six ounce Big Swig was starting to slide off the stacks of books she was carrying, threatening her with a headache-inducing caffeine-free day, she lurched forward to jam the books against the closed door. Deftly snatching her precious cherry soda before it could complete its trek to the ground, she grinned. It was all in the reflexes.

Her cell phone rang.

"God Bless America. Seriously?"

Realizing there was no way she'd be able to answer the call unless she was willing to sacrifice her soda (let's face it, she'd sacrifice the stack of books first), she frantically pushed the heavy door open and plopped the awkward load down in the bin just inside the door. Hurrying over to the alarm's keypad, she punched in the disarm code while simultaneously setting her drink down on the counter. One hand now free, she shrugged her right shoulder and caught her purse as it went flying off her arm. She pulled out her cell and glanced at the display. She sighed. Her second job was calling. It was time to put on her receptionist hat.

"Thank you for calling the Computer Handyman, this is Lia, how may I help you?"

The business she managed, the Cookbook Nook, also housed a second business, one that wouldn't be apparent to the casual observer. Whereas the specialty kitchen store was owned and operated by Sarah Miller, the second business belonged to her husband, Steve. It was his suggestion that she field any afterhours tech calls to make some extra cash.

Steve used the store for his own business, even though it had nothing to do with his wife's. He was a computer tech, and a damn good one, even though she'd deny that statement under the most heinous of torture. He had personally rescued her own laptop after she had killed it a few times playing Terra Troubles, a massive online game. Steve had set up the shop's wireless network, encrypted it, and even set up the phone system. Sarah let her husband use her office whenever he needed. While the occasions were rare, every so often one of his clients would want to meet in person so he would use the store. As a result, the shop periodically received mail addressed to "The Computer Handyman." It was a title that suited him perfectly.

Focusing her attention on the call, Lia's eyebrows shot up as one of Steve's clients had the tenacity to gripe at her before she had her morning caffeine fix. Unfortunately, she knew this voice well. It was the cantankerous Mr. Summers, an arrogant octogenarian who was regrettably one of Steve's oldest and best clients. The complaint today was that, apparently, his email program wasn't delivering his emails (again) and he naturally wanted it fixed. Yesterday.

"Hello Mr. Summers. I'm sorry to hear about your email. Are you still using Speedy Mail? Okay, perfect. Are you connected to the Internet? Remember, your computer is old. Haven't I been trying to get you to replace it? Anyway, think of it like you. You don't just spring out of bed, do you? Give it some time. Close everything out. Now, click your mail icon and wait. Don't click anything else, just wait. It's working now? That's fantastic. You have yourself a good morning."

Rolling her eyes, she again questioned the logic of handling Steve's tech calls. At least she was getting compensated for it. In fact, with the extra money that she earned by covering the calls, it more than paid for her entire cell phone bill. Besides, it was rare that she actually had to call Steve; the majority of problems were classified as NBE, or No-Brainer Emergencies. If she could answer the call, great; if not she'd give the client the opportunity to schedule an appointment.

She moved to the bank of light switches and began flipping them on. She then proceeded to awaken the wireless router, enabling Internet access for her customers. Clutching her keys, she walked down the main aisle toward the front door. She sighed. There were already five people outside waiting to come in. So much for a quiet morning. She plastered a smile on her face.

"Good morning! How is everyone today?"

Since accepting this job four years ago, she never would have imagined a specialty kitchen shop in a quiet resort town such as Coeur d'Alene doing quite so well. Sarah Miller had created a store that catered to the kitchen and everything pertaining to it. The shop carried cookbooks, kitchen utensils, and gadgets. Sarah had even installed a small commercial kitchen and work area upstairs for the occasional catering job, custom cake order, or cake decorating class, as the store was known as an authorized distributor for a line of popular cake decorating supplies.

Lia never imagined she would become the manager of the shop when she started working there. She remembered that day well. She had decided a rapid change of pace from her previous employer was needed before someone in that medical office turned up missing. Or dead. There were so many incompetent people at that office that, even if she recalled her past experiences there, she would end up giving herself a headache. Therefore, seeing how she had no desire to see the insides of a jail cell, she tendered her resignation and abruptly left.

In less than an hour, she had found herself on the doorstep of a recently opened specialty store that offered cookbooks and various knick-knacks for the kitchen. The woman that had opened the store was younger than herself; then again, after hitting the dreaded 4-0, most everyone was younger than her these days. She and Sarah became instant friends. Since the store's popularity had been steadily increasing, an extra set of hands was deemed useful, and the rest, as they say, was history.

Lia had been born and raised in Coeur d'Alene. There wasn't anyone in this small town she didn't know. As a result, she couldn't step out of her house without bumping into a friend or someone she knew. In turn, that made dating difficult. She began entertaining the notion of joining an online dating site when she started corresponding with a man via email named Adam. While he lived in Ohio, hundreds of miles from her, once the two of them finally agreed to meet in person, it was love at first sight. Within a month, he had packed all his belongings into his car and had moved to Coeur d'Alene.

It was Lia and Sarah's animated talks about their significant others which prompted the start of their friendship. Same height, same weight, same hair color, many previous employers of the same type. It was eerie! Now, she and Adam were frequent visitors to the huge manor on French Gulf Street. If only she could inherit a house like that!

While she had been unsure at first about working for a friend, her doubts had been quickly put to rest as she learned Sarah was a very gracious, if not firm, employer. Tardiness was not tolerated, nor was laziness, which worked well for Lia as she had never been either. As long as she showed up in plenty of time to open the store, and kept herself busy, she was given free rein to oversee the store.

She logged into the store's online account and printed off the Internet orders. Filling the orders usually took an hour or so, and it would allow her to keep an eye on the customers already in the store, so she abandoned the counter and started moving through the racks. As she pulled books to fill the orders, she caught sight of a familiar black SUV pulling into the parking lot. Sarah got out and opened the hatch. She caught Lia's eye through the window and motioned for help to carry her recent acquisitions into the store. Lia shook her head and mouthed 'customers.' Sarah nodded.

Moments later, a big dark blue quad-cab truck pulled in next to Sarah's SUV. Lia smiled. Steve was here. He'd make sure Sarah didn't have to carry those heavy boxes inside.

They came in together, with Sarah holding open the door for her husband as he was carrying three heavy boxes of books balanced precariously on top of each other.

Lia grinned. "You can make more than one trip, ya know."

Steve peered around the stack of books and grinned back at her.

"Why would I do that when I can get everything in just one?"

"Sooner or later you are going to throw your back out."

"Perhaps." Steve smiled. "But not today."

Lia gestured to the boxes that Steve dumped on the counter. "Whatcha got for me this time?"

Sarah pushed by her husband and opened the first box. "I found some really good foreign cookbooks in Phoenix. I was thinking about starting an International section."

Lia, who fancied herself a decent cook, gleefully rubbed her hands together. "Ooooo, recipes I can't read! Awesome! Let's see what we got. Here's one in French. This one's in Italian. I might have to hold on to that one. What about this one?" Lia squinted at the book. The pictures of the dishes, while intriguing, were unknown to her, as was the language.

"I'm told that one is Romanian," Sarah explained. "I was told it came all the way from Prague. The previous owner told me he took it in trade from a Romanian man who wanted to learn how to cook Chinese food."

"You just made that up."

"Yeah, I did."

Both women laughed as Steve headed up the stairs to the office.

"How was your trip to Arizona? Did you have a great time? How was the Grand Canyon?"

Sarah smiled. "It was a trip I won't soon forget. Steve and I have seen the canyon before, but Mikal hadn't. We caught the Grand Canyon train that departed from Williams. It took us all the way to the south rim. Mikal loved it. He hadn't ever been on a train before."

"But you guys went to Disneyland, right?" Lia was incredulous.

Sarah nodded. "Yes, we did. We tried to get him on the Disneyland Express but he flatly refused. Steve finally convinced him to give the Grand Canyon train a try. Turns out he loved it."

"That kid sure did lead a sheltered life before you adopted him. Where was he from again?"

"Nebraska."

"Ah. 'Nuff said."

Lia pulled out another book and opened it. A slip of white paper fluttered to the ground. She retrieved the paper and handed it to Sarah, but not before she glanced at. It was the sales receipt, dated from last night at seven. Wait. Last night? How could she have made it back so fast? They must have taken a red-eye flight. Admirable. Had she taken a flight that left that late, and then come in this early the following day, she would have been beat. Neither of them, Lia noted, acted like they were tired.

She chalked it up as being yet another quirky observation she had made about this husband-and-wife team and stored it away, not knowing that in less than forty-eight hours, she would be rapidly recalling each and every unusual observation she had ever made about her friends.

"Is it getting hot in here or am I just having a hot flash?"

Sarah paused in her attempt to make room on several shelves. "It is getting a little warm. You can turn on the AC, if you want."

"Hey down there."

Sarah looked up at Steve on the second-floor balcony.

"Hey yourself."

"I wasn't able to talk to Tristan. He's still sick. I don't think that chicken Kiev he ate is sitting well with him. To top it all off, I think he's picked up a cold."

Lia looked up at her boss's husband. Out of the corner of her eye, she saw Sarah silently mouth *calm down*. Funny, he didn't appear agitated to her.

"I told him that he shouldn't trust those microwave dinners. Poor thing. He's probably just trying to give Annie a break."

Lia took a long swallow from her Big Swig. "I knew it. It just goes to show you that you can't leave a man alone in the house without direct female supervision."

Sarah took a sip of her iced tea and nodded. "True story."

"When will she get back?" Lia asked.

"She and Christopher will be back from Sacramento in a couple of days."

"That has to be rough, flying with a two-year-old."

"It's not as bad as you might think," Steve observed, smiling down at the two of them.

"Do you like having your sister living so close to you?" Lia asked, sliding a stack of the new cookbooks into place.

"I do. We have plenty of room on the estate, so it's not like we're intruding on one another."

"When are she and Tristan going to get married?"

Sarah sighed. "It's complicated."

"They have a son together, with another on the way. How complicated could it be?"

"They're together, and that's what's important."

"If you're happy, I'm happy."

"To see them together, I definitely am."

An hour later, Lia watched a dozen women carry their hard plastic totes full of cake decorating supplies into the store and up the stairs. This next cake class was supposed to be devoted to the art of making sugar flowers, but Lia had pulled Sarah aside after this group of students' last class and advised her boss that they were nowhere near ready to tackle the fine art of working with sugar paste. None of the students could properly crumb-coat a cake, as evidenced by the torn and uneven nine-inch rounds that had been presented for inspection at the end of the last class.

"Today, we're going to review the proper procedures for preparing a cake for crumb-coating," Lia began, opening her own decorating kit and taking out her cake leveler. "The first thing we're going to do is turn the cell phones off and put them away." She plastered a neutral expression on her face and waited until the two red-faced teenage girls returned their phones to their purses.

She set the cake leveler to the desired height and indicated the students should follow her lead.

"The first step when making a cake should always be to ensure you're working on a flat surface. As many of you are aware, cakes don't bake evenly, so that's why these guys were invented. See the wire? Make sure both sides are even, and we're ready. All you need is a gentle sawing motion to get through the cake. Don't force it or it'll tear. Jill, your wire is lopsided. That's why your cake now looks like a ramp. Angie, it's a wire, not a knife. You can't force it. That's why your cake ripped. Grab another round and try again."

Fifteen minutes later, a dozen adequately leveled cakes were sitting on the large metal table. The students who had previously destroyed their cakes had been required to frost the remains and add them to the display case downstairs as free samples.

"Now that the cakes are level," Lia continued, "it's time to crumb-coat. Grab your angled spatula and … Sarah? What's the matter?"

Sarah was rifling through her kit and had an irritated expression on her face. "I can't believe I forgot my favorite spatula."

"The purple one?"

"Yes. That irritates the crap out of me. I just used it a few days ago. Let me see if I have a spare in my office. I'll be right back."

Chuckling to herself, Lia returned her attention to her students and started walking amongst them, giving helpful pointers to those who needed the help.

"Crumb-coating means you put a thin layer of buttercream on, then scrape it thin. The frosting is at least an inch thick up here, Mae. Scrape some of that off."

A few minutes later, the office door opened and Sarah came back out. She was holding the purple spatula!

"Thought you said you forgot it."

"Nope, I was wrong. I must have left it in my office."

"Mm-hmm." Lia didn't buy it. Unless she had more than

one of her custom ordered purple-handled spatulas, then something was up. Either that or her friend's memory was shot. How many times had Sarah been missing things only to have them end up in her office? It was always the same thing. Her boss would excuse herself to go search her office and voila! She would come out with whatever she had been searching for.

The class finished with mixed results. While the majority of the students now had a decent understanding of how to prepare a cake to be professionally decorated, there was no hope for the teeny-boppers. They clearly lacked the attention span, as well as the patience level, necessary to pass the class. Lia had already spoken with Sarah about the possibility of refunding the class fee for the two girls. Sarah had agreed to offer store credit in exchange for the girls withdrawing themselves from the class. There was no point in teaching someone who didn't want to learn.

Several hours later, Lia was restocking the local authors section of the store when Sarah approached, keys jingling in her hand.

"I'm meeting Steve for lunch at the Hacienda. Care to join us?"

"What about the store?"

"Just put the 'Out for lunch' sign on the door and lock up."

"Are you driving?"

"It's only a few blocks away. Come on, we'll walk."

"We're not driving?"

"Nope. Walking is good for us. Come on."

Lia grabbed her purse and set the alarm, slapping the 'Out to Lunch' sign on the front door as she left. Locking the door and then verifying it was secure, she turned to see Sarah regarding her.

"What?"

"Would you seriously drive over there?"

Lia pulled out her car keys. "I'm still planning on it."

Sarah snatched the keys from her palm. "Oh no you don't. Come on, it'll be good for us."

"Swell. Let's walk." Automobiles were invented for

the sole purpose of getting you where you need to go, Lia thought angrily. The distance involved was irrelevant.

"Those school cookbooks are really selling well," Sarah commented, slipping her arms through her brown leather Dooney & Bourke backpack purse.

"Some of those recipes are questionable," Lia commented, still a little annoyed she was being forced to walk. "But it's a good idea. Most kids love seeing their names in print. Naturally, every kid's family wants to buy a few copies. We can't keep enough of them on the shelf."

They approached the Mexican restaurant just as Steve pulled up in his truck.

"Afternoon, ladies." Steve reached out and held the door open for them to enter.

"Why thank you, kind sir." Sarah gave him a kiss hello.

Lia strolled past them through the open door and nodded her head in approval. "You're learning."

Steve's hand sprang open. The door had just enough weight to it that it might smack the facetious manager on her backside before she made it indoors, but Sarah caught the door first.

"Hey, play nice."

"She started it!"

Lia cackled as she followed the hostess to a table. "Sweet! Got you in trouble!"

Thirty minutes later, Sarah was going over her plans for the new International section with Lia when her cell rang. She glanced at her husband, who was just finishing up his caramel empanada. She looked down at the display and frowned before answering the phone.

"Hello, Mrs. Vandersloot. How are you today? Mmm-hmm, he's here. He—what? Hold on, let me put him on the phone."

"What's going on?" Steve whispered as he set his soda down. "What'd she call you for?"

He took the cell and held it a few inches from his ear. Mrs. Vandersloot was a little tone deaf and tended to talk in a very loud voice.

"Who is Mrs. Vandersloot?" Lia wanted to know, watching

as Steve winced and held the phone farther away from his ear.

"It's our neighbor. Well, she's the closest thing we have for a neighbor. She's about a mile away from us. She said she thought she saw a bear in her backyard and it was heading for our house. She's calling to warn us."

"A bear? Black or grizzly?"

"She said she thought it had to be a grizzly. It was big, had brown shaggy hair, and it ran off on two legs."

"Bears don't run on two legs," Lia clarified. "They can prop themselves up on their hind legs, maybe even take a step or two, but they don't run on them."

"Well, obviously this one did."

"Okay, thanks for letting us know, Mrs. Vandersloot. I said thanks for letting us know." Steve sighed. "No, I said thanks. Thanks! THANKS!" He snapped the phone closed. "She seriously needs to change out the battery in her hearing aid."

"Did she tell you the bear ran off on its hind legs?"

Steve frowned. "Yeah, she did. Grizzly bears don't run on their hind legs."

Lia sat back in the restaurant booth and smiled victoriously. "See? I told you they didn't."

Ignoring her, Sarah looked at her husband. "Is it possible that one could?"

Steve shook his head and shot a worried glance at his wife. "Something big, with brown shaggy hair, and walking around on two legs? Heading toward the manor? Are you thinking what I'm thinking? Mikal is back there."

"Tristan is there. I'm sure he'll be fine."

"Tristan is sicker than a dog. He can't get more than ten feet away from the toilet."

Lia jammed her fingers in her ears. "TMI people! TMI!"

Steve was still staring at Sarah. "Something's not right. I think … I think I need to go. Now."

"I, uh, will walk you out. Lia, wait here for me, okay?"

"Aren't we leaving?"

"You and I are leaving in just a little bit. Steve is going to check out this bear sighting, but he has to do so now."

Sarah and Steve disappeared around the corner, heading

toward the restrooms and the front entrance. Less than twenty seconds later she was back. Alone.

"What does Steve think he's going to do against a grizzly bear?"

"You'd be surprised," Sarah casually remarked, dropping some cash on the table and tucking the receipt into her purse.

"It's a bear. This is not something he should be messing with. Maybe we should call the Fish and G— what's his truck still doing here?"

"He, er, told me he had to run over to the sporting goods place there and pick up a few things."

Lia spun on her heel and looked across the street at the retail store.

"Why wouldn't he drive over there?"

"Same reason we didn't drive. He wanted to walk."

Something wasn't adding up.

"It sounded like he was in a rush. People who are rushing around don't walk. Besides, what's he picking up? A gun? Steve hates guns."

"True," Sarah agreed. "The store owner is a friend of his. I think he's was going to ask for some advice."

"Mm-hmm."

* * *

"Tristan! Mikal, are you here?"

Steve bolted through the front doors and ran to the rec room. Mikal wasn't there. He took the stairs two at a time as he checked the second floor. Tristan wasn't in the library and Mikal wasn't in his room. The house was deathly quiet.

Red flags were going up left and right. He had to find Mikal! Could Tristan have secured him in the panic room? Located deep underground, and only accessible through his office on the main floor, the manor's newest addition had only been built last year. Steve bolted back down the stairs and headed to his office. He strode to the bookcase against the farthest wall and slid two books, *Demon Gates* and *Hemlock and the Wizard Tower*, two of his favorite fantasy books, off the shelf. He pressed the small button that had been concealed.

There was a soft click and the bookcase swung out just a few inches. Steve gripped the right side of the bookcase and gently pulled it forward, revealing an illuminated tunnel that spiraled downwards.

The lights were on! That meant it had to have been recently used. Steve fervently hoped everything was alright. How had Tristan known to come down here? Had there been an attack? Had he suspected something? Following the tunnel as it spiraled down, he eventually came to a solid steel door. Steve tapped in an access code on the massive door's keypad and waited for the communication panel to appear. He punched in a second code and waited while the screen powered up. Within moments, Tristan was looking back at him from the inside of the room.

"Tristan, it's me. Are you guys okay in there?"

"We are fine, Sir Steve," Tristan assured him. His face was pale and he had beads of sweat dripping down his brow. He looked terrible.

"Stay in there. Take care of Mikal. Or vice versa. Dude, you look like hell."

Tristan mopped his forehead with a back of his sleeve and sat weakly down on the nearest chair.

"As you would say, I look about as well as I feel."

"Just stay sitting before you collapse. Mikal, can you hear me? Did you guys see anything out there?"

The teen's eager face replaced Tristan's on the view screen.

"Aye! Trolls! We saw two of them! We came down here as soon as they were spotted."

Steve cursed; his suspicions confirmed. Their neighbor hadn't seen a grizzly bear but a Lentarian troll! What was it doing here? Better yet, *how in the world* did it get here?

"Stay put. I'll take care of this."

"I can help you! Let me go with you!"

"Not on your life, kiddo. Listen to me. I appreciate the thought, I really do. But your safety is more important than mine. Besides, I can deal with this. Where's Peanut? Is she in there with you guys?"

Mikal nodded, briefly looking off screen. He turned back to face Steve once more. "You need to hurry. I think Peanut has to go to the bathroom."

Steve laughed. "She farted, didn't she?"

Mikal was fanning the air in front of him. "Aye. It smells horrible."

"I'll be back as soon as I can. Promise me you'll stay in there and look after Tristan and Peanut."

The teenager's brow furrowed. The boy clearly did not want to stay put.

"Don't fight me on this, sport. Promise me you'll stay in there until I say the coast is clear."

"Fine, I promise."

"Good. I'll be back as soon as I can."

Steve jogged back up the curved tunnel and emerged into his office. He pushed the bookcase back into the wall and kept pushing until he heard the latch click. With the hidden tunnel secured, he sat down at his desk and brought up the feed from the security system on the flat panel screen opposite his desk. A quick perusal of all twenty-four zones revealed absolutely nothing. If the trolls were out there, they could be hiding just about anywhere on the property. He had to find a way to lure them out into the open, but how?

Wait. Trolls are monsters. They're living creatures. They had to eat, didn't they? Steve abandoned his office and headed into the kitchen. He opened the large stainless steel, Sub-Zero refrigerator and instantly saw the package of rib-eye steaks he and Sarah were planning on grilling that night.

"Sorry, babe." Steve tore off the cellophane wrapping on the expensive package of meat. "It's for a good cause."

He grabbed the double handful of raw meat and bolted out the front door, circumventing Sarah's extensive garden and entering the forest proper. How should he go about this? How do you get a troll to come to you? Hesitating a few seconds as he considered his options, he grinned: an idea had just presented itself. What could it hurt to give it a try? He whistled.

"Rib-eyes! Come and get your lovely, disgustingly raw rib-eyes right here! Dinner time! Where else are you gonna get a free dinner? Come and get it! Fresh meat! Where are you, you ugly sons of —"

Tree limbs cracked; something large was crashing through the trees at an alarming rate. That was quick. Steve dropped the steaks and used his jhorun to ignite both hands. Whatever it was, it was close. Too close. Branches and tree limbs continued to snap loudly as the creature moved closer. Had it smelled the raw meat? What if it was a grizzly after all? He couldn't possibly hurt a bear, but if it came to it then he'd … The winds shifted and all thoughts of wild bear vanished. Unfortunately, he recognized that stench!

"That's it, come and get me, stinky! I don't know how you got here, but you sure as hell —"

Once again, he trailed off as the troll emerged from the trees. It was bigger than he remembered. Much bigger. The troll roared and lunged for him, its long hairy legs closing the distance between them unbelievably fast. Without thinking of what he was doing, he created a jet of fire and refrained from giving it a target, thereby arming himself with the fire rope. Thanks to an Indiana Jones movie marathon a few years ago, as well as a desire to fulfill a lifelong dream of becoming the swashbuckling archaeologist, Steve had become fairly proficient with a bullwhip. Cracking the fire whip above his head, he lashed it out at the rapidly approaching troll.

The ugly brute skidded to a stop, avoiding the strike from the whip, but howling in pain as Steve blasted a jet of fire point blank with his left hand. Roaring in pain, the troll lunged for him again. Steve's right arm snapped up into a defensive block, causing the fire whip to lash out and coil itself around the troll's neck. Surprised, Steve stared at the troll. He wouldn't be able to do that again if his life depended on it.

The troll bellowed with rage and threw itself backwards, violently shaking in an attempt to free itself of the deadly rope of pure fire that was securely fastened about its neck. Steve was forcibly yanked off his feet and dragged along the ground as the huge troll fled the area. Faster and faster it ran as it tried to put as much distance between itself and the flames scalding it. The troll kept digging at its neck as it ran, but only succeeded in singeing its fur whenever contact was made.

Small twigs, dried leaves, and several unidentified substances (that Steve fervently hoped wasn't what he thought it was) flew into his face at an alarming rate. His right arm ached horribly. It felt as though it was going to be ripped from his shoulder! He grunted in pain as the troll jumped over a fallen tree branch in its path. Suddenly, for a few seconds, Steve was airborne. Landing so hard on his chest that his breath whooshed out of him, he glared at the troll. Then he saw something that made his eyes open wide: the troll veered toward several fallen trees. Broken tree limbs were protruding up at all angles. If the troll jumped that, he'd be run through multiple times on the first tree alone. This wasn't good. Fearing for his life, Steve rolled onto his back and yanked back with his right arm.

He was free! That was easy! What happened? Had the troll managed to free itself? Dazed, Steve painfully rolled to his knees and looked at the inert troll. It was standing about ten feet away. Something wasn't right. It was hunched over, or else looking at something on the ground. It had also gone strangely quiet. The troll then toppled over. Right about this time, Steve noticed a misshapen lump on the ground, not too far from his feet. It was the troll's head. Apparently, when he had yanked back on his arm, he had inadvertently blasted jhorun through the rope, decapitating the troll.

"Whoops, my bad."

Another roar met his ears. The second troll had caught up. It emerged from a copse of trees twenty feet behind him. Its black eyes spied Steve. The troll roared again as it lumbered his way.

"I am so done with this. Hasta la vista, sucker."

Steve raised both arms and blasted the troll with everything he had.

During his last trip to Lentari, Steve had experienced firsthand what it was like to battle a troll. He had blasted it with jets of fire but only scored glancing blows and in no way had impeded the troll's furious attack. However, in the last four years, Steve had practiced using his jhorun whenever he could in an effort to increase the intensity, as well as his control, over those blasts. He was a quick learner.

The troll didn't stand a chance. A super-heated wall of flames appeared out of nowhere and encompassed the howling monster. Within moments, the charred corpse had dropped to the ground. Backing well away from the remains of the two trolls, Steve continued to watch the second troll burn, refusing to extinguish the flames. He couldn't let any trace of the creature remain. He eyed the carcass of the headless troll. Pulling his tee shirt up over his nose, he incinerated the first troll as well, including the head. Lucky for him distance wasn't an issue when it came to making something burn. He had just caught a whiff of the smoldering remains and nearly gagged.

He turned and slowly headed back to the mansion.

"Did you get 'em? Tell me you got 'em!"

"Yes, Mikal, no more trolls."

"Woo-hoo! Way to go, Steve! I wish I could have seen it!"

Steve flexed his right arm and rubbed his shoulder. He was definitely going to be feeling the effects of this battle tomorrow. He wished again that Sarah's healing potion worked here, or that Annie could use her healing jhorun on him. However, the only magic that existed here in their world was his and Sarah's jhorun, as well as the portal on the top floor of the manor. No one else could tap into their magical abilities nor would any magically enhanced items work here, and unfortunately that included Sarah's vial of healing elixir that was tucked safely away inside her amulet. Peanut started barking. A car was approaching. Good, Sarah was home.

Sarah was out of the car and inside the house in a flash.

"Is everyone here? Is everyone okay? Steve, what about you? Are you okay?"

"Everyone's good. I'm alright, just a little sore. My right arm hurts, though."

"What happened to your arm?"

"Let's just say I found something that wasn't a bear, and he and I had a disagreement. It was a troll."

"A troll? Here? What on earth is a troll doing here? Are you okay? What happened?"

"He wanted to make me into lunch and I disagreed. Ever see those western movies where the cowboy is lassoed and then dragged along behind a horse? It was something like that."

"So, you took care of the troll? Was there only one?"

Steve shook his head. "Actually, there were two and I stress the word *were*."

"I don't understand how a troll could be here."

"*That* is the million dollar question I'd like an answer to."

Tristan, pale and weak, agreed. "If someone is sending trolls after young Mikal, then the Kri'yans could very well be in danger, too."

Steve scowled. "I want to know how. How in the hell did someone from Lentari manage to teleport something all the way here? Not to mention the fact that they were two huge trolls!"

"Lady Sarah, besides yourself, there is no one who can teleport anything from our world to here, correct?"

"Right. According to the official records kept by the king and queen, there are no other teleporters strong enough to do it. Why do you ask?"

"Because someone has clearly found a way."

"That explains those monkey things in the Grand Canyon," Steve muttered.

Sarah looked at her husband and nodded. "I thought they were Lentarian, too."

Tristan looked from husband to wife in bewilderment. "What monkey things? What has happened? Were you attacked in Arizona?"

Steve nodded. "I was going to tell you, but you were under the weather."

"I was what?"

"Sick," Mikal translated.

"Be that as it may, if you were attacked, I need to know! What happened? What attacked you?"

Steve relayed the events of their hike and finished only when he reported the creatures rapidly disappearing as they caught fire."

"Malwerns."

"Aren't they the flocks of things that were going to attack the castle the last time we were there?"

Sarah nodded. "That's right. I remember. Three groups of them. One was headed to Donlari, one for the castle, and the other unwisely chose to fly over dragon territory."

Tristan sneezed and reached for a tissue.

Steve grimaced. "Seriously, man, you need to get your butt back to bed. You look like crap."

"I do not feel as though I am at my best," Tristan admitted. "What will you do?"

"I think we need to pay a visit to R'Tal. Mikal's parents need to know what's going on here. If we are being attacked here, as you suggested, then there's a strong possibility they might be targeting his parents as well."

"Agreed, Lady Sarah. I will be ready in—"

"Nuh-uh. You're sitting this one out, Tristan." Steve turned to Mikal. "We have to make certain your parents are alright. Somehow, and I don't know how, someone in Lentari is sending these things after you. This has to be dealt with. There."

Mikal's face lit up. "Excellent! Then I can —"

"You can redeem yourself by staying here and giving me your word that you won't try to sneak back," Steve finished for him. Mikal's face fell.

Sarah went over to the boy and hugged him. "Tell you what. The only way in which we'll give permission to use the portal is if something here is threatening you and it's a life-or-death decision."

Mikal smiled. "I understand."

"Wipe that smile off your face, sport," Steve warned. "If you use that key, then you'd better have a dragon on your ass, is that understood? You shouldn't have any need to use it."

"But what if something attacks me here? With Tristan ill, what am I supposed to do?"

Sarah turned to her husband. "What *is* he supposed to do if he's attacked? How do we know this isn't what they want us to do? Split us up? We are his protectors. He has to stay with us."

Mikal whooped aloud and punched his fist triumphantly

into the air. "Finally! I get to accompany you!"

"Okay, okay, you win this round. Just remember, this isn't going to be a vacation," Steve clarified, laying a hand on Mikal's shoulder. "You're going to need to be on your toes the entire time, agreed?"

The teenager glanced down at his feet. "What do my toes have to do with anything?"

"No screwing around, no exploring, no seeking out your friends. This is dangerous, Mikal."

"I understand."

"Good." Steve looked over at his wife. "What do we do about the house? Tristan is too sick to do anything and Annie is due back tomorrow. Think you can convince her to stay with your mom for a few more days?"

Sarah nodded. "Yes, she'll be safer up there. In fact, I'll take Tristan up there, too."

Tristan rose from the couch and protested. "I am not so ill as to be rendered useless. The prince is in danger. I will not stand idly by. You will not—" he trailed off as a nasty coughing fit forced him back onto the sofa.

"Okay, that's it." Sarah leaned forward to grasp Tristan's arm, but the savvy soldier deftly yanked his arm out of her reach. "Tristan, don't be a big baby. You need someone to look after you." Again, Sarah reached for his hand and again he backed away from her.

"Lady Sarah, I will not allow myself to be taken from Mikal's side."

Sarah smiled at him. "That's so sweet. Like you have a choice in the matter. Do you think I need to touch you?" She gave her husband a quick peck on his cheek. "Be right back."

Tristan and Sarah vanished, all without her making physical contact with the sick man. Several minutes later, she reappeared.

"Annie is sick, too. Morning sickness. My mom says that we owe her big-time."

Steve grinned. "I'll give her that one. Now what about the house? Think we can get Lia to watch it again?"

"Only if you call her."

"I called her last time. It's your turn. Besides, I bought

lunch for you today."

"No, you didn't! Wow, your memory stinks! You left early and I ended up paying. I still have the receipt. Want to see?"

Husband and wife stared at each other and sighed in unison. A rapid rock-paper-scissors session was held. As was usual in these types of situations, Steve lost.

Scowling, Steve pulled out his cell and punched in a number.

"Hey Lia, it's Steve. Listen, could you—yes, we need you to watch the house again. Yes, something has come up and we need to leave town. As soon as possible." Steve muted his cell and turned to his wife. "You're right. She definitely suspects something. I can't say that I blame her. We'll just have to deal with her later."

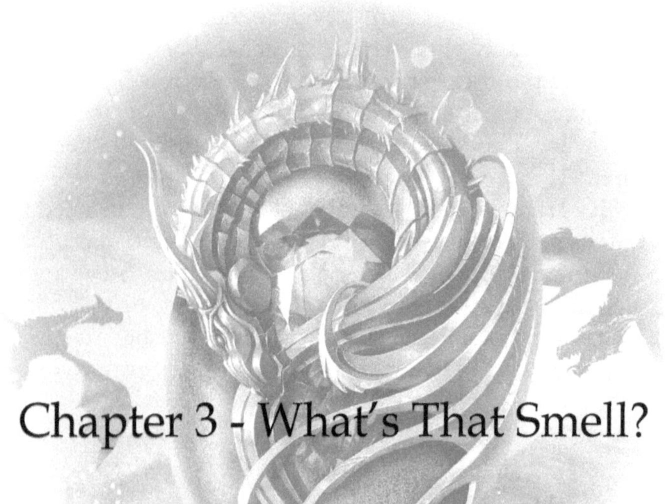

# Chapter 3 - What's That Smell?

Steve approached the massive ten-foot-tall doors and pushed them closed, sealing off the mansion's master bedroom. He absentmindedly adjusted his sword belt again as he struggled to find a comfortable position for the large green-bladed broadsword presently strapped to his back. Mythrin had been a gift from the Kla Guur of the Bohani mountain dwarves after the now-legendary battle to eradicate the dreaded guur on their first visit. He had been surprised to learn that the mystical sword possessed the ability to facilitate contact between the holders of the other two specially commissioned weapons, even if the owners were worlds apart. That was how he had been alerted to the queen's abduction four years ago. Steve had decided from then on, whenever Mikal was with him, the sword would be nearby. Now that he had to return to Lentari, he sure as heck was not going to show up without it.

Sarah approached the carved doors, holding one of the two portal keys in their possession. Inserting the purple key into one of the windows carved into the castle, she activated the portal and stepped back. The familiar chiming sounded; the doorframes fuzzed out, and then … went dark.

Steve walked up to the threshold of the portal and stared at the dark opening. Was something wrong with it? Why wasn't it showing them the small portal chamber adjacent to the throne room?

"What are we looking at? What's going on?"

Comprehension dawned and Sarah smiled. "It's covered. Remember when we first saw the castle's portal? There was a huge tapestry draped over it. I'll wager that the portal has been covered again."

Mikal tried to grab a handful of the tapestry so that he could yank it off its holder, but the tapestry was too thick, the fabric too stiff; his hands were unable to find purchase. Annoyed, he pushed against the thick fabric, hoping to knock it from the wall. Steve leaned his right shoulder up against the fabric and together they pushed. The tapestry bulged slightly outward at the center, but again resisted being removed from its holder.

"I remember your dad simply yanking this thing down last time," Steve complained, turning to look at Mikal. "What's the catch?"

"I do not know the unlock spell," Mikal confessed, letting the tapestry fall back into place with a solid thump. "Shardwyn enchants all valuables in the castle to ensure nothing goes missing."

"Now *that* is a clever idea," Sarah observed, nodding her head. "But is that really necessary? Do you guys have that many problems with thieves in the castle?"

Mikal thought for a moment. "If there has been, my father has never told me about it."

"Okay, get ready to put your back into it." Steve braced his shoulder against the heavy tapestry and gestured for Mikal to join him. "We need to give Sarah enough room so that she can get out. Hurry, I don't want to be caught halfway through the portal when it fuzzes out."

"Why did we not just have her take us straight there? Why did we have to use the portal?"

"That's a huge jump for her. Why waste jhorun when you don't have to?"

"True story," Sarah agreed, nodding.

Together, Steve and Mikal pushed the heavy, resistant tapestry out and away from the wall. Sarah squeezed by and slipped out from behind the wall hanging, pulling Mikal with her. Steve gave the tapestry a final violent shove and darted out just before it thumped back into place.

The portal chamber was quiet. Eerily quiet. At no point could either of them ever remember any part of the castle being vacant, not even in the middle of the night. The door leading into the throne room was closed. Quietly, Steve opened the door and poked his head through. Two gilded thrones glittered in the flickering torchlight as the three of them beheld the empty throne room. No guards and no servants.

Puzzled, Steve turned to his wife. "What time is it? Where is everyone? I don't think I've ever seen the throne room empty before."

Sarah automatically glanced at her left wrist, momentarily forgetting she had taken off her watch. She moved over to the closest window and peered outside.

"It's dark outside, but that's because it's overcast out. I don't think it's that late." Sarah inhaled, taking a deep breath. "Smell that? It's going to rain. God, I love that smell."

A pair of soldiers, undoubtedly on patrol, suddenly appeared in one of the three doorways leading in from the Great Hall.

"Halt! Who are you? How did you—"

Both soldiers had drawn swords and rushed to intercept them, but both caught sight of Mikal and came to a sliding halt.

"Kre'Mikal! What are you doing here?"

The two guards turned to Steve, who had deliberately stepped in front of his wife and Mikal, both hands curled tightly into fists.

"Sir Steve! Lady Sarah!" One of the guards turned to the other. "Fetch the captain at once!"

After the second guard vanished through the doorway,

the first turned back to face Steve. He bowed.

"You are lucky I recognized you, Sir Steve," the guard scolded, smiling fleetingly as he did so. "Our orders are to use any means necessary to see to the safety of the Kri'yans. I would have felt terrible had I injured you."

Steve visibly relaxed. His dark red fists slowly morphed back to a healthy pink as he unclenched his hands and wiggled his fingers.

"In that case I'm glad you recognized us, too. You seem like a nice guy." Steve ignited both hands and smiled as the guard instinctively jumped backward. "I would have hated having to turn you into a French fry."

Footsteps clattered nearby. The second guard reappeared, followed closely by —

"Pheron! How the hell are you, buddy?" Steve stepped forward to grasp the forearm of his friend. "You're a captain now? Congrats!"

The tall officer noticeably relaxed. He turned to the guard who had summoned him. "Wizards be damned. You were not jesting. The Nohrin and the prince." Pheron turned back to Steve. "Sir Steve, Lady Sarah, glad to see you!" The tall soldier turned to the prince and bowed. "Kre'Mikal, are you well?"

Mikal formally bowed back. "I am, captain. Can you please tell me where my parents are?"

"The Reckoning has called them away."

"The Reckoning?" Steve repeated, puzzled. "As in, 'there can be only one?'"

Sarah slapped his arm. "That was the Quickening."

Steve looked at his wife and grinned. "I'm so proud of you right now."

Sarah let out an exasperated sigh. "Do you have any idea how much useless movie trivia you've crammed into my head?"

Pheron leaned toward the prince and whispered, "Do they always veer off subject like this?"

Mikal held back a laugh. "You have no idea."

"So what is this Reckoning thing then?" Steve wanted to know.

"It is the time of year when my parents travel to each village to meet with the people, listen to suggestions, complaints, and so on," Mikal explained.

"You mean the king and queen are out gallivanting about the kingdom without protection?"

"Of course not, Sir Steve. Commander Rhenyon and two full squadrons also accompany the Kri'yans. Is there a problem? Why are you here? We have all been told that is it not safe for the prince to be here."

Steve scowled. "It's not safe for him in our world, either. We were attacked by a group of malwerns and then by trolls, on two different occasions. Someone from here is sending these things after us in our home world."

Pheron stared in shock at the Nohrin as the implications of that statement sunk in. He whirled to the two guards standing quietly nearby.

"Assemble the men. Two full squadrons will be here in no less than ten minutes, is that understood?"

Both guards snapped to attention. "Aye, captain!"

Pheron's face was grim as he turned his back on the departing guards. "How is this possible? No one has access to your world but the two of you!"

Steve scowled again as he fidgeted with Mythrin on his back. If he didn't know better, he'd say the green-bladed sword was growing heavier. "Well, someone clearly found a way."

Concerned, Sarah turned to her husband.

"What's the matter? Why do you keep fidgeting? Are you okay?"

"I don't know what the deal is with this thing," Steve complained, loosening the buckle on his baldric. He repositioned and retightened it for the umpteenth time. "It just doesn't feel right. At times it's too heavy, and other times it seems like it's purposely jabbing me in the back. Like right now, for instance. It feels like the damn thing has tripled in weight."

"You're probably just tense," Sarah suggested.

Inspiration struck. Steve grabbed the sword hilt with one hand and the base of the scabbard with the other and used his sword as a scratching post.

"What would Master Kharus say if he saw you using Mythrin to scratch an itch?" Sarah asked, smiling.

Steve gave her a sheepish grin. "This will be our little secret."

"Have you looked at the blade, Sir Steve?"

Sarah looked at Pheron and raised an eyebrow. "Why? What does that have to do with anything?"

Pheron lowered his voice to a whisper. "Commander Rhenyon has told a select few of us that the Mythra weapons can be used to contact the Nohrin in their home world. He also told us how you found his sword when he lost it in the woods. It seems to me that your sword might be trying to tell you something. The commander told us that the blades will glow."

Shrugging, Steve pulled the green sword free of its scabbard.

"Well, there's your problem right there," Sarah quipped, leaning over her husband's shoulder.

Mythrin was glowing.

Steve whirled around to stare at Pheron. "So what does this mean? That Rhenyon's in trouble."

"Or Breslin," Sarah added.

"True. But more than likely it's Rhenyon."

"Unless your sword can sense something amiss with someone other than the holders of the Mythra Triad?" Pheron asked as he glanced again at the glowing green blade in Steve's hand.

Steve opened his mouth but then closed it with an audible snap. He looked at Sarah and shrugged. "Could be. It would make sense that it only is affected by the other two. But I guess it's possible."

"Could the sword perhaps be sensing the danger to the prince?"

Sarah nodded, looking over at Mikal, who was sitting sullenly on the closest chair. "I'd say anything's possible at this point."

"I am so tired of this."

Everyone turned to regard the prince. Mikal was frowning.

"We know you are, Mikal," Sarah began, coming up to the teenager and putting an arm around his shoulder. "That's why we're here. We need to end this once and for all."

"Agreed," Steve agreed. "Listen, I know you hate hearing this, especially from me, but we're going to need you to stay put for a while."

"But I want to fight! You taught me your fancy fighting moves last year. I can take care of myself!"

"Taekwondo is no match against bows and arrows, or swords for that matter," Steve corrected. "Trust me, I get it. You're tired of being away from home and away from your parents. Am I right?"

Mikal nodded his head.

"Then I need you to humor me. Do me a favor, no questions asked. Go with the captain. I trust he will keep you safe."

Pheron nodded. "Indeed, I will. No one will hurt you, Your Highness. I will have several squadrons surrounding the Antechamber. No one will lay a finger on you. Speaking of which…" The captain angrily turned to face the door that the departing soldiers had run out of. "Where are —"

As if on cue, fully armed soldiers began streaming into the throne room. Within moments fifty men were standing stiffly at attention.

The two bodyguards nodded. Both Steve and Sarah trusted the captain implicitly. If Pheron was satisfied, then they were satisfied as well. With Mikal's safety in good hands, Steve turned to his wife.

"So, any ideas where we need to go first?"

"If they are planning on visiting all the villages, then it's just a matter of hit or miss until we get the right one. Let's try Donlari first. Mikal, stay here, stay safe. Promise me."

Steve smirked, happy to not be on the receiving end of one of Sarah's promises for once. Mikal's eyes narrowed. He had caught his bodyguard's quick smile. Both Steve and Sarah knew that if Mikal gave his promise, he would rather stuff an apple into his mouth and offer himself as lunch to a hungry dragon, than to break his word. Mikal hesitated for a few moments longer, searching furiously for a response that would satisfy Sarah, yet refrain from him having to promise anything.

"Don't even think about it," Sarah warned. "I know you're trying to find a loophole that won't get you in to trouble. Well, forget it. I want you to promise me you'll stay here and do as Pheron says."

Mikal shifted his weight from leg to leg, exasperation clearly showing on his face.

"Come on, promise me!"

"Fine! I promise! Are you happy now?"

Sarah smiled. "As a matter of fact, I am."

Mikal scowled at his foster parents as he was led by the soldiers into the small chamber specifically enchanted to repel all but the strongest of jhorun. Only a select few, Steve and Sarah included, had jhorun powerful enough to defeat the protections in place and had full use of their abilities inside the Antechamber.

"That's one pissed off kid," Steve commented as he watched the heavy wood door swing shut.

"I know, but it has to happen. I want him safe."

"As do I. Come on, let's find the king. We're off to Donlari?"

"Yes. It'll be nice to see Thacken and Bolli again."

"Works for me. We did promise them we'd visit the last time we were here."

Sarah clasped her husband's hand and brought up a mental image of the inn's interior. Selecting a location near the large hearth inside the great room, she teleported the two of them directly into the mayhem that called itself Thacken's Lodge. Unfortunately, they appeared directly in the path of a serving girl whose arms were laden with food.

"Aiiieeeeee!!"

The platter went airborne as the girl threw up her arms and bolted under the nearest table.

"Oh, this isn't gonna end well," Steve muttered, as he watched bowls of glop fly through the air.

Just as the items neared the apex of their arc, the stew and other various airborne foodstuffs abruptly froze in place. Steve blinked a few times. This was new.

Sarah smacked his arm. "Don't just stand there. Grab those bowls and see if you can get the contents back into them before they hit the ground!"

Sure enough, the airborne food wasn't really frozen, more like it had been placed into super slow motion.

"How are you doing this?" Steve asked, gently swatting a slow-moving roll out of his way. Having second thoughts, he snatched the roll from the air and placed it on the closest table.

Concentrating as she watched the contents of the tray slowly tumble end over end, Sarah smiled.

"It was easy. Since I really can't freeze anything in place, I just instructed everything to move toward that table, but to do so very slowly."

Steve nodded his head in approval. How cool!

Together he and Sarah scooped up the swirling mass of thick lumpy liquid, restoring it back to the four bowls it had originally come from. With plenty of time to spare, Steve noted.

"When it's in the bowls, it looks fine. Streaking through the air, not so much."

Sarah laughed and swatted her husband's arm. "We've had their stew before, remember? It tasted fine."

"Well, I should say so, Lady Sarah!"

Smiling, Sarah turned to behold Bolli, Thacken's wife. She was tugging on the arm of her serving girl, trying to get her to come out from under the table.

"Will you come out from under there? What are you afraid of? I know these two well! They are the Nohrin!"

All traces of hesitation vanished. Within moments the starstruck girl was standing by Bolli's side, beaming at them.

"My most humble apologies for blocking your way," the girl curtsied. She took the large platter Bolli handed her and efficiently reloaded it, determined to deliver the meal to the intended recipients.

"Sorry about that," Sarah said, smiling at the innkeeper's wife. "I chose a spot I thought would be vacant."

"Think nothing of it, dear." Bolli turned to see where her husband was. She was surprised to learn he was standing right behind her. Thacken handed her a roll that Sarah had missed, who in turn started to hand it to the serving girl, but hesitated. "Thack, did you pick that up off the ground?"

Thacken shook his head, sending a mass of black curls tumbling about. "I did not. Plucked it out of the air, I did."

"Nice catch!"

Thacken turned to Steve. "Glad to see the two of you! Steve, Sarah, welcome back to our humble inn! It has been a while, has it not?"

"A few years," Steve admitted, smiling. He turned to Bolli. "Listen, have the king and queen been through here recently?"

"The Kri'yans? Aye, perhaps four days ago. The queen sampled my stew. *My stew*! Can you believe it? She even told me that she loved it and wanted the recipe! I told her that the secret is in the—"

Thacken laid a hand on his wife's shoulder, cutting her off. He had detected the look of alarm that had passed over Steve's face.

"What is the matter? Are you looking for them? Why are you here?" Puzzled, the burly innkeeper gazed at both of the Nohrin, staring first at Steve, then Sarah. "You are the royal bodyguards to the young prince. If you are here, then that can only mean—"

This time Bolli elbowed her husband in his ample gut to shut him up. She leaned toward the Nohrin.

"Has something happened? Is the prince safe?"

Steve nodded. "For the time being, yes, he's safe and sound. The problem is, we've identified a possible threat. His parents need to be told, so we have to find them."

Thacken scratched his thick black beard as he attempted to remember if he had overheard where the Kri'yans were headed next. Hadn't he heard the queen say something about the trees of the high north?

"Verdayn! Hah! That's it. They were going to Verdayn next."

Bolli shook her head. "I just told them that. Did you not hear me? Were you not paying attention?"

The big man shuffled his feet. "I was not."

Steve grinned. "Don't sweat it, Thack. Happens to me all the time."

Thacken smiled as well and wisely decided to keep his mouth shut.

Sarah nodded. Verdayn. That was the quaint village in the forest that reminded her of Placerville, a small town in northern California that she frequented often whenever she and Steve attended the Apple Grower Festival to pick up some truly killer apple pies.

"Hey fire thrower, what say you conjure me a fire ball!"

As one, the two Nohrin, along with the barkeep and his wife, slowly turned to the drunken man trying unsuccessfully to push himself away from the bar. Unfortunately, the man was at least three inches taller than Steve's six-foot three frame and probably outweighed him by a good hundred pounds. The inebriated peasant managed to detach himself from the long counter and finally made it to his feet, only to sway dangerously to the left as soon as he tried to take a step.

"That will be quite enough, Marik," Thacken snapped, pushing Bolli behind him. "You have had enough. Collect your brothers and be on your way."

"Home? Wha' fer? Ain' got nothin' ta drink there. We are gonna stay righ' here, whatcha say boys?"

Marik's three brothers all pushed themselves away from the bar, angry at the prospect that they were going to have their supply of ale taken away. Naturally, all three brothers were even larger than Marik.

"Now look what ya did, oaf!" one of the brothers bellowed, cuffing his little brother on the back of the head. He turned to Thacken and banged his empty tankard noisily on the counter. "Just ignore him. Come on, another round!"

"You are the fire thrower, are you not?" Marik took a few more hesitant steps toward Steve, ignoring his brothers' continued jeers at the innkeeper who now stood facing them from behind the counter, arms crossed over his chest. "I wan' tuh see a fire ball!"

The other two brothers also thumped their tankards to signal more ale.

"Another round! We ain' leavin' 'til we are ready!"

Four chasers surged into existence and zoomed to hover in front of each of the shocked brothers. Marik turned to regard the fire thrower, whose hands were lit while he casually spun a fifth fireball on his right index finger. The chaser spun neatly in place, glowing brightly in the darkening room.

"You heard him. You've had enough. Leave."

Too drunk to consider the ramifications of what he was about to do, Marik lurched forward, angling straight toward Sarah, intent on talking some sense into the fire thrower's wife. It wasn't the wisest move he could have made.

Marik squawked with surprise as he was yanked violently upside down by some invisible force and suspended high, up in the air, far enough away where he would be unable to grab on to anything for support.

Sarah smiled sweetly at her husband before her gaze slowly traveled up the tavern wall to land on the upside-down patron. "I'm sure he just wants to go home and get away from here. Isn't that so, Mr. Marik?"

"Get that crazy wench!"

Two of Marik's brother lunged for Steve while the third leapt at Sarah. The man gunning for Sarah only made it about three steps before one of Thacken's beefy hands smashed into his solar plexus, dropping him like a sack of potatoes. He didn't get back up. The innkeeper angrily looked at the other two brothers, ready to jump to Steve's defense. However, he didn't need to, as both men were standing motionless. A large net composed of woven tendrils of fire had surrounded both brothers and was only inches from making direct contact. And, the net was slowly shrinking.

"Nobody calls my wife names but me, dude, and even I do that only sparingly. So, I do believe you owe her an apology." Steve reduced the net by a few more inches. "I'll give you guys about five seconds to decide."

"You have our apologies," one brother instantly blurted out, thumping the other in the gut before he could protest. "We had too much to drink and we were just leaving. With your kindest permission, we will take our leave."

"Wise choice, Derik," Thacken scowled, cracking his knuckles as he did so. "Collect your brothers and be off."

Sarah lowered Marik to the ground where he took off like a shot, disappearing through the open door as though he was afraid he'd have to spend more time hanging upside down twenty feet in the air. Steve extinguished the fire net he had perfected several years ago and watched the brothers help the one that Thacken had felled.

Together, the two brothers, with the third supported between them, ran for the front door. Unfortunately for them, only one of the front double doors was open, the other held securely in place with several deadbolts in the bottom and top of the door frame. Arithmetic not being one of their strong suits, the three men tried to maneuver through a doorway designed for one. At high speeds. The resulting crash stopped brothers one and three dead in their tracks, while brother two was hurled through the doorway as though he had been shot out of a cannon. Fortunately for Thacken, the door and its frame were unharmed.

Picking themselves off the ground, Derik and his brother beat a hasty retreat and vanished outside.

"You must forgive us," Bolli began, mortified that the famous Nohrin had to help break up a brawl with several of their patrons. "I had no —"

"Don't apologize for them," Sarah said, glancing over at her husband, who nodded in return. "No harm done, right? Are you ready to go?"

Steve nodded again. "Yeah, ready as I'll ever be. The sooner we know everyone is safe, the sooner we can figure out what's going on."

Thacken extended his arm. "Safe journey to you. Keep 'im safe. The prince I mean. The Kri'yans can fend fer themselves."

Steve grasped his friend's arm and gave it a firm but friendly shake. "Absolutely."

Sarah took his hand. "Off we go. Thacken, Bolli, until next time!"

They both vanished, this time reappearing in front of a two-story wood and stone building. The design reminded Steve of the inns and taverns he had seen while playing the latest expansion pack to Terra Troubles. The building had three wide stone steps leading up to the single wooden door. A rustic metal lantern hung from a hook above the door to the left, no doubt to avoid having anyone hitting their heads while entering or exiting. Off to the right, below the roofline of the first floor, hung a wooden sign with the words "The Flaming Fighter" clearly visible in bright green paint. Also painted on the sign, next to the title, was the unmistakable image of a human with his hands on fire. The northern corner of the inn had a round tower that jutted out well above the rest of the structure. Maybe it contained a stairway leading to the second floor? A single chimney was visible from the front of the inn.

Whereas the rest of the buildings that comprised the village appeared to be several centuries old, this structure was by far the newest building in the village. Steve figured someone must have won the equivalent of the Lentarian lottery to afford something this nice. The clean, sharp building definitely contrasted with the rest of the drab, rundown structures found in the village.

"What a pretty inn!"

"We're in Verdayn, right? I realize we haven't been here in a long time, and my memory is worse than yours, but do you remember this place?"

Sarah shook her head.

The front door of the inn banged open and a balding, portly man in his mid-fifties emerged, all but jumping down the steps in his haste to greet his potential guests. Steve squinted his eyes. He had to be wearing the brightest purple tunic he had ever seen.

"The Nohrin! Wizards be damned! Thank you so much for gracing my inn!"

"I'm sorry," Sarah began, "do we know you?"

"We have not met, no," the man admitted, smiling broadly as he looked at the two people before him, "but I personally feel as though we are family!"

Sarah nervously eyed her husband. "That's just, um, just —"

"—splendid," Steve finished for her, nonchalantly stepping in front of his wife, "Mr.—?"

"You can call me Anton! We finally meet! I have the two

of you to thank for my new-found fortune!!"

"Come again?" Puzzled, Steve looked at his wife, who shrugged. "How are we involved?"

"My old tavern was the site of your famous duel with the evil wizard. When the king offered to rebuild my tavern, my wife suggested we turn the place into an inn. People now come from all over the kingdom to see for themselves the exact spot where the wizard was defeated by our famous fire thrower. And we must not forget the dragons and the role they played!" The innkeeper proudly pointed at a spot thirty feet away near a copse of evergreens. A large marble statue, depicting two dragons, one rearing as if ready to take flight, and the other baring its fangs, met their eyes. "There. Right there. Two dragons actually graced our village with their presence!"

"We know," Steve muttered. "We were there."

"We have become the most famous tourist attraction Lentari has ever seen! In honor of that fateful day, I have named my new inn *The Flaming Fighter.* What do you think?"

Steve pointed at the figure painted on the sign. "Is that supposed to be me?"

Anton proudly gestured at the inn's sign. "Painted that myself. My wife said I should put a picture of a dragon on there, but I asked her if she had any idea how difficult it was to paint a dragon on a small surface and have it look like a dragon and not a smudge of paint. Oh no, I tell her, the fire thrower played a much more significant role in the wizard's defeat. I tell her —"

In unison, both Steve and Sarah jerked their arms up, palms facing out, in twin "please stop talking" gestures.

"Mr. Anton," Sarah began, "are you familiar with the Reckoning?"

The innkeeper nodded. "Aye. Happens every year. Our village is preparing for the Kri'yans' arrival in a few days."

"So, they're not here now?"

Anton looked at Steve and shook his head. "Their majesties have not yet arrived. Do you need to seek an audience with the king? You like the name of my inn, yes? You don't want me to change it, do you?"

Steve shook his head and blew off Anton's concerns.

"Hey, it's fine. I'm honored. If the king doesn't have a problem with your inn's name, then neither do I."

Anton lurched forward to embrace Steve, encompassing him in a surprisingly strong bear hug.

"Wizards be damned! Are you saying — that is, are you telling me you like my inn? I have your personal endorsement??" A single tear fell down the old man's cheek. "I must go tell my wife! She will be so thrilled!"

The chubby man in the bright purple get-up disappeared back into the inn, calling loudly for his wife.

Steve groaned. "I figure we have about ten seconds to beat a retreat before he gets his wife to come out."

"In that case, we're off." Sarah took her husband's hand once more.

"Where to now?"

"We'll try Capily next."

The tall, majestic pine trees winked out, to be replaced by an endless expanse of open water. Both Steve and Sarah inhaled sharply.

"Smell that? Oh, I love the smell of the ocean."

"Reminds me that I'm hungry."

Sarah paused. "The smell of the ocean makes you hungry? Why?"

"The air is salty. So are French fries. Ergo, it reminds me that I could go for lunch."

"Do you always think with your stomach?"

"I do when I'm hungry."

"Let's just find the king and queen. As soon as we do, we'll get you something to eat, okay?"

Steve nodded. "Sounds good to me."

He yawned and stretched his back, looking around at the quaint cottages lining the cobblestone streets. He couldn't recall ever visiting this village before, so he took his time looking around. Trees were scarce, with only a few of the fat, squat pines pushing past the rooflines of the single-story homes. It also appeared as though most everyone lived in town, as he could see only a few houses off in the distance.

Steve noticed there was one main avenue which housed

the business district. Small shops and carts lined both sides of the street for at least several hundred feet. He could see two residential roads running parallel to the main street, one on either side. Apparently, the villagers wanted to live as close as possible to their businesses. The surprise came, however, as he looked west toward the open sea. He counted no fewer than fifteen piers, with enough berths to hold twenty boats apiece, stretched out for nearly half a mile.

Interspersed here and there were smaller piers, each capable of holding an average of five small boats. A quick glance through the many rows of boats confirmed there were only three or four open berths. There were small rowboats, dories, and dugouts; nearly every type of boat imaginable was accounted for. The furthest southern pier drew Steve's eyes. It was easily the largest. A huge three-masted galleon sat majestically in one of the large berths. The other two were empty.

Clearly this village's main industry had to do with the sea. Judging by the size of the village versus the number of boats presently docked, Steve figured every family must own at least two boats. With that many boats, the seafood must be truly awesome here. Steve's mouth watered as he fantasized about a huge basket of fish and chips. Trying to get his mind off of food, he turned to his wife.

"So, where do we go from here? Why did you choose this as your safe zone?"

Sarah turned to point at the closest building. "That's the constable's office right there."

Steve looked at the large two-story green building with the bright yellow roof.

"Whoever picked out those colors should be shot."

At that moment the front door of the constable's office opened and a young girl of about thirteen or fourteen descended the steps. She was wearing a brown outfit consisting of light brown blouse and darker brown trousers. Looking closely, Steve thought he could see several clumps of dirt on her knees. Had she been digging in the dirt? The girl abruptly stopped as she noticed the two strangers.

Sarah smiled and waved. "Hello! Could you please tell us

if the constable is in?"

Apparently, they were deemed harmless as the girl smiled back and shook her head no.

"My father is accompanying the Kri'yans as they tour the countryside."

Sarah grabbed her husband's arm.

"The king and queen are here? That's great! We need to find them as soon as possible. Can you tell us which way they went?"

A shout drew their attention to the main street. A group of five men had just exited a tavern across the street and were angling their way. All five of the men were huge, muscular, and looked mean. They fanned apart as they rapidly approached. Steve turned to the frightened woman.

"If the king is here, then that means he should have some of his soldiers with him, isn't that right?"

The girl nodded, nervously watching the gigantic men approach. "Most accompanied the king, but there were some that stayed behind."

"You might want to track them down," Steve casually remarked as he turned to the girl. "Don't worry about us, we'll be fine. Hurry!"

The teenager darted off, disappearing from sight as she ducked into one of the busy shops. Sarah tensed, ready to teleport the two of them to safety should the need arise. Steve looked at his wife and grinned.

"Want to do the honors or shall I?"

Sarah gestured at the approaching men. "Knock yourself out. Just be careful."

"Will do." He faced the men and smiled. "Hello. Something we can do for you?"

"Who are you? Why are you asking about the king?"

"How did you know we were asking about the king?" Steve smoothly returned.

The group's spokesman gestured at the man nearest to him.

"Because Tam here heard you. Thanks to his jhorun, he can hear an arrow whistling through the air six hundred feet away. Now answer the question, dolt. What business do you have with the king?"

"The better question would be," Steve began, "is what business is it of yours? You're clearly no soldier. You're dressed as a common street rat, have the manners of a pig, and you stink like one."

A small giggle sounded from behind him.

The ruffian's face turned purple with rage while his companions all snickered loudly. He opened his mouth to spew an angry retort when he was shoved rudely aside and an even bigger man took his place.

Steve whistled. "Damn! Are all you guys on steroids?"

Surprisingly, the leader smiled. Coldly.

"This village is being evacuated. Leave now, while I still allow it."

Steve turned to look back at his wife. "What do you say, should we follow Tweedledee's orders?" Without waiting for a response, he turned back around to face the group of men. "Okay guys, I see your offer of evacuation and raise you one terrifying sprint for your life."

"Go ahead and flee, coward," another man snarled, hoping to provoke the peasant into an attack.

"Oh, sorry, that wasn't directed to me, it was for you. Instead of us leaving, it'll be the five of you running like hell away from here. What do you say?"

All five men burst out laughing.

"Go ahead, runt, let's see what you got!"

Sarah shook her head. She had already noticed that her husband's hands had turned that ugly shade of red she was quite familiar with.

The five thugs eyed each other. This wasn't going as planned. The peasant couple was not fleeing! Instead, they acted as though they had the upper hand. Could they not see that they were outnumbered and outmatched? Cracking his knuckles, the gang leader smiled again.

"Last warning, runt. Leave."

"As enticing as your offer is," Steve began, igniting both hands, "it'll be you guys who will be doing the leaving, not me."

Gone were the confident smiles. Now looks of alarm

passed quickly amongst them. Always one to continually poke the bear, Steve continued.

"Perhaps an introduction is in order. Back home my name is Steve. Around here, I'm called Fire Thrower."

Five sets of eyes widened with disbelief.

"The Nohrin! Run! Flee while you can!"

The tough-guy facade was finally abandoned as all five men shouted with alarm and fled the scene.

"To the boat! Hurry!"

True to his earlier prediction, both Steve and Sarah watched, bemused, as five fully grown men ran in a panicked sprint toward a dilapidated, oversized rowboat mired to an ancient pier. Four piled in as the fifth pushed the boat off, not bothering to cast off the rope; one slash with his dagger and they were away. As the gentle lap of the incoming waves drew the boat away from the shore, two of the men took to the oars and the small boat took off through the waves. Steve generated a large chaser and contemplated whether it was worth it to sink the craft. It'd be his luck that no one would be able to swim and their deaths would be on his head. Sarah laid a hand on his shoulder.

"Don't worry, I've got this."

There were shouts of surprise as the small skiff came to a very sudden stop. After a moment's hesitation, the boat was yanked back so forcefully that the boat's four oars snapped in half.

"What is happening?" one man shouted, panic evident on his face. "Why are we going back?"

"Something's got us!" another shouted, peering fearfully over the side of the boat into the water.

In just a matter of a few seconds, the boat was pulled clean out of the water and about twenty feet up the rocky embankment. Jets of fire sprang into existence and encircled the boat.

"Everyone get out of the boat," Steve ordered. "Lie face down on the ground. Now."

No one moved.

"Final chance, guys."

The men again refused to cooperate.

One of the jets of fire thickened somewhat and twirled about high in the air for a few seconds before it came slamming down through the boat, slicing it neatly in two.

The occupants of the boat dove to the ground and were now lying face-first on the sandy terrain.

"All right, that's better."

"Now that we have them," Sarah began, "what do we do with them?"

Steve looked at his wife. "I'm not sure. I say we turn 'em over to the soldiers as soon as they get here."

Sarah sighed. "I hope that doesn't take too long."

In actuality, it only took three minutes. Once the alarm had been raised, the village guards, aided by a full squadron of the king's personal soldiers, had the five ruffians trussed up in only a matter of moments.

Once the men had been taken away, two soldiers approached. One was wearing maroon, evidently an officer from R'Tal. The other was wearing a deep azure blue uniform commonly found on Capily's soldiers. Both gave a short bow. Unclear of what the expected response should be, Steve bowed in return while Sarah gave a small curtsy.

The maroon-clad soldier bowed again. "Nohrin, I am Lieutenant Bairn. I am in command of the 4th Regiment. This is Talin, in command of the local brigade."

The soldier in blue nodded.

"We are deeply mortified that you were accosted by these cretins. Let us offer our —"

Steve held up a hand, cutting off the lieutenant in mid-sentence.

"Don't apologize. Their actions are entirely their own."

Both Lentarians nodded gratefully.

"Did those men say anything to you?" Bairn wanted to know.

"They told us that the village was being evacuated," Steve answered, looking in the direction the men had been led.

"Evacuated? That makes no sense."

"Sure it does," Sarah countered. "The king and queen are here. Then these guys show up and try to shut down the village? I'm guessing they underestimated the size of the force the king travels with."

"We take no chances," Bairn confirmed. He turned to Talin. "Did you recognize any of them?"

Talin shook his head. "No. They are not from this village. I know everyone here."

"Could there be more of them hiding about?" Sarah wanted to know. "You don't try and kidnap the king with only five men."

"The rest of their band has already been apprehended. Ten others. They were *persuaded* to surrender." At that both Bairn and Talin slowly smiled.

Steve nodded. "Good."

"What are you doing here, Sir Steve?" Lieutenant Bairn asked. "I thought you were supposed to be in your home world with the prince? Has something happened to him? Is he safe?"

"Safe and sound, back at the castle."

Lieutenant Bairn froze. "The prince is in the castle? Unsecured?"

Sarah shook her head. "No. Lieu-- I mean, Captain Pheron is with him, along with several squadrons. He's safe in the Antechamber."

Bairn visibly relaxed and nodded his head.

"That is good. Would he not be safer in your world?"

Steve grunted. "One would think."

"Am I to understand he is not?"

"He is not," Sarah confirmed. "We've been attacked on our home world by someone here. The king and queen need to know."

Talin paled as he turned to watch the prisoners being herded into a squat stone structure just on the village outskirts. He turned back to Bairn.

"Sir, do you think the events are related?"

"Aye, I do. I agree with the Nohrin. We must find the Kri'yans. Immediately."

Steve nodded. "Now we're talking."

Lieutenant Bairn turned to his companion. "I was only told that the king was headed out to Pyke Farm. I am not familiar with its location."

Talin spun to his right and pointed. "Pyke Farm is way off to the south. That farm is the largest supplier of par bark in the entire kingdom."

"Par bark?" Sarah briefly looked at her husband before returning her gaze to the soldier in blue. "Sounds like a spice. Is that from a tree?"

"Aye. Par trees only grow in this climate, therefore the bark is highly coveted. Many villagers grind the bark to powder and add it to hot beverages."

Sarah turned to her husband. "Sounds like cinnamon, doesn't it? Wouldn't it be nice to get some so that I could—"

Bairn held up a hand. "I will be the first to procure you a sizeable amount once we ascertain the king is safe."

Steve grinned. Sarah smacked him on the arm.

"We best get started," Talin advised. "Even on horseback the journey is nearly an hour. The farm is large and encompasses an enormous area."

Sarah snapped her fingers to get Bairn's attention. "I can teleport us, you two, and about ten of your men all at the same time. Trust me, I can get all of us there faster than any horse."

"But you haven't seen the farm before," Steve protested. "How do you plan on getting us all there?"

"There are barely any trees. I'll take us as far as I can see each time. If I can see where I'm going, I'm guessing it'll take three or four jumps."

Five minutes later Sarah, Steve, Bairn, and Talin, along with ten soldiers from both of their units, huddled together. Sarah turned to look south.

"Talin, do you see that rock formation way out there? The one that looks like a huge bird sitting on the rocks? I think it looks like a sea gull."

Talin shaded his eyes as he squinted. "I know not what a 'sea gull' is, Lady Sarah, but I do see a formation that looks like a dragon head. Is that what you are referring to?"

"A dragon head? Yeah, I guess it kinda looks like a dragon head. That's where we're going. Teleporting is a strange jolt to the system, so everyone take a deep breath. Ready?"

Everyone took a deep breath and held it. The present

scene winked out and was replaced by a similar one: rocks and water. Only this time they were now about five miles away from where they began.

Steve turned to look at the peculiar rock formation they had all spotted prior to the jump. "Take it from someone who's seen several up close: that really doesn't look like a dragon head."

"Doesn't really look like a sea gull either," Sarah added, smiling. She turned to Talin. "Which way now?"

Breathing heavily and ordering his lunch to stay put, Talin turned and pointed to a single bump on the horizon, about ten miles out. "Do you see that tree? It marks the northern border of Pyke Farm."

"Deep breath, everyone," Sarah warned, staring at the distant tree. "Ready? Here we go."

Suddenly they were all staring at the lone birch tree directly before them. Off in the distance they could see the beginnings of several huge fields with the short par trees. Even farther away they could see the actual ranch, with at least four or five large buildings.

Not bothering to see how the troops were holding up, Sarah took her husband's hand. "Final jump. We're almost there. Here we go!"

Pyke Farm materialized in front of them. One large two-story residential structure met their eyes, with a smaller two-story building sitting several hundred feet away. There were also three large warehouse-type buildings set about three hundred feet apart from one another and well away from the two residential structures.

Three soldiers fell to their knees and retched on the ground. Steve instantly backed off and started walking away, humming loudly to himself.

Lieutenant Bairn looked at the three soldiers with pity. Fortunately, the three fallen soldiers were all wearing blue. He looked at Talin, who rolled his eyes and shook his head.

"Let's give them a few moments to collect themselves. Where is Sir Steve going?"

Sarah turned to watch her husband as he put more distance between himself and the retching soldiers.

"In our world it's called sympathetic puking. If he smells or hears someone getting sick, he'll get sick himself."

Both Bairn and Talin quizzically looked at the fire thrower still walking in the opposite direction. Talin stifled a chuckle.

Sarah smiled. "Just take my word for it. Now, which way should we go?"

Talin turned to point at the largest building.

"We should check there first. That is where the harvested bark is washed, dried, and cut into strips. Most of the farm's workers are there, so more than likely that's where the king and queen will be."

Sarah whistled, catching her husband's attention. She pointed at one of the buildings. Steve nodded and began walking in that direction.

A soldier emerged from the open double doors, evidently hearing Sarah's whistle. He blinked in confusion for a couple of seconds before striding over to grasp Steve's outstretched arm.

"Rhenyon! Nice to see you, buddy!"

"Sir Steve! You are the last person I was expecting to see here."

Sarah approached. "Hello, Rhenyon. This was an unplanned visit."

"Wizards be damned. Kre'Mikal. Where is the prince? Is he safe?"

"Yes. He's back in the castle. Pheron is with him."

"Kre'Mikal has returned? Again?"

"Not by choice," Steve muttered.

"What has happened?"

"We were attacked."

Rhenyon cursed. "By whom?"

"More like by *what*. Malwerns and trolls."

Rhenyon stared in shock. "In your world? How is that possible?"

"I wish I knew. Someone from here is sending these things to our world."

"That is supposed to be impossible."

"You won't find malwerns or trolls in our world," Sarah pointed out. "They had to have come from here. Therefore, someone has clearly found a way to reach our home world."

Bairn approached and bowed. Rhenyon gave a curt nod of his head in acknowledgement.

"Commander, we have apprehended a band of men in the village who were planning on holding Capily hostage to lay in wait for your return. The events must be related."

"I would agree, Lieutenant. Come, we must inform the king."

"You must inform the king of what?" an all too familiar voice asked.

Rhenyon and Bairn both turned and bowed deeply. Talin and the rest of the soldiers followed suit a few seconds later.

"Sir Steve, Lady Sarah. A pleasure to see you both again."

Steve bowed and Sarah curtsied.

"You're really getting good at that," Steve whispered to his wife. Sarah playfully slapped his arm. He straightened and met the king's eyes. "Your Majesty. Nice to see you again."

Ny'Callé and the rest of the castle personnel appeared.

"Lady Sarah! Sir Steve! What are you doing here? Has something happened to Mikal? Where is he? Is he safe?"

"You cannot expect the Nohrin to answer when you do not give them a chance to respond, dear."

The queen blushed. "Of course, my apologies."

"He's perfectly safe, Your Majesty," Steve assured the queen.

"If he is safe, then what are you doing here?" Kri'Entu asked, alarm still evident on his face.

"He's safe for the time being," Steve amended. "He's back at the castle."

"We were attacked in our world," Sarah explained, drawing gasps of astonishment from Mikal's parents.

"By whom?" the king wanted to know.

"By *what*. Several malwerns in Arizona and two trolls outside our home in Idaho."

"But how is that possible?" Callé protested. "He should be safe there!"

The king was silent as he considered the ramifications of what he had just learned.

"We will return to R'Tal. Immediately. I trust this not.

Commander, we leave for the village in ten minutes. I wish to be back in the castle in no more than hour."

"I can have you back there in five seconds flat."

The king turned to Sarah and smiled. "Why do I keep forgetting about your remarkable jhorun?"

"Wait a moment." Steve pivoted in place as he counted everyone present. "There are about fifty people here. That's too many for you. You're good, but not that good. Besides, what about Talin and the soldiers from Capily? We'd have to stop there first."

"On behalf of my men," Talin began, "we will be more than happy to walk back to the village rather than be teleported again."

Steve chuckled. "It takes some getting used to, doesn't it?"

"I do not see how you can ever get used to the feeling that your insides were left behind."

"All those going to the castle, step forward. Make haste!"

Thirty people stepped forward.

"Umm, I think that's still too many. How many can you take at a time?" Steve asked his wife.

"Not that many. Perhaps twenty."

Bairn stepped back out of the group and gestured for his men to join him.

"With your leave, Your Majesty, my company will return to the village and use the portal to return to R'Tal."

"Appreciated, Lieutenant. Lady Sarah, if you please."

Sarah glanced around at the group, which had now been reduced to nineteen. This would still be the largest group of people she'd ever attempted to teleport. She looked worriedly at her husband. Steve grinned and flipped a mimet at her. Sarah caught the power crystal and nodded appreciatively. She would most certainly need it.

"I have another ready when we get there. This is going to completely drain you; you do realize this, right?"

"It's for a good cause. Okay everyone, deep breath. Here we go!"

The surrounding farmlands with the fragrant par trees vanished as the group was physically wrenched sideways.

Not one person managed to stay on their feet. Fortunately, Sarah had chosen the castle's drawbridge as her safe zone. Thankfully there was no one entering the castle as nearly twenty people appeared out of thin air and stumbled to the ground together, becoming tangled with each other's arms and legs. Muted laughter was heard by all.

"I am so very sorry, Your Majesty."

"I am terribly sorry, milady."

"You lost your crown, Your Majesty."

"Where is it now?"

"I have it over here, sire."

"Can someone help me up?"

Steve rose to his feet and pulled Sarah up with him.

"Are you okay?"

Sarah blinked her eyes. The weariness was setting in. Substantial as her jhorun was, teleporting nineteen people had depleted all of it. She pulled the power crystal out of her pocket and clenched it tightly. The disc grew warm as it released a steady stream of power to replenish hers.

Sarah smiled. "I really needed that. I'm still tired, but at least I'm not as exhausted as I was."

Steve pushed another mimet into her hands. "Well, use this one, too. The more the merrier, right?"

"No, thanks. Save it. I'm okay."

Steve slipped the nine-sided crystal disc back into an empty pouch on Mythrin's scabbard. "Got it if you need it."

"Thanks. If I do, I'll let you know."

Everyone had finally disentangled themselves from one another. Those that were standing helped those that weren't rise to their feet.

"Is everyone okay?" Steve asked, giving several soldiers a hand up.

One of the younger soldiers suddenly swatted at his thigh and let out an exclamation of disgust. Rhenyon was at his side in a flash.

"What is it, soldier?"

"My apologies, commander. I seem to have lost my dagger when we teleported."

"Unlikely," Rhenyon remarked, before Sarah could

interject a complaint. "Lady Sarah's teleportation does not work that way. Either you did not have your dagger when you were teleported or else you lost it upon your arrival here."

Still annoyed at (almost) being accused of being responsible for a lost dagger, Sarah automatically started scanning the surrounding terrain. The likeliest place to conceal a knife would be in the bushes at the moat's edge.

She ambled over to the dark green foliage lining a twenty-foot section of the moat and started poking around. She gently pushed aside several colorful flower stalks and stared intently at the ground. There, nestled amongst the base of several plants was the missing dagger. As she took the knife and started looking for the owner, she froze. Alarmed, she slowly turned back to the tall flower stalks of purple, blue, and white. She leaned forward to inspect the stalks up close. Yes, the flowers were open, containing a single follicle instead of a cluster. Her eyes slowly scanned the area.

"What's the matter?"

Sarah looked at her husband, worry evident on her face. She gently ran her fingers down the stalk, careful not to disturb the delicate purple flowers.

"Do you know what these are?"

The queen approached, followed by the king and the rest of their group.

"Lady Sarah. Is there a problem?"

"Your Majesty, do you see these flowers? Look around. They are everywhere."

"Aye, they are," the queen agreed, looking around at the numerous tall flower stalks. "They have always been there as far as I can remember. Is that important?"

Sarah nodded. "These are larkspurs."

Kri'Entu stiffened with surprise. "Celestia. It's her favorite flower. I am surprised no one has noticed before."

Callé looked up. "Who?"

"I'm sure you remember me telling you about the two sisters who are sorceresses."

"Aye, you did. The one who was good and the other who wasn't?"

Entu nodded. "Those are the ones."

Sarah turned to give the king an appraising smile. "I'm surprised you remembered."

"As it happens, Lady Sarah, I have Shardwyn searching relentlessly for confirmation of Celestia's death."

Everyone stepped out onto the drawbridge and headed inside the castle.

"Has he had any luck?" Steve asked, holding out his hand and waiting for Sarah to take it.

"None. He believes Caladonia's sister is still alive."

"Is that even possible?" Queen Callé asked, following Sarah's lead and taking her husband's hand. Surprised, the king glanced down at their joined hands before answering.

"Shardwyn has already confirmed both sisters had several jorii in their possession."

Steve nodded. "So, teleportation inside the castle is possible if someone has a jorii?"

"It is aye, but why would she not have done so earlier? There were plenty of opportunities to do so."

"I'd say she was clearly waiting," Steve hypothesized. "Whether she couldn't teleport something then, and can now, remains to be seen. Either way, someone clearly can and I'd wager all the tea in China that it's her."

The Kri'yans stared blankly at him.

"Ummm, I'd be willing to wager all the grifs in the kingdom that Celestia is responsible," Steve corrected.

The king gave an affirmative grunt as he pictured all the golden grif coins in the kingdom's treasury.

They approached a closed set of double doors. The two guards standing on either side of the doors snapped to attention and hurried to pull them open.

"Everyone be still! No one moves! Does anyone else smell that?"

The commander's sharp outburst had silenced everyone, even the Kri'yans. A breeze wafted through the open door, alerting Steve to that which had alarmed Rhenyon: a sharp, acrid stench, reminiscent of a landfill on a hot summer day.

"Holy crap," Steve swore, yanking his undershirt up to cover his nose. "Is that what I think it is?"

"There are trolls in the castle!" Rhenyon snapped.

"Flanking positions. Protect the Kri'yans! We go to the Antechamber!"

The soldiers Sarah had teleported back from Capily instantly drew their swords and formed a circle around the Kri'yans. The farther inside the castle they went, the more soldiers joined the armored circle protecting the king and queen. By the time they arrived at the Antechamber, the ring of soldiers were three deep and progress with that many people moving in tandem was slow.

"I simply do not understand how trolls made it inside the castle! How is that possible?" the queen asked, clutching her husband's arm tightly. One of the queen's biggest fears was the vicious, shaggy haired monsters from the high north. "There are supposed to be enchantments in place that prevent any unauthorized teleportations!"

"Be that as it may, Your Majesty," Rhenyon said, as he physically pushed the king and queen into the Antechamber, "these abominations are in the castle. We will deal with this."

Mikal, who had been dozing in one of the plush recliners in the room, leapt to his feet.

"Mother! Father! It is not my fault! You cannot blame me for—"

"Mikal, be silent!" Kri'Entu ordered, taking his son's arm and guiding him out of the way.

Pheron snapped to attention as both the king and queen entered the room. At the same time, he noticed the stench that had followed them into the chamber. Incredulously, the captain stared at his superior officer.

"Commander! Do you smell that? Are there trolls in the castle?"

Rhenyon whirled around to face Pheron. "Wait. You just now smelled them? So they appeared recently? Just as we returned? Wizards be damned. Two full squadrons will report to me and will be assigned to protect the Kri'yans. Four others will search the castle. The rest will take up position outside the—"

A young soldier suddenly darted into the room.

"Commander! A troll has been sighted on the upper floors! It has already destroyed one of the guest chambers."

"How many have engaged the troll?"

"As many as would fit in the room, sir."

"How many trolls?"

"We have only sighted one, sir."

"Make that two, sir!"

Rhenyon spun around just as two additional soldiers entered the room, both out of breath.

"Where?"

"Kitchens."

"Dungeons."

Both messengers eyed each other nervously, clearly alarmed that they were not talking about the same troll.

"Three trolls," Rhenyon repeated, cursing softly to himself. "Captain, take as many men as you can and deal with the troll on the upper floors."

Captain Pheron nodded and pulled several men along with him as he ran from the room.

"You take the one in the kitchen," Steve told Rhenyon, igniting his hands. "I've got dibs on the one in the dungeon. I already took out two earlier today. What's one more, right?"

Rhenyon looked at his friend and nodded. "I do not have many men to give you."

"I only need one."

"One man? That's it? Are you sure? I can pull some men from outside."

"Nope, just the one will do. If I knew where the dungeons were, I wouldn't need any. As it is, I'm not about to trust my sense of directions, especially when a troll is involved. I need someone to guide me down there."

Rhenyon nodded again. "Very well." He faced the ten soldiers before him. "I need a volunteer to lead Sir Steve down to the dungeons."

All ten men raised their hands. The commander singled out a boy of seventeen. "What is your name, soldier?"

"Nolun, sir."

"Are you familiar with the dungeons?"

"Completely, sir. My brother and I explored them countless times when we were lads."

"Perfect. You will aid the Nohrin in locating the troll. Do

not attempt to engage it in any fashion. Sir Steve is more than capable of taking care of it himself. Understood?"

"Aye, sir. Follow me, Sir Steve."

As he turned to go, Steve leaned forward to kiss his wife. "Stay safe."

"You, too."

"Love you."

"I know."

"Your line is, 'I love you more'."

"I know."

Steve laughed and jogged after the young soldier who was already disappearing through the doorway leading into the Great Hall. The entrance to the dungeons was in the Great Hall? That couldn't be right.

Nolun continued jogging through the enormous chamber and into the service corridor leading past the massive kitchens. He could hear the sounds of Rhenyon's troops as they engaged the kitchen troll. How many men did it take to kill a troll, anyway? Steve chuckled. That sounded like the start of a bad joke.

The kitchens fell behind as they continued running through the corridor. It dead-ended into a larger hallway running east and west.

"To the right will take you outside to the stables," Nolun told him, turning left. "We are almost upon the first checkpoint before we descend into the dungeons."

"How many levels are there?" Steve wheezed. Running was not one of his favorite activities.

"Three. Minor offenders are on the first level, prisoners serving long term sentences are on the second, and the lowest level of the dungeon is reserved for—"

"I get it. It's reserved for the worst of the worst, right?"

"Aye. The troll was seen heading for the third level."

"Of course it was. Why wouldn't it be?"

They passed through the first heavily fortified checkpoint and started down the stairs. Once they reached the bottom, Steve drew up short.

"Wait a moment. Those guards had to unlock that heavy iron door to let us onto the first floor of the dungeon, right?"

"Aye. Why do you ask?"

"I'm thinking the troll didn't politely ask to be let through."

"But that would indicate the troll did not traverse the stairs, Sir Steve! How is that possible?"

"It means it was teleported straight to the dungeons."

"Sir Steve, no one can teleport inside the castle."

"My wife can do it," Steve countered.

"Lady Sarah is one of the Nohrin. Of course, she can do it."

Nolun was off like a shot again. Cursing silently, Steve trudged after him. They approached the second checkpoint cautiously. The heavy metal door had been forcefully ripped from the wall and cast aside, revealing a winding staircase leading down to the final level. There were several torches on the wall to illuminate the stairs, but they were out.

Steve squinted at the three torches he could see. All three simultaneously erupted into flames. Nolun started to descend the stairs when Steve pulled him back.

"Do you smell that? It stinks like rotten garbage. It's down there, all right. Are there any prisoners down here right now?"

"There have been no prisoners on the third level for several years."

"That's definitely good to know. Okay, it's time for you to head back."

The soldier hesitated, unwilling to desert one of the famous Nohrin in a time of need.

Anticipating his thoughts, Steve smiled and clapped the young man on his back.

"Don't worry about me. Get going."

"Good luck, Sir Steve."

Nolun vanished back up the stairs. Steve turned back to face the darkened room. What he needed now was more light. He ignited both hands and increased the amount of jhorun flowing into them. Both hands blazed brightly, bringing the room's visibility up to around twenty feet.

Steve cautiously walked along the far wall, following the directions his nose gave him. Fortunately, it wasn't difficult to determine which way the troll went. It didn't take a bloodhound to follow this trail. The stench was so bad he could almost see it.

"Come on, ugly. Where are you? You have to be here somewhere."

A loud noise sounded off in the distance. Problem was, the sound was receding. Steve cursed to himself. He should have asked Nolun how big this level was. He turned to look longingly back at the distant stairs leading up to the second level. He better not get lost down here.

He jogged toward the sounds of the fading disturbance. Just in case he needed to call up a huge reserve of jhorun, he pulled two mimets off their holders on Mythrin's scabbard and clutched one in each hand.

There it was again! The troll had made another noise. It clearly was not trying to move about in stealth. At least he was headed in the right direction. What was the troll doing? If there were no prisoners on this level, what was it looking for? Shouldn't it be coming after him?

He needed more light. Forgetting he was holding a power crystal in each hand, he blasted more jhorun into his hands. The surrounding shadows decreased noticeably as his flames grew brighter.

A loud clatter sounded, and it was much too close for his liking. Steve paused only long enough to determine which direction the troll was fleeing. Wait. Fleeing? Why was it running? Then again, for the first time since he could remember, more than his hands were on fire. He saw that his arms were burning brighter than his hands, and since it wasn't affecting him in the slightest, he let it be. Speaking of being affected, this was why the troll was fleeing! It was afraid of fire!

He took off after the receding footfalls and started firing off quick bursts in random directions, which gave him enough of a picture to see which way he had to go. Thankfully, his jhorun allowed him to see when he finally caught up to the troll. Caught at a dead-end, the monster roared its displeasure.

Cornered, the troll took a few steps toward him. Steve didn't even consider his actions. He generated a chaser and threw it at the troll. With nowhere for the troll to go, he waited for it to be over. However, the troll leapt nimbly aside a split second before impact. The chaser, unable to alter course at such close proximity, slammed into the rock wall. Large slabs of stone fell away, breaking apart noisily as they struck the floor. A huge plume of dust rose off the ground, threatening to remove what little visibility he had left this far down in the dungeons.

"Where are you … you ugly son of a—"

Steve pumped more jhorun into his flames in an attempt to make it as bright as possible. Through the swirling dust, he could just make out the shape of his adversary, only with the increase of light, it could now see him, too. It lunged toward him, arms outstretched.

The explosion knocked Steve onto his butt while further weakening the wall that had already taken a hit from his earlier chaser. Several chunks of stone fell from the deep gouge where the fireball had struck, sending even more dust into the air. Steve wrapped his arms around his head and waited for the sounds of falling rocks to stop.

Eyes screwed shut to avoid getting dust in them, and with his shirt pulled up over his nose to try and mask the overpowering stench of toasted troll, he rolled to his knees. He coughed a few times and scowled. He was beginning to hate dungeons.

The pain in his knees forced him to switch to a sitting position, only he immediately recoiled in pain. Had he just sat on a tack? He felt around on the floor to see if he could find the offending object. What he found was a sharp piece of rock in close proximity to where his butt would have landed. Had he landed on that? He rubbed the welt forming on his butt.

"That's gonna be a tough one to explain."

The dust finally cleared and Steve rose to his feet. He looked at what was left of the troll and nodded. But, as he rose to his feet, a brief flicker of light caught his attention. He paused, waiting to see if the light reappeared. He gingerly stepped over the fallen troll and peered at the rubble on the rocky ground. There was some type of metal object embedded into one of the broken rocks.

Both of his knees protested loudly as he squatted down low to examine the object. Whatever it was, it was the size of a quarter. A letter, or maybe a rune? What about some type of symbol? As soon as he reached out to touch it, the metal sigil flashed angrily and glowed with an eerie blue light. Scowling, he tried again to touch it again. This time the sigil flashed and generated an unknown barrier, preventing contact.

"Okay, so you want to play? Fine. Let's play."

Steve focused on the metal symbol and began to channel his jhorun at it, intent on heating the metal to its melting point. The sigil flared brightly and stayed lit. Whoever put it there clearly didn't want it removed.

He calmly stood up, backed several feet away, and blasted two jets of fire at it. One jet missed, the other didn't. As the fire jet made contact with the unknown symbol, an earsplitting screech tore through the air. Steve was so surprised that he inadvertently snuffed out both hands. The screeching stopped.

"Well, that was unpleasant. Whatever you are, you can't be good."

He reignited both hands and hit the sigil dead on with both fire jets. The deafening screech once again assailed his ears. Steve blasted away for all he was worth.

Just as suddenly as it had started, the shrieking stopped. A thin trickle of molten metal flowed off the surface of the broken rock to collect on the ground. The entire wall he was facing shimmered several times before it vanished completely, revealing a smooth, polished stone wall with a single arched doorway. Through the doorway he could see a staircase leading down.

"Well, well, what have we here?"

Distant shouting could be heard coming from behind him. Someone was approaching, and fast. In fact, he could make out multiple voices now.

"Sir Steve!" a familiar voice called out. "Are you down here?"

"Rhenyon! Yeah, I'm here! I found something you need to see!"

"Where the blazes are you?"

"Hang on, I'll make something you can see."

Still holding on to both mimets, Steve reignited his arms and hands and increased them as much as he could.

The shouting voices neared.

"Decrease your flames, Sir Steve. We cannot approach."

"Sorry."

Steve let his flames resume torch levels and watched Rhenyon, along with a squadron of twenty soldiers, enter the room. Each was holding a torch.

"What happened in here?"

"The better question," Steve countered, "is where exactly do you think that goes?"

# Chapter 4 - Oldest Cougar Ever!

She was living in the castle?" Kri'Entu asked again as he descended down the stairs to the third level of the dungeon. "Right under our very noses? This disturbs me greatly, Shardwyn."

"I understand, Your Majesty. I feel the same."

"And there is no chance she is lying in ambush, waiting for the most opportune moment to strike?"

"None whatsoever, Your Majesty. I had several kytes, trained to vocally react to any other person they encounter besides their handler, sweep the area no fewer than five times. None have given any indication of alarm."

"Could she have sabotaged her lair before she fled?"

"Aye, she might have, Your Majesty. That possibility is being explored. Strong levels of jhorun have been detected, so we are taking no chances."

"I am hoping Sir Steve's battle with the troll surprised her enough to flee. Unprepared," Rhenyon added, drawing nods from both king and wizard.

"The problem there, young sir," Shardwyn said, "is if she fled, then where did she flee to? Somewhere else in the castle?"

"I hope not," Rhenyon muttered darkly.

"That makes two of us," Kri'Entu agreed.

"What do you expect to find down here?" Steve wanted to know. He, Sarah, and an entire squadron of fully armed soldiers followed Shardwyn and the king into the third level of the dungeon.

Shardwyn turned to look back at him. "Answers, Sir Steve. If Celestia is responsible for sending those monsters to your home world, then I would like to know how that was accomplished."

"I want to know why she waited so long to go after Mikal."

Kri'Entu came to an abrupt stop on the stairs and twisted around to stare at Sarah. The rest of company came to a halt as well.

"Think about it, Your Majesty," Sarah persisted. "She's probably been living here for hundreds of years. Why did she wait so long to grab him? She could have snatched him before we even came into the picture."

"A valid point, Lady Sarah," Shardwyn conceded.

"There must be a reason," the king finally said. "It's up to us to discover why. I want to know everything there is to know about her, is that understood?"

Shardwyn nodded. "Completely, Your Majesty."

"Do you really think we'll find a portal down there?" Sarah asked.

"Maelnar assures me teleportation was not Celestia's jhorun," Shardwyn said, turning to follow the king back down the stairs. "Therefore, she must have had other methods to satisfy her teleportation needs. A portal is the most logical assumption, milady."

"Wouldn't you guys have been able to tell if another portal was in the castle?" Steve asked from behind them.

"Observe how far down we are, Sir Steve," Shardwyn pointed out, pausing long enough to rap his knuckles several times on the closest stone wall. "These stones were more than adequate to shield Celestia's activity from us."

"Chances are," Sarah theorized, "she's been using her portal long before anyone of us was born."

"Another valid point, Lady Sarah," Kri'Entu acknowledged from up ahead.

They arrived at the scene of Steve's battle with the troll. Fortunately, the troll's carcass had been removed. Most of the debris littering the rocky floor had also been removed. Armed guards were posted everywhere.

"Has anyone been down there yet?" Steve inquired, leaning closer to the stairs for a better look.

"Just the kyte handlers," Shardwyn informed them. "The area is safe to proceed."

"Sir Steve and I will take point," Rhenyon declared, pushing his way to the front of the procession.

Steve's surprised eyes found his wife's. Sarah smacked him on the arm and pushed him toward the stairs.

"Well? Get going! Everyone's waiting on you."

Already anticipating how the fire thrower would react, Rhenyon's two pre-selected soldiers took up position on either side of Sarah. Both nodded their heads. It was nothing personal, but she would be allowed down once the area was secure. Sarah rolled her eyes.

"Light any and all torches that you see, Sir Steve," Rhenyon began, slowly inching down the stairs.

"They said the area was clear. Why are you moving so slow? Come on, old man, let's speed it up!"

Rhenyon scowled as he turned to face his friend. He held out an arm, inviting Steve to take the lead.

"Be my guest."

Steve hooked his thumbs in his pockets and swaggered down the stairs to join him.

"Don't mind if I do. Just to let you know, I *am* going to cheat a little."

A large chaser appeared several feet in front of them. The fireball hovered there until Steve directed it to slowly pace them out front. If something was going to jump out and attack them, let whatever it was hit the chaser first.

Rhenyon nodded. That would work.

They made it to the bottom of the staircase unmolested. Steve figured they were now at least fifty feet or so below the dungeon's third level. How much farther would they have to go?

Torches hung in their holders every five feet or so along the walls. All were out. The large chaser sped along the walls, lighting torches as it passed. Once they all were lit, the fireball poofed out. Properly illuminated, the full scope of Celestia's lair was revealed to them.

It was roughly a thousand meters squared. Tables, crates, and bookcases were everywhere. Several open books lay forgotten on one table. Another had a complicated apparatus setting with scattered papers all over the place. In the far corner was a simple straw-filled mattress with a few blankets strewn about. Several stale pieces of bread and a flask of water were on the floor near the mattress.

One table had a large piece of parchment spread out over it. Steve angled over to take a look. What he saw chilled his blood. The parchment had a hand-drawn map of the continental United States of America! Sarah joined him moments later. She gasped with shock as she stared at the crude map.

"Where did she get this?"

"Looks like she drew it."

Steve tapped a finger on an area of the map marked with an X. His eyes slowly scanned the rest of the map, noticing at least five other Xs. A horrifying thought just occurred to him. He turned to his wife. "In the last year or so, point out on the map everywhere we've been."

Sarah looked at the marks on the map. She noted an X on the left portion of the map, right about where Northern California would be. Sacramento? Then she tapped her finger on an X down south, in Arizona. Phoenix? She looked at the other marks and was shocked to discover that she recognized all five locations: Moses Lake, Washington; Twin Falls, Idaho; Sacramento and Los Angeles, California; Phoenix, Arizona. They'd been to them all. Remembering the weekend trip to New York City to see a live show on Broadway, she glanced at the east coast. Sure enough, there was an X over the spot where New York City should be.

Kri'Entu approached and stared down at the map. He gently touched a tiny figure of a troll in the northwestern corner of the parchment.

"Would this area on the map indicate where the two of you live?"

Steve was staring at the map, fury in his eyes. He nodded.

The king tapped another section of the map and indicated another tiny figure, unmistakably a malwern.

"And would this indicate where you were when we were attacked by the malwerns?"

"Yes, that's Arizona. We were there just a few days ago."

"We have seriously underestimated her," Shardwyn admitted with a sigh.

Steve rounded on the wizard. "You think? Do you see these Xs? That's everywhere we've been in the last couple of years."

"Everywhere we've been with Mikal," Sarah corrected, concern evident on her face.

Kri'Entu looked horrified. "She has been tracking you? In your home world? How is that possible?"

"I'm really hoping we find the answer somewhere in here."

"Honey, look!" Sarah pointed at small table against the back wall, near the makeshift bed. On the table was Steve's old cell phone, the same one he lost on his first visit to Lentari when he and Sarah were prisoners in the slaver's hut. Next to the cell phone was an instantly recognizable gray sphere the size of a walnut: a jorii. The large marble was sitting on a small tripod device that lifted it up off the table by several inches. The cell phone and the jorii were the only items on the table and they were sitting a few inches apart from one another.

Steve leaned over the table for a closer inspection. "What the hell is that doing here? I never thought I'd see it again."

"You're missing the obvious! It has power! Do you see the power indicator? Your old phone flashed green every ten seconds or so. There, it just flashed again. Did you see it?"

"Yeah, I did. I don't get it. How is that even possible?"

Steve snatched the phone off the table. He flipped open the display in time to see the display blink off. The phone was dead.

"It was just working! It just now decided to die?"

Sarah shook her head. "Wait a moment. Move it back to the table, so it's close to the jorii."

Steve reached out and held the phone next to the jhorun-enhancing sphere. He pressed the power button. The cell phone chimed and the display flashed on. He turned to his wife, inadvertently taking the phone away from its alternate power source. The phone died. Again.

"She found a way to power the cell phone using the jorii? How?"

"Simply incredible!"

Steve and Sarah turned to see Shardwyn leafing through one of the many notebooks. The king and his entourage wandered closer.

"What do you have there, Shardwyn?"

"They appear to be notes, sire. However, they do not make sense. These two entries are many years apart. This one," Shardwyn tapped the entry on the left page, "references Kri'Fallum, Kre'Mikal's grandfather. And this one," the wizard tapped the right page, "talks about her displeasure with Kri'Entu's willingness to create an enormous underground cavern for the dragons to use when they visit the castle. She goes on to mention her extreme dislike of dragons. I think it is clear. Celestia was frightened away. She would not have left this behind for us to find."

"I could have told you that," Steve pointed out, hooking a thumb back at the small table. "Check it out. She left a jorii."

The king's head snapped up. "What? A jorii? Where?"

Sarah pointed to the table. "It's over there. Celestia was using it to power Steve's old cell phone."

"What is a 'sell fone'?" Kri'Entu asked.

Steve held the dead piece of electronics out to the king for his inspection.

"It's a device that enables two people to communicate regardless of how far apart they are. Fortunately, there is no service here so this thing would have been useless to her."

"She was clearly using it for something," Sarah observed, turning to look back at the table. "What else is on the phone that she might be able to use?"

Kri'Entu handed the phone to Steve, who walked back to the table with the jorii on it. Once he was close enough, he powered it up one more time.

Sure enough, the black cell phone searched for a signal, found none, and eventually gave up. Steve flipped up the display and searched through the applications to see what was installed on the phone. The first was the navigation app. His breath caught in his throat. He had forgotten that he had pre-loaded maps of the west coast in preparation for their ten-hour drive from Twin Falls to Coeur d'Alene back on that fateful day he learned they had inherited a house. The map that loaded showed a zoomed-in image of Northern Arizona.

"I'll be damned. The Grand Canyon."

Careful to keep the phone next to the jorii, Steve rotated the phone so that the others could see the map of Flagstaff and the surrounding areas. "I still don't understand how she knew we were going to be there."

Sarah stared at the map, deep in thought.

Flipping through his old phone's apps, Steve stopped once he got to the stored text messages. Could there have been something in there that Celestia could have used? Fortunately, the majority of them were either from Sarah or to her. There were a few from his mother, back when she was learning how to send a text. Nothing helpful there.

"I think I have it."

Steve turned to his wife. "Have what?"

"She was tracking jhorun. In our world. Somehow, she used her jorii and her own portal to track us in our world, and then used the maps on your old cell to plot out where we've been, where we live, and so on."

"Fine, if that's how she's doing it, then where is it? Where's her portal?"

"Excellent question, Sir Steve," Shardwyn piped up, closing the notebook he had been leafing through. "Her notes do confirm the existence of a portal, but does not indicate its location."

"It must be here," the king declared, staring hard at the subterranean chamber that Celestia had called home for more than four centuries.

Rhenyon walked the perimeter of the room, running his left hand along the walls as he did so. "Nothing out of the ordinary. Lady Sarah, would you be so kind as to try? You did it before when we searched for the entrance to the dwarves' realm."

"Ummm, okay, I'll give it a go."

Sarah methodically repeated Rhenyon's experiment, walking slowly around the perimeter of the square room. She was frowning before she was halfway through checking the first wall. Her pace quickened, her hands skimming delicately along the uneven surface. With a sigh, she turned to her husband.

"Find something?"

Sarah helplessly shook her head. "All I get is a buzzing in my head. I'm sorry."

"Something is blocking you, milady?" Rhenyon turned to stare at the rock walls surrounding them.

"Remember that chest with Caladonia's journal? I couldn't see into that one, either. This reminds me of that."

"They are sisters," the king reminded her. "They must have found a way to prevent something from being teleported."

Sarah nodded. It made sense.

The king turned to the wizard. "Shardwyn, what do you say? How do we reveal the portal? Celestia must have it disguised in some fashion. Shardwyn?"

Steve looked over at the quirky wizard. He was holding something metallic in his hand, twisting this way and that, frowning down at it.

"Shardwyn, you okay?"

"Your Majesty," Shardwyn began, ignoring Steve, "can you remove the jorii? I believe it is interfering with my readings."

"What are you trying to do?" Kri'Entu asked, looking down at the odd device the wizard was holding. It was no more than three inches wide, five inches long, had several complicated dials and knobs. A single tiny pendulum was swinging rapidly from side to side. It chimed every time Shardwyn held it toward the jorii, yet every time he moved it away, it would chime again.

"For those special occasions when I need a more reliable method to detect jhorun, I sometimes use this. I simply refer to it as my FJT. Foolproof Jhorun Tester."

"Original, Shardwyn," the king said with a smile. He turned to Rhenyon. "Commander, take several men and secure the jorii in the vaults."

Rhenyon nodded. "Aye, sir."

Having no desire to touch the jorii, and therefore be tempted by the smoky gray sphere, the commander tore off a small piece of bedding from the mattress and used it to scoop up the powerful talisman. Tying the makeshift pouch securely closed, he bowed to the king before he exited the chamber, followed closely by the two soldiers he had chosen.

Steve picked up his old cell phone and approached the king.

"What do you say we make certain this never falls into the wrong hands again?"

"What do you have in mind, Sir Steve?"

In response, Steve ignited both of his hands while still holding the cell. Kri'Entu nodded his approval. Walking over to an empty corner of the room, Steve gave his jhorun permission to destroy the object he was holding, simultaneously blasting extra power through his right hand. In a flash, the black cell phone broke apart. The unmistakable scent of burnt electronics filled the room. Sarah glanced over and nodded approvingly at the destroyed cell.

"The jorii is gone, Shardwyn," Steve reported. "So is my old phone. What does your tester thingamajig tell you now about the jhorun in this room?"

"I expected the jhorun to drop, but that is not the case. Observe."

The odd mechanical device in Shardwyn's hand was still chiming. The closer he walked to one of the many bookcases, the louder the chiming became.

"Chiming and bookcases. I'm having a serious case of déjà vu right now," Steve joked. No one laughed.

Shardwyn stopped in front of one of three identical wooden bookcases and paused; the device in his hand was chiming so fast that all anyone could hear was a continuous note. Shardwyn stowed the jhorun detector back inside his robes as he carefully skimmed a long, thin finger over the books on the shelf.

Finding nothing that piqued his interests on the first shelf, Shardwyn moved to the second. The instant his finger made contact with a thick, cracked leather-bound book, a warning klaxon began wailing. Everyone, save the wizard himself, slapped their hands over their ears. Giving no indication that the shrill noise was inconveniencing him in any way, Shardwyn slid the thick tome off the bookshelf and into his arms. Chanting softly to himself, he traced a finger over several imaginary symbols on the book's cover. The incessant wailing ceased instantly.

Steve's jaw dropped. Shardwyn looked over and smiled.

"That was nothing, Sir Steve," he explained as he gently opened the musty book. "A simple intrusion alarm, easily nullified. Hmm, what have we here?"

Sitting directly inside the hollowed-out volume was a much smaller book, one that appeared to be constructed entirely by hand. The small book was bound by threaded leather laces spaced half an inch apart down the entire length of the seven-inch-long spine. Shardwyn recited several more disarming spells, just in case. Fortunately, nothing happened. Evidently Celestia never counted on someone finding her lair, let alone detecting the existence of the enchanted, hollow book.

Shardwyn delicately opened the hand-crafted book and scowled with irritation. It was illegible. Whatever was contained in the book was deemed so important that it had been secured with an enchantment which prevented unauthorized access. He could only speculate as to what was contained within its pages. Detailed notes about her plan? Future goals?

"Clever, sorceress," Shardwyn softly muttered to himself. "However, easy to nullify. We must find the unlock key."

Celestia's notes were blurry, as though she had composed

everything in ink that hadn't had adequate time to dry, and had therefore become smudged. Shardwyn tapped his long fingers on the table's surface as his eyes started skimming over the myriad objects within the room.

"What now?" Steve asked, leaning over his shoulder to look at the notes. "Everything's smudged? How are we supposed to read that?"

"Her notes are perfectly fine, young master," Shardwyn corrected. "I have seen this before, although not for some time."

"You know what it will take to clean that up?"

"This book has a symbiotic relationship with another item. Think of it like a quill and its ink. The two go hand in hand. Do you follow me?"

Steve and Sarah both nodded. The king approached and nodded as well.

"When Celestia wrote this, she employed a lesser-known spell which linked her notebook with another object. If the two are in close proximity, then the notes would be legible. Otherwise, we have this."

"That's easy enough to solve," Sarah said, straightening to look around the chamber. "Can't we just move the book from item to item and see if it becomes legible? Then we'll know we have the right object."

"It wouldn't be that simple, would it?" Steve frowned as he glanced around the room, mentally tallying several possibilities. "It sounded like she was adamant about people not discovering what she was doing. I mean, we pick up her book and just walk around until we can read it? Wouldn't that be too easy?"

"Easy?" Sarah countered, pulling on her husband's arm until he turned to face her. "What if the item we need was something she was wearing? Like a necklace? Or maybe a ring? Ever think of that?"

"It appears to me," Kri'Entu began, "that Caladonia's sister was arrogant. She believed no one could match her abilities; therefore, it was beneath her to even try. She clearly thought no one would be able to defeat the protective measures she had in place for her journal. Yet within a matter of a few moments, we have gained access to her private lair and discovered her notes. Observe. Think. She left behind a jorii. All her spell books, notes, and experiments were left out in the open. My friends, she fled, and she did not give a second thought about the possessions she left behind. Her survival was more important to her. She may be able to count more than four centuries in age, but her actions define her as a juvenile. Look closely. I believe you will find that which you seek."

Steve hesitated a few moments before wandering over to where Kri'Entu sat. He slowly leaned down and stared at the king's ears.

"Sir Steve, are you well?"

"I'm sorry, Your Majesty, I was just checking to see if you have pointed ears."

"Pardon?"

"You don't look like a Vulcan, but just then you sure sounded like one."

Quizzically, the king turned to Sarah, who smiled and shook her head. The king returned her smile.

"Well, let's get started," Steve declared, leaning over to snatch the leather book out of Shardwyn's hands. "You figure out where her portal is and I'll see if I can find this missing item that will let us read this thing. Deal?"

Shardwyn's bushy eyebrows shot up. Slowly he smiled. "You have yourself a deal, young master. Unlock her notes and I will find her missing portal."

While the wizard began withdrawing various objects from the recesses of his robes and setting them up on one of the tables, Steve began by taking the book over to a table that had a bottle of ink and several quills nearby.

Steve sat down, opened the book to a random page and slid the ink bottle closer. Nothing. He took all four quills from their holder and placed them on the open page. Nothing.

In the meantime, while Steve experimented (unsuccessfully) with various objects, Sarah began selecting objects at random and bringing them over to the open journal. With her fourth selection, she hit the jackpot.

"Omigod! I've got it! I found it!!"

Steve had been leaning back in his chair, trying to reach several small glass bottles when he whipped his head back. The chair clunked noisily on the ground as all four chair legs regained contact with the floor. He squinted at the book. A tarnished gold tube, about three inches long and half an inch in diameter, was resting on the book. Steve blinked. There had been nothing but smudges and indecipherable writing in the book before; now the penmanship was neat, clean, and quite legible.

"What's that? Where did you find it?"

"It's my old lipstick! I found it over there by the mattress." Sarah uncapped the tube. "Look! The lipstick is gone. This girl had a serious fascination with anything from our world. Besides, watch this!"

Sarah gently lifted the empty lipstick tube from the book and put it in her pocket. The elegant writing reverted back to the smudges they had seen earlier.

"That's awesome! Good job!" He picked up the small object and stared at it. He slowly handed the tube back to his wife. "My old cell. Your old lipstick. You know who had this last, right?"

Sarah nodded. "I do. That kidnapper. He had to have been working for Celestia." She paused. "Or else ran into her and the meeting did not go well for him."

"Either way, I'd love to run into him now. At any rate, good job! Now that we can read it, is there anything good in there?"

"May I?"

They turned. The king was standing before them, holding out a hand. He wanted the journal.

"By all means, Your Majesty." Sarah passed him the book, making sure to keep it level so that the empty lipstick cylinder remained lodged in the open seam of the book.

"Excellent work, Lady Sarah. Let us see what Celestia has to say."

Sarah smiled. Her good mood was infectious. Steve was whistling to himself as he put the various items he had tried back where he had originally found them. Kri'Entu slowly paced about as he read through the journal, every so often commenting softly to himself. Sarah watched him for a few moments. Several times the king frowned, while at other times he nodded his head.

"Finding anything good?" Steve asked, moving to stand beside the king. He started to lean over the king's shoulder to read it himself when he caught Sarah's horrified look. She violently shook her head no. Steve straightened up and approached from the front.

"Celestia appears to be responsible for stirring up the dragons in the north. Apparently, one of her hobbies is to create havoc amongst peaceful species. She has been working to destroy the alliance I have made with Rinbok Intherer, Lord of the Dragons."

"How could she do that?" Steve protested. "She's only one person!"

"She's just one person, aye," the king agreed, "but she has had plenty of time to set her plans in motion. This explains much."

Steve waited, curious to see if the king would elaborate.

"Our alliance with the dragons is in danger," Kri'Entu explained, sighing heavily. "The people of Verdayn have lost entire herds of animals. Dragon scales were found nearby. Several residences have burned to the ground, while numerous villagers say dragons were seen in the area."

Instantly defensive, Steve rolled his eyes. "That doesn't mean that the dragons were responsible. It just means one was out flying around. It's their home, too."

Kri'Entu laid a hand on Steve's shoulder in an effort to calm him down. "Be at ease. I have people secretly watching both parties, and thus far, neither has violated the truce. I had often pondered how that could be so, but now I see that Celestia has been playing us both for fools."

"Now that we know this, how does it help us?"

"I have to try and arrange a meeting with the Dragon Lord and show him what I have discovered. It will not be easy, but I must try."

The king resumed reading Celestia's journal so he wandered over to where Sarah was standing. She had been skimming through the titles on one of the bookcases when

Steve approached.

Steve held a finger to his lips and inclined his head toward Shardwyn. Sarah glanced over at the wizard, surprised that he had emptied his pockets onto one of the tables and was in the process of setting up yet another instrument to do who knows what.

"I think we should go help him. Come on."

She took her husband's hand and pulled him over to the wall.

"Shardwyn, have you had any luck?" Steve asked, tapping the wizard on the shoulder when he didn't turn around. "It's been about thirty minutes. Can we give you a hand?"

"Tell you what, just tell us which wall haven't you checked yet, okay? We'll start working on that one."

Shardwyn sighed. "I have checked them all, milady. I do not believe her portal is down here."

"It has to be," Steve argued, as he ran his hands over the wall closest to the stairway leading up. "It's a perfect hiding place. Right under everyone's nose!"

"Sir Steve is right," the king agreed, looking up from Celestia's diary. "She has foolishly chronicled her efforts in obtaining my son. There are quite a few entries referencing her portal. In fact, one of the first references to the portal indicates she acquired it from Maelnar himself!"

Steve, Sarah, and Shardwyn all spun around to stare incredulously at the king.

"Maelnar gave it to her? No way! He sure left out that tidbit, didn't he?"

"I cannot believe Maelnar intentionally gave Celestia a portal," Shardwyn said.

"I would like to believe so as well," Kri'Entu added, looking up from the book he was reading.

"Well, what do you say we ask him?" Sarah pulled a blank piece of parchment from a stack next to a bottle of ink. Selecting a quill from one of the four Steve had tested earlier, she uncorked the small bottle of ink and dipped the quill into the black liquid. Everyone was silent as the soft scratching of the quill on paper could be heard as Sarah composed her message to the dwarf key maker:  We're having trouble locating the portal you gave Celestia in her lair. Can you tell us what it looks like?

Leaning over her shoulder to read the note, Steve nodded. "That ought to get a reaction out of him."

"What did you ask him, Lady Sarah?" Kri'Entu asked.

She relayed the message.

The king's eyes widened with surprise and he slowly smiled. He nodded his approval.

Sarah waited a few moments for the ink to dry and folded the parchment into thirds. She brought up an image of the council chambers deep underground in Borahgg and dropped the message directly on the table.

"How long will you wait for a response?" the king inquired without looking up.

"I'll give him a few minutes," Sarah answered, wandering over to one of the many bookshelves and pulling out a book. "I imagine it will take a while for word to reach him that he's got a message. He'd have to get to the council chambers, read the message, and then write his response. Hopefully it won't take too long."

As luck would have it, Borahgg's Council of Elders was celebrating the completion of the latest set of excavations in the heart of what used to be guur territory. Sarah's message literally dropped right onto Maelnar's lap, causing the key maker to leap to his feet in surprise. Unfortunately, his goblet was full of ale; the dark brown liquid ended up splashing all over not only his chest but that of his two neighbors as well.

While she was waiting for Maelnar to respond, Sarah opened the book she had pulled from the shelf and rifled through a few pages. Strange formulas and complex equations met her eyes. One particular notation caught her attention. She squinted at the page.

*Malwern — these airborne beasts are notoriously difficult. The potion requires the blood of three different kytes, followed by two griffin feathers, and five pounds of bolger meat. Also required are ...*

Sarah held the open book up and approached the Lentarian wizard.

"Shardwyn, what do you make of this?"

Shardwyn took the book and read the passage. Mumbling

softly to himself he turned the page, and then the next. He looked up at Sarah.

"Where did you find this, milady?"

Sarah pointed at the bookcase closest to the mattress.

"There, on that one. It's a spell book, isn't it?"

Shardwyn walked over to the book shelf and selected another. He skimmed a few pages. After a few moments he replaced the second book and selected another to repeat the process.

Sarah turned to the king and shrugged her shoulders after Kri'Entu sent her an inquiring look. He then cleared his throat.

"What have you got there, Shardwyn? What are you reading?"

"She would not have wanted this left behind," Shardwyn muttered softly to himself. He turned to look at the king. "Lady Sarah is right. This is a spell book."

"Where did she get them?"

"She wrote them herself, Your Majesty! See? The writing in these books is a match for Celestia's encrypted journal."

Kri'Entu turned to examine the bookcase-lined walls. There had to be over a hundred books full of nothing but spells!

"Well, now we know what a sorceress does when she has too much time on her hands," Steve observed. "Bet she's pissed she had to leave all those behind."

Kri'Entu smiled. "Indeed. She will be even more displeased to know they have all been confiscated."

"I can burn 'em," Steve offered, igniting a hand. "Just say the word."

"Shardwyn will study them first," the king decided. "If the spells they contain are revealed to be too dangerous, then they will be destroyed."

Ten minutes later Sarah decided the dwarf had had enough time to respond to her message, so she retrieved the paper. She unfolded it and sat down at the closest table to read the single sentence response. Both Steve and the king leaned over her shoulder to see what the dwarf's answer was:

I did no such thing.

Sarah turned to look up at the king and raised an eyebrow. With a stern expression on his face, Kri'Entu opened the journal and found the passage which clearly stated she had acquired the portal from the dwarf. He turned the book around and held it down low so Sarah could read it for herself.

Dipping the quill back into the ink, Sarah composed her response: Celestia's journal says otherwise.

"We'll give him another minute."

It only took a few seconds.

I had suspected she still lives. Come get me, lass.

Kri'Entu smiled. "It would seem you get to revisit Borahgg."

"Apparently. Don't go anywhere, I'll be right back."

Sarah vanished, reappearing ten seconds later with the dwarf clutching her arm. Maelnar turned to the king and bowed.

"Kri'Entu. It is an honor to see you again, lad."

"It is we who are honored by your presence," the king formally answered back.

Maelnar fell silent as he turned to scrutinize the cluttered room where Celestia had spent so much time. The dwarf's brow furrowed as he slowly pivoted in place. His eyes were instantly drawn to the wall opposite the stairs. He slowly walked the length of the wall and then turned in place to eye the room once more. With a grunt, he turned to face his audience. He bowed to the king once more before his eyes alighted on Steve. The dwarf grinned and gave the fire thrower a bow, too.

"Sir Steve. I did not see you there. A pleasure as always, my friend."

The tiniest of coughs sounded from somewhere behind him. The dwarf rolled his eyes and turned to behold Shardwyn.

"Wizard."

"Dwarf."

Sarah sighed. "Really? Are you guys seriously back to this?"

"By that do you mean has the wizard admitted his mistake? No, he has not. Nevertheless," Maelnar turned back to the stone wall, "you asked where Celestia's missing portal is hiding? I would say right there." The dwarf rapped the wall with his knuckles. "There is an unsettling feeling of imbalance here. Besides, this wall is false."

"What?" Steve approached the wall and ran his hands along the surface. "Feels like a stone wall to me."

"How can you tell?" Sarah asked, knocking a few times with her own knuckles. "It sounds solid to me."

"The senses can be deceived, young lass. Do not trust them."

"Why do you keep staring at this one spot?" Steve asked, leaning in to inspect the wall up close. Nothing but solid rock met his eyes. "There's nothing here. No hidden doorway this time."

"I was not looking for a doorway." Maelnar turned to look up at the tall human and tapped a slight indentation on the surface. "I was looking for this."

Steve and Sarah both leaned closer to inspect the tiny indentation no bigger than a thumbprint while Shardwyn and the king continued to pore through Celestia's notebooks, although Sarah noticed the king was constantly glancing their way as if to keep an eye on them. The indentation was no more obvious than any other mark or depression on the wall. Confused, both of them looked down at the dwarf as though he had just sprouted wings.

Maelnar sighed. "When you have worked with stone as long as I have, you become an expert at noticing any irregularities. Observe."

He withdrew a dagger from his belt and scraped along the length of the groove. A thin film of gray paste was scraped away, revealing a glint of metal below. Once all the stone-colored paste had been removed they could see a small metallic symbol of a flower. A larkspur.

"What now?" Kri'Entu asked. "That is her symbol. What does that mean?"

"We remove the mark and reveal the portal which I did *not* give her."

"Why would she say that you did?" Sarah countered. "It's mentioned in her own journal in her own writing!"

"I have no idea, lass. There were only two portals in existence back in her time. Both are still accounted for."

"How do you remove the mark?" the king asked, anxious to see this mysterious portal. "Can you scrape it off with your dagger?"

"No." Maelnar turned to stare at the fire thrower. "But an idea on how to accomplish that has just presented itself. Sir Steve, if you would be so kind?"

"No problemo. Melted one before to find this place, I don't see why I can't do it again. If this one is like the last, you had all better cover your ears."

"May I suggest we all wait outside until Sir Steve removes the mark?" Kri'Entu suggested, already moving toward the stairs.

When he was alone, Steve turned back to the wall, zeroed in on the metal image of the flower and blasted twin jets of fire at it, being careful not to ignite anything else in the room.

Steve winced as the screeching klaxon sounded once more. However, this time he was prepared, having stuffed his ears with some small pieces of fabric he had torn off the nearby bedding.

Fifteen seconds later it was over. The larkspur symbol was gone, having melted and run down the wall to become a tiny pool of molten metal on the floor. The false stone wall had vanished, revealing the authentic wall several feet away. The others rejoined him.

Celestia's elusive portal was finally exposed, however several differences were apparent right from the start. The other portals had all been ten feet tall and at least that many feet wide. This one was shorter, at seven feet tall, and only four feet wide, and appeared to be a single door model. There were no symbols adorning this portal's frame, nor were there any decorations on the surface. It almost looked like a normal door, only it was comprised of stone and not wood. It was the smallest portal any of them had ever seen. All save one.

Maelnar whistled. "Wizards be damned. I thought this had been destroyed."

"You recognize this portal?" the king asked.

"I should say so. I had a hand in its creation."

Confused, Steve looked at the dwarf, who was running his hands over the surface of the door. "I thought you only made portal keys."

"I am the only *maker* of portal keys, Sir Steve. However, I am not the only maker of portals. There are others more skilled than I."

Steve sighed loudly. "Allow me to venture a guess. Those two sisters."

"On the contrary, neither sister could ever master portal creation. I showed them on one occasion. This portal was the result."

"So, you did give Celestia a portal?"

"For the second time, I did no such thing. The portal was dismantled and previously thought to have been destroyed."

"My, my, my. What have we here?"

Everyone turned to see Shardwyn inspecting one of the tables full of complicated devices. Also on the table were four or five small flasks of multi-colored liquid. The wizard was holding one of the bottles and had carefully sniffed the contents. He looked up to see everyone regarding him. He held up the beaker and swished the bright blue liquid around in a circular motion.

"Phisur potion."

"What's that?" Steve asked. "What does it do?"

"This potion has been known to place whoever drinks it into a stupor, becoming highly susceptible to suggestive commands. Very difficult to make."

Sarah pointed to a flask containing a small amount of the brightest yellow fluid she had ever seen. "What about that one?"

Shardwyn replaced the blue potion and picked up the yellow one. He cautiously sniffed the contents. He frowned.

"I do not smell anything, milady."

"So why is that a bad thing? Why are you frowning?"

"Because, Lady Sarah, the more vivid the potion color is, the stronger it is. And usually," he added, "potions such as this are very aromatic."

"That's a bright yellow potion," Steve observed, walking up to put an arm around his wife. "It's almost fluorescent."

"I'd like to know what it does," Sarah added. "Is there some way we can find out?"

"To test a potion's potential requires a safer environment than this." Shardwyn handed the yellow potion to Steve and indicated he should put it back on the table.

Steve turned, his foot clipping a chair leg. Realizing he was about to stumble while holding the yellow potion, he lurched forward to slap the glass flagon back on the table before anything could happen to it.

"Careful!" Sarah scolded. "What would you have done had you dropped that?"

"Sorry. Didn't see that there."

"Obviously. I *so* married a klutz."

"Snot. Bite me."

Sarah giggled and turned back to watch Maelnar as he inspected the small portal up close.

The sudden flash behind her had her gasping out loud as she whirled around to stare at the table. Steve had also spun around, both hands blazing brightly. Kri'Entu had a ring of guards surrounding him as every soldier in the room leapt to his protection.

"What was —"

There was another flash behind them, followed immediately by a shout of alarm. Maelnar dove under the closest table. The small portal was activated! The frames were glowing bright white. Just as suddenly as it had activated, the portal quickly returned to its dormant state.

"What the hell just happened here?" Steve demanded. "First something flashed on the table, then that portal lit up like a Christmas tree. Maelnar, you okay? Did you do anything?"

Steve pulled the dwarf to his feet. Surprisingly, Maelnar wasn't scowling, but instead staring with rapt fascination at the small portal.

"I was inspecting the frame. Visual inspection only. I had not touched anything."

"Your Majesty," Shardwyn suddenly interjected, "I believe

you ought to see this!"

Everyone spun to face the table where the first disturbance had happened. Shardwyn was leaning over the table, slowly rotating the now-empty glass flagon. Several spider-thin fracture lines covered the lower half of the flask. The bright yellow liquid was gone. A dark, circular scorch mark marred the table where the yellow potion had drained out of the flask.

Two hands appeared between two of the guards and gently pried them apart. Once the gap was large enough, the king squeezed through and approached the table.

"What happened? Shardwyn, report."

"Sir Steve appears to have broken the flask," to which Steve squawked with surprise. "The potion drained out and made contact with the table."

"Was there something on the table that it reacted to?" the king wanted to know.

Steve leaned closer for a better look. He slipped a small dagger off his belt and scraped along the wood. Several flakes of a dried greenish substance appeared on the blade. Steve turned to the wizard and offered him his dagger.

"What do you think this stuff is? The king was right. There was something on the table that that reacted to the yellow potion."

"There's a green spot over here, too," Sarah observed, pointing to the far-left corner of the table.

"There's a drop or two left in that thing. Let's drop it on that spot and let's see if something happens."

Sarah nearly choked. "Are you kidding me? We don't really know what type of reaction happened. You want to cause another one?"

"You remember how much potion was left in there, right? There are a couple of drops left. I say we give it a try. We have to know what happened to the portal and why it turned itself on."

"How do we conduct the test safely?" Kri'Entu asked, frowning. "Unless you can convince me no one will be hurt, then I say we leave everything be and it will be thoroughly investigated at a later time."

"I suppose I could do it from the other side of the room."

The king stared at her while he considered. "Very well. Proceed."

"Everyone stand back. Just in case."

With everyone safely on the other side of the room, Sarah instructed her jhorun to gently pick up the fractured flask and hold it over the small spot of dried green potion. The flask slowly rotated, coming to rest upside down. Several drops of the yellow liquid raced down the sides of the glass, collecting on the lip of the flagon. In a moment the first drop touched the table's surface; half a second later, the second drop made contact. The two drops flashed brightly, sending two tiny puffs of smoke spiraling into the air.

The portal's frame flashed twice, exactly half a second apart.

Maelnar dragged a chair over to the table and nimbly jumped up. He leaned forward to inspect the residue from the chemical reaction. He pulled one of his own daggers off his belt and scraped a few flakes onto its surface. He held the blade up to his nose and gently inhaled.

"I can smell ryalallodil. And seuliria."

Annoyed that the dwarf's olfactory senses were better than his own, Shardwyn huffed out an irritated sigh. Maelnar's eyes shifted over to his.

"For once, I will not mock you for not knowing that, wizard. Ryalallodil and seuliria are incredibly rare subterranean herbs found only in a select few caves in the Selekais."

"For what purposes are those herbs harvested?" Shardwyn asked, still annoyed that the dwarf's knowledge of herbs surpassed his own.

"Those herbs are no longer used. We used to use them as guur repellant. Grind the ryalallodil into paste and smear it all over the tunnel floors. Then, since the guur usually descend from the ceilings, we would take iral, or adaisuir, or seuliria, and do the same thing, but only for the walls and ceilings."

Kri'Entu nodded. "Brilliant. As the guur descend down the walls, the potion would adhere to its legs, then as soon as they tried entering one of your tunnels, the two herbs would come into contact with one another."

Maelnar nodded. "Precisely. The resulting reactions would alert us to imminent guur attacks. However, once the guur learned to approach either by ground, or else confine their movements to the walls or ceiling, that particular defense mechanism became nullified."

"How did she get the portal to react to those, well, reactions?" Steve asked, pointing back at the portal.

Maelnar shrugged. "I wish I knew, Sir Steve. If given enough time, perhaps Shardwyn and I could ascertain —"

"Another time, perhaps," Kri'Entu interrupted. "We know the potions and the portal are somehow linked. How has she managed to open the portal into the Nohrin's world?"

Silence ensued as the group pondered. Maelnar, still standing on his chair, suddenly twisted around to stare at the portal. A few seconds later he returned his gaze to the scorch marks on the table then twisted once more to stare at the portal.

"What are you thinking there, buddy?" Steve asked, coming to stand beside him. "You're on to something. Care to share?"

"I have a hypothesis. I believe Celestia was marking different creatures with one potion and then introducing a second potion at a later time which activated the portal. Therefore, she could teleport anything she wanted to wherever she wanted, and quite possibly, whenever she wanted."

"In this case," the king began, "she would have had to tame a troll—"

"Two trolls," Steve interrupted, receiving a thump in his gut from his wife.

"Don't interrupt him," Sarah whispered. "It's rude."

"Two trolls and several malwerns," Kri'Entu corrected with a smile.

"Could she have hit one with an arrow tipped with one of those potions?" Sarah asked.

"And risk damaging the creature?" Kri'Entu shook his head. "I sincerely doubt it. I believe she found some way to overpower it, apply the first potion, and then find a way to apply the second when she was ready to send the creature through the portal."

Sarah and Shardwyn locked eyes.

"The disgusting cookbook! That recipe! It talked about malwerns!"

"Where?" Steve asked. "Which book?"

Sarah pointed to one of the bookcases. "Top shelf, all the way on the right."

Steve retrieved the book and handed it to Sarah, who in turn handed it to the king.

"Do you remember where you found the passage, Lady Sarah?"

"See the bent page there in the middle? That's where it opened for me."

The king flipped open the book and began to read.

"Are these things relevant?" Steve suddenly asked.

Sarah turned to see him reach into an open blue ceramic jar. He pulled out what looked like a two-inch-long yellow marshmallow. A closer inspection revealed it to be a packet of gelatinous substance, encased in plastic. The bright yellow color caught their attention first.

"I'd say we found the rest of that yellow potion."

"I wonder what she was going to do with this?" Sarah reached into the jar to retrieve one of the yellow packets when Steve let out a shout.

"No! Don't touch it!"

Quick as a snake, the king's arm grabbed Sarah's wrist and yanked it out of the jar. Alarmed, Sarah looked at her husband.

"Honey? What's the matter?"

Steve was violently shaking his right hand. The packet had adhered to Steve's fingers and refused to be dislodged.

"This freakin' thing won't let go! It's like I super-glued it to my hand."

"That's how she does it," Kri'Entu whispered. He indicated the packet stuck to Steve's fingers. "She tames the creatures enough to apply the first potion to their skin by attaching one of the yellow packets. Whether it dissolves on its own or she invokes some type of spell to puncture the pouch remains to be seen. Once the two potions come into contact with one another, the portal is activated."

"She managed to tag two trolls and a bunch of malwerns? Could she have managed to tag anything else?"

"An excellent question, Lady Sarah," Kri'Entu said, shaking his head. "We may never know."

"In the meantime, how does he get that off his hand?" Sarah asked. In response, a brief burst of fire and heat flashed from Steve's hand. Problem solved.

"So as long as the portal is active, isn't there a chance that anything else she has tagged could use it?"

Wizard and dwarf both nodded.

Steve ignited his hands again. "Then let's make sure that doesn't happen. I say we destroy it."

"You could blast everything you have at that and you would be incapable of leaving so much as a mark upon its surface."

Steve turned to the dwarf. "Then what would you suggest?"

"How do you deactivate a portal?" Shardwyn asked, curious despite himself.

"Every portal that originates from dwarven hands, or from dwarven design," Maelnar began, pulling a set of small tools off his belt, "has an athe crystal embedded somewhere in the frame. Remove the crystal and you will have yourself a useless portal."

"An athe crystal?" Sarah repeated, looking at her husband, who shrugged. "How does a simple crystal provide power for a portal?"

"A simple crystal?" The dwarf shook his head. "They are anything but, Lady Sarah. Athe crystals are only found in our deepest mines. They will fracture if any part of the crystal is exposed to daylight. Once the crystal has fractured, it becomes useless."

"So, we have to find this power crystal thing and then get it outside?"

"Aye, Sir Steve. The crystals are fireproof, so you would not be able to destroy it."

"Is it, er, teleportable?" Sarah smiled and shook her head. "Sorry. I don't even know if that's a word."

"Hey, I know what you meant. Good question, though.

Is it?"

Maelnar paused in his attempts to remove a section of the portal's frame as he answered. "I am not certain. I do not recall anyone ever having tried before."

"I'll try it as soon as I see it," Sarah vowed. "I don't want this particular portal to ever be operational again."

The dwarf scowled with frustration. He had both hands around a small section of the frame, near the lower right corner that was in contact with the floor, and was pulling for all he was worth in an effort to pry a piece of the frame off the wall.

"I do not understand it. I located the panel, tripped the release catch, yet the panel does not open."

"If Celestia helped create this portal," Kri'Entu reasoned, "then we can assume she knew where the power crystal was. She probably took measures to see to it that her portal remains functional."

The dwarf finally gave up and glared at the portal. With a sigh, he straightened back up.

"I cannot get the blasted panel off. The crystal remains secure."

"Honey, hand me a mimet."

Surprised, Steve looked at his wife's outstretched hand. He slid Mythrin's scabbard across his belt and removed a power crystal from one of the many pouches sewn into the leather sheath. Sarah took the mimet and replenished her jhorun. Just in case.

Steve dropped to the floor and tried to peer behind the frame, hoping that maybe Maelnar might have missed a handhold. However, the dwarf had been thorough. Besides, the portal was flush against the stone wall; for all intents and purposes, the frame might as well have been part of the wall.

"Trust me, Sir Steve, Celestia has sealed the access panel. We will be unable to—"

"Stand back," Sarah instructed, moving to the other side of the room. "I can get that thing off, but if she's set some type of booby trap, I don't want anyone near that thing when I do this."

Kri'Entu made eye contact with one of the guards.

"Lieutenant, tell your troops to clear the room. Lady Sarah is right. If she attempts what I think she will, then we will take no chances."

"Agreed, Your Majesty." The soldier turned to the closest guard. "A possible trap might be sprung. Everyone will clear out of this room. Back up the stairs. Hurry!"

The guards broke rank only to reassemble moments later on the staircase.

Sarah took her husband's arm and guided him to the stairs, catching and holding on to Maelnar's along the way.

"Come on, we're all going to wait on the stairs."

"What are you planning to do, Lady Sarah?" The dwarf was clearly confused. "The access panel has been sealed shut. You will not be able to teleport the crystal out."

Sarah smiled. "Trust me."

Once everyone was safe in the tunnel, Sarah began. She took several calming breaths as she focused on the small section of the frame that Maelnar had been tinkering with. It shouldn't be too difficult. It was an inanimate object. It wasn't that big. She should be able to easily pop the cover off.

Readying herself, she ordered her jhorun to slide that part of the panel over to her. The portal groaned in protest and remained in place.

"Hold on, no one move. I'm going to try again."

Sarah concentrated. Both of her hands started tingling like crazy, signaling her jhorun was ready to try again. Focusing all of her jhorun onto the task at hand, she again ordered the panel cover to separate from the rest of the frame while remaining in her sight.

A five-foot section of the portal's frame, including the piece that had the power crystal in it, was wrenched loose from the wall and collapsed to the ground with a loud crash.

Fanning the air in front of her, Sarah inspected her work. The left side of the portal was still intact. The right side, however, was now mostly on the ground. Whatever adhesive—or spell—the sorceress had used to keep the portal attached to the wall had clearly not wanted to relinquish its grip.

Using a small hammer and chisel that he must have had

somewhere on his belt, Maelnar chipped the excess rock away from the broken piece of frame. Surprisingly efficient with the tiny chisel, the dwarf removed all the broken rock in just a matter of minutes. Returning his tools back to his belt, he then selected a small wood-handled tool with a thin metal wire topped with a small barbed hook. It reminded Steve of lock pick tools commonly used by movie and television burglars to open doors.

Slipping the tool into a tiny concealed hole on the back of the access panel, Maelnar grunted with frustration as the panel again refused to open.

"Blast. Perhaps if we—"

The access panel popped off, as though a powerful air compressor had just given it a mighty blast from within.

Maelnar turned to regard Sarah. "I suppose you could have done that at any time, eh?"

Sarah smiled. "I tried the first time with no luck. I increased my jhorun the second time and the whole thing broke. Then I focused on just a tiny spot on the panel, the same spot you inserted that thingy into, and voila! It was just a matter of knowing where to aim."

Maelnar reached into the open panel and withdrew a dark, blood-red crystal the size of a standard computer mouse. As soon as the crystal cleared the portal frame, it instantly began buzzing like a swarm of angry bees.

"What's it doing?" Steve asked, alarmed. "Is it supposed to be making that noise?"

"No." Maelnar turned and shoved the crystal into Sarah's hands. "Get this into the sunlight. Hurry!"

Sarah reached out, snagged her husband's hand, and teleported the two of them outdoors, choosing the front of the dragon cave in the northern orchards.

They both heard it: a soft tinkle of glass, as if the most delicate champagne flute in the world just broke. The buzzing stopped instantly. Sarah dropped the crystal shards to the ground where they continued to fracture until nothing but fine powder remained, which eventually blew away in the gentle breeze.

Sarah took her husband's hand once more. "Back we go!"

The deep recesses of Celestia's lair appeared around them. Maelnar hurried over.

"Were you successful, lass? Did the crystal shatter?"

Sarah nodded. "It did. It kept shattering until there wasn't anything left but red powder, and even that blew away."

"Excellent, Lady Sarah." The dwarf turned to the king, who had resumed reading Celestia's private journal. "Your Majesty, the portal has been disabled. Permanently."

Kri'Entu said nothing. He was gripping the small book so tightly his knuckles were turning white.

"Your Majesty?" Sarah asked, concerned. "Are you okay?"

The king did not respond.

Concerned, Sarah caught the wizard's attention and tilted her head in the king's direction. Shardwyn glanced over at the king, who was still standing completely motionless. The wizard's bushy eyebrows shot up. He swallowed nervously.

"Sire, are you alright? Your Majesty?"

"I believe I can answer your question, Lady Sarah."

Surprised, Sarah looked up at the king's stern face. What was the last question she had asked? She hoped he would elaborate.

"You wanted to know why she waited for so long to try and take my son. It's because she did not know of Mikal's existence until five years ago."

"What? How is that possible?" Steve demanded. "She's been alive and living in the castle for centuries!"

Kri'Entu nodded. "She has, aye. But unfortunately for the sorceress, she kept fairly detailed notes."

"On what?" Steve wanted to know.

"On how many times she placed herself in stasis in anticipation of my son's birth."

"She put herself in stasis?" Confused, Steve turned to his wife. "Does that mean suspended animation?"

Sarah nodded. "I think so. She did that to herself several times?"

"On multiple occasions," the king confirmed, glancing down at the journal in his hands.

"For years at a time, Your Majesty?" Shardwyn asked as he joined the impromptu meeting. "Why?"

"Her own journal confirms my earlier observation: she's brash, impatient. Prior to her last awakening, she was previously active before Callé and I were joined. That was nearly fifteen years ago."

"Self-imposed suspended animation." Steve shook his head. "That makes her a certifiable whack job."

"How long has she been active this time around?"

Shardwyn consulted the spell book he was holding. "At least five years. From what I can determine, it is the longest she's been awake for at least three centuries."

"The news worsens."

They turned to the king.

"Now what?" Steve inquired.

"I believe I know why she wants my son. *She wishes to marry him.*"

# Chapter 5 - The Jig is Up!

Ewww! I don't care who you are. That just ain't right."

"Remember, she ages very slowly, Sir Steve."

Steve snapped his fingers. "That's right, I forgot. That still doesn't make it better. So, what, she wants to wait for Mikal to come of age, marry him, and then use whatever she's been taking to keep him young?"

"That would appear to be her plan."

Sarah pointed at the book. "Does she just come out and say she wants to marry him?"

Kri'Entu shook his head. "She did not say she *wants* to marry my son, but that she *will*. I will not allow this."

"Nor should you," Steve agreed. "I'll be damned if Mikal comes anywhere close to that mixed bag of nuts."

"Your Majesty," Shardwyn suddenly interrupted, "I think you need to see this."

"What is it?" Kri'Entu asked, setting the small book down and turning to see what the wizard had found.

"This appears to be her newest spell book," Shardwyn

began. "But you will see here that the most recent spell was completed nearly a year ago."

"When, exactly?"

"Near the end of summer."

"How is this important, Shardwyn?"

"Observe, Your Majesty. Every other spell book is filled with spells and experiments she was working on. Every waking moment she devoted to crafting more spells to accomplish her goals. Would you agree, Your Majesty?"

"I would, Shardwyn. Get to the point, please."

"As I mentioned, this is her most recent spell book. Do you see? The last entry was dated from the end of last summer!"

Steve approached. "So?"

"She's stopped trying to figure out what she needs to do," Sarah observed, shaking her head. "That can only mean she's created all the necessary spells. What was the last spell she worked on?"

Shardwyn turned to read from the book.

"She does not have a name for this particular spell. However, I recognize several elements from others. This first part deals with conjuration. See this? She's calling upon ancient deities not even I have heard of, begging them to come to her aid and to gift her with a token of their appreciation. She does not indicate whether she was successful." Shardwyn rapidly skimmed through a few more paragraphs. "Ah, here we go. She alleges she had a brief moment of enlightenment, which according to her was due to a trance she placed herself in. Personally, I concur with Sir Steve. Her mental faculties are not to be trusted."

Kri'Entu nodded, indicating he should continue.

"Very well. It says here that after she awakened from her trance, she was able to conjure, or create, a creature that feeds on the blood of others and is attracted to fire. Where the creature originates is unclear, only that it does her bidding."

"What manner of creature?" Kri'Entu asked, already knowing that no description the wizard could give him would make him feel any better.

"One that attaches itself to the host victim. Once

attached, a slow and painful death is all but assured."

Sarah clapped her hands over her mouth. "That's horrible! Does she really hate Steve that much?"

Shardwyn glanced at Sarah. "Sir Steve is not the intended target."

"How can you be sure?"

"Because, milady, these creatures are the size of a trebuchet stone."

"The rocks that are flung out of a catapult? Are you serious?"

"Oh, son of a—she's going after the dragons, isn't she?" Steve whirled back to the king. "Didn't you just say that relations with the dragons were worsening? Sounds to me like since she hasn't had much luck breaking the dragon alliance, she's now going to resort to her backup plans. Do we know if she's used these damn things yet?"

Everyone turned to the king.

"If they have, I have not been made privy to that information."

"What else does that spell do?" Sarah asked, pointing at the forgotten spell book. "You said there were other parts, right?"

Startled, the wizard returned his attention to Celestia's book.

"Let's see. After this creature was conjured, the spell moves to the next part. Apparently when these creatures appeared, she unwittingly created a bond with it. Flesh and blood creatures do not require such a bond, but a construct would."

"A 'construct'?" Sarah repeated, puzzled. "You're saying she built something and brought it to life?"

Shardwyn nodded. "The more I think about this, the more I believe she must have, Lady Sarah, because to the best of my knowledge, there are no parasitic creatures that size in any period of our history. How, then, would you account for creatures such as this? She *had* to have created them."

"But you don't know for certain," Steve insisted, unable to accept that Celestia was capable of breathing life into inanimate objects. "This could just be something you guys have never encountered, right?"

"What difference does it make?" Sarah countered. "Whether they're flesh and blood or made of metal, either way, she's responsible for these things, so we have to assume she's pulling their strings. Do we have any idea of how many?"

While Shardwyn consulted the notebook to see if he could determine how many of the creatures existed, Steve wandered over to one of the large work tables and peered under it at the large pile of discarded objects. He waved Sarah over.

"I really don't want to touch any of that stuff under there, but I also want to take a look. Can you do your thing and wiggle your nose to make that stuff move around?"

"I do *not* wiggle my nose, thank you very much."

Steve grinned. "Maybe you could. You know, just this once. For me?"

Sarah tried to force herself not to blush, but the more she thought about scrunching up her face to recreate Elizabeth Montgomery's famous nose wiggle, the redder her face became. Did she really do that? She was pretty sure she didn't. She tried not to smile as she held out her right hand, palm up. A small crystal atomizer appeared in her palm. Steve paled.

"Hey! Play nice!"

"Apparently, you'd like to smell pretty for the rest of the day."

Steve held up both arms as though a gun was trained on him. "I'm sorry, I so apologize. I really don't want to smell like a girl today or any other day."

Sarah giggled. "You sure? It sure sounds like you do."

Steve made a cross over his heart. "Cross my heart and hope to not smell like Chanel number five."

The perfume bottle vanished.

"Was that really necessary?"

"You just implied that I was a witch."

"Water under the bridge. Can you move that stuff for me?"

"I'd like to move it, alright. May I suggest—?"

"No, you may not. Now, what's in that pile of crap?"

Reminding herself to revisit this particular topic once

they were alone, Sarah squatted so she could see under the table. Deliberately conscious of her expression, Sarah ordered her jhorun to scatter the pile of debris. Several rusted shields clanked noisily along the ground as the large pile of various artifacts was thrown in every direction. Steve bent down to retrieve a scrap of rope that had wrapped itself around his boot. He squinted at the frayed ends. Whether or not the rope had been recently restraining something, he couldn't tell. The rope rejoined the other detritus on the floor. One of the dented, tarnished shields slowly rose from the floor and spun in place while Sarah leaned closer to take a look.

"What is it?" Steve asked, coming to stand beside her. "What do you see?"

"Nothing. I was just looking. Do you see anything?"

"Nothing but a bunch of crap. I was hoping there might have been some clues in there as to what else she's been doing, but all I see is just pieces of junk."

Sarah lowered the shield back to the ground and then turned to watch Shardwyn skim through several paragraphs.

"Well? Have you figured out how many of those, er, nasty bloodsucking creatures she has at her disposal?"

"She does not say, only that once she figured out how to make them, she made enough to confront *them*. We can only assume she was referring to the dragons. Then she began to work on the final part of the spell, which was to sever the link between herself and the creatures."

"Was she successful?" the king inquired.

"She does not say," Shardwyn reported.

Steve shrugged. "Maybe that means if we take out these RICs, we could —"

"Did you say 'rics'?" Sarah interrupted.

"Yeah. RICs. Really Icky Creatures."

"Surely we can come up with a better name than that."

Steve shrugged. "The floor is now open for ideas. Let's hear your suggestion."

Sarah sighed. "Fine. RICs it is. It just doesn't sound right."

"It doesn't matter. Whatever we call them, they're clearly a threat. We need to find them and destroy them before they can be used on the dragons."

"That's if she hasn't already," Sarah clarified.

"If she has not already confronted the dragons with these things, then she certainly plans to soon." The king turned back to the wizard. "Shardwyn, dispatch a message to Kahvel. If Celestia is planning on using these creatures to attack the dragons, then they must be warned. They must know that she does not act on behalf of R'Tal."

Shardwyn bowed. "At once, sire."

"Have you guys seen this?" Sarah suddenly asked, peering into one of the crates she had just opened. Several more were stacked nearby in the northwestern corner of the room. "I'm pretty sure she's not trying to make it look as though the humans are responsible for these RIC things."

"How can you be certain, Lady Sarah?" Kri'Entu asked. He strode purposefully over to the crate and peered inside. Maelnar joined him moments later. With a surprised expression on his face, the dwarf pulled out a several gray smocks, complete with metal shavings on them.

"I've seen those before," Steve began, leaning over to pull out a chipped double-bladed axe. "It's —"

"Dwarven," Maelnar finished for him. "If she leaves enough of this lying around, then it could convince just about anyone that the dwarves are involved. If the dragons see any of this, then they will attack my brothers. Of course, the dwarves will retaliate, and it will lead to all-out war. This is not good, lads. You must take me back, Lady Sarah. I must consult with the Council at once!"

Sarah nodded. She took the dwarf's arm and vanished, reappearing moments later.

"Did you get the sense that the dwarves were ready to go to battle?" Steve asked. "I sure hope not. I really like those guys and don't want to see anyone get hurt."

"They didn't look any different from when I was there earlier."

Steve turned to the king. "Maybe she's trying to pin this on a different clan of dwarves. Do you know how many live in the area?"

"There are three that I am familiar with. There's Kla Guur, Kla Narrus, who live in the western Bohanis, and finally

Kla Chanus, who live under the lake." The king sighed and sank heavily into the closest chair. "Which clan she accuses is irrelevant. The dwarves and dragons must not go to war, not over the whims of this girl. Fortunately, I do not believe Celestia has used her newest creation. I would like to think the Dragon Lord would have informed us about it if they had."

"Then we still have time. If we can find these RIC things before they're used, we can still avoid war." Steve sighed. "Damn. Why couldn't she have pitted the trolls and malwerns against each other? She could have done us all a favor and gotten rid of both of them."

The king laid a friendly hand on Steve's shoulder. "If only it were that easy."

One moment Steve was facing the king and the next, some unknown force spun him around roughly a hundred eighty degrees so that he was now facing a darkened corner of Celestia's chambers.

"Whoa! What the hell just happened? Something just—"

Whatever had spun him did so again. He let out a surprised squawk as he found himself facing the king.

Steve rubbed painfully at his right shoulder. It had felt as though someone had reached out to snag his sword belt and used that to spin him about.

"Man, whoever's doing that needs to stop. I already have enough bruises."

Sarah pointed at Mythrin, still strapped to Steve's back.

"I think you need to check your sword."

"My right arm hurts. I can't get it unless I unbuckle my baldric. Can someone get it for me?"

Kri'Entu gently turned Steve so that he was facing away from him and carefully pulled the green-bladed broadsword out of its sheath. Sarah had guessed correctly; Mythrin's blade was glowing.

"Let me see it. Usually if I hold on to the thing, whoever's trying to contact me will do so telepathically."

The king presented Steve his sword, hilt-first. As soon as Mythrin was in his grasp, Steve heard the voice of Maelnar's son, courtesy of his own unique Mythra weapon, Mythryd the axe:

*You took your ruddy time, Sir Steve. Have Lady Sarah come get my father at once.*

"It was Breslin. Hon, go back and get Maelnar."

Sarah nodded and vanished.

"Is it safe to assume we have learned all we can in here for now?" the king asked Shardwyn, rising from his seat.

"I believe so, Your Majesty."

"See to it that everything in here, and I do mean *everything*, is confiscated and properly secured. Take as many men as you see fit."

"I will, Your Majesty. Fear not. I will document everything."

"Do that, Shardwyn. I wish to leave this place. As soon as Lady Sarah returns, we will resume these talks in the Antechamber."

Thirty minutes later, Steve, Sarah, and Maelnar were all sitting quietly in the enchanted chamber, waiting for the king to arrive.

"What do you think happened?" Steve softly asked his wife.

"What do you mean?" Sarah whispered back.

"What do you mean what do I mean? Just before we got here the king was pulled aside and hasn't been back since. That was at least fifteen minutes ago. It's quiet. Too quiet. Something's happened. You can feel it in the air. I keep waiting for someone to come barging through that door and give us some really bad news."

As if on cue, Kri'Entu strode through the door, followed closely by the commander and Shardwyn. They didn't look happy. As soon as they had taken their seats Kri'Entu turned to the guards stationed around the perimeter of the room and dismissed them. Once all the doors were sealed shut, he turned back to face his guests.

"We have received word from the dragons," the king reported, his face grim. "Kahvel was just here. The last two hours have seen some very disturbing activity. The dragons have destroyed several of the dwarves' hidden subterranean entrances in direct retaliation to several of their kind falling victim to, in their words, 'the new parasitic threat awakened by the dwarves'."

Steve cursed softly to himself while Sarah looked truly horrified.

**Alas, I have tried to convince them the dwarves are not responsible, but they will not listen this time.**

Startled, Steve straightened in his chair. It was the voice of Kahvel's mate, the dragon who had saved his life.

*Pryllan? Are you in the area?*

**Aye.**

*For how long?*

**As long as necessary to rectify this situation.**

Oblivious to Steve's mental conversation with the dragon, Sarah continued to vent her outrage.

"She's used them! Several dragons have already fallen victim? That's horrible! What can we do?"

"We have been warned not to interfere," Kri'Entu stated, locking his hands together and letting them fall into his lap. "They are correct. We are officially stepping aside to let the dragons and dwarves work this out themselves."

"What are the dwarves going to do?" Sarah wanted to know, turning to the dwarf sitting in his chair and puffing away silently on his pipe. "They couldn't possibly hope to face the dragons, could they?"

Maelnar's beard fluttered outwards as he let out a loud sigh of exasperation. "The ruddy hell we can. You might not think so, Lady Sarah, but we are more than capable of defending ourselves against the likes of the dragons. That is why open hostilities *must* be avoided. At all costs."

"Your son wants to be included."

Surprised, Maelnar turned to Steve, who had removed his baldric and now had Mythrin stretched across his lap. "What was that, Sir Steve? What did you say about my son?"

"Breslin is formally requesting that Sarah go back and get him. He wants to help."

"He does, does he? And how does he know …" The dwarf's eyes fell on the jade-colored broadsword on Steve's lap. "Never mind. Your Majesty, what would you say to an additional member to our group?"

"Officially, I know nothing about this. Unofficially, I welcome the help."

Sarah nodded and vanished, appearing moments later with not one but three heavily armored male dwarves. Instantly recognizable was the third member of the Mythra triad: Breslin, son of Maelnar. Dressed in dark studded leather armor with the striking red double-bladed axe, Mythryd, strapped across his back, Breslin detached himself from Sarah's grip and turned to face the group. He bowed.

"I do not believe we have met, master dwarf," Kri'Entu formally declared, giving Breslin a curt nod of his head.

"Kri'Entu, may I present Breslin, my first born." Maelnar turned to face his only son. "Son, this is Entu, human King of Lentari."

All three dwarves bowed again. Breslin approached and bowed a third time.

"I am honored, Your Majesty."

"Would you kindly introduce us to your companions?" the king asked.

"Aye. Allow me to present Athos and Venk, sons of Tobin."

Athos was dressed in heavy black leather armor, with a single-bladed black handled axe strapped across his back. His long black hair had been neatly braided and fell halfway down his back. His beard was also braided and was tucked into a thick leather belt. Venk was similarly dressed, only his leather armor had been dyed a deep maroon color.

Steve sidled closer to inspect the axe. All the axes he had ever seen the dwarves use had been double-sided. This was the first single-bladed version he had ever seen. The axe head resembled that of a poleaxe, which consisted of a curved crescent blade used for downward thrusts on one side as well as an armor-piercing spike on the other. There was also a spike at either end of the haft for thrusting at enemies.

Athos glanced up at the tall human and bowed. "Nohrin."

"Sorry, I was just admiring your axe."

"Don't let him get too close," Sarah warned, smiling at the dwarf. "He collects weapons and he'll do everything he can to talk you out of yours."

Athos smiled, although it was lost behind his beard. "Once the threat has been neutralized, you may have my axe, Nohrin."

Triumphant, Steve turned to his wife. "Woo-hoo! Did you hear that?"

Exasperated, Sarah approached the dwarf. "Athos, you don't need to give my husband your axe just because he expresses a little interest."

"Hey, speak for yourself, woman!"

Sarah smacked her husband on the arm, eliciting a throaty chuckle from the dwarf.

"Think nothing of it, milady. I made this axe. The ultimate compliment to my work would be to see it in the hands of the famous Nohrin. I am honored."

Grinning broadly, Steve turned back to his wife, who rolled her eyes at him.

"You may have mine once I am done as well," Venk added, removing his axe from its holder and presenting it to Steve for his inspection. "My brother may be more talented than I when it comes to blacksmithing, but mine will last longer. My axe is more substantial than that light thing he uses."

Steve accepted the axe and admired the craftsmanship. The haft was tightly wrapped in dark leather. Each of the curved blades, while scarred and chipped in several places, was razor sharp. Unlike many dwarven axes, this one did not have any other decorations. It was exactly as it seemed, a weapon that was meant to be used.

"I'll make a deal with you. Well, both of you. I'll gladly accept your axes, but you have to let me do something for you. A favor for a favor. What do you say?"

"Eradicating the guur that had been plaguing our Kla Guur brothers was more than payment, Sir Steve," Athos answered, receiving a nod of agreement from his brother. "No other payment is necessary, nor will be accepted."

"You do realize that I'll do my best to try and convince you two otherwise, don't you?"

"You can try, Nohrin, but you will be unsuccessful."

**They always were stubborn.**

Steve had forgotten about the dragon. *Are you hearing this?*

**Aye. Our senses are shared, remember?**

*I thought that only worked for me. I didn't know you could hear what I was hearing, too. How cool!*

Sarah raised her hand. "I have a question."

Kri'Entu nodded. "Aye, Lady Sarah, go ahead."

"The dwarves have sent, unofficially I'm sure, three to help discreetly handle this situation." Sarah's voice dropped several decibels. "Are you going to do the same?"

The king smiled cryptically. "As I mentioned before, we are officially stepping aside to let the dwarves and the dragons come to an amicable solution themselves."

"And unofficially?" Steve prompted, leaning forward in his chair. "What are you gonna do?"

Even though the Antechamber had been sealed, and they were alone, the king's voice dropped so low that his voice was the barest of whispers.

"I will be *damned* if I step aside and let a human be responsible for this mess."

Matching the king's tone, Steve glanced around the room and repeated his question. "So, what are you gonna do?"

Kri'Entu sighed. "While I cannot officially dispatch any militia, what I can do is suggest a course of action for any *non*-Lentarians that may or may not be present."

"Then it's your lucky day, Your Majesty. It just so happens you have two here, and we're both all ears."

"Two non-Lentarians and one former commander," Rhenyon added, rising to his feet. "Your Majesty, I resign my commission, effective immediately."

Surprisingly, the king nodded. "Temporary, I am sure."

Rhenyon nodded. "Of course."

"Very well. The six of you have a very volatile situation to defuse. You must act quickly. You must prevent the dragons and the dwarves from going to war at any cost. Get to Verdayn as quickly as you can. Investigate Lake Raehón and the surrounding valley. I am told there are more entrances to the dwarves' demesnes than anyone realizes up there. You must prevent the dragons from further antagonizing them."

"How many are there?" Steve asked, turning to Maelnar.

"Twelve in the valley alone. Seven have been destroyed."

Kri'Entu's gaze locked on his former commander. "She's up there somewhere. Find her. Stop her."

Rhenyon nodded. "Understood, Your Majesty."

*If you only knew that there were* seven *of us dealing with this little predicament,* Steve mentally chided the king.

**I know you wish to inform your companions that I am in the area. If you trust those present, then you may announce my involvement. However, refrain from telling anyone about riding on my back. Dragon riding is still forbidden.**

Steve cleared his throat and hesitatingly raised a hand. Kri'Entu turned to the fire thrower.

"Sir Steve? You wish to add something?"

Steve nodded. "Yeah. There's actually going to be seven of us heading north."

The king was in the process of sitting down when he hesitated. "Oh? Who is the seventh?"

"Pryllan."

The king nodded approvingly. "Kahvel's mate. I have no objections to a dragon's involvement. In fact, I welcome it."

"A dragon wants to join us?" Breslin asked, incredulous.

"She's been a loyal friend and is invaluable to us," Steve remarked, looking hard at the three dwarves. He had caught the derisive tone coming from the dwarf and didn't like it. "You guys aren't going to have a problem with her, right?"

"Do you trust this dragon, Sir Steve?" Breslin asked, motioning for his two companions to remain silent.

"Implicitly."

"Then that is good enough for the likes of us," Maelnar interrupted, silencing the two brothers with a single glance. "The dwarves are honored a dragon would have the courage to right this injustice and join our troupe."

**It is I who am honored. They have my thanks.**

"She says she's honored as well, and offers her thanks."

"How is it you can speak to this dragon?" Athos demanded, looking about the room fearfully as though Pryllan might be hiding in a darkened corner.

"I have a mental connection with her," Steve explained to the dwarf. "I can sense her thoughts and she can sense mine. In this case she can hear the same thing I do. She's been listening."

"So, where is this dragon now?" Venk asked, mirroring his brother's nervous behavior.

"As I said, her name is Pryllan," Steve clarified, giving both dwarf brothers a scowl. *Pryllan, where are you right now?*

**In the subterranean cavern built by the humans.**

"She's out in the dragon cave, just north of the castle," Steve answered.

**The circumstances are becoming dire. We must be off. Rinbok has summoned all dragons that call the Bohani mountains home.**

*Who's Rinbok?*

**Rinbok Intherer is known to the humans as the dragon lord.**

"We have to get going," Steve added. "Pryllan says things are deteriorating quickly. If she says we need to hurry, then we need to hurry."

"Indeed," Kri'Entu agreed, turning to his former commander. "Seeing how I have no knowledge of what you are about to do, I will be on my way."

The king rose from his chair and exited the room, leaving three humans and four dwarves staring at one another. Slowly, Maelnar rose from his chair and hopped down.

"For the same reasons, I also must be off." Just before the dwarf left the Antechamber, he turned to face the six of them and bowed. "May luck favor the courageous. Or was that the foolish? I can never remember."

Once the dwarf key maker had departed and the Antechamber was sealed once more, Steve turned to the former officer. "What now?"

"We prepare ourselves," Rhenyon answered. "Our orders are to do everything in our power to prevent open hostilities between the dragons and dwarves, but we must be ready in case we are unsuccessful."

They detoured to the armory (which was conveniently unguarded) so that Rhenyon could properly arm himself. Watching Rhenyon pull a suit of armor off one of the racks, Sarah teleported hers and Steve's from their private chambers in the castle. After Steve had strapped the last greave into place and had buckled his baldric over his shoulder, with Rhenyon mirroring his actions, the three humans glanced at their dwarven counterparts. Since the dwarves had arrived in full armor, they had only chosen a few daggers and short swords to complement their existing weaponry. Once everyone's armor was properly fitted, and they were all adequately armed, Sarah instructed her jhorun to teleport the six of them to the dragon's location.

Everyone braced themselves for the inevitable jolt and loss of balance that always ensued after Sarah's teleportation jumps.

"I do not believe I could ever get used to that method of transportation," Venk muttered, rising slowly to his feet. He pulled his brother upright before both lent a hand to Breslin.

Facing the mouth of the enormous subterranean tunnel, Steve turned to look back at the castle sitting majestically in the distance and let out a heavy sigh. Moments later Sarah approached and embraced him from behind.

"Are you okay?"

"Yeah, I'm just nervous. I always am when things are going to get ugly."

"You think it will?"

"Without a doubt. Celestia has already used the RICs. She's obviously prepared for us. Since she's gone after us in the past, we have to figure she knows all about us and what we can do. Quite honestly, that scares the hell out of me."

"I know. Me too."

**She is but one girl. You should not be afraid of one human female.**

Sarah gasped aloud. "Okay, I heard her that time!"

**As I mentioned to Steve, the time for discretion has passed. If we are to succeed in this clandestine endeavor, we must be able to communicate at all times. Also, I have never communicated with sons of earth in this manner before, and I wanted to try. I trust you can follow along?**

"Aye, that we can, dragon," Breslin confirmed.

**I will call you by your designated name if you will**

**extend me the same courtesy.**

Forgetting Pryllan was still absent, Breslin bowed. "Agreed."

The ground trembled as the dragon stirred deep in the underground cavern. The tremors grew in intensity as the enormous dragon ascended the tunnel. Pryllan's sleek reptilian form emerged out of the darkness and towered over them. Having never been this close to a dwarf before, she lowered her massive head to inspect the three diminutive figures, breathing in their scent so as to better familiarize herself.

Athos took several tentative steps back. Friend or not, being that close to a dragon was unsettling.

Pryllan chuckled. "Be at ease. It is only disturbing because the two of us are not yet acquainted, son of earth. Besides, dwarves taste worse than humans."

Athos, Venk, and Breslin stared at the dragon in shock. The gigantic emerald dragon returned the stare.

"I think she's joking, guys," Steve offered, slapping Breslin on his back. "You can trust her with your life. I have. Several times."

Wait.

*You are just joking, right?*

**Of course. Humans taste much better.**

*Excuse me?*

Pryllan swayed gently from side to side as her rumbling laughter was felt by all.

Recognizing the rumblings for what they were, Breslin turned back to the dragon and stared up at her. He hadn't known that dragons could have a sense of humor. "You will have to forgive our hesitation. We have never been in such close proximity with a dragon before. Voluntarily, that is."

The dragon nodded. "Likewise."

Pryllan had started to raise her head when she noticed the third dwarf staring at her with rapt fascination. She paused while she studied the dwarf wearing the dark red armor.

Breslin turned to Venk and nudged his shoulder.

"What are you doing? Why are you staring?"

Venk mumbled something before he dropped his eyes to the ground.

Athos approached and smacked his brother on the back of his head. "Eh? No mumbling. Speak up."

Venk sighed and looked back up at the dragon. He opened his mouth, but nothing came out.

"What about your offspring?" Pryllan asked, still picking up the dwarf's thoughts.

Curiosity piqued; Athos turned back to his brother after craning his head up at the towering dragon. Why would she mention his niece and nephew? "What about Lukas and Madisonia?"

"Ask and be done with it," the dragon demanded.

"I, er, promised my children that if I ever encountered a dragon that I would try and procure a dragon scale for each of them."

Athos sighed in exasperation. "Are they still going on about that?"

Venk nodded. "Lukas got the idea from one of his friends and now will not let it go. Naturally Madisonia wants whatever her brother wants."

Pryllan's head instantly dropped to ground-level and met the dwarf's eyes. "You promised to acquire dragon scales? Exactly how did you plan on fulfilling that particular promise?"

"I do not know," Venk admitted. "I had assumed my only chance would be to steal a scale off the carcass of a dead dragon. If I ever found one, that is."

"Impossible. Our dead are burned."

There was a pregnant pause as dragon and dwarf stared at one another.

Pryllan's expression was unreadable. "You appear to have a dilemma, son of earth."

"I am Venk, son of Tobin."

"Very well, Venk, son of Tobin. We have been acquainted."

The dwarf bowed in response.

"How old are your kids?" Steve suddenly asked.

"Lukas is nine and Madisonia is seven."

"And they want a dragon scale? Why?"

"They *each* want a dragon scale. Why, I cannot fathom."

"Did you know there'd be a dragon with us today?"

Sarah asked.

"I did not. When I heard Breslin and Athos talk about the possibility of battling dragons, I knew I had to try. For their sake."

Pryllan eyed the nervous dwarf a few moments more before she whipped her tail around and caught the tip in her mouth just before it would have knocked the dwarf flat. Spitting her tail out on the ground at the feet of the three dwarves, Pryllan straightened and stayed stock still, pointedly looking off in another direction.

**The scales on my tail sloughed off several weeks ago. Perhaps there might be one or two left?**

Steve grinned. *I get it. You want him to steal some scales from you?*

**All the better to impress his offspring. Stolen from a live dragon sounds better than stolen from the burnt carcass of a dead one.**

Steve sidled up close to Venk. He knelt down and motioned the dwarf over.

"Now's your chance, man. She's looking the other way. Check her tail. You might find a few scales."

"But she's awake! How could I possibly—"

"She's giving you the opportunity to impress your kids. You'd better hurry before she changes her mind."

Pryllan rolled her closed reptilian eyes as she watched (through her shared visual abilities with Steve) the uncharacteristically timid dwarf inspect the tip of her tale and gently remove two scales that were ready to fall off of their own. Even though they were some of the tiniest scales on her body, the two scales Venk selected were each the size of a frisbee. Typically, she didn't care what happened to any of the scales that sloughed off, so if a dwarf wanted a few so that he might shine that much brighter in the eyes of his offspring, so be it. She inspected her tail to see how many had yet to fall off. Only a few remained. That was good. She noticed Steve had surreptitiously leaned around his mate and was inspecting her tail as well.

Sarah smacked her husband on his arm. "Don't even think about it."

Tucking the precious cargo safely away inside one of his many inner pockets, Venk resumed his place next to his brother.

Athos nodded. "That should keep 'em occupied."

"For a while at least," Venk agreed.

*That was very nice of you.*

Pryllan grunted in acknowledgement, eliciting puzzled looks from both Sarah and Rhenyon.

"So how do you want to do this?" Sarah asked, glancing over at Rhenyon before she looked up at Pryllan. "I can jump us all the way to the valley where the lake is."

"Couldn't you just take us to that fake boulder that was the dwarf door from before?" Steve asked, eliciting a frown from Rhenyon. "What's the matter? What's wrong with that idea?"

"It is said that several doors were destroyed. We must assume that is one of them. Besides, there is no cover. Any passing dragons would easily locate us."

"What about you?" Sarah asked, still staring up at the dragon. "I don't think I can teleport you there. Sorry, but you're just too big."

Pryllan shook her head. "Fear not. A healthy dragon can make the journey in about an hour. I can be there sooner if I push myself."

"That means we're going to be on our own for an hour," Steve muttered, not looking forward to being in the heart of dragon territory without a friendly dragon around. "Well, you'd better get going. The sooner you're up there, the better I'll feel."

"Agreed. Until we meet again."

Humans and dwarves alike were thrown to the ground as Pryllan explosively launched herself straight up and disappeared high into the clouds.

Sarah regained her feet first. "Okay, here we go. The safe zone I'm going to use is right at the forest's edge. The valley will be to the north and the lake will be about twenty miles off in the distance. Is everyone ready?"

Steve grasped Sarah's left arm while Rhenyon took her right. The dwarves looked about uncertainly until Steve pulled Breslin over and motioned for Athos and Venk to grab on as well. Screwing their eyes shut, the dwarves flinched as they were wrenched sideways. This time all three managed to stay on their feet, but only because Breslin retained his vise-like grip on Steve's arm.

Once he was certain the dwarves weren't going to topple over, Steve pulled his arm free and rubbed it in an attempt to restore circulation. The dwarves might be small in stature, but they definitely weren't weaklings. Steve sighed. That would be another bruise to add to his growing collection.

Rhenyon instantly crouched behind several tall ferns and pulled both Steve and Sarah with him. Following his lead, the three dwarves knelt down behind their own bushes and peered intently at the valley floor.

"What do you see?" Breslin inquired, unable to locate anything threatening in the immediate vicinity.

"Dragons. Two of them circling high in the sky."

Squinting up at the sky Steve could just see two swirling specks of color disappearing in and out of the clouds. One dragon was black, the other a dark green.

"We should be safe," Athos declared, rising to his feet. "Those overgrown reptiles should not be able to see us all the way down here."

Steve hooked two fingers on the dwarf's breastplate and yanked him back down.

"Trust me, pal, they can. They could see every strap of leather holding your armor in place. Their eyesight is a helluva lot better than yours and mine."

"How can you be certain?" Venk asked, crouching lower so he could better conceal himself from the prying wyverian eyes he was certain was staring straight at him.

"Oh, trust me, they can. Shared senses, remember? Pryllan could not only look through my eyes but I could look through hers, too. She could spot a tiny kyte flying several miles away."

"Do you think they have seen us?" Rhenyon whispered, peering up at the circling dragons.

"If they were looking straight at us, then we'd be toast. As it is, I'd say they haven't. They're probably circling over the area that had the dwarf doors in the hopes that some foolish dwarf would poke their heads up."

Athos and Venk both turned to stare at the fire thrower. "Sorry, no offense."

"None taken," Breslin assured him.

"What do we do now?" Sarah wanted to know. "Do we just sit here and wait for something to happen?"

"I don't see any movement out there," Steve reported, shading his eyes while he scanned the area.

"Is there not a human settlement nearby?" Breslin asked, turning to stare at Rhenyon. "Could she have gone there?"

"Aye, Verdayn is less than an hour's walk from here. There are no dwarves there, so I do not see why she would bother with the village."

"Would you really put it past her to not try and do something to the village?" Steve asked. "Can we really take that chance?"

"Blast. You are right. Should Celestia pay a visit, the village must be prepared. Lady Sarah, if you please."

Sarah leaned in and gave her husband a quick peck on the lips. "Be safe. I'll be back as soon as Rhenyon finishes whatever he needs to do. Here, take this." She unfastened her medallion, a gift from Shardwyn several years ago, and hooked it around Steve's neck. "Just in case."

"I'd rather you have it," Steve protested, reaching up to unfasten the necklace.

"No. I can get myself to safety faster than anyone. You can't. If it can help protect you, or if you need the vial of kaormac nectar for any emergencies, then at least you'll have it."

"Fine. You just stay safe, okay?"

"I will."

Rhenyon took Sarah's arm without being asked and the two of them vanished.

"Do you believe the sorceress is hiding in the village, Sir Steve?" Breslin asked, pulling Mythryd off his back to check the sharpness of its twin red blades. As always, the mythical axe was razor sharp.

Steve shook his head. "No, I think she's hiding here somewhere. Maybe those dragons have to be closer in order for her to dispatch a RIC after them. It's hard to say."

Steve was unsure how much time had passed. Maybe an hour? Two? Without a watch it was hard to say. Either way he was tired of sitting, his butt having fallen asleep a while ago. The dwarf brothers were whittling. Breslin appeared to be asleep. Nothing was happening! They were supposed to be trying to prevent a war and here they were, twiddling their thumbs. Where was the blasted sorceress, anyway?

He detected movement in his peripheral vision. What had caught his attention? He glanced up and saw that the two dragons from before, the black one and the green one, had been replaced by a single red dragon circling lazily, way above the highest clouds. The red dragon had started spiraling in tighter and tighter circles. Steve blinked a few times. Was the dragon descending?

His gaze snapped down to the valley floor. There was something moving about! A single dwarf was moving amongst the large boulders as he inspected the damages inflicted by the dragons earlier. Several of the massive boulders had fractured in multiple places, as though someone had hit them with an enormous sledge hammer. The stones that were still intact had been blackened to the point of resembling large charcoal briquettes.

"Are you kidding me? Take cover!" Steve nervously glanced up at the slowly descending dragon. "Guys. Heads up. We have trouble."

In a flash the three dwarves were on their feet and were staring intently at the solitary dwarf walking amongst the boulders. They were too far away to render any assistance, nor were they in shouting range. Steve squinted at the distant boulders. They were at least a mile or two away.

"The dragon's getting closer. What the hell is he doing? Get out of there! Come on, we have to go help him!"

"That's no dwarf," Breslin declared, catching a hold of Steve's arm and pulling him to a stop. "It's the sorceress. She's baiting the dragon!"

"What? That's totally a dwarf. Look at the clothes. He has

an axe strapped to his back, just like you guys do."

"A single dwarf not bothering to conceal himself?"

Steve was silent as he stared at the lone dwarf. "It does look as though he's swaggering about a bit," Steve conceded.

"Precisely. He's making sure he's seen."

"You would think he would be worried about the dragon," Breslin argued. "If it is Celestia, she has to see that the dragon *is* getting closer."

"In that case we should warn the dragon." Steve ignited his hands. "If that is Celestia in disguise, then she clearly wants the dragon to come closer so that she can sic the RIC on him. We can't let that happen!"

Breslin and the brothers nodded their heads. "Agreed. We must draw the dragon's attention!"

"What do you think is going to happen when the dragon sees you three? He's gonna go after the three of you instead of Celestia. Plus, since we don't have Sarah to get you guys to safety, you run the strong risk of being turned into French fries. Nuh uh. I'll do it. If I'm roasted, I stand the best chance of surviving." Steve turned to scowl up at the sky. "Where the hell is Pryllan? She should have been here by now."

When the red dragon was close enough that they could hear the beat of its enormous wings, the lone dwarf quickly reached down to the ground and flung a large oblong item up into the air. Two sets of wings, the larger primary wings being a dull mottled brown and the smaller secondary wings being the same brown but with streaks of dark red running from wingtip to body, unfurled and began flapping so fast that they became a blur, much like a hummingbird. However, this thing wasn't after nectar. It zeroed in on the large red dragon and sped off in hot pursuit. Fortunately, the dragon had noticed the artificial winged monster and had instantly reversed course and sped off into the clouds.

"She's gone! Celestia has vanished!"

Steve's gaze dropped back to the valley floor. Sure enough, the sorceress in disguise was nowhere to be seen.

"Dammit! Where'd she go? Did anyone see which way she went?"

The three dwarves silently shook their heads.

"Well, that's just—"

Steve was violently thrown to the ground, along with all three dwarves, as one moment they had been facing an empty valley and the next they were staring straight into the face of an enormous gold dragon. The dragon's impact had even dislodged several of the blackened boulders nearly a mile away!

"Whoa! Kahvel, give a little warning next time, okay? You just scared the—"

"There is no time," the gold dragon snapped, silencing the human instantly. "Pryllan has been attacked by one of those creatures. I am unable to remove it without inflicting further damage."

"Son of a …! What do you need me to do?"

"You have small appendages. You might be able to attack its undersides. I cannot. Get it off of her and I will destroy it."

"Sarah's not here," Steve began. "I don't know how I can get to—"

"Do you really think I am unaware of her taking a human rider?"

"Ummm …"

"I will forgive this transgression once. Let us be off."

"Are you suggesting what I think you're suggesting?"

In response, Kahvel deftly plucked Steve from the ground and placed him squarely on his back.

"Not one word of this to anyone, is that understood?"

"Mum's the word."

"Now let us be off."

"Keep your eyes open," Steve warned the three dwarves. "Celestia is still out there somewhere. I will be back just as soon as I can."

"We will, Sir Steve," Breslin assured him.

Kahvel's ascent into the air was much the same as his mate's. Before he knew it, Steve once more found himself airborne, but this time the senses were not shared, nor was he going to inquire about the possibility. Kahvel's right wing dipped, turning them gently eastward.

"So what happened to Pryllan?" Steve asked the dragon.

As before, when he first rode her years ago, the words were whipped out of his mouth and lost to the wind.

Steve sighed. Until they landed, or else Kahvel chose to share his wyverian senses, he'd be unable to communicate with the dragon.

Kahvel lurched suddenly, sending Steve to his knees. Kahvel lunged to his right; Steve grabbed the most secure handholds to try to hold on. The dragon banked sharply to his right once more. Gripping one of the smaller bony plates running down Kahvel's spine as tightly as he could, Steve leaned out over open space as much as he was able to, desperate to see what Kahvel was trying to avoid.

There, about a hundred feet below them was a RIC. Its four wings were beating smoothly as it maintained its pace with the fleeing dragon.

Kahvel banked sharply to the left. A second RIC had joined the pursuit and both were closing.

"Kahvel, can you hear me?"

The dragon did not respond.

Steve took a deep breath and shouted.

"KAHVEL, IF YOU CAN HEAR ME, GIVE ME SOME TYPE OF SIGN!"

The dragon spat a small fireball in response.

"FLY STRAIGHT! NO SWERVING!"

Kahvel again lunged to his right.

"TRUST ME! I'LL TAKE CARE OF THOSE THINGS!"

The dragon had to have heard him as his flying leveled off and became much more pleasant. Letting go of the small spinal plate, Steve ran along the dragon's back until he was as close to Kahvel's tail as he dared. He ignited a chaser and flung it at one of the RICs. The chaser covered the short distance to its target in less than two seconds and slammed into the RIC. Flames erupted from the damaged creature and it began emitting dark black smoke. However, the RIC was still in pursuit.

The second chaser punched through the thin metal skin of the RIC and a split second later, the giant metal tick exploded.

Steve gave the second RIC a malicious grin and ignited two chasers, hurling them one right after the other.

"Yippee kai yay, you ugly son of a —"

The remaining RIC exploded the instant his second chaser struck.

"I GOT 'EM!"

Kahvel banked slightly right as he started spiraling down toward a tiny lake not five miles from the valley. Landing on the southern edge of the small lake, Kahvel folded his wings and squatted down low. Steve slid down the dragon's back and landed on his feet. Pryllan, however, was nowhere to be found.

"Are you okay? None of those things got you, did they?"

"They did not. You have my thanks for eliminating that threat."

"Anytime, my friend. So where is she? Could she have flown off?"

"No. She lacks the strength to camouflage herself, so I had to do it myself."

Steve watched Kahvel stare hard at a group of rocks and boulders that looked as though they had spilled into the lake from a recent landslide. Steve swallowed. He hoped she wasn't buried under that! Wait. A landslide? From where? There's nothing but trees around and only a few scattered boulders. The rocks abruptly vanished and were replaced by the motionless form of the green dragon.

"Pryllan! Oh, man, are you okay?"

Kahvel's mate did not respond.

"The creature is there, on her back just above her wings. Do you think you can remove it?"

"I sure as hell can try. Lift me up there. Hurry!"

Kahvel held out his right forearm and waited while Steve hastily hopped on. He gently held his arm over his mate's back and waited for the human to jump off.

"So where is the—" Steve trailed off as he detected the faint coppery stench of blood in the air. Steeling himself, he moved up Pryllan's back, toward her head. He hated seeing her like this, in pain. The sooner he got that blasted RIC off her back, the sooner Kahvel could squash it like an ant.

There, above her right wing on the equivalent of her right shoulder blade, Steve saw something that had chewed its way through several layers of scales and was now embedded into the dragon's skin. Sarah was right. It was just like a tick! The head was concealed beneath the dragon's skin, and the two sets of wings were laying so flat against the RIC's back that it had all but disappeared into the creature's body. With its wings concealed, it looked like a giant, squashed, metallic drop of rain, with the point of the teardrop being the head.

Venturing closer, Steve inspected the RIC. It was roughly the size of a wheel barrow from his world. It couldn't be that heavy if Celestia was able to fling it up into the air. That had to mean the RIC was predominately hollow. How was he supposed to eradicate this thing?

Steve pondered a moment before he shrugged. The ticks from his home world really didn't care for fire, so what could it hurt to see if these things behaved the same?

Steve ignited his hands and blasted the creature from above, watching with satisfaction as the two smaller wings melted off. The RIC stirred; it started buzzing. The creature lurched forward, burying another foot or so of itself into Pryllan's body. The dragon groaned in pain as the parasite burrowed deeper into her flesh.

"Okay, so I can't burn you off, but unfortunately for you, sucker, I've learned that I can get things a lot hotter if I touch them. Let's see what you think of this." He turned to look at Kahvel, who was eagerly watching from above. "I'm going to get its attention. Are you ready?"

"Aye. As soon as it comes free, get clear."

Steve nodded. "You got it. Here we go."

Steve lit both hands and sprinted toward the creature, slapping both hands on the RIC's smooth carapace. The RIC was definitely metallic! It was confirmed, it *was* a construct! The RIC began glowing red almost instantly. The buzzing grew stronger. It was working! The RIC slowly extricated itself from Pryllan's skin, intent on finding a more hospitable locale.

"It's coming up!" Steve called out. "Watch me! As soon as it's clear, I'm going to jump out of the way!"

"I am ready."

Blasting twin jets of flame as well as instructing his jhorun to heat the creature just as hot as he could get it, he saw the RIC finally pull its head free. Its four artificial eyes fixated on Steve and the buzzing became higher in pitch.

Steve let go and launched himself backward, scrambling to put as much distance as he could between himself and the creature. At that instant, a huge golden claw appeared and plucked the RIC off of Pryllan's back. Kahvel dropped the mechanical bug on the ground and raised a foreleg so that he could smash it flat.

"No!" Steve warned, drawing the dragon's attention. "Don't touch that thing if you don't have to!"

In the instant the dragon had hesitated, the RIC unfurled its undamaged primary wings and took to the air. It managed to retreat about twenty feet into the sky before Kahvel grabbed two boulders, each the size of a swimming pool, and smashed them into it from either side. The two massive stones broke apart from the impact and crumbled to the ground. Pieces of the RIC also fell to the ground, demolished by the impact.

"I'd say you got 'em," Steve observed from Pryllan's back. He started working his way back to her right shoulder blade when Pryllan groaned again.

Steve paused. She had groaned like that when the RIC burrowed deeper into her skin. Was there another one? He could still smell blood in the air, but then again, she had an open wound on her shoulder. Then he heard it: a faint buzzing sounded nearby. There *was* another one!

"Heads up! We've got another one to take care of!"

Kahvel was by his mate's side again in a flash. "Where?"

"I'm not sure. I can hear it, and I heard her groan again."

Kahvel growled, low and ominous. "Here. The other is just below her left hind leg. This one is buried even deeper."

Steve hurried over and cursed softly. There was only a foot or so of metallic skin still visible. If he burned it from above, and if the RIC chose to burrow even further, they'd be out of luck and Pryllan would be doomed.

As if sensing his thoughts, Kahvel shook his head. "Do it."

"You sure?"

"Aye. You have her trust, and you have mine. Do what you can."

"If it does start to come out, be ready."

Kahvel selected two more enormous boulders and set them nearby. He nodded at the fire thrower.

Steve hurried over and slapped his hands on the tail end of the creature. As before, the RIC was glowing red within seconds. The buzzing grew louder as the creature stirred. It was working! The mechanical tick was slowly withdrawing itself!

"Here it comes! Get ready!"

Kahvel tensed, ready to snatch the foul creature off his mate's back just as soon as he was able.

"There it goes! Grab it!"

As before, Kahvel snatched the RIC before it could fly away and smashed it to bits by slamming the two gigantic rocks into it. Kahvel gently brushed bits of broken rock off Pryllan's body and inspected the wound on her leg.

"She has lost a lot of blood. I am not sure she will recover."

"Oh, yes she will."

Steve strode over to Pryllan's inert form and used her large spinal scales to climb onto her back. He gingerly pulled Sarah's medallion from around his neck and activated the hidden compartment. There, nestled inside, was the precious vial of kaormac juice, an elixir known for its remarkable curative properties. He pried the stopper off, placed his index finger over the opening, and then held it upside down. Righting the vial, he smiled as he noticed a single glistening drop of the elixir on the tip of his finger. Squatting down on one knee, he placed his finger on the gaping shoulder wound.

Bones and muscle tissues regrew. The torn skin sealed itself right before his eyes and glossy green scales sprouted to replace the damaged ones. Within seconds there was no trace a RIC had ever been embedded in Pryllan's skin.

Steve hurriedly returned to her flank to inspect the second injury. Repeating the process, he applied a single drop to the ragged wound. Since that RIC had clearly been attached longer, the wound was much more severe, taking three times as long to regenerate damaged tissues, muscles, tendons, and scales. In the end, Steve administered a second drop of the healing elixir. Just to be certain.

Pryllan finally stirred. Her green eyes opened and fixed on her mate.

"It feels as though my strength has returned. How is this possible?"

"The creatures have been extricated."

"You were successful after all? I told you all you had to do was try."

The gold dragon huffed irritably. "I did try. I was unsuccessful."

Pryllan's nostrils flared. Her gaze dropped and fell on Steve.

"So, you were able to —"

Pryllan's eyes widened as she realized Sarah was not present. She flicked her gaze back to her mate. How did Steve get here? That could only mean—

Kahvel nodded. "Aye, I know of your rider. I have known for some time now."

Pryllan's shocked eyes swiveled back to Steve's.

"Hey, I didn't tell him. I swear."

"Kahvel, you must know that I—"

"Next time," the gold dragon growled, "wash the scent of the human off of you."

"Hey! Are you saying I stink?"

Kahvel's neutral gaze rested momentarily on him. Was he smiling? Was he upset? Steve couldn't tell.

The two dragons suddenly snapped their heads around to stare off to the south. Both dragons growled so low and deep that Steve felt it before he heard it.

"What's wrong? Do you guys hear something?"

"How many?" Kahvel asked, once again ignoring the human.

"How many what?" Steve wanted to know.

Pryllan was silent for a few seconds as she gazed off into the distance. "By my count, at least forty."

Steve waved his arms. "Guys? Down here please. What's

going on?"

"Did you not hear the call?" Kahvel asked, looking down at the human. "Rinbok has sounded the attack."

"No, I didn't hear any—wait. Did you say forty? Forty what? RICs?" Steve whistled. "Why would there be that many unless …"

Kahvel shook his head. "Forty of our brothers have taken to the sky. The dwarves must have finally revealed themselves."

"But the dwarves aren't responsible for this! It's that damn sorceress!"

"We know this and you know this," Pryllan gently added, shaking her head. "But no one else does."

"What can we do?"

"We must obey the summons. We go to battle."

"What about those RIC things? With that many dragons in the air you have to figure that Celestia will unleash her bloodsuckers on you guys."

"We will destroy them as best we can."

"You two need to think about this!" Steve insisted. "Celestia designed those things to specifically kill dragons. Two got you, Pryllan! Two almost got you, Kahvel. No, don't growl at me. It's true. You guys can't beat these things. Even if you flee, they'll catch you!"

"We are dragons," Kahvel proudly declared. "We are not afraid of any creature, be it natural or unnatural. We do not flee."

"What a crock! When those two were chasing us, weren't you doing just that?"

Kahvel's long golden neck whipped around until he was practically nose to nose with the human.

"I was *not* fleeing. I was biding my time until I could determine the best course of action to eliminate the —"

Kahvel trailed off as he noticed the look that passed between his mate and the human. His large golden eyes narrowed with annoyance while the other two wyverian eyes sought out something else to look at. Sighing irritably, Kahvel straightened and extended both wings as he prepared to take off.

"Hey, don't leave me here by myself! I can cover someone's back if one of those things gets too close!"

Kahvel hesitated a few seconds. While he detested the thought of his mate allowing a human rider, he couldn't dismiss the added security the human fire thrower could provide if she was attacked again. Why Pryllan was so attached to this human, he couldn't say. At least the biped did seem to care about her welfare, and that could not be discredited, no matter how much he wanted to think otherwise.

Kahvel stretched out a foreleg, picked Steve up off the ground, and dropped him onto Pryllan's back. Once again, he went nose to nose with the human.

"Protect her. Do not let any of those creatures near her."

Steve nodded. "You got it, buddy."

Kahvel blasted into the air. A second later Pryllan joined him. Within moments they were both hundreds of feet above the ground, heading back toward the valley.

Warmth spread throughout Steve's body as Pryllan shared her wyverian senses with him. The howling wind died away. His eyes stopped watering, and everything leapt into incredible detail. He wished for the umpteenth time that his visual and auditory acuities were one tenth of what the dragon possessed. One moment he was inspecting the valley floor hundreds of feet away and the next, their combined gaze shifted skyward as Pryllan searched for signs of Celestia's lethal devices.

Kahvel broke off and joined five others circling high above the valley floor. Steve leaned out, over Pryllan's back, and cursed softly to himself as he watched hundreds of dwarves stream out of several large openings in the earth. Makeshift shelters were rapidly constructed as at least two full clans of dwarves prepared for an aerial assault. He hoped the Kla Guur were not involved.

"At least there are no signs of RICs," Steve commented.

Pryllan nodded. "For now."

No sooner had he made the comment about the absence of the RICs when they both saw a swarm of small winged creatures emerge from the edge of the forest several miles away and streak toward them. Pryllan growled and banked sharply to her left.

Within moments five RICs were buzzing steadily behind her. Fortunately, they weren't gaining. However, they weren't falling away, either. No matter how much they swerved and rolled, ducked and dodged, the RICs deftly maneuvered themselves to stay dangerously close to Pryllan's tail.

"You need to tell the others how to kill those things!" Steve shouted as the huge green dragon continued to swerve erratically through the air as she evaded the mechanical monsters.

"Which is how, precisely?" Pryllan inquired, firing off a huge fireball toward one of the metallic creatures that was in pursuit of a large white dragon with jagged stripes on its abdomen. The RIC darted out of the way; Pryllan's fireball missed its target and, thankfully, slammed into a vacant stretch of open grassland far below.

"You have to hit 'em twice. Like this. Watch."

Steve cocked back his arm and threw a chaser at the RIC still in pursuit of the white dragon. A moment later a second chaser sped out after its twin, veering straight toward the aberration, intent on bringing it down. As before, the RIC swerved to avoid the chaser, but this time the chaser swerved as well, and slammed into the metal tick. The two smaller wings started fluttering erratically. Smoke streamed out from the two secondary wing holes, leaving a dark trail, reminding Steve of daredevil pilots who would leave similar trails in the sky. Several seconds later, the chaser's twin caught up and slammed into the creature's carapace, punching a hole through the metallic skin. The RIC exploded, sending chunks of twisted metal falling harmlessly to the valley floor.

"Hit them twice," Steve instructed again. "I don't know why it happens, but the first hit must nullify some type of protection spell on it, 'cause the second hit punches through the skin like a hot knife through butter."

Not really understanding Steve's analogy of a warm dagger through butter, whatever that was, Pryllan mentally relayed instructions for destroying the RICs to her fellow dragons. How were they supposed to destroy these creatures? Her shots wouldn't curve on their own accord, so how were they supposed to hit a moving target, let alone twice?

A dragon roared in pain as one of the RICs made contact. Pryllan's head snapped around to search for the victim. A dark green dragon, with white wing tips, had not managed to shake one of its pursuers. The RIC had latched on to her back just below her left wing. Pryllan roared in frustration. If only she could —

"Don't just stand there, get me over there!"

"We are hundreds of feet in the air. What do you think you will be able to do?

"Get me on that dragon's back and I'll kill Celestia's creation. I have a ton of mimets, so I won't be running out of jhorun anytime soon. Hurry! Get me over there before another one latches on someplace where I won't be able to reach!"

Pryllan hesitated. It was one thing to defy Rinbok Intherer, their leader, by taking a rider, but to deposit a human on one of her brethren's back would be a bold announcement to everyone that, quite literally, she had turned her back on her own culture. That sort of behavior had led to the downfall of many a dragon.

"Pryllan, I'll take full responsibility for this," Steve called to her from her back. "We cannot let that dragon die, not while I can kill that thing. Come on, just get me over there!"

Resigning herself to disciplinary actions which could result in her banishment, she flew toward the injured dragon. She stretched her left foreleg behind her and up as high on her neck as she could and waited for Steve to climb up her back and slide into her open claw. Increasing her velocity, she easily overtook the injured dragon and passed as close as she was able without disrupting either of their flight paths. She dropped Steve on the green dragon's back and flew off to monitor the scene from a safe distance. She didn't personally know this dragon, but she did know it was a female, and the females could be even more dangerous than the males if they felt provoked. Or insulted by having a human dropped on them.

Picking his way around the large spinal plates, Steve hurried toward the dragon's wings. He had to act fast, as this dragon was losing speed and it was only a matter of time before it was attacked by another RIC. Steve knelt down and inspected the artificial tick. It had just wrapped its four wings tightly around its body and had already chewed its way through the scales and had hit the soft tissue underneath. The dragon groaned in pain as the RIC shifted slightly and burrowed even deeper into the dragon's body.

Hesitating only long enough to determine that his jhorun was still running at optimum levels, Steve slapped both hands on the RIC and heated it as hot and as fast as he could. The RIC buzzed angrily as it detected it was rapidly approaching the point in which it would melt. Its sense of self-preservation kicked in and it began withdrawing itself, unsure why this location had become suddenly inhospitable.

Just as soon as its narrow head had extricated itself completely from the dragon's skin, Steve focused all his jhorun into one hand, dropped as low as he could, and blasted the RIC from underneath. He watched with satisfaction as the RIC was flicked off the dragon's skin, as if a wasp had landed on his own arm. Steve threw two chasers in rapid succession. Several seconds later the destroyed RIC was falling to the ground in pieces.

Being careful not to drop the tiny vial or its stopper, Steve withdrew the kaormac elixir and administered a drop to the injured dragon's back. In just a few moments the dragon's skin was blemish free.

Regaining its strength, the newly healed dragon ascended higher into the sky. It was unsure how it had regained its strength, but it wasn't about to argue the point. The dragon hesitated. Having a sense of smell much greater than practically every other living creature in Lentari, the dragon now knew it still carried a visitor on its back.

It still amazed Steve how fast a creature as large as a Lentarian mountain dragon could move. One minute he had successfully dispatched the RIC and had healed the wound, and the next he was staring at the green dragon face to face. The supple reptilian neck had allowed the dragon to bend all the way around so that they were now looking at each other straight in the eyes. A tiny wisp of smoke trickled out of the dragon's left nostril.

"Look, I don't have time to be scared. Want to be mad at me? Fine. Do so later. I got that thing off your back and destroyed it. I even healed you."

The dragon said nothing. A second tiny tendril of smoke escaped from the dragon's nostril. Could it even understand him?

"Okay, you're pissed. I get it. I don't care. Worry about it later." Steve turned to point at a small red dragon that had just roared in pain. "Fly over there. That one has been hit and I need to get that damn thing off its back as soon as possible."

The massive horned head finally moved as it turned slightly to observe its injured brethren.

Steve stomped the dragon's back with his right foot, causing those disconcerting slitted eyes to refocus back on him.

"If we wait any longer, it'll get hit by another. Come on, move it!"

Incredibly, the dragon banked to the right. It was working! He was being escorted to the red dragon!

"Fly as low as you can and I'll just hop off. Remember, it takes two blasts to take these damn things out. Spread the word. And don't let them touch you!"

Steve slid down the green dragon's side and dropped off just as the red dragon passed underneath. It was a drop of about ten feet but luckily, he was able to avoid the massive spikes and jagged plates scattered along its back. He quickly rolled to his feet and sprinted up the dragon's neck and slapped both hands on the RICs back. Within moments he had blasted the metal monster off the dragon's back and destroyed it with two well aimed chasers. A tiny drop of the healing elixir restored the dragon to full strength and it, too, whipped its head around to inspect its savior.

Steve waved a hand. "No need to thank me. If you'd like to file a complaint, find me later and we'll sort it out then. Who's next?"

This dragon wasn't as thankful. Both nostrils closed with a ping and its jaws opened. A faint orange swirl appeared at the back of the mouth.

**Jump off. I am underneath.**

*Beautiful timing. I don't think this one likes me.*

**Are you surprised? Dragons do not tolerate riders.**

*You do.*

**Be that as it may, he is ready to fire. Jump now!**

Steve flung himself off the red dragon's back just as it unleashed a jet of fire at him. Flames licked at his back and he felt the intense blast of fire as he started speeding toward the ground many hundreds of feet below. Where the hell was Pryllan? Wasn't she supposed to be right below him?

**Fear not. I had to deviate for a few moments. I finally destroyed one of those creatures. It was very difficult. I fired off at least ten —**

*Hello! I'm kinda falling to my death here! Would you mind coming to get me?*

In the blink of an eye, Steve's freefall was cut short as the dragon swooped out of nowhere and deftly plucked him from the air. Pulling out of her steep descent, she leveled out just long enough to let Steve climb onto her back.

"If you please, would you kindly dispose of the creature that is now following us?"

Steve turned to look back behind them. There, about fifty feet behind them, and closing fast, was another RIC. Two chasers brought it down.

Pulling out a mimet to recharge his tiring jhorun, Steve watched the frantic activity around them. Thus far, the dragons were doing an admirable job of avoiding the deadly RICs. They hadn't managed to score many kills, but at least they were making progress. One jet black dragon just streaked by him with two RICs in hot pursuit. A second black dragon trailed behind. The second dragon spat a well-aimed fireball that was strong enough to hit the first RIC and bounce over to the second. Both of the artificial bloodsuckers began emitting smoke. A second fireball fired by the dragon hit one of the RICs, destroying it, but missed the second. The remaining RIC edged closer to the first black dragon. The second black dragon fired again, but missed. In just a few seconds it would be close enough to latch on!

Steve generated a large chaser and threw it at the RIC. He watched as it streaked toward the damaged machine. Five seconds later, it struck its target and the metal tick exploded.

**That was not intelligent.**

*You said it yourself. The time for discretion is over. I'll be damned if I let one of those things hurt a dragon if I can help it.*

**Observe. He is now searching for you. He knows it was not dragon fire that destroyed the creature.**

*Then get us out of here!*

**The point is moot. We have been seen. His mate is watching us.**

Steve swallowed nervously. He had forgotten about the dragon that was being chased. Its neck was turned and its head was staring straight at him. Not at Pryllan, but him. He looked at the dragon's mate. It, too, was now staring at him.

The black dragons were motionless for a few moments before they banked sharply south and sped off.

Steve rubbed his temples and sighed. They were probably going to punish Pryllan. He'd just have to convince their leader, Rinbok whatshisname, that she was innocent. There was certainly nothing he could do about it now. He had other dragons to save.

*Look at that big one over there, the big green one with black stripes all over him. He just got hit by two RICs.*

Pryllan hesitated.

*Look, I know the other dragons probably know about us by now, but dammit, we'll have to worry about that later. First things first. We need to help that one. Let's go.*

**But that is —**

The massive striped dragon roared in pain as a third RIC attached itself to its lower back.

*Pryllan, there's more of 'em on its tail! MOVE!*

As before, Pryllan overtook the ailing dragon and flew over just as Steve dropped off her back. Gripping a curved scale tightly, Steve carefully scanned the area. One RIC had attached itself just below the dragon's left wing. That was the first one to be evicted. A quick drop of elixir had the wound completely healed.

Steve nodded his head and smiled as new scales sprouted

and covered the previously torn skin. At that moment, two more RICs came swooping in from above and landed nearby, one ready to latch on to the right wing and the other was ready to chew through the new scales that had grown to replace those that had been damaged in the previous attack.

"Really? Do you not see me right here?"

Steve dropped flat on his stomach and blasted the closest RIC from beneath, sending the monster tumbling through the air while it desperately flapped its four wings to try and right itself. Two chaser blasts later and the RIC was destroyed.

A flash of fire behind him caused him to whirl about, halfway expecting to find himself face-to-face with yet another ungracious victim. What he found was the second RIC had been blasted off the big dragon's back by a well-placed shot by Pryllan. Steve threw a chaser to finish the job.

Working quickly, Steve evicted and destroyed the last two RICs and administered two more drops of kaormac juice to completely heal the enormous dragon.

**Get off my back, human.**

Steve paled. That wasn't Pryllan's thought he had just picked up. It didn't sound thankful, or grateful, but annoyed. Angry. Powerful. Male.

*Pryllan, I think it's time to go!*

Pryllan's urgent command stirred him into motion.

**Hurry, get off his back! I am close.**

*You sure? You said that before, remember? You weren't there.*

**Do not argue with me! Get off his back! Now!**

Steve rushed to the edge of the dragon's back and leapt out into open space. True to her word, Pryllan was waiting for him.

*He spoke to me!*

**I know. I heard him, too. He made sure of it.**

*Is that a bad thing?*

**Very.**

*Why?*

**That was the dragon lord.**

*What??*

**You just met Rinbok Intherer.**

*Why didn't you say something?*

**I tried. You did not let me finish.**

*So, what does this mean?*

**Our fates have been sealed.**

*Don't be so melodramatic. We just saved his life. That has to account for something.*

**I would not be so sure.**

*So, what's going on? Are the dragons attacking the dwarves?*

**As luck would have it, no. My brethren have been preoccupied with the metal creatures.**

*What have the dwarves been doing?*

**Constructing shelters. They appear to be waiting for the most opportune time to strike.**

*With what?*

**Unknown.**

*Where's Celestia?*

**I am not familiar with her appearance. I cannot say.**

*She's going to be disguised. Look for a single dwarf off by himself. That'll be her.*

Pryllan shifted her gaze to the distant ground and began searching for any solitary dwarves that stood out from the others. Unfortunately, there were many candidates. However, they were all collectively working on fortifying their makeshift shelters against any aerial attacks. If the sorceress was down there, then she'd be forced to do manual labor with the others or else risk blowing her cover. Therefore, she would probably be off by herself as far away from the dwarves as possible.

*Try by the trees*, Steve suggested. *That's where all those RICs seemed to come from.*

Pryllan slowly moved her gaze along the forest's edge. Tall, majestic pine trees ringed the valley perimeter. Waist high spindly bushes were also interspersed every twenty feet or so.

**I think I see him. Or her.**

*Where? I don't see anything.*

**Apologies. One moment.**

She had inadvertently withdrawn her wyverian senses from Steve as she searched for the sorceress. She activated her senses one more time and gazed at a point several miles away.

*That's her! Look! She's holding an inert RIC. What is she doing with her right hand?*

**It would appear she is clasping something. A medallion?**

The image shifted as it zoomed closer. The dwarf they were watching was staring intently at the sky, waiting for the most opportune time to launch the next RIC. She was clutching some type of pendant in her right hand. A closer inspection of the dwarf's face revealed unblinking eyes and moving lips. He/she was chanting!

Steve generated the biggest chaser he could and flung it at her. Moments later Pryllan fired off one of her own fireballs. Together they watched as chaser and fireball sped toward the phony dwarf. His chaser struck first, however a blue shield appeared and deflected his attack. Pryllan's fireball met the same fate.

*There's your target! Hit her again! Spread the word!*

Steve fired off chaser after chaser at the sorceress, while Pryllan launched several additional shots, all to no avail. The balls of fire bounced harmlessly off the protective shield Celestia had cast about herself.

Loud whooshing noises sounded from all around them. Bursts of light shot through the clouds, from the ground, from everywhere there was a dragon. Each and every dragon had targeted the sorceress and had unleashed everything they had at her. Multiple times.

The first dozen fireballs slammed into Celestia's shield, overloading its protective capabilities. The image of the dwarf disappeared, replaced by a furious girl in her mid-twenties, wearing an ankle-length white robe. Her lips were curled back in a snarl as she stared straight at dragon and rider. Quick as a snake, she whipped her long braided hair out of the way, reached into one of her many pouches, and threw some type of black powder into the air. A ball of black fire, easily the size of his pickup truck, formed in the air and sped straight toward them.

It was over in less than five seconds. The dark fireball sped unerringly toward the two of them, setting off an explosion many times more powerful than Steve had ever generated.

The rest of the dragon shots struck their target as well, but Celestia was gone. When the smoke finally cleared, Steve and Pryllan had vanished as well.

# Chapter 6 - Teleporter Troubles

Sarah stared at the open space in shock. All traces of her husband and the dragon had completely disappeared. She felt a lump form in her throat. Deep down she knew something bad had just happened. What had Celestia done to Steve?

The world started to spin and Sarah discovered she really needed to sit down. She felt strong arms hold her steady and lower her to the ground. Rhenyon. Rhenyon was here. That was good.

"Do not believe it," the former commander ordered, staring again up at the open expanse of sky. "Did you see the black fireball? Celestia is responsible for this. Somehow, she has banished them."

"To — to where?"

Rhenyon sighed. "I know not, milady. We have to assume that wherever they are, they are safe."

"If that psycho sorceress did this, do you really think they're safe?" Sarah snapped. She was instantly sympathetic.

"I'm sorry, Rhenyon. I didn't mean to bite your head off. I'm worried."

"They are alive, milady. We just have to find out what happened to them."

Sarah's eyes were close to filling. "How can you be so certain?"

The commander took a deep breath. "Please accept my apologies for having to say this, but if you observe the evidence?"

"*What* evidence?" Sarah asked, trying her hardest to keep an edge from her voice.

"My point exactly. There is no evidence. Do you see their remains anywhere? You saw what I saw: an exploding black fireball. There would have been some type of remains, yet nothing fell to the ground. *Nothing!*"

Sarah blinked away her tears. He did have a point. She shuddered to think it, but even if her husband's body was incinerated by that blast, there was no way the explosion was powerful enough to dispose of Pryllan's body. Celestia *had* to have done something.

"There! In the trees!"

Sarah whipped her head around. No more than fifty feet away she saw a young woman's face briefly appear as she peeked between trees. Sarah squinted. Was that Celestia? The woman staring up at the sky with a victorious smile on her face was young, maybe in her mid-twenties. The woman heard the shouts, looked over at the rapidly advancing group of men and dwarves, and flung the inert RIC she had been holding up into the air. The RIC disappeared in the sky while the woman sped off into the trees, clutching a medallion around her neck.

"After her! She must be stopped!"

Blind hatred had Sarah following the soldiers and dwarves running into the forest. She had to know what Celestia did to her husband. If the sorceress had transported her husband somewhere, then she sure as heck could bring him back. If not, no amount of magic would be able to bring her back from where Sarah would teleport her.

"Halt! Who goes there?"

The command drew her up short. All she could see were trees. Was someone speaking to her?

"I'm—"

"I am Balos, of the Kla Chanus. Identify."

"Commander Rhenyon, from R'Tal."

Sarah resumed her trek forward, intent on finding the owners of the voices.

"Human. You seek the sorceress, do you not?"

"Aye. We're track her south."

"We came from the south. My troops and I were tracking her north."

Another voice chimed in. "We were following a human woman from the east."

"The ruddy wench is playing us for fools!"

"Then which blasted way did she go?"

"She's already long gone, lads," a familiar voice said.

"Sir Steve and the green dragon have disappeared," she heard Rhenyon say, eliciting gasps from many of the dwarves.

Sarah briefly smiled. Her husband was very well known amongst the dwarven population. Rounding a bend, she arrived at a small break in the trees and saw at least thirty armed dwarves.

"What did she do to them?" Breslin demanded. The dwarf pushed by his companions and rounded on Rhenyon, as though he was responsible for more than being the bearer of bad news.

Rhenyon shook his head. "Unknown."

"There's no sense looking for her in here. Let's return to the valley."

Emerging from the confines of the dense forest, Sarah gasped and came to a sudden halt. So did everyone else. It was so quiet they could have heard a pin drop. Directly in front of them, wings spread as though it might return to the sky, was a dragon so huge that its wingspan alone had to be over a hundred fifty feet. The dragon's sleek body was dark green, almost black, and its wings had jagged black stripes, much like a tiger's, all over his body, including his wings. Just behind it and to its right was a familiar gold dragon. Scattered behind them were at least thirty other dragons of various hues and colors. All were waiting, motionless, as they stared at the two humans.

The dwarves leapt into formation behind Sarah and Rhenyon, forming an armored semi-circle. The dragons ignored them. Four mounds of earth inexplicably rose into the air as four subterranean tunnels were revealed, scattered along the forest's edge. Dwarves began pouring out, fully armed. More dwarves streamed out of the forest, taking up positions by their companions. In a few minutes there were over five hundred dwarves standing motionless behind Sarah and Rhenyon. Grim faced, the dwarves stared at their reptilian adversaries, who continued to ignore them. All wyverian eyes were focused on one person: Sarah.

"Why are they staring at me?" Sarah whispered to Rhenyon.

The big green dragon in front took several thundering steps forward and stretched its long neck out. When it became clear that the dragon was intent on getting closer to the two of them, Rhenyon pushed Sarah behind him. Sarah looked at Kahvel, hoping to make eye contact, but the gold dragon refused to look at her. In fact, Kahvel's eyes never strayed more than a few feet from its front talons.

The big dragon sniffed the air. It continued to stare at Sarah for a few moments before it finally withdrew its head and resumed its imposing stance at the head of the … of the … Sarah hesitated. What do you call a group of dragons? A coven? Flight?

"Human, do you know who I am?"

Both Rhenyon and Sarah shook their heads no. Surprised, the dragon hesitated a few moments.

"I am Rinbok Intherer. I am Dragon Lord over all wyverians in these mountains."

Sarah and Rhenyon remained silent.

"I smell the human who rode on my back, but do not see him. Produce him. Now."

Sarah swallowed nervously. She didn't know what to say. Steve rode on that big dragon's back? He clearly must have done so without its permission. Why would he do that? What was he thinking? He knew better than to hop on a strange dragon's back, especially since Kahvel warned him all those years ago that dragon riding was forbidden.

"I cannot say why Sir Steve was on your back, dragon," Rhenyon began, glancing quickly back at the woman he was guarding. "But if he did, then he must have had a good reason to do so."

"No human rides a dragon. Ever."

Several of the dragons were slowly moving closer. Sarah heard a rustling of movement behind her as the dwarves who weren't holding their axes pulled them off their holders. Rhenyon held up his hands.

"Wait. Just wait. There's no need to —"

One of the dragons spoke up. "My lord, do not place fault with the humans. I knew of the human rider and did nothing to stop it. The fault lies with me."

The big dragon turned its massive horned head to regard Kahvel, who was still staring at the ground.

"Speak, Kahvel. What do you know about this?"

"My mate was the one who allowed the human rider. I cannot say why she did, only that she did. I learned of it later, but seeing how the human went back to his world, I assumed the problem had resolved itself."

"The human was not from this world?" The huge head swung back around until it was facing Sarah again. "You have his scent all over you. Are you his mate?"

Sarah didn't trust her voice to not come out as a squeak, so she just nodded. She wanted to teleport out of there, badly, but somehow she knew if she were to vanish with Rhenyon, it would go badly for the humans in the dragons' eyes. Not to mention she wouldn't abandon the dwarves, whom she viewed as family even though she didn't know any of them.

Kahvel finally stirred, moving around his leader's right wing and positioning himself in a spot where he and the humans could be seen without Rinbok having to swing his head back and forth.

"My lord, this is Sarah, mate of Steve. They are the Nohrin, sworn protectors of the little human prince, Mikal."

Rinbok flicked his irritated eyes to Kahvel's. "The fire thrower was the rider?"

Kahvel nodded.

The Dragon Lord lowered his head once more to stare at Sarah up close. "That makes you the teleporter, does it not?"

Again, Sarah nodded.

"Why do you not just leave, teleporter?"

Sarah found her voice.

"To leave would be admitting guilt. I am not guilty of anything. Yes, my husband rode on Pryllan's back. Yes, he knew it was forbidden. But both he and Pryllan knew that they worked better as a team and, as a result, they were able to help save the life of the queen the last time we were here. Besides, I will not leave here and let you think the dwarves are responsible for creating those horrible metal things."

"Enlighten me. Who is?"

"A human sorceress intent on destroying the alliance between humans and dragons."

Rinbok angled his head slightly to observe the many rows of silent dwarves standing behind them.

"If what you say is true, then why involve the dwarves?"

"Humans and dwarves are also allies," Sarah explained. "How do you top ruining one alliance? By ruining two. She found a way to kill two birds with one stone."

Thin wisps of smoke trickled out of both nostrils as Rinbok stared at her.

"By that, I mean, she found a way to accomplish two goals by only doing the work to accomplish one."

"Where is this human sorceress now?"

"We were just searching for her," Rhenyon explained. "She fled into the forest. We pursued. We then encountered several clans of dwarves, who indicated they had been in pursuit as well. However, she must have doubled back at some point as we all came from different directions."

"Therefore, you were not successful in apprehending her?"

Rhenyon shook his head. "We were not."

Rinbok turned to study the hundreds of silent dwarves. "Why mass for battle if you have done nothing wrong?"

"Because you destroyed several of our hidden entrances, dragon."

Pushing his way through the rows of stationary dwarves was none other than Maelnar, celebrated key maker of the Kla Guur. He pushed his way past Sarah and Rhenyon and glared at the creature that towered over his head. Sarah was bewildered. Where had Maelnar come from? There must be another entrance to the dwarves' realm nearby.

"Do not play coy with me, dragon. You know damn well why we are here. Ten of our stairways have been decimated. We have our own methods for dealing with wyverian assaults."

Rinbok snorted with mirth. "Indeed. I do believe I would like to see what you can—"

"Rinbok, Maelnar, enough of this!"

A male voice, calm and collected, rang out, silencing the dwarves' chatter as well as catching Rinbok's attention.

Kri'Entu, decked out in his finest armor, emerged from the forest. He stepped around Sarah and stood beside the dwarf.

"Entu."

"Rinbok Intherer."

"You come unarmed? Unwise."

"I am not unarmed."

"Then have your soldiers reveal themselves."

"Very well." The king gave no audible or visual signal, yet several hundred armed soldiers emerged from the trees and formed ranks right beside the dwarves.

Men and dwarves alike eyed each other briefly before returning their attention to their respective leaders.

"For two species to claim innocence in these matters, you certainly do appear to be prepared for battle," one black dragon muttered.

Rinbok's head whipped around until he was nearly nose to nose with a small black dragon that had been continuously edging closer. The Dragon Lord growled his displeasure at his subordinate. The black dragon lowered its head to the ground and kept it there.

"What can I do to convince you of our good intentions?" Kri'Entu asked. "The girl acts on her own behalf, and in no way should it be construed that her insane behavior is typical of all humans."

"Prove it," Rinbok sneered.

Kri'Entu nodded. "Very well. Commander, I believe you have a missing sorceress to locate. Take the men and find her."

Sarah's eyes widened as she looked at Rhenyon. The commander was scowling, clearly not happy leaving the king unprotected.

"As you wish, Your Majesty."

Turning his back on one of the most dangerous situations he had ever been witness to, Rhenyon gave orders to split into teams of four and fan out. Dedicated and loyal, the soldiers obeyed instantly.

Once all of the human soldiers had departed, leaving only Sarah, the commander, and the king, she nervously looked at the leader of the dragons. Those unnerving green slitted eyes had shifted to the dwarf. Stroking his beard thoughtfully, Maelnar followed Kri'Entu's example and ordered the dwarves to conduct searches as well, and also to aid the human soldiers whenever and wherever they could. Before dismissing the hundreds of dwarves, Maelnar turned to Rinbok.

"Can I assume that they will have nothing to fear from the dragons as they search the valley? That conniving wench is out there somewhere and we must be allowed to conduct a thorough search."

"No dragon will harm human or dwarf while this search is being conducted," Rinbok agreed, impressed that the soldiers were leaving the human king and dwarf council member alone.

"Now, I would say we have taken several steps toward proving our innocence in these matters," Kri'Entu stated, staring up at the enormous dragon. "I challenge you to reciprocate."

The huge dragon studied the king. "Very well. Search from the ground; we will search from the air. There is a lone human female out there," the dragon informed his followers. "Find her. Report to me the instant she is located."

Kahvel's headed snapped up.

"If I may, my lord."

"Speak, Kahvel."

"If more of the metal beings are encountered, I would suggest we travel in pairs. To destroy the creatures, they must be hit twice."

"Agreed. In pairs. Be gone."

The dragons all launched themselves up, flattening the surrounding grass as thirty pairs of wings furiously beat the air. Once the dragons cleared the tree tops, they paired up and vanished into the clouds. Within moments the only dragon still present was the Dragon Lord.

Kri'Entu looked up at Rinbok. "With all due respect, my friend, I must be off. I fear the sorceress will target my son next."

Curiosity piqued, Rinbok looked at the human king. "Why does the sorceress want your offspring?"

"She intends to marry him."

"I assume you do not approve?"

"You assume correctly. I do not."

"Are you going to search for the fire thrower?"

Kri'Entu nodded. "I am, aye."

"Then, I expect to be notified once his location is known."

"What are you going to do to him?" Sarah asked, getting defensive even though the huge dragon scared the bejesus out of her.

Rinbok Intherer had started to turn around to depart when he paused and looked back at her, lowering his multi-horned head to get down near her eye level. "Your mate will answer to me for two reasons. First, to answer for the offense of riding a dragon. As for the second, I will disclose that as soon as the first has been dealt with."

Sarah stared into the dragon's dark green eyes. Was she mistaken? It looked as though Rinbok's eyes had softened somewhat. She couldn't begin to imagine what must be going through that reptilian brain of his.

"Lady Sarah," Kri'Entu said, tapping her on the shoulder. "If you would be so kind as to return us to the castle?" The king turned to look up at the Lord of the Dragons. He nodded. "Happy hunting."

"You do understand that I do not plan on turning the

sorceress over to human custody if she is apprehended."

The king shook his head. "My apologies, but I did not hear you."

Rinbok's slitted eyes narrowed. "I said, I do not —"

At the slight nod of the king's head, Sarah took his and Rhenyon's arms and teleported them straight to the throne room. The Dragon Lord stared at the recently vacated spot a few moments. If a dragon could smile, Rinbok Intherer would have been sporting a grin from ear to ear.

* * *

The normally pristine valley was a hive of activity. Groups of humans and dwarves dotted the valley and surrounding forest, looking for any clues to indicate what had happened to the missing Nohrin and dragon. Pairs of dragons swooshed by overhead, ensuring the skies were free from any threats, as humans and dwarves alike investigated and inspected every tree and rock within a five-mile radius around Celestia's last known location. The snapping of branches and the crackling of dry leaves sounded from all directions.

"Forest border, north, clear!" one group called.

"Forest border, northeast, clear!" another called out.

Three groups of dwarves approached. They bowed and gave their reports: no traces were found. One by one the groups of searchers returned to their starting points and reported the same results: there were no traces of the sorceress anywhere, let alone any indications on what had happened to Steve and Pryllan.

Celestia had escaped.

It was decided that, since there were so many dwarven tunnels crisscrossing underneath the valley and forest, there should be patrols in the area at all times, in case Celestia returned for any reason and knew of the tunnels. Half the dwarves formed back into their groups of four and split up, some returning to the forest and others spreading out across the valley.

Sarah and Rhenyon appeared out of thin air, with a group of ten human soldiers clustered around them.

"There's always a chance, Rhenyon," Sarah was saying. "That's all I'm trying to tell you."

"Do you really think," the commander argued, "that she would be foolish enough to try?"

"What do you think? She knows the castle much better than anyone else. What if there are other ways to get in that no one knows about?"

Rhenyon conceded the point as they turned to look at the large group of assembled humans and dwarves. One human soldier stepped forward and saluted.

"Commander, with regret, we have had no luck in locating the sorceress."

"How big of an area was searched?" Rhenyon asked, looking off into the distance as several groups of dwarves emerged from the forest and began patrolling the valley's perimeter.

"The original search area was a radius of two miles. We have since enlarged that area to five. No luck. What are your orders, commander?"

"I do not believe the sorceress will return here, nor do I believe she'll try to infiltrate the castle," he added, turning to look at Sarah. "However, I will defer to Lady Sarah and will not ignore the possibility. Break off into teams of —"

Rhenyon trailed off as a gold dragon appeared in the skies and rapidly approached. It was Kahvel, and he was on a direct intercept course. He landed silently nearby and approached Sarah and the commander.

"Hello again, Kahvel." Sarah smiled up at the dragon. "Is everything alright?"

"I came as soon as I could," the dragon began, staring with unblinking eyes right into Sarah's. "Several of my brethren —"

"What's the matter?" Sarah interrupted, instantly concerned.

Kahvel tried again. "Several of my brethren —"

"Are missing? Are hurt?"

The gold dragon let out an irritated huff, inadvertently releasing two jets of smoke from his nostrils.

"Three separate reports of —"

"Sorceress sightings? RIC destruction?"

"Will you kindly allow me to finish?"

"Sorry. Go ahead."

"Pryllan is much the same. Oftentimes she interrupts to share her thoughts. There is such a thing as an unspoken thought."

Sarah crossed her arms over her chest. "Tell me you didn't say that to her."

"About having unspoken thoughts? Reckless I may be at times, but foolish I am not."

"So, what were you going to say?"

"Will you allow me to finish?"

"Yes. Stop stalling. Is this about Steve?"

Kahvel studied her for a few moments. If Sarah didn't know any better, she'd say the dragon just rolled his eyes at her.

"Several of my brethren," Kahvel began again, eyeing Sarah as if he was daring her to interrupt, "have made observations, and I do believe you might want to hear it. The human sorceress was not responsible for Pryllan and Steve's disappearance."

That got Sarah's attention.

"What? Are you sure?"

"Three separate reports all have the same facts. Pryllan and your mate vanished before the dark fireball exploded."

Rhenyon tore his eyes off the dragon to stare incredulously at Sarah. The nearby soldiers, human and dwarf alike, also turned to stare at the female Nohrin. "Did you send Sir Steve and the dragon someplace safe?"

Sarah looked down at her hands as though she'd find evidence suggesting just that.

"If I knew the answer to that, then we wouldn't be having this discussion now, would we?"

Breslin approached and bowed.

"Milady, is it possible to accidentally transport someone without knowing where it is you sent them?"

Sarah shook her head. "No."

"What about —"

"Look, Breslin," Sarah snapped, acknowledging later that

she could have used a gentler tone, "I know my jhorun. When I accidentally teleported Mikal and myself several years ago, I was just learning. I have more control now."

Breslin held up his hands. "Please forgive me, milady. I did not mean to offend."

"No, that was my fault. I don't know what's happened to my husband, and I'm not handling it well."

"As to be expected, Lady Sarah," Rhenyon added, glaring around at the group as if to challenge them to distress her further. "Recall what happened. We just teleported from Verdayn." He began to pace, as was his custom. "The metal creatures were attacking the dragons. We saw Sir Steve destroy several of the metal beasts that were pursuing two black dragons."

"He saved those two dragons," Sarah sniffed, her eyes filling as she recalled the last moments she had seen her husband.

"Incidentally, they are very grateful," Kahvel added. Sarah smiled fleetingly. "Sarkan and his mate, Arealin, kept an eye on Pryllan and her rider afterwards. They were the first to approach me with information about the circumstances of Pryllan's disappearance."

"What did they see?" Rhenyon inquired.

"Just what I have already told you. They disappeared prior to the explosion."

"Then we must assume that Lady Sarah somehow teleported them."

Sarah sighed. "If I did, then I'd like to know where."

"I can tell you he is nowhere close," Breslin confirmed.

All eyes turned to the dwarf.

"How?" Sarah wanted to know.

Breslin pulled his red-bladed axe off his back and held it up. "This tells me. When I have it, I can sense the proximity of the other Mythra weapons. And I can prove it to you. Commander, if you will, please walk about in circles. Behind, near, far, it does not matter."

The dwarf closed his eyes and tipped his helmet down so that there were no chances of being able to see anything. He held out an arm and spun until he was pointing straight at

Rhenyon. The commander began moving about, all the while Breslin kept his finger pointing straight at him. Even when Rhenyon doubled back and walked behind him, the dwarf rotated in place until he was facing the correct direction.

"I will have to try that sometime," Rhenyon added, giving Breslin a slap on the back. "I hope you can teach me, my friend."

"I will," Breslin promised.

Sarah was nodding. "Okay, you made your point, Breslin. What can you tell me about Steve's location? He is not anywhere close?"

"I would go so far as to say he is no longer in Lentari."

Rhenyon turned to Sarah. "Could you have teleported them to your world?"

Sarah considered. It was possible. She did recall recoiling in terror as she had watched the black fireball speed toward her husband. She had screamed a warning but he was too far away to hear her. Then he was gone. She had done an accidental teleportation once before when Mikal had been threatened with a possible kidnapping years ago. She had been just as scared then as she had been during the battle. But to teleport an entire dragon? If she was truly responsible for their disappearance, then the one place she would have thought would have been safe would be their home. In Idaho. That had to be it.

Sarah's eyes widened. That meant she had just teleported a live dragon to her world. Her world! She had to get home. As soon as possible!

She spotted a fallen log and slowly lowered herself down. If she was going to her world, without a portal, that meant she needed to have a clear image of her home. It was already difficult enough to teleport from one world to the other. The only way she'd done it in the past was to completely empty her mind of all thoughts so she could acquire a mental picture of her intended destination. How was she supposed to do that now? With concern for her husband running foremost in her thoughts, it would be extremely difficult to calm down enough to still her mind.

She took several deep breaths and closed her eyes.

Behind her she heard someone (a dwarf?) ask another what was happening.

"Quiet," Rhenyon's voice ordered, in a hushed whisper. "Let Lady Sarah concentrate."

"What is she doing?" Another voice whispered. This time it was Breslin.

"Teleporting between worlds is very difficult," Rhenyon explained, his voice so low that only a few others in close proximity could make it out. A few dwarves leaned closer. "She has to empty her mind of all thought, and you know how difficult that is for—"

Eyes still closed; Sarah held up a warning finger. "Careful."

"Anyone to do." Rhenyon finished, casting a worried look over at her. The commander smiled as he saw the corners of Sarah's mouth curve upward.

Sarah sighed again. She didn't think this was going to work. She was just too worried about her husband. She could only hope that she sent the two of them to someplace safe at home.

The log vanished and she dropped several feet to the ground, landing on her rear.

"Ow!"

Sarah stood, and tenderly rubbed her backside. What happened? How did she manage to fall off the—

Her eyes widened and her pain disappeared. She was sitting on a tiled floor, in a darkened house. It was the foyer! She was in her home!

She instantly teleported to the master bedroom on the top floor and called for her husband. No answer. She teleported to several other rooms on different floors to see if there was any indication he had been there. He hadn't.

She teleported back downstairs and opened the back door leading out into the west side of her gardens. A quick perusal of her extensive gardens revealed no damaged plants, no blackened sections of earth. Pryllan hadn't been here. If they were here, where would Steve hide the dragon? The garage! It would be a tight fit but he might be able to get Pryllan inside.

She teleported to the side door leading into the large detached garage and tried the door. It was locked. She cursed to herself. She knocked and then laid her ear on the door. She couldn't hear anything. Sarah teleported inside the garage and flipped on the overhead fluorescent lights. She saw her black SUV in the first bay. The second bay was for Steve's truck, but it wasn't there. The third held two all-terrain vehicles, and the fourth held a large fifth wheel trailer.

She flipped off the lights and teleported back to the other side of the door. She was ready to jump back inside the house when she saw the water on the ground and noticed a smell which reminded her of rotting garbage. She carefully walked around the side of the garage and noticed Steve's truck. Water was dripping from the open bed. Small black lumps of some unknown substance were on the ground directly beneath the open tailgate. Whatever it was, it must have been washed out of the truck's bed. She jogged around the truck and came to a stop. Lia's FJ was parked on the side of the garage. Had Lia driven Steve's truck home, or had Steve??

A light flicked on in the manor; she spun around in surprise. It was the kitchen light. Someone was in her house!

# Chapter 7 - How to Feed Your Dragon

He was uncertain how long he had been unconscious. Five minutes? Five hours? His head was swimming; it was hard to think straight. Steve slowly sat up and looked around. He and Pryllan were still hundreds of feet up in the air. Memories of the dark ball of energy came rushing back at him. What had happened to it? Had it exploded?

"Pryllan, what do you—" His unfinished question was ripped out of his mouth and lost to the winds tearing by him at extreme speeds. Apparently Pryllan had withdrawn her senses again.

*What happened? Where do you think we are?*

No response. Pryllan was silent.

*Pryllan? Are you okay?*

The emerald dragon continued to ignore him as she glided through the air. She wasn't beating her wings and she wasn't talking to him. That could only mean …

*Pryllan! You need to wake up! Come on, snap out of it!*

Steve slowly picked his way along her back and carefully climbed up her long neck. Inching forward on his belly, avoiding the sharp edges of her scales, Steve finally lay stretched out on the top of her head, nestled between the two spiraled horns protruding from her skull. He gently leaned forward for a better look. The dragon's eyes were closed.

*I really need you to wake up right now!*

Still no acknowledgement from the dragon. Steve cursed to himself. Here they were, gliding through the air, heading toward—what *were* they heading toward, anyway?

He leaned out over Pryllan's side and looked down. Lake Raehón and the valley before it were gone, replaced with miles and miles of semi-arid desert. Bisecting the bleak countryside was a two-lane highway running straight as an arrow from north to south. An occasional car could be seen, as they were travelling much faster than what the land-bound cars were capable of going.

Cars? Highway? Uh oh.

*You really need to wake up. Right now. We have a problem!*

Igniting both hands and laying them directly on Pryllan's head, he sent two gentle blasts of fire down into Pryllan's skull, thankful that dragons were fireproof.

Pryllan's eyes snapped open. She lurched ungracefully in the air as she detected a myriad of unfamiliar scents.

Holding on to her head as though his life depended on it, which he was certain it did, Steve waited for the confused dragon to regain her orientation.

**What has happened? Where are—why are you on my head?**

*I had to wake you up somehow.*

**I have never been rendered unconscious before.**

*I have and it's not fun. Listen, I hate to interrupt, but we have a huge problem here.*

Pryllan instantly whipped her head around to see if they were being pursued by one of the dreaded RICs. Thankfully there was nothing else in the sky besides them. Her eyes widened as she took in the changed landscape. Gone was the lush green valley she had been flying over just before the black fireball would have impacted them. Gone were the comforting voices of the other dragons in her mind. Far below, she could see more of the mechanical beings scooting along a straight path through a parched, desolate landscape. Unfamiliar clumps of ugly grass, tiny pungent yellow flowers, and scraggly bushes were visible as far as the eye could see.

Pryllan inhaled, ready to spit fire at the distant bugs.

*No! Wait! Those aren't bugs! That's what I was going to tell you!*

**Where are we? What has happened to the landscape? Where are the trees, the grass, and the water?**

*We're not in Lentari anymore. We're in my world.*

**Are you certain?**

*Yes.*

**How is that possible?**

*I wish I knew. How we got here is the least of our problems. There are no dragons here. At all. People are going to freak out if they see you. We need to figure out where we are and get back to Idaho.*

**Where the two of you reside when not in Lentari?**

*Right. And it gets better, I'm afraid.*

**There's more bad news?**

*I have the* worst *sense of direction.*

**So, you are saying that you do not know how to find your home?**

*Ummm, right. You sound just like Sarah.*

**Can you not ask for directions?**

*I suppose I could—*

At that moment the flat land disappeared and they went flying out over a canyon a half mile wide and hundreds of feet deep. It was a canyon Steve knew all too well.

*It's the Snake River Canyon! Do you have any idea how many times I've gone across that bridge over there? That means the city to the south is Twin Falls. Look, there's the mall right there. This is my old home!*

**Be that as it may, you mentioned humans have never beheld a dragon before, correct?**

*You're right. We need to find a place to hide, and fast. The Snake River is down at the bottom of the canyon. There are tons of trees there to hide in.*

Pryllan dipped below Perrine Bridge and spiraled down to land silently at the edge of the river. Steve cautiously looked around. Thankfully no one was present. He briefly wondered how long it'd take for videos of them to show up on the Internet. They would have to be careful and avoid being seen at all costs.

Once the solid unfamiliar ground was beneath her, Pryllan withdrew her wyverian senses and looked at the human.

"This is your world. How would you recommend we proceed?"

"Well, we're in the right state but the wrong part of it. Our biggest problem is you. We need to keep you concealed until it gets dark. Then we should be able to head north."

"How do you plan on finding your way when you just admitted you did not know how to find your home?"

Steve sighed. "If I had my phone with me, I'd use the GPS capabilities and just follow that back to Coeur d'Alene. Problem is, my phone is at home."

"Can you not acquire another?"

Steve was silent as he considered the dragon's suggestion. "As a matter of fact, I think I can. Good idea. I can get one of those pre-paid phones with data plans and use that. I just need to get some cash as I don't have my wallet on me." He looked up at Pryllan and grinned. "There's a bank on Blue Lakes Boulevard. If Chuck is still working there, then we're good.

"Who is Chuck? What is a bank?"

"He's an old friend of mine. He used to work for the same company I did, but he didn't like the work. So he got a job at the bank. It's a place where, umm, humans keep their gold. If my friend is working today, then he should be able to help me convince them I am who I say I am and then we're golden."

"You can be golden if you prefer. I am green."

"No, that's not what I meant. It means—forget it. Not important. Let's see, I'd say there's at least two hours of sunlight left. If you carry me up to the top of the bridge I'll just walk into town. You keep yourself concealed, okay? Keep an eye on the bridge up there. I'll flag you down once I get everything I need."

"Agreed."

"Think you can see me up there from all the way down here?"

"Easily. I see several humans now, walking along the edge of the path."

"Perfect. Remember, no flying. Dragons don't exist here. It would freak people out. Also, there are devices here that can spot something as large as you from many miles away. We have to keep a low profile."

"One of the humans appears to be in distress."

"What? How so?"

"I believe the human has suffered a horrible defeat at the hands of a barbarian horde and has been taken prisoner."

"Say what? Why would you say that?"

"He wears a metal collar. He has several chains wrapped around his torso. I can also see that various metal implements have penetrated his body."

"Is his hair sticking straight up?"

Pryllan's eyes narrowed as she gazed at the distant bridge far above their heads. "Aye. And it is blue. How did you know this?"

"Call it a hunch. Not to worry. Believe it or not, he chooses to dress like that."

"Indeed. He also appears to be unarmed."

"As he should be."

Pryllan's gaze dropped down to land on him. "The other humans I observed were not armed. If I am not mistaken, you *are* armed."

"I am not."

"And strapped to your baldric is …?"

"Oh, that. Yeah, probably shouldn't wander into town wearing a sword on my back."

He unbuckled Mythrin and gently placed it on the grass before the dragon. Gently patting himself down as he searched for other weapons, he suddenly realized, garbed as he was, he would stick out like a sore thumb. Leather armor, gauntlets, cuirass, and several daggers were discarded and placed next to his sword. Looking down at his brown leather trousers and heavy boots, he tucked his green tunic into his belt. He nodded. It would have to do.

Stashing his weaponry and armor behind a large stump, he climbed back up Pryllan's back.

"Tally ho!"

Two reptilian eyes stared at him.

"Sorry. Couldn't resist." Steve pointed up at Perrine Bridge five hundred feet above their heads. "Top floor, please."

Pryllan launched into the air and rose straight up, directly under the bridge. When she was close enough, she latched ahold of the bridge's steel support beams that were anchored into the canyon walls. Holding her foreleg out behind her, she grabbed Steve and swung him up and over the rim of the bridge.

With a surprised yelp, Steve landed on the pedestrian walkway running the length of the bridge. At either end of the walkway were viewing points where tourists could snap pictures of the impressive bridge as well as the legendary locale where a certain famous daredevil had tried unsuccessfully to jump the canyon in a rocket car back in the year 1974.

Steve rose to his feet and came face to face with an elderly couple that were clearly out taking in the sights.

"Hi there! Bridge climbing. It's an exciting new sport!"

Both seniors stared at him in shock.

"I think I'll take the elevator down. If you'll excuse me."

As Steve turned to make his way toward the southern rim of the canyon, he heard the elderly woman arguing with her husband.

"Bill, he came from under the bridge!"

"Bonnie, you heard him. He was climbing the bridge."

"Do you hear yourself? Climbing a bridge?"

Steve moved out of earshot and stepped off the bridge onto a sidewalk heading south into town.

*Still with me?*

**Always.**

*Awesome. I'm off.*

**I will remain concealed.**

Steve strolled into the biggest bank in Twin Falls and looked around. He sighed. He couldn't see his friend anywhere.

"Good afternoon, sir. Can I help you?"

Steve turned to observe a young woman in her twenties. Her hair was up in a tight bun and she was wearing an elegant cream-colored business suit. Her name tag identified her as the assistant branch manager.

"Can you tell me if Chuck, er, Charles Cartwright is working today?"

"Mr. Cartwright is no longer affiliated with this branch. Is there something I can help you with?"

Figures.

"Ummm. I don't think so. Thanks anyway. Listen, can you tell me where I can find the closest pay phone?"

"Absolutely. You can find one right across the street at the Square L store."

Steve thanked the woman and went back outside. He watched the people milling about for a few minutes. Twin Falls had definitely grown in the years since he had lived here. He couldn't recall if he remembered seeing so many people walking along the sides of the street. One of his favorite restaurants, The Prime Cut, was no longer there. It had been replaced with a franchise burger joint. Farther down the road, he could see two other franchise restaurants found in practically every other town. No doubt the big-name restaurants were responsible for driving out the smaller family-owned establishments.

Sprinting across the street after spotting a lull in traffic, Steve walked up to the pay phone and hesitated. He had never placed a collect call in his life and naturally his first one had to be *her*.

"Thank you for calling the Cookbook Nook, this is Lia, how can I help you today?"

"Do you accept a collect call from ..." the operator hesitated as Steve spoke up.

"It's Steve, Lia. Please accept the charges."

"Well yeah, I suppose so."

There was a click as the operator exited the line.

"Hi there, Stevie-boy. Whatcha doin' placing collect calls?"

"Lia, I don't have time to explain. I've got a very peculiar situation going here."

"Are you okay? What's going on?"

"Listen. This is going to sound strange, and I'll be more than happy to explain what's going on at a later date. Right now, I need you to find a store within walking distance of my exact location that has a prepaid cell phone you can purchase right over the phone using the store's credit card and that I can pick up. You're going to have to tell them that I will be in there to get it and that I don't have my wallet on me, so no ID. Did you get all that?"

"What the hell happened to you? Did you get mugged?"

"No. Trust me, I'll explain later. Oh, I almost forgot. You have to make sure they charge it for me."

"You owe me big, you know that, right? There's something weird going on with you. You have to tell me what's going on. So, you and me? Answers. Agreed?"

"Agreed. For the record, we were already planning on telling you."

"What? You were planning on telling me *what?*"

"I'll tell you face to face. Right now I need that phone, Lia."

"God bless America. Fine. So where are you?"

Steve took a deep breath.

"I'm in Twin Falls."

"Twin Falls? What are you doing down there? How did you get there? By the way, your truck is still parked in front of the Hacienda. Oh, don't tell me. You can't explain now, right?"

"Right. If you get time after all of this, I'd really appreciate if you stop by the house and pick up the spare set of keys hanging by the door and see if Adam will drive the truck back. I know I'm asking you to take a lot on faith, Lia, but I need you to just humor me for now."

"Fine. How do I reach you?"

"Tell you what. I'll give you a little bit and then I'll call you back."

He told her where he was and hung up the phone. Fifteen minutes later Steve called her back with a second collect call.

"Okay, you're in luck. There's one of those huge

department stores not far from you on Cheney Road. Go north on Blue Lakes, as though you're heading toward the mall. Is that close to you?"

Steve turned to look back down the busy street toward the bridge.

"Close enough. I know where it's at. Then what?"

Lia gave him directions how to find the gigantic department store. True to her word, the store was less than mile away, just a little west of the Magic Valley Mall. Tracking down an associate by the name of Willy, in the electronics department, Steve picked up the (mostly) charged phone. Willy assured him he had full coverage in Twin Falls and that the cell phone should have good coverage for most of the state.

"Any way I can get you to print me out a map of Idaho's coverage area?"

The associate eyed him suspiciously. "Yeah, I suppose I can do that. Going to a costume party?"

Steve shrugged. "Kinda."

Pocketing the map and the phone, Steve exited the store and stepped out into the fading sunshine. He looked off to the north, toward the distant canyon and bridge, and sighed. He trudged off, cutting through the parking lot, heading back toward the highway.

"You're not from around here are you, fella?"

Steve turned at the friendly voice and saw a man younger than he was. He had a shaved head, sported a goatee, and had on a white Metallica tee shirt and black shorts. He was pushing a shopping cart with a case of bottled water, a family sized bag of crunchy Cheetos, and two bags of beef jerky.

"Believe it or not, I used to live here. I don't anymore, though." He eyed the contents of the cart. "Are you just passing through?"

The young man smiled. "Guilty as charged. What gave me away? The name's Jared."

Steve shook the proffered hand. "Steve. Nice to meet you, buddy. Where are you from?"

"Rocklin. That's in —"

"Northern California," Steve finished for him. "My wife's

family lives in Sacramento. At one time, they lived in Rocklin."

"Really? Small world, man."

"Tell me about it."

"Do you need a lift?"

"I appreciate the offer, but I just need to get back to the bridge. I'm meeting my, uh, friend there."

"Well, hop in. We've got plenty of room. My wife wanted to stop there and take some pictures with the kids."

"Thanks, I appreciate it."

They approached a red Chevy van with windows tinted so dark that no one on the outside could see into the inside of the vehicle. The sliding door opened and a young blonde girl of about twelve years jumped out and ran to her father.

"Dad! What took you so long? Did you get the Cheetos?"

"Got 'em right here, princess."

The young girl looked up at Steve and smiled. The passenger window rolled down and a young woman with shoulder length brown hair, wearing a blue summer dress and retro tinted sunglasses, leaned out.

"So, who do we have here?"

"This is Steve," Jared answered as he loaded the supplies into the back of the van. "We're going to give him a lift to the bridge. He's meeting a friend there and we're going to save him a long walk."

"Oh, okay. Hi, I'm Randi."

Steve shook Randi's hand. "I'm Steve. Thanks for the lift."

"No problem. Terrence, move to the back."

A boy, about eight years old, was sitting in the seat directly behind Randi and was totally involved with his handheld video game.

"Terrence, back seat. Now."

"Looks like he has his earphones on," Steve offered, looking at the sulking boy.

"He's pretending he can't hear us," Randi argued, scowling at her son. "Watch this. Terrence, if you're not out of that seat in two seconds, then I'll personally donate that video game to the closest Salvation Army."

As slowly as he could, without getting into further trouble, the boy tipped up the arm rests to his chair and climbed out, settling himself into the bench seat in the back of the van. Not once did he raise his eyes off his game or utter a word to his mother.

"Have any kids?" Randi cheerfully asked him.

"Yeah, you could say that. One. He's fourteen now."

"Want another one?"

Steve laughed and took the recently vacated seat. The daughter went around to the other side of the van and took the seat behind her father just as he slid behind the wheel. Steve looked at the girl and held out a hand.

"Hi. I'm Steve."

The girl shyly offered her hand. "Missy."

"Nice to meet you, Missy."

Twenty minutes later he was stepping out of the van and following the family down the steps to one of the two observation points, set about fifty feet below street level. Steve casually glanced around. There was no sign of Pryllan anywhere.

"Who're you meeting here?" Jared asked. "Wife? Friend?"

"A friend. We're heading back north, to Coeur d'Alene."

"That's way the hell up at the top of the panhandle, isn't it?"

"Yeah. If you're ever there, look me up. I'll show you around."

"Deal. Yo, Randi. You get your pics, babe?"

"You know I did."

"Terry still acting like a dork?"

"You know he is."

"What say we toss him over the edge?"

The boy snapped his head up and met his father's eyes with a horrified look, his video game forgotten.

"I'm thinking about it," his mother admitted, still frowning at her son. She held out her hand. She wanted the video game.

The boy shuffled over to his mother and plopped his precious game down onto her palm.

Steve had leaned out over the safety railing and was inspecting the ground far below. He couldn't see Pryllan anywhere. From his vantage point below the bridge, he could see the support beams that she had latched onto earlier today. She wasn't there, either. Now what was he supposed to do?

"Are you gonna be okay, bro?"

Steve turned back at Jared. "Yeah, I'll be fine. I just bought one of those prepaid cell phones. I'll give 'em a call."

"Good luck! Have a safe trip!"

"You, too. Nice meeting you guys."

Randi waved and pushed her petulant son in front of her. Jared looked back and spotted his daughter staring at the undersides of the bridge.

"Missy! Shake a leg! Let's go, princess!"

Steve turned to see for himself what had attracted the girl's attention. There, up on the rocky canyon wall, directly underneath the surface of the bridge, was a bulky formation of rocks that was staring back at them. Steve blinked a few times as he squinted at the rocks. Sure enough, two green reptilian eyes were either staring straight at him, or straight at the girl. From this distance, he couldn't tell.

Missy turned to him. She tapped him on the shoulder. "Look! The rocks have eyes!"

Steve met the girl's eyes and smiled. He winked and held a finger to his lips.

"Can you keep a secret?" he whispered to her.

Missy leaned toward him and emphatically nodded her head, her blonde ponytail bobbing up and down.

"That's my friend. She stays hidden because no one besides me has ever seen one. Now you have, too."

"Missy! Move it, girl!" her father called from above.

"I'm coming, Dad! Gawd! Just a second!"

She turned back to the wall. The eyes had vanished.

"What was that?"

*Pryllan, can you reveal just your head?*

**As you wish.**

A section of the irregular canyon wall slowly morphed into the dragon's massive head. Missy gasped with surprise. She turned to Steve, her eyes as big as saucers. Once more Steve held a finger to his lips.

"Remember, this is a secret."

"Is that a dragon? I thought they only lived in faerie tales!"

"Typically, they do. This one is just visiting. Say hello to Pryllan."

The girl waved shyly at the dragon, who winked back.

*Ok, that's enough for now. You'd better vanish.*

Pryllan's head melted back into the rocks.

Steve turned to Missy and smiled. "You just helped me out. I appreciate it."

"I did?"

"I wasn't sure where she was. She and I are headed back north. She's the friend I'm waiting for. Thank you for finding her for me."

The young girl looked with amazement at the canyon wall where she knew the dragon was hiding and then back at the man before her. She smiled. "Thanks for showing me."

"You're welcome. Don't tell anyone, especially your dad, okay? She has to be kept safe."

Missy held out her pinkie. Steve rolled his eyes.

"You have to," the girl insisted. "If you want me to promise, then we need to pinkie-promise."

"Okay, fine. Pinkie-promise it is."

He hooked his right pinkie finger with hers and shook.

"I gotta go. Thanks! Bye Steve! Bye Pryllan!"

**Farewell, human girl.**

*I don't think she heard you.*

**I know.**

He watched the girl dart back up the stairs and vanish from sight.

**Did you get the device you needed?**

*Yep. Got it right here.*

Steve pulled out the phone and activated the GPS app. A spinning circle appeared on the screen as the device attempted to ascertain his present location. After a couple of moments, the phone beeped and a map of his current location appeared.

"Jackpot. Okay, now all I have to do is tell it where we want to go."

He set the destination as his home address in Coeur d'Alene and waited while the phone downloaded the necessary information from the Internet. A progress bar appeared and slowly inched along the screen.

**Is the device satisfactory?**

*Yeah. It's almost ready.*

The phone beeped again. The maps were downloaded and an overlay of their route appeared on the screen. The first set of instructions appeared a moment later. An arrow appeared, directing them north, across the bridge. For kicks and giggles, he downloaded a free compass app and made certain it would work without a satellite signal. It did.

*Got the directions loaded. We just need to wait for dark.*

**Light or dark, will we not be seen regardless?**

*True. Can you camouflage yourself when you're flying?*

**Interesting question. I have never tried.**

*It should be dark soon. We'll experiment once it does.*

**Agreed.**

* * *

With the lights of Twin Falls fading rapidly beneath them, Pryllan gently banked right.

*Just a little bit more.*

Pryllan's right wing dipped low for a few moments before leveling off.

*Perfect. Right like that. Stay like that and we should be good.*

**How long will we head in this direction?**

*I'd guesstimate, at the rate we're going, it'll take at least five hours*

**Guesstimate? I am unfamiliar with that word.**

*It means I'm giving an educated guess.*

**Understood.**

Steve leaned back against one of Pryllan's spinal plates and sighed contentedly. This was the way to travel. No loud thrumming of an airplane's engines. No screaming kids bumping into his seat. It was peaceful and completely relaxing. He pulled out his cell and checked their location. Right on course. Perfect. Then Steve caught sight of the battery indicator. About half the cell's battery was discharged! That wasn't good. They'd only just started their flight! He sat up with alarm. Pryllan's head turned to regard him.

**Are you alright?**

*We have a new problem. My cell is gonna die within two hours. We need to get where we're going before it does.*

**What do you suggest?**

*Can you speed up like you've done before?*

**For how long?**

*I'd say at least two hours.*

**I will not be able to maintain that velocity and attempt to camouflage myself at the same time.**

*Then focus on getting there as soon as possible. Can you fly that fast for that long?*

**Doing so will deplete my resources. I am already famished. I will need to feed once we arrive.**

*You leave the food appropriation to me. Get us there and I'll take care of the rest.*

**Agreed.**

*Don't accelerate just yet. We still have a decent signal here and I need to make a phone call. Hoo, boy, she's gonna love this one.*

**Who?**

*Lia. She's someone who works for us.*

Pulling out his cell once more, he dialed Lia's personal cell.

"I almost screened this call," Lia scolded, once she answered. "I didn't recognize the number."

"Hello to you, too, Ms. Grumpypants."

"I take it you got the phone?"

"Obviously. Ummm, listen. I have —"

"Are you kidding me right now? Seriously? Are you going to have me do something else that's really strange and unusual?"

"Yeah, I'm afraid so."

"Awesome! I *so* wanna know what the two of you are up to."

"The deal still stands. I'll tell you everything as soon I'm able."

"I'll hold you to it. What do you need me to do?"

Soaring through the air, passing over the small town of Gooding, Idaho, Steve grinned. "Here's what I need you to do."

* * *

Lia hung up the phone and stared incredulously at the list of instructions Steve had given her. Buy all the sides of beef and pork that she could? Drive out to the lake on their property? What was going on? Was Steve arriving with a pride of lions?

She drove back to the Cookbook Nook and retrieved the company credit card from the safe one more time. Turning on the lights in the upstairs office, Lia flipped open the phone book and looked up the phone number to the local grocery store. One of Steve's clients was the manager of the store and she desperately needed to get him on the phone. Immediately.

She dialed the number and waited for someone to answer.

"Hello, may I please speak to Robert Patterson? His shift just ended? Is there any way I can get you to check the store to see if he's still around? It's really important that I talk to him. Yes, I'll hold. Thank you so much."

Her luck held. The manager hadn't made it to the door, having stopped to get a latte at the in-store coffee bar.

"This is Robert. How may I help you?"

Lia explained who she was and who had asked her to call. She steeled herself and took a breath.

"I need to purchase every side of beef and pork you can spare. I kid you not. That's what I was told."

Patterson said nothing for a few moments. Hopefully he was mentally tallying up what was in the freezer.

"That's an unusual request, Ms. Manning. You said this is for Steve Miller?"

"That's right."

"What does he need that much meat for?"

"Believe me, I'm wondering that myself."

"Give me the number you're at right now and I'll go check with my butcher. I have to hurry. They usually clean up and leave around this time."

Lia gave him her cell number and hung up. Ten minutes later her cell rang.

"Okay. Ordinarily I would pass this type of request off as a simple prank, but I do know Steve, and if this is what he wants, and he's willing to pay for it, we will fulfill that request. Here's what we can give you."

Lia listened as the manager listed off various cuts of meats. Her eyes widened as four complete sides of beef were added to the list and three sides of pork. He even included five legs of lamb.

"If you can give me another day or two, I can get a lot more here."

"Sorry, this has to be picked up right now. Can I give you a credit card number?"

"Don't you want to know the total?"

"No, it's a company card."

"And you have their permission?"

"I do. I'm the manager at Cookbook Nook. Steve and his wife, Sarah, own the store."

"Oh, okay. What is the number? And when will you be here to pick this up?"

Lia gave him the store's credit card number and thought about how she was going to pick up that much meat. She'd be damned if she'd let raw meat touch the insides of her Toyota FJ. A grin slowly spread across her face.

"I'll have Steve's truck. Can I pull up to the back?"

"I'd recommend it. I already have three guys pulling the order now. We'll be ready for you."

"Thank you so much. I'm on my way."

Lia drove to the Miller's mansion, parked her car off to the side of the garage and climbed into the truck after retrieving the keys from where she'd dropped them on the kitchen counter just over an hour ago.

Lia's mind was whirling with questions. What was Steve up to? Why did he need all that meat? Where was Sarah? And what the blazes was he doing in Twin Falls earlier today? And more importantly, how did he get there? Sarah's Santa Fe was parked in the garage. She knew, seeing how she had checked to make sure it was there herself.

A moment of realization struck. He didn't have his wallet. No ID. No money to buy that phone. Something seriously didn't add up.

She pulled the truck up to the back of the grocery store.

One of the large delivery doors was wide open, spilling bright fluorescent light out into the darkening loading zone. She spotted several people stacking slabs of raw meat on the dock.

A portly man in his fifties, black hair and thick mustache, appeared at her window. She rolled it down and smiled at the man.

"Are you Robert?"

He smiled. "Ms. Manning, I presume?"

"That's me."

"Do you have something to line the bed of the truck with?"

Lia shook her head. "His exact instructions were to get this meat to a certain spot and dump it on the ground. If I didn't know better, I'd say he was going to feed a bunch of lions."

"So, you just want us to dump it in?"

"Yes, please."

"Just dump it in, guys," Robert ordered the three courtesy clerks.

The truck shook as various chunks of meat were thrown in. Something slammed onto the bed and shook the truck so violently that the air freshener flew off the rearview mirror.

Lia twisted around to see what the source of the impact was. The truck shook violently again. And again.

The three clerks had collectively pushed one of the huge sides of beef off the dock and into the truck. One after another they were all heaved in. The final leg of lamb was thrown on the pile as the store manager approached her window. He handed her the credit card receipt and a pen. Lia glanced at the total.

"Twenty-two hundred dollars? Are you serious? Wow!"

"I have to say, this is the largest consumer order I've ever received," Robert admitted, taking back the slip of paper and the pen. "I hope he has enough meat here."

"Good lord, so do I."

"If you ever find out what he needed all this meat for, be sure to let me know."

Lia nodded. "Will do."

The manager waved as she drove off. Driving back to the mansion, instead of parking the truck in front of the quad RV garage, she continued around the house and took the gravel road that bordered the forest.

Driving down the unpaved road, headlights barely illuminating what lay before her, Lia followed Steve's directions until she found the small lake she hadn't known existed. She put the truck in park and stepped out, grabbing the flashlight from the glove box Steve had said she would need.

She switched it on and swung it around. Half of the tiny lake had trees on the northwest border. The rest of the area was open grassland with an occasional pine tree scattered here and there. The gravel road dead ended at the lake.

She pulled out her list of instructions and looked at what she had written down. 'Dump the meat out into the open.' How in the world did he think she was going to be able to lift those sides of beef out of the truck? It was raw meat. She wasn't about to handle raw meat. Forget it!

As Lia stared at the truck, inspiration struck. She'd seen a particular maneuver performed on television and in the movies. Why wouldn't it work for her, too? She got back in the truck, drove carefully over the grasslands to the west of the little lake and smiled. Right about here will do. She continued to drive west for another ten seconds before putting the truck back into park, got out to drop the tailgate down, and then took her seat again. As an afterthought, she reached over and pulled the seat belt across her lap. Once it was securely fastened, she put the truck in reverse and stomped on the gas.

The truck actually peeled out as it sped backwards. She gave it a few seconds then slammed her foot down on the brakes. Sure enough, hundreds of pounds of raw meat slid out of the truck and fell to the ground. She parked a final time to close the tailgate when a curse so vile a sailor would have blushed escaped her lips. One of the legs of lamb had not slid out. It meant she was going to have to touch it.

She found a broken tree limb and spent ten minutes poking the stick at the grisly piece of meat, from the truck's cab, until it plopped onto the ground. Dropping the branch, she slammed the tailgate closed and covered her nose. Phew! Apparently, the meat was starting to thaw. If bears were in the area, then this was going to attract each and every single one of them.

She drove the truck back to the house, parked it just outside the garage and hosed out the bed. She went inside the house and deposited the keys on the granite kitchen countertop. She turned toward the door and screamed in surprise, eliciting a scream from Sarah, who had just come in the back door.

"Sarah! What the hell!"

"Lia! You scared me!"

"What are you doing here?"

"What am I doing here? I live here. What are *you* doing here?"

"Your crazy husband had me —"

"What! You talked to Steve? Is he okay? Where is he now?"

"I believe he's on his way here. He called me earlier, from Twin Falls."

"What?! How long ago?"

"I talked to him a few hours ago. You didn't know he was in Twin Falls? Where have you been? I haven't seen or heard from you all day."

Sarah rubbed her painful temples and groaned.

"What's the matter? Do you have a headache?"

Sarah nodded. "Yes, and it's getting progressively worse."

Lia automatically turned and went to the fridge. She pulled out a soda and slid it across the counter toward her. "Here, drink this."

Sarah cracked the can open and sipped some of the fizzy drink. "I need to know everything. What did Steve want you to do?"

"Well, first off he had me purchase a prepaid cell phone that included a data plan that he could pick up in person, without having to pay for it."

Sarah nodded and drank more of her soda.

"He said he didn't have his wallet, ID, or anything. No money, either. I had to accept a couple of collect calls from him. You'd think he —"

"Lia," Sarah blurted out. "It's okay. What happened next?"

Lia proceeded to fill Sarah in on everything she talked to Steve about, concluding with her hosing out his truck after dumping the raw meat on the ground out at the small lake. She reluctantly handed the exorbitant receipt from the grocery store over to her friend. "Sorry. It's what Steve told me to do."

Sarah's eyes had filled with tears. She glanced once at the receipt and nodded, saying nothing. Lia instantly went sympathetic.

"Oh, honey, are you two okay?" She handed Sarah a paper towel from the kitchen countertop.

Dabbing at her eyes, Sarah nodded. "Yes. Everything is perfect. Now. I was so worried. How long ago did you dump the meat?"

Lia glanced over at the clock on the double wall oven.

"About thirty minutes ago."

"Okay, I have to go. Right now. Lia, thank you so much. For everything."

Lia put a restraining hand on her friend's shoulder. "Look, I know something is happening. Steve said he'd tell me as soon as he was able. Can you tell me what's going on?"

Sarah shook her head. "I can't Lia, not right now. Look, I really have to get going. Thank you so much!"

Lia watched as Sarah ran to the door, snatched the keys to one of their all-terrain vehicles off the row of hooks, and bolted out the door. Within moments, Lia watched the ATV tear around the side of the garage and disappear up the gravel road.

"Not this time, missy." Lia reached for the keys to the second ATV and ran out to the first bay of the huge garage. Good. Sarah had left the door up. Thanking her lucky stars that Steve and Adam had convinced her that driving one of these ATVs was just as easy as driving a normal car, she fired up the second vehicle and tore off after Sarah.

Dousing the headlights, she cut the motor when she got within a hundred yards of the lake. Lia pulled the ATV off the road and stashed it behind a clump of trees. Retrieving the borrowed flashlight from her jacket pocket, she crept toward the lake, taking care to stay off the road and, instead, stayed concealed within the trees.

She carefully pushed a few branches aside and peered through the foliage at the clearing. There was Sarah's ATV, so the lake must be close. Then she saw the reflections of the stars in the glassy surface of the water, so she knew she was in the right place. It was only a few days away from the scheduled full moon, so there was plenty of light in which to see the huge pile of meat. Actually, she smelled it before she saw it. There was Sarah, pacing nearby, acting like the rapidly thawing raw meat wasn't bothering her in the slightest. Sarah was staring at the sky.

"What in the world are you doing out here?" Lia softly murmured to herself. "What do you think you're going to find out here, aliens?"

Thirty minutes later, Lia was sitting on a fallen log, still watching Sarah pace around the lake. She was hungry, cold, and she was sure her butt had completely fallen asleep. She was about ready to sneak back to her ATV, and return to the manor, when a loud thunderclap scared ten years of life off her. It was followed by a blast of wind so strong that it blew her off the log and onto her back.

"What the—?" Lia struggled to regain her feet. Rising painfully, she peered through the trees to observe Sarah also regaining her feet. However, something else was now out in the clearing. Something huge. Then she heard the sickening crunch of breaking bones. Whatever that thing was, it was eating the meat!

She dropped to all fours and crawled closer to the forest's edge. She had to know what the creature was. Hearing voices, she pulled a few branches out of the way and stared at the scene before her. There was Steve! He was embracing Sarah and acting like they hadn't seen each other for several weeks. And behind them, just finishing up the last of the meat, was …

"You've *got* to be kidding me."

A dragon! An actual flesh and blood dragon! And it was

huge!! It towered over the two humans beside its left front foreleg. Clearly, Steve and Sarah didn't have any fear of it. Wait. Did that mean Steve had ridden that dragon here?

Just when she thought she couldn't have any more questions swirling about in her head, a million more erupted. She couldn't stop staring at the dragon. She heard her two friends begin an animated conversation. Sarah kept pointing at the dragon and then back at her husband. Lia could only catch snatches of their conversation.

"We need to get back … has demanded a meeting …"

The end of Sarah's comment trailed off. Did she just say the name of a popular shoe manufacturer? Why would they want a meeting with Steve? That didn't make sense at all.

"We have to go. ASAP."

Steve nodded. He said something and gestured to the dragon. It was slowly moving its head as it looked around.

"She's too big …"

Lia had resumed her stealthy approach when she looked up. She? The dragon was a she?

"Take a couple of mimets …"

Lia hesitated again. What was a mimet? She watched Steve hand something to Sarah. Lia smiled. She was close now. Almost close enough to touch the dragon's tail. Only a few more feet to go.

Steve and Sarah fell silent. The dragon was motionless, too, the tip of its tail now less than a foot away. She leaned forward and gingerly touched the scaled tail. It was cool, and sleek to the touch, much like the body of a snake. She grinned. She was definitely looking forward to having that conversation with Steve and Sarah now.

Suddenly Lia felt dizzy and stumbled forward, landing flat on her face. She was nauseous and disoriented. What had happened? Had the chimichangas she ate for lunch caused some sort of allergic reaction?

"Never have I been so glad to see this valley as I am now."

Lia paled. That wasn't Sarah's voice, and it certainly wasn't Steve's. The voice was female. Powerful. She had felt the rumble of the voice just as easily as she had heard it. It had to belong to the dragon!

Wait. Valley? What valley? Lia turned to the north. By the light of the moon, she beheld a large lake, bordered by mountains to the north and east. Open grassland as far as the eye could see stretched to the south and west. She turned to look behind her. Trees the size of sequoias met her eyes. The dragon's voice drew her attention once more.

"I must be off. I must locate Rinbok Intherer and explain my actions."

"We both will, Pryllan," Steve corrected. "You're not facing this hotshot dragon by yourself. End of discussion." He turned to his wife. "Where do we have to go?"

"R'Tal," Sarah answered. "The king wants to be included in whatever this Rinbok character wants to do. So he's waiting there for word on you two."

Steve turned to the dragon. "Will you come to the castle with us?"

Pryllan nodded. "Until Rinbok summons me, I have nowhere to go. I must wait for him to initiate contact."

"If you guys are all telepathic, wouldn't he already know you're back?"

"Aye, he knows I have returned. I can feel his anger. He has not decided what to do with me."

"You're not alone in this. I'm just as guilty as you are. Let's get this over with."

The dragon nodded gratefully. She spread her wings and prepared to launch into the air. Pryllan's nostrils flared as she picked up an unfamiliar scent. She disregarded it for now. Her tail was still stretched out behind her, with the tip resting just inside the forest's edge. Pryllan's tail twitched as she launched herself up into the air.

Lia, still crouching on her knees, hidden just inside the forest, looked down as the tip of the tail whipped up, knocking her out. Cold.

# Chapter 8 - Lia in Limbo

The dagger whistled through the air, thrown with a precision not typically found with most people, especially humans. End over end it tumbled through the air, finally making contact with its target. The solid jeweled hilt of the dagger thunked into the prone figure's stomach, eliciting no response from the unconscious woman lying on the forest floor. Had the thrower wanted to inflict a wound, he would have. As it was, a simple test to determine whether the figure was alive or dead was needed.

"It must be her," one dwarf whispered to another, a second dagger clutched tightly in his fist. "One throw. I can end this now with one throw. We would be known as the ones who killed the sorceress! They would write songs about us!"

The other dwarf shook his head. "As much as I think that would be a grand idea, we must not. Think how courageous we would appear if we were able to capture her alive!"

"Is she alive? She looks dead."

"There! She lives! Did you see her take a breath? She

must be immobilized immediately!"

Athos looked at his brother and nodded. "How much rope do you have?"

"Enough."

"We should gag her as well."

"Good idea."

Venk tore a strip of fabric from his inner tunic. He coiled it tightly around his right hand and slowly followed his brother through the tall grass until they were less than ten feet from the unconscious woman. Athos waved his left arm around in a wide arc, indicating Venk should approach from the other side. When both were in position, less than five feet from the still figure, Athos gave the signal.

Both dwarves pounced on the woman, quickly flipping her onto her stomach to immobilize her arms. Together they flipped her onto her back. Venk started to unwrap the makeshift gag that was tied around his hand when the figure stirred. Athos noticed their prisoner's movement first.

"Hurry, you blathering idiot! Gag her quick!"

The woman's eyes opened in shock as she discovered two figures practically sitting on top of her.

"Are you freakin' kidding me? Get off me you stupid —"

Lia's angry retort was abruptly cut off as a dirty piece of fabric was stuffed in her mouth and promptly tied behind her head.

"Muh fuh ah-huh, guh hiss ing udda muh ouff!"

Venk worriedly eyed his brother.

"If we cannot understand the spell, then it will not work, right?"

"I do not see you sprouting horns or a tail, so clearly, she is powerless. We did it. We captured her!"

Both brothers leapt to their feet and hooked their arms together to dance a jig around Lia's body.

"We got the sorcer*ess*! We got the sorcer*ess*!!"

"What's all this hubbub about?"

Venk and Athos turned to the newcomer.

"Breslin! Look! You were right to look over here. We caught Celestia!"

Breslin looked at the furiously struggling human who

continued to spew nonsensical rants at them. He knelt down in the grass to study the woman who glared back at him. Athos and Venk joined him moments later.

"Look at her attire!" Athos remarked, pointing at the light black windbreaker Lia was wearing. "Look how she struggles. Clearly, she wants to kill us."

"It was wise of you to gag her," Breslin praised. "She must not be allowed to speak."

"What do we do with her now?" Venk wanted to know.

"She must be secured," Breslin decided.

"How? Where? The human king said that she was capable of bewitching all manner of creatures. Who knows what might be coming to her aid."

"That is precisely why she must be secured," Breslin pointed out, turning to look behind them at the beginnings of the forest. "We need a pole, Athos. Venk and I will remain here to secure the prisoner."

"How long?"

"Eight feet. Go."

"Aye. Give me ten minutes."

Their prisoner gasped with shock as Breslin promptly sat on her chest and Venk sat on her legs.

Breslin pulled out his pipe and held his pouch of tobacco out to his companion. "Fancy a smoke?"

Venk pulled his own pipe out. "Excellent idea."

The two dwarves chatted amicably about the ease of Celestia's capture while they waited for Athos to return with a suitable tree to be used as a yoke to transport their prisoner. True to the request of his brethren, Athos arrived with a three-inch diameter, eight-foot section of a tree trunk that had been stripped of all its branches. He laid the pole next to their prisoner and took off a coil of stout leather cord that had been wrapped around his torso.

Lia's legs were tied together at the ankles and then together at the knees. With a dwarf on each arm, they untied Lia's hands from behind her back and forced her to clasp her hands together around the pole. Retying her wrists together, several loops of the leather cord were wrapped around her waist, knees, and ankles, and were all fastened to the pole.

"That ought to do it," Breslin announced, looking with pride at their work. "They will have feasts in our honor, lads!"

"Are we going to Borahgg or should we head to Graun?"

"Graun is closer. As much as I would love to parade her through our own city, we must secure her as quickly as possible."

Wistfully dreaming of the gallons of ale that they were sure would be bestowed, Venk and Athos each took an end of the yoke and lifted Lia up into the air. Whistling merrily, the three dwarves turned sharply south and ventured into the forest as they headed toward the closest entrance that would take them to the vast subterranean realms below.

It wasn't until they were well below the topside world when Breslin grunted with annoyance. Athos turned to his friend.

"What is it?"

"We should tell the humans. I will contact Rhenyon and let him know we have captured their renegade sorceress."

"And let him take the credit for her capture?"

"The credit is all ours, I assure you. However, the humans want her much more than we do. They are our allies. We will hold on to their prisoner until they can collect her."

Breslin pulled the famed Mythra axe from his back.

"Do we stop?" Venk asked, peering around the swinging form of their inert prisoner. In the hour since her capture, their prisoner had yet to cease her struggling or stop her incessant chanting. "Be silent, will you?" Venk deliberately lurched forward and watched with satisfaction as the prisoner swung outward on the yoke and smacked her backside into the tunnel wall.

"Muh fuh, ah gomfa keh yuh en yuh sluh!!!"

"Not necessary," Breslin answered, ignoring the prisoner's outburst. "Besides, contacting him will not take long."

The red axe began to glow. Within moments Breslin was smiling.

"I send greetings, Commander Rhenyon."

Venk looked at his brother.

"He's lost it. He's talking to people who are not here now."

"I wish to inform you that Celestia has been captured. Aye, that's right. We are taking her to Graun. What's that? Verdayn? It can wait. Dragons are never on time. Aye. Have Lady Sarah take you there and we will escort you down. Until then, my friend."

The red axe lost its glow and returned to normal. Breslin turned to look back at Venk.

"Rhenyon has been informed. He will inform the human king."

"Lady Sarah is a teleporter, is she not?" Athos asked. "Could she not teleport directly there?"

"Not until she has stepped foot there and can see for herself what it looks like," Breslin explained, smiling fleetingly as he recalled the guur battle from several years ago and how Sarah had teleported all the human soldiers but one from the heat of the battle, much to their dismay.

They arrived at the dwarven city of Graun less than an hour later. Emerging into the naturally large cavern, Breslin dropped his axe handle on the signal plate just outside the tunnel entrance and announced their arrival. Armed soldiers appeared instantly. While weapons weren't drawn, they weren't exactly welcomed with open arms either.

One dwarf stepped forward. His uniform was more decorated than the others. "Identify."

"Breslin of the Kla Guur, at your service."

"Ehren, of the Kla Chanus. What can we do for you, brother?"

"You have no doubt heard of the search for the human sorceress, Celestia?"

The dwarf nodded. "We have." Ehren's eyes suddenly opened wide as he noticed a shoulder pole with a bound human woman attached to it.

"Is that her? You captured the sorceress?"

Breslin smiled proudly and held his arm out to indicate his companions.

"*We* have captured her, aye. We ask for help securing her until the humans can retrieve her."

"Granted."

Ehren motioned to his companions to relieve Athos and

Venk of their heavy burden. Once the prisoner was safely in the hands of the Chanus guards, the three Guur clansmen breathed a collective sigh of relief. Now it was up to the humans to take her off their hands.

The dwarves turned and effortlessly marched to a large domed structure located nearby, at the entrance of the city. Breslin would have thought it more prudent to locate their council chambers away from the outskirts of the city, but it wasn't his problem. Let them worry about defending the structure should they ever be attacked by outsiders.

They approached the thick marble doorway leading into the chambers just as a group of elders exited the building. Several old dwarves approached and bowed before Breslin, who bowed in return. One dwarf, gnarled with age, hair and beard as white as snow, pointed a wrinkled finger at the prisoner.

"This is the human causing so many problems?"

Ehren turned to the newcomer and nodded. A split second later his eyes opened with surprise as he recognized Sautin, revered clan leader of the Chanus. Ehren bowed his head in respect. Following his lead, the Kla Guur clansmen bowed their heads as well.

"It would seem so. The human king has been informed of her capture. The female Nohrin will be taking him to the valley to await escort here."

Sautin nodded. His heavily wrinkled face turned to Ehren's.

"Go to the valley. Make contact with the human king and escort his entourage here."

Ehren nodded. He and his guards retraced their steps and vanished back into the tunnel from whence they came.

The wizened eyes studied the human who was desperately trying to free herself, an angry look of defiance still visible in her eyes. Sautin turned to point at an empty cold hearth with two wooden braces already in place on either side of the enormous fire pit. The hearth was large enough to support a spitted animal easily the size of an adult griffin.

"Put her there."

Breslin approached and bowed again.

"With respect, you do not plan to eat her, right?"

Surprisingly bright and clear eyes sparkled with merriment as one of the oldest dwarves Breslin had ever seen turned to regard him.

"Our hunts have been unsuccessful as of late. We thought perhaps a bit of fresh meat might—"

Lia screamed into her gag and struggled furiously with her bonds as the yoke was placed down into the support braces, effectively stretching her out across the fire pit. She struggled so much that the pole started thumping up and down on the braces, threatening to dump her into the soot and ash piled deep beneath her in the hearth.

"Kah suh-huh, yeh cah kish muh ash! Ahh hoah yeh choa!!!"

"What better way to greet our human visitors," Sautin began again, ignoring their prisoner's outbursts, "than to present the source of so much stress and trouble for all the world to see?" The old dwarf chuckled. "Fear not, son of Maelnar, she will remain unharmed while in our custody. What happens to her once the humans arrive is entirely up to them."

This seemed to placate the prisoner for a bit as her struggles lessened somewhat, but her muffled rants continued.

* * *

"I can't believe they caught her so easily."

"Neither can I," Rhenyon admitted. "I would have thought she would have put up more of a fight."

Steve, Sarah, Rhenyon, Kri'Entu, and a contingent of ten soldiers, all followed the flickering torchlight as they were led down into the realm of the dwarves. Walking between his wife and the king, Steve ignited both hands to provide more light.

"I still do not think this wise," the commander muttered under his breath, but loud enough so others could hear. "Celestia's supporters may be hiding just around the next bend. We could be ambushed at any moment."

"Hence my proximity to both fire thrower and teleporter,"

the king answered with a smile, turning to look back at the commander. "If ambushed, we are well protected, and if it is proven to be beyond our control, then Lady Sarah will escort us to safety."

"In the blink of an eye," Sarah agreed. "Umm, excuse me? How much farther is it?"

"Not far," the lead dwarf answered, without breaking stride.

"You said that nearly an hour ago."

Accustomed to the dislike most humans felt toward enclosed areas, the lead dwarf smiled.

"Fear not, milady. We are nearing the bottom of these stairs. Just beyond is the gateway to Graun."

"If we could just get some more light in here," Sarah complained, "then I could see where we're going and I could get us all there faster. Can we light a couple of more torches?"

"Even if there were more torches, milady, they would do you no good. There are no unauthorized teleportations here."

"That's what the Kla Guur said."

"And?"

"I was still able to do it."

One of their escorts turned to study her.

"You were able to teleport to Borahgg? Through their barrier? Our own enchantments are modeled after theirs."

Sarah nodded. "Whether I'm on the surface, or in R'Tal, or pretty much anywhere, I can teleport right to their council chambers if I wanted to."

"Whether snacks from the castle or vials on a rack, or even plucking me off a big dragon's back …" Steve murmured, sounding an awful lot like he was quoting a children's nursery rhyme.

Sarah shook her head. "That's it. It's official. I married a dork."

"Just remember no one forced you to say 'I do'!"

"You weren't this crazy when I met you."

Steve laughed.

Following their three guides through the large arched gate, Steve came to a halt as his eyes adjusted to the extra light in the great cavern. Once again, he tried to identify the source of the light but was unable. Whether illuminated by concealed lights, bioluminescent moss, or some form of jhorun, the light was just there and easily enabled him to see how massive the cavern was.

Steve glanced down at the glowing metal plate just as the lead dwarf dropped his axe handle on it, sending out a loud crack. Dwarves started pouring out of the big domed building they were walking toward. Steve also noticed that off to the side of the council chambers was a large communal fire pit where many dwarves had gathered around. As they approached the crowd, the dwarves parted right down the middle, revealing a figure tied to a pole carrier. The carrier had been set down in two wooden holders on either side of a large fire pit. Steve squinted at the figure. It was a blonde woman who was twisting to look at something behind her, so he was unable to get a good look at her face. It didn't really look like Celestia but who else would be struggling that hard to escape? The gag in her mouth prevented him from understanding anything she was shouting. As if sensing others were present, the woman whipped her head back around to stare at him straight in the eyes.

Lia. Gagged, tied to a pole carrier, and shooting daggers at him.

Steve burst out laughing. He laughed so hard he couldn't breathe. One look at Lia trying to chew through her gag sent him spiraling out of control again and he collapsed against the side of the closest building.

Kri'Entu turned to Sarah.

"I take it she is an acquaintance?"

Sarah pushed past the king and her husband to stare, open-mouthed, at the woman the dwarves had apprehended.

"Omigod! It's Lia! I know her! *We* know her. Trust me, she's not Celestia. Cut her down!"

"But it may be Celestia in disguise!" Athos protested.

Sarah threw him a dirty look.

"We will trust Lady Sarah to know who her friends are," Breslin hastily added, cuffing Athos soundly on the back of his head. "If she says that is not Celestia, then we have made an alarming mistake. Please offer my most profound apologies to your friend."

Steve sauntered over to the hearth and squatted down so that he was eye-level with Lia.

"Howdy. How's it goin' down there?"

Steve untied Lia's gag and pulled it out of her mouth.

"Are you just going to stand there or are you going to get me down?"

Steve straightened and ignited his right hand. "I really wish I had a camera with me. So, whatcha doing here, Lia?" He walked along the length of the pole and gently touched his flaming hand to each knot securing her in place. Within moments Lia was free. A dozen dwarven hands reached out to help her to her feet.

"Don't touch me! You hairy midgets have some nerve! You never once asked me who I was!"

"Well, in their defense," Steve began, "they really couldn't take any chances when —"

"I'll kill you all in your sleep!"

Lia suddenly found herself staring at the business end of countless swords, spears, and daggers as every dwarf within earshot took notice of her threat. She offered a sheepish smile. "Okay, perhaps that wasn't the best choice of words."

The dwarves lowered their weapons somewhat but kept them trained on her, just in case any further threats presented themselves. Lia rounded on Steve and held up an accusing finger.

"And you, Chuckles! If you had just told me what was going on, then I wouldn't have had to take it upon myself to see what you guys were up to!"

"Oh, I get it. You get all nosy and then try to blame this on me?"

"Precisely!"

"You must have been nearby when I teleported everyone back here," Sarah accused.

"Close enough to see the dragon Steve rode in on," Lia admitted, briefly frowning at Steve before she returned her attention to Sarah. "I couldn't believe what I was seeing. I had to know if it was real, so I snuck forward to touch its tail."

"You followed me from the house, didn't you?"

Lia smiled at Sarah. "Guilty as charged."

"It would seem Celestia has not been apprehended after all," Kri'Entu broke in.

"Yeah, sorry, all we got was a stubborn friend of ours from our world," Steve explained.

"Stubborn? Really?" Lia placed herself directly in front of Steve and put her hands on her hips. "After all I've been through, that's the game you want to play right now?"

"After all you've been through? Is that the best you can do? Puh-lease."

"Now that you're here," Sarah interrupted, giving her husband a conspiratorial wink, "we need to get you to safety. If Celestia learns you're a friend of ours, then you'll become a target. We have enough to worry about without having to protect you, too."

"Awww, that's so sweet."

The sarcasm was so thick it could have been cut with a knife and served for breakfast.

"You know," Steve said, coming to stand next to the king, "she'd be safest if she was with Mikal. The two already know one another."

Kri'Entu nodded. "Perfect. Lady Lia will be secured in the Antechamber."

"You're not—wait, what did you call me? Lady Lia?" Lia suddenly smiled. "I can get on board with that."

"Sorry," Steve apologized to the king. "I guess introductions are in order. Your Majesty, may we present Lia Manning, a friend of ours from our world. Lia, this is Kri'Entu. He's the King of Lentari."

"Lentari?"

"That's the kingdom we're presently in."

"So, you can teleport things while Mr. Hothead over there can light things on fire?"

Sarah laughed. "Yes."

"Dragons, magic, and kings," Lia ticked off on her fingers. She looked at her two friends. "You two have some 'splaining to do."

Sarah nodded. "And we will, I promise you. As soon as—"

**Rinbok Intherer has arrived. He waits for you east of**

**the settlement.**

" —things calm down," Sarah finished.

Steve's head had snapped up.

"Time's up. Pryllan says the Dragon Lord just made it to Verdayn."

"The Dragon Lord?" Lia whispered to Sarah.

"The dragon king," Sarah explained. "Dragon riding is very taboo, yet Steve did it anyway. Both he and Pryllan are in trouble."

"Holy crap! Are they going to be okay?"

"They better be. Steve saved the Dragon Lord's life."

"How?"

Kri'Entu cleared his throat. "Lady Sarah. We must be off to Verdayn. Lady Lia will have to wait until after the proceedings before she can be secured in the castle."

"Does she come with us?" Sarah asked.

The king nodded. "Sir Steve is correct. Since she is an acquaintance of the Nohrin, then she has, unfortunately, become a potential target."

Sarah looked back at her friend. "Sorry. Looks like you're coming with us for now. Stay close."

"If you say so."

Sarah looked around the room. "Okay, everyone who is going to Verdayn gather close, please."

Steve, Rhenyon, the king, and his contingent of soldiers, all stepped forward to crowd around Sarah and Lia. Breslin nudged Venk and Athos and stepped forward as well.

"If you are able, Lady Sarah, we would like to accompany you."

Sarah eyed their party. "There's still less than twenty. I can do it."

The king nodded. "Excellent. Whenever you are ready."

* * *

"Look at the size of that sucker! It's huge! That's got to be the biggest dragon I've ever seen!"

Sarah turned to Lia.

"You make it sound as though you've been observing

dragons your whole life. You've only seen Pryllan and Rinbok, right?"

"Well, yeah. Still. He makes the other dragons look tiny."

Standing on the outskirts of the town, the massive jade dragon, with jagged black stripes, towered over all present, including Kahvel and several other smaller dragons in attendance. Just outside Verdayn's gate was the farthest eastern stretch of Lake Raehón's valley. A mile and a half past the east gate was where Rinbok and the dragons had decided to touch down. Kri'Entu and the human contingent were closer to the town's gate than the dragons, but still far enough away to show their wyverian counterparts that they would not be relying on the townsfolk to come to their aid should they need it.

Lia sidled up next to Sarah as she watched the strange proceedings. She was pretty sure she had overheard she'd be joining Mikal in some safe room, but the sudden announcement from Steve that this important dragon had arrived to conduct this hearing had trumped her departure. It still amazed and fascinated her to see an actual dragon in person. While she could tell that these proceedings were not meant to be taken lightly, she couldn't help feeling giddy as she realized she was in another world. A world where dragons and magic were everyday occurrences! Standing next to the dragon she had touched was Steve, and next to him was the ruler of this kingdom. An actual king! Lia trembled with anticipation. Hopefully everything would turn out okay.

A deep voice suddenly rang out across the vale.

"Pryllan, offspring of Caradoc, offspring of Lorcan, step forth."

With her head hung low, Pryllan presented herself before Rinbok Intherer.

"I have called you—"

Steve took several steps forward as well. "Nuh-uh. Wait a minute, pal."

Sarah gave a tiny jerk. She swallowed noisily. Lia took her hand and held it.

Rinbok twisted his neck to see around Pryllan's body, searching for the speaker. He spotted the small group of humans and growled.

"Identi—" the Dragon Lord suddenly inhaled. His slitted eyes narrowed and focused on Steve. "You are the fire thrower."

Steve nodded. "I am. You will not accuse her without accusing me first. I was the one who convinced her to fly over you so that I could remove the RIC."

Rinbok stared at him, unblinking. "Clarify. What is a ric?"

"One of those ugly metal suckers that landed on your back and burrowed its way into your skin."

"Be that as it may, human, you are charged with the offense of riding a dragon. It is a well-known fact that dragon riding is forbidden, fire thrower."

"I know. I'm aware."

"Are you now? You knew this and yet you still dared step foot on my back?"

"Yep, and I'd do it again."

"Bold words, human."

"I would rather get in trouble and break a few rules than idly stand by and allow a dragon, *any* dragon, to succumb to those metal blood suckers."

Rinbok's gaze shifted to Pryllan.

"How was it that a dragon was overpowered by a mere human?"

"I was not overpowered," Pryllan said quietly. "I could have said no, or else refused his request."

"But you did not."

"Correct. I did not."

Steve stepped between the two dragons and whistled.

"Mr. Reebok, you …"

**Rinbok.**

*Whatever.*

"… want to be mad at someone? Fine. Be mad at me. Punish me, not her. Don't punish her for dropping me off on a dragon when the end result was that dragon's life being saved."

Sarah groaned. If her husband somehow managed to get out of this predicament, she was going to kill him herself.

"Punish? You think I am going to punish her? I owe my

life to the two of you. Zabbe, Sarkan, his mate, and all the others you helped by telling us how to defeat the creatures and, ultimately, who was responsible. Nay, fire thrower, I will not dispense any punishments."

Taken aback, Steve took a step back. "Okay, I'm a little confused here."

The ground shook as Rinbok moved closer to the small party of humans. Steve stiffened with surprise as the massive dragon approached. He quickly glanced up at Pryllan to judge her reaction. He hadn't ever seen fear on a dragon's face, but he was looking at it now. Pryllan was cowering under the much larger dragon's fierce stare. Steve worriedly looked at the king.

"Hold your ground," the king softly murmured to him.

Lia tensed. She was unsure if things were going well or not. On the one hand, the dragon seemed to be appreciative of what Steve had done, but on the other, he still acted supremely ticked off. And now he was moving closer! This couldn't be good. She looked at Sarah, who had a stern expression on her face. Sarah met her eyes and shook her head.

"If things turn ugly," Lia whispered, leaning close to Sarah, "can you get us all out of here?"

"If I need to, I can. And I will."

A sudden commotion had Lia returning her gaze to the dragon king. It was now lowering its head to look Steve directly in the eye. No one spoke for a few moments and then, much to her surprise, the big dragon bowed its head to Steve. Lia inched closer so that she could better hear what the dragon was saying.

"Your past transgression will be overlooked," Rinbok was saying, giving his undivided attention to Steve. "I must now decide what I am to do. Riding a dragon is still forbidden."

Steve nodded. "I understand."

"Will you continue to ride Pryllan, if given the opportunity?"

"I could lie and say that I won't, but the way I see it, I shouldn't have to lie. Not to you. So my official answer is 'probably'."

"Steve!" Sarah hissed with shock.

"Nay, do not reprimand him, female Nohrin," Rinbok admonished. "I appreciate his honesty."

"But you just said dragon riding is forbidden!" Sarah protested from her position next to the king, who had his hand on her shoulder to prevent her from attacking her husband. "I don't want him doing something that will just get him into trouble again."

Steve scowled. "Would you give me a little bit of credit here?"

Sarah looked as though she was ready to break the king's grip so she could smack some sense into her husband.

"Steve, zip it. And you!" Sarah turned back to the dragon king. "My husband is fascinated by dragons. Can you just picture it? He thinks he's allowed to jump on any dragon's back and ends up getting himself eaten. I can't have him killed by a rogue dragon when I'd much rather kill him myself!"

Rinbok snorted out two quick jets of fire before he was able to compose himself.

"This is my token of appreciation I hereby give you, fire thrower. For saving the lives of countless dragons, as well as my own life, and for preventing us from going to battle against our dwarven brothers, I proclaim you friend to all the wyverie I rule over and grant you permission to ride Pryllan."

Steve gasped with shock.

"But," Rinbok cautioned, lowering his massive horned head to once more look Steve in the eye, "only if she allows it. You will not ride any other dragon, even if they do not object, unless you receive permission from me alone. In the presence of all that are here, I ask you, fire thrower, do you understand me and will you comply with my wishes?"

Steve smiled. "I do and I will. I'm honored. You have my word that I will only ride Pryllan and that's if, and only if, she gives me permission."

"Very well. It is settled. I will be off."

"Excuse me, my lord."

Rinbok's long neck swung around to look at Kahvel. "Speak."

"You had indicated earlier that I was to abandon my

duties as liaison to the humans. Did you have some other —"

"I did no such thing. You will continue to speak on my behalf to the humans. Kri'Entu, until next time."

All dragons save Kahvel and Pryllan took to the air and disappeared into the clouds.

Kri'Entu turned to stare at the Nohrin. "Sir Steve, Lady Sarah."

Steve and Sarah approached the king and bowed. "Yes?"

"The two of you have an uncanny ability of staving off the threat of war. This time, you have prevented open hostilities between dragons and dwarves."

"My question is," Steve began, taking his wife's hand, "what is Celestia planning in order to sever the alliance with the dragons and dwarves? She was almost successful and damn near took out the alliance with the humans and dwarves while doing so. She's gotta be stopped."

"What do *we* do now?" Sarah clarified.

"Return to the castle."

Everyone turned to Rhenyon.

"Her plan has been foiled. Mikal is at the castle and we know Celestia has escaped. The most logical step for her now is to take the prince. By force if necessary."

Kri'Entu stared at the commander. "Mikal is secured in the Antechamber. He should be safe."

Steve nodded. "He should be, yes, but we also know if anyone can infiltrate the castle, or find a way to sneak in, it'd be her. Rhenyon is right. We need to get back there."

Breslin approached the king and bowed. The acceptable method for a dwarf seeking atonement was to present themselves to the appropriate authority for disciplinary action. Breslin continued to stare at the ground as he waited for the human king to acknowledge his presence. Kri'Entu finally noticed the dwarf.

"Breslin, of the Kla Guur, I do not hold you responsible for apprehending the incorrect person. It could have very well been Celestia, therefore I absolve you of any wrongdoing."

Breslin finally straightened, sighing with relief. "We thought it was her."

"You could've just asked," Lia grumped, folding her arms

across her chest and lifting her nose into the air.

Ignoring Lia, Breslin kept his eyes on the king. "I, and my fellows, would ask that we be allowed to accompany you back to R'Tal. We would see the threat to your son eliminated once and for all."

Kri'Entu nodded. "Granted, master dwarf. I hope you are ready. We leave for R'Tal now."

* * *

Lia tried hard not to stare. She was in a castle! An honest-to-goodness castle! The room she had just passed through even contained two golden thrones! It must be where the king and queen held court. If only the king would slow down so that she could properly check out the sights for herself. She briefly wondered if they offered tours.

A group of five soldiers approached and bowed; their own group came to a halt. Commander Rhenyon approached the second group and nodded his head in acknowledgement. A tall officer stepped forward to face the commander.

"You sent for me, sir?"

"Aye, Captain. We need to increase the number of guards protecting the prince."

"The guards have already been doubled, Commander."

"I do not care if the guards have been doubled," Rhenyon snapped. Sighing, he took a breath and pulled Captain Pheron aside and out of earshot of the rest of the men, but still within hers. "Celestia was unsuccessful in starting a war between the dragons and dwarves. She will retaliate. The most logical target will be the prince. I want an armed presence at all times, is that understood?"

Pheron nodded, understanding. "Completely. The guards will be tripled."

"We must be off," the king interjected. "Report to the Antechamber as soon as you are able, Commander."

"I will, Your Majesty."

Rhenyon and Pheron stood stiffly at attention as the king led the group past the kitchens and into the heart of the castle.

"Who was that blonde woman with the Nohrin?" Pheron asked, turning to follow the group with his eyes until they disappeared down the hall.

"That was Lady Lia. She is from the Nohrin's world and is a friend. She was accidentally transported here when Sir Steve and the dragon were teleported back."

"Teleported back? A dragon went to their world? Was it the sorceress's doing?"

Rhenyon shook his head. "It was Lady Sarah."

"Really? What dastardly deed did Sir Steve do to incur her wrath?"

Rhenyon laughed and slapped the captain on his shoulder. "This time, nothing. Lady Sarah only reacted when she saw him in danger. Now if you will excuse me, I must be off. Three reserve squadrons have just arrived and I must assign them to protect Kre'Mikal."

"I understand. Good luck, Commander."

Rhenyon nodded and disappeared into the Great Hall. Just as he approached the Antechamber, he heard the prince laugh, followed closely by a sharp outburst from a female voice. He paused to listen at the door.

"Are you freakin' kidding me? Take it back. Give me something different."

"I cannot. Once a jhorun has been given, I cannot take it back. I think."

"You think? You don't know? If ever there was a time to try, it's now. You have to give me something else!"

"Why?" Mikal asked, perplexed. "I have given you a jhorun! I thought you would be happy!"

"Happy? *Happy*? I can now point to three small objects and get them to juggle on their own and you think I'd be happy?"

"All I am saying," Mikal's voice said slowly, "is that you would be a great jester."

"If you ever tell Steve or Sarah that, then I'll personally feed you to that big dragon I saw earlier. A jester. Hmmph. Little punk. Why would you say that?"

The teenager laughed again. "Because you are funny and can make me laugh like no other." Mikal raised an eyebrow.

"Besides, I am a prince. You are in my home. You have to do what I say!"

"Kid, I'll kill you in your sleep."

Once more Lia found herself staring at the business end of a sword. Rhenyon had leapt from his position just outside the room and rushed inside, drawing Mythron as he did. A split second later he had intercepted the foreigner before she could get close enough to strike. Lia backtracked a few steps and held up her hands. Mikal jumped between Lia and the commander, arms outstretched.

"She does not mean it! She was jesting!"

Rhenyon's eyes narrowed as he stared the woman down. "You may be a friend to the Nohrin, but that does not give you the right to threaten our prince."

"It was a joke! Geez, switch to decaf, okay?"

Rhenyon blinked in confusion. He slowly slid Mythron back into its scabbard. "Decaf?"

"She's suggesting you drink too much dujari juice," Mikal translated.

Rhenyon rounded on Lia. "You accuse me of using narcotics?"

"Who said anything about doing drugs? Take it down a notch."

Rhenyon turned to the prince again. "What did she say?"

"She's not accusing you of anything. She is trying to help you relax."

"Why not just say so?"

"I did say so," Lia grumped.

"Lady Lia, you will need to remain in here for the time being."

"I have to stay in here? Seriously? I want to look around! This is a castle, for crying out loud!"

"Aye, it's a castle," Mikal agreed. "It's absolutely fascinating. There are hidden passageways, dank dungeons, stables, moats, moat monsters, and so on!"

"You're killing me, kid."

Mikal grinned. "I can keep going."

"You do and you're dead."

Rhenyon's eyes darted back and forth between the two.

Chuckling softly, the commander departed, but not before stationing four guards inside the room.

"Oh, this just keeps getting better and better," Lia complained. "I don't need no stinkin' babysitter!"

* * *

Finally able to claim an hour to themselves, Steve and Sarah enjoyed a fine meal served by the king's personal chef. Hand in hand, husband and wife strolled down the wide corridor. They had just checked in on Lia and Mikal and discovered them in a heated debate on who was better at Rock Group. Leaving the argument over who was the better guitar player, they headed outside, eager to claim as much downtime as possible. After all that had transpired since their arrival, they were both mentally and physically exhausted.

"What do you think Celestia will do next? She's not stupid enough to go after Mikal now, is she?"

Sarah leaned up against her husband as they stopped along the water's edge in the inner bailey. As they stared down into the moat's dark murky water, ripples appeared and a large serpentine head slowly rose up from the surface. Clumps of stringy green moss clung to the enormous snake's head as it rose out of the water. Once it was at eye level with them, it flicked its tongue several times in rapid succession. Steve returned the stare and ignited both hands.

"I don't think we've been introduced, Bredo. My name is Steve and this is my wife, Sarah."

The giant snake eyed the flaming hands.

Steve ignited a chaser and spun it on his finger. "If you're entertaining any foolish notions about attacking us, then now would be a good time to let them go."

Bredo flicked his tongue a few more times before sinking back into the depths of the moat.

"I don't think I've ever seen Bredo in the flesh before," Sarah admitted.

"That would make two of us."

As Sarah leaned over to watch the ripples become smaller and smaller, she gasped and pulled herself sharply backwards, gripping Steve's arm tightly as she did so.

"What's the matter? Did you see Bredo again? Did he try something?"

Sarah vehemently shook her head and pointed at the water's edge. Steve leaned out over the water to see for himself what had spooked her, however only his own image looked back at him. He scratched his chin. Man alive he could use a shave. Whenever he let his beard grow unchecked for a few days, the salt and pepper jokes always followed shortly thereafter.

"There's nothing there, hon. Nothing but my ugly mug, that is."

Sarah shook her head. "No. No, she was there. I think it was Caladonia!"

"What? Where? In the water?"

"Yes. When I looked down, I didn't see my reflection at all. Then another face appeared and it wasn't mine. She was young. Mid-twenties, I'd say. Her hair was brown and it was elegantly braided. She looked sad."

"Can you still see her?"

Composing herself, she leaned over the water's edge to look. Sure enough, her reflection wasn't there. The brown-haired woman looked back at her and gave her a fleeting smile.

"Are you Caladonia?" Sarah whispered.

The woman's head nodded.

Steve leaned close and looked down at the water. All he could see was his and Sarah's reflection.

"You can still see her? I can't. Can she hear you?"

"Shush! Hang on a second." Sarah looked back down at the water. "Can you understand me?"

Caladonia nodded again.

"What do you want? Is there something we can do for you?"

Caladonia looped her fingers under the silver chain encircling her neck and pulled until a pendant appeared in her hand. She glanced down at it and visibly sighed.

"What is it?" Sarah whispered, more to herself than to anyone in particular. "What do you want to show me?"

The sorceress held up the pendant and let it gently sway

back and forth. Sarah focused on the amulet. It looked broken. She studied the shapes on the amulet, trying to determine what she was looking at. It had to be a dragon. She could see a pointed tail as well as the lower portion of the dragon's body. The head must be on the other half.

"Your amulet? Is that what you're trying to show me?"

Caladonia smiled and nodded again, swinging the broken piece a final time. She looked at Sarah and bowed her head slightly. Then she looked over at Steve, and even though he couldn't see her, she bowed to him, too.

Her image melted away and was replaced by Sarah's own reflection.

"She's gone," Sarah told her husband. "She saw you, too, you know."

"Really?"

"She looked straight at you just before she disappeared."

"Did she tell you anything?"

"I couldn't hear her. She wanted to show me her pendant. She made certain I saw it."

Steve gave a jolt of recognition.

"Was it broken?"

Sarah spun around. "How could you possibly know that?"

"I've seen Celestia clutch something around her neck a couple of times. It must be the other piece of that amulet!"

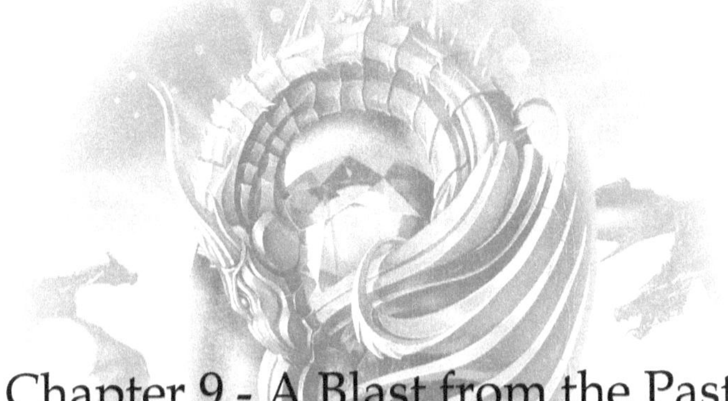

# Chapter 9 - A Blast from the Past

They rushed back inside, bowling over peasants, soldiers, and anyone else who got in their way. Husband and wife burst into the Great Hall and scattered a group of soldiers that had just exited the dining area. One soldier had his back to the door. It cost him. Sensing a disturbance coming from behind, the soldier had tried leaping out of the way, unfortunately choosing the same direction Steve had leapt. Both men went down in a tumble of arms and legs. Sarah glanced back as Steve painfully regained his feet.

"I'm fine. Keep going, I'll catch up!"

Sarah nodded and sprinted toward the Antechamber, hoping that at least one of the monarchs would be present.

Steve watched Sarah disappear through one of the many doors leading out of the hall before he turned to the fallen soldier.

"Sorry about that. Never pays to rush, right?"

He extended a hand and waited for the soldier to roll onto his back. When he did, Steve did a double take.

"Darius! I'll be damned! It's been a few years, bud! How are you?"

"A pleasure to see you again, Sir Steve."

Steve pulled the soldier to his feet. "You okay? I hit you kinda hard."

"It was my fault. I should have—"

"Your fault, nothing. You weren't even facing me. I'm the one who hit you."

"Where are you off to in such a hurry?"

"The Antechamber. We need to talk to the king and queen immediately."

"The king is in a meeting with Commander Rhenyon and Captain Pheron."

"Important?"

"I know not."

"Okay, what about the queen?" Steve wanted to know. "Is she in the Antechamber?"

"I believe the queen was seeing to several peasant complaints."

"Where's Shardwyn?"

"In his workshop."

"That'll have to do. Do you know where that's at?"

Darius nodded. "Aye. I used to be a runner. I was responsible for personally hand delivering all communiqués from the king."

"Beautiful. Come on, we have to find Sarah. She should be at the Antechamber by now."

They arrived at the protected chamber just as Sarah appeared at the door with a frown on her face.

"Neither one of them is in there, just Mikal, Lia, and so many guards that it's standing room only. Why didn't we just teleport?"

Steve laughed. "Umm, caught up in the moment?"

Sarah noticed the soldier standing next to Steve and smiled brightly.

"Darius! Hello! It's good to see you!"

Darius bowed. "Milady. As always, a pleasure."

"So where is everyone?" Sarah inquired, looking at Steve.

"The king's in some meeting with Rhenyon and Pheron,

and the queen is dealing with some bickering peasants."

"Okay, the queen's out. The king is tied up in meetings. We should tell someone, right?"

"I will send word for her," Darius informed them, signaling to one of the guards standing quietly at attention to the left of the Antechamber's main door. "Once the queen is finished with her business, inform her that Lady Sarah and Sir Steve request an audience at her earliest convenience. If she asks, tell Her Majesty that I will escort the Nohrin to Shardwyn's workshop."

The guard bowed. "Aye, lieutenant."

Steve grinned and slapped Darius jovially on the back. "How long have you been a lieutenant?"

"About two years. This way to the north tower."

Husband and wife followed Darius back through the kitchens, through the Great Hall, and out into the bailey. Darius headed north as soon as they were outside, angling for a massive stone tower at least five hundred feet away.

"Why's his tower so far away from the castle?" Sarah asked, turning to look back across the keep and up at the formidable fortress. "Wouldn't he want to be closer to everyone else?"

"You have met Shardwyn, have you not? This was not by his choice, but by the king's decree."

Steve laughed. "That bad, huh?"

"After he destroyed his workshop for the third time, the king relocated him to the tower. Had to think about the safety of others, he said."

"Did Shardwyn have a problem with that?"

"Not at all," Darius reported. "He said he enjoys the freedom to conduct his work without interruption."

"How many accidents has he had?" Sarah asked, taking Steve's hand.

"Not many," Darius admitted, smiling. "He has been incident free for close to a month now."

Steve and Sarah nervously eyed each other. Only a month?

Entering the base of the stone tower, they ascended the gently spiraling stairs. Once they reached the top, Darius knocked politely on the thick wooden door and waited. They all heard a loud clatter come from somewhere within, followed by soft tinkles of broken glass being swept together, all while a low voice muttered incoherently. The bolt was pulled back and the door creaked inward.

"Lady Sarah! Sir Steve! What a pleasant surprise! And Lieutenant Darius! Pleased to see you again, m' boy!"

Darius bowed. "Good afternoon, Shardwyn. The Nohrin urgently request an audience."

"Splendid, splendid! Right this way."

"Sir Steve, Lady Sarah, I must be off." Darius turned toward the stairs before he turned around and bowed once more. "I hope you find whatever you are looking for."

"Thanks." Steve clasped Darius' forearm. "Me, too."

"So! Sit down, sit down." Shardwyn plopped himself down on a chair so covered in purple cushions that he was practically swallowed up by the colorful pillows. "An urgent meeting, you say? What can I do for you?"

"I saw Caladonia," Sarah announced, eliciting a gasp from the wizard.

"What? How is that possible? Where did you …? How did you …?"

"Let me just tell you what happened," Sarah interrupted.

Shardwyn leaned back in his chair. "Very well. Proceed."

"We were outside by the moat," Sarah began excitedly. "Steve and I were walking along the water when Bredo stuck his head up. Steve scared him off. Then I leaned over the edge to watch him sink back into the moat. I looked down and noticed my reflection was gone."

"Go on," Shardwyn prompted with his eyes closed.

"After a few seconds a woman's face appeared. Younger than me. Fair complexion. Long brown hair braided down the back. It was her eyes that got me. She looked so sad. She looked straight at me and pulled on a silver chain she was wearing until some sort of pendant appeared."

Both of Shardwyn's eyes snapped open. "A pendant, you say?"

Sarah nodded. "Right. I saw wings and a tail end of what had to be a dragon. I'm assuming, based on the shape of the piece I saw, that the overall shape of the amulet is a vertical ellipsis."

"And the woman you saw?" Shardwyn prompted. "You believe her to be the sorceress Caladonia? Why?"

"Because I asked her. She nodded her head."

"Wait a moment. You asked her a question and she responded? Did she speak?"

Sarah shook her head no.

"She just nodded her head when I asked her if she was Caladonia. She dangled the pendant in front of her and let it swing back and forth to make sure I saw it. I asked her if that's what she wanted to show me and she nodded yes. That has to mean something, doesn't it?"

The eccentric wizard sat back in his chair, sinking down a few more inches in the heaps of pillows as he did so.

"Do you think you can describe it to me?"

"Well, it looked like it was broken. Steve said he had seen Celestia clutching something around her neck before and just figured it might be the other piece of—what's wrong?"

Shardwyn had jumped up out of his chair so fast that purple cushions went flying everywhere. Steve batted one pillow out of the way before it had a chance to bop Sarah on her face.

"Was it something we said?" Steve asked as they watched Shardwyn snatch books off different shelves. Shardwyn briefly glanced at the titles before the books were haphazardly dropped to the floor.

"I take it you're looking for a book?" Sarah asked, squatting down to inspect a few of the titles Shardwyn had discarded.

"Aye. At the king's request, I searched for any and all references to Celestia in the library. While there, I discovered a copy of one of our oldest historical volumes. If you get a chance, you should read it. Very fascinating."

"I'm sure it is," Steve muttered.

"Would you like me to write down the name of the book? It is quite long and easy to forget."

"Perhaps another time," Sarah suggested. "You were saying?"

"Indeed. The tome was written by a lesser-known historian who lived nearly seven centuries ago. He wrote of a king breaking an amulet in twain as it was too powerful to be possessed by one person."

"What? That has to be it!"

"We will not know for certain until I can find the picture of it. Zinn, that would be the historian, included a sketch of the amulet. Nothing fancy, but it—aha!"

Shardwyn let out a victorious shout as he turned back around with a thick dusty leather-bound book that looked as though it had seen better days. Parts of the leather binding were falling off. Several sections of the book's pages were sticking out past the cover, giving the appearance that the pages had fallen out and someone had shoved them back in. He gingerly set the damaged book down on one of his many worktables and carefully opened the cover.

"Let us begin. I do not remember where—"

Sarah deftly ducked under Shardwyn's arm and came up between the wizard and the book.

"Would you mind if I looked?"

Shardwyn took several steps back. "I do not think you can decipher ancient Lentarian script, so maybe it would be better if I—"

"I don't need to decipher anything," Sarah interjected. "You said there was a sketch. So, I'm going to look for a drawing."

Surprised that he hadn't thought of that, Shardwyn withdrew his objections and moved to stand next to Steve.

"You must have very interesting arguments with her."

"Dude, you have no idea."

"I can still hear you," Sarah reminded them, keeping her eyes on the book as she flipped through the pages. "Don't forget my ears are better than yours."

"You're right," Steve said, turning to Shardwyn. "We have some *very* interesting arguments at our house. One-sided, but interesting."

"It's not my fault you can't keep up," Sarah quipped, earning herself a grin from her husband.

Sarah skimmed through nearly a third of the book and had just picked up several of the loose pages when she stopped. She looked up excitedly.

"I think I found it! Look!"

Steve and Shardwyn eagerly crowded around the open book and inspected the rudimentary sketch. Sarah was smiling. It was clearly the same amulet that Caladonia had been holding. Well, a piece of it anyway.

The Amulet of Aria was about four inches in diameter and was elliptical in shape. The illustration clearly depicted a dragon sitting on its haunches, clutching a large jewel. The wings were jutting up into the tip of the amulet and were extended, as though the dragon was ready to leap into the air. The dragon's head was looking to the right while its front forelegs were wrapped around the large gem nestled in the curve of its body. Sitting astride the dragon's back was an unmistakable figure of a man.

Steve nudged Sarah in her ribs.

"Check it out. That could be me and Pryllan."

Sarah turned to the wizard.

"This doesn't have any type of hidden meaning to Steve, does it?"

Shardwyn shook his head. "Back in the day this was created, dragon riding was very popular."

"Rinbok Intherer said that dragon riding had been forbidden," Steve reminded them. "I got the impression it's been that way for a long time."

"The amulet is very old," Shardwyn pointed out. "There are several powerful talismans in our history, Sir Steve, but none as powerful as this amulet. That's why it was deliberately broken. It was said the king thought it best that a single person did not have access to that much power."

"Who was Aria?" Sarah asked.

"No one really knows," Shardwyn admitted. "For all we know, it could be the first human to have ever ridden a dragon."

"This pendant, how powerful was it?" Sarah asked. "How did it work?"

"Much the same as the joriis. In fact, their properties were modeled after the amulet. You are familiar with the characteristics of a single jorii? A single piece of the amulet has the strength of at least ten joriis. Perhaps more."

Steve whistled in amazement. Shardwyn slapped his thigh and grinned.

"This is simply amazing! What a find! That amulet was thought to have been lost centuries ago. Most believed it had been destroyed. You are certain, Lady Sarah? This is the amulet you saw in your vision?"

Sarah covered the upper portion of the sketch with her hand, concealing the dragon's head, front forelegs, and all traces of the human rider.

"I saw this part of it," Sarah confirmed.

"Logic would suggest Celestia holds the other piece, Lady Sarah."

"Logic schmogic," Steve harrumphed. "I *know* Celestia not only *has* the other piece of the amulet, but I've seen her *use* it."

Shardwyn gasped and stared at Steve as though he had just sprouted wings.

"What? How long have you known of this? Why did you not tell me?"

Steve scowled. "What was I supposed to tell you? That I saw Celestia grab something around her neck? How was I supposed to know it was that amulet thing?"

"Never mind that for now," Sarah said, brushing aside Shardwyn's indignant outburst. "What does it say about this? What can you tell us about it?"

Shardwyn smiled. "I fancy myself an expert in the subject. Ancient historical oddities are a passion of mine."

"You don't say," Steve quipped. Sarah shushed him.

"What would you like to know?"

"How long ago was the amulet broken? By whom? What happened to the two pieces? How did Caladonia and her sister end up with it?"

Shardwyn opened his mouth to speak, hesitated for a few seconds, then closed it with an audible snap. He gestured at the open book.

"Let me see what Zinn had to say about the matter."

"Can you read this?" Steve asked, looking down at the illegible lines of text scribbled above, below, and even to the right of the illustration. "Looks like Greek to me."

"While I may not be the most proficient person when it comes to deciphering ancient script," Shardwyn began, rolling up his sleeves, "I do have my methods. Unorthodox as they may be at times."

"What are you going to do?" Steve asked. The quirky wizard had resorted to unconventional methods before and Steve wouldn't put it past him to try again. The wizard had something up his sleeve, and that alone had prompted him to grab Sarah's wrist and slowly move backward.

"Fear not," Shardwyn assured them, noticing the distance between them was slowly increasing. "This should be perfectly safe."

"Should be? *Should be*? We're going to wait outside."

Once the two of them were safely outside of Shardwyn's laboratory, Sarah slowly sank down to the ground and leaned up against the cold stone wall.

"What do you think he's going to do?" Steve quietly asked. "Cast some type of spell?"

Sarah shrugged. "If I were to venture a guess, I'd say he's going to do some type of experiment. Some *make-me-read-ancient-Lentarian* spell maybe?"

"What would that —"

There was a brief flash of super bright white light. Fluffy white smoke wafted out from under the door.

Sarah was on her feet in a flash. "Omigod! Is he okay?"

Steve pushed the door open and fanned the air. Thick white smoke was everywhere. He couldn't even see his hand in front of his face.

"Yo, Shardwyn! You okay?"

"I am perfectly fine! No windows are broken. No fires. That went well!"

"No fires? What was with the flash of light? What about all this smoke?"

"The smoke is a consequence of mixing kober root and scullie weed," the wizard's voice informed them.

"And the flash?" Sarah prompted. She was still waiting at the door. Until she could see where she was going, she refused to step foot inside his lab.

"That was the flash of enlightenment, Lady Sarah."

Sarah pulled Steve back out the door and tugged him down until she could whisper in his ear.

"Was he insulting me or was he serious?"

"Probably serious," Steve whispered back.

The smoke finally cleared enough so that they could make out the wizard, still leaning over the table and peering intently at the book. Shardwyn skimmed his finger along a page, pausing only long enough to gently flip the torn page over. He was acting as though explosions, such as what had just happened, were everyday normal occurrences, which they probably were.

"Can you read that now?"

"Of course, I can. Was that not the purpose of the enlightenment spell? You saw the flash, did you not? The spell worked like a charm!"

"If it worked like a charm, then why is the tip of your beard green?"

"Hmmm?" Shardwyn looked down to inspect his facial hair and grunted with surprise. The last three inches of his beard was now a vibrant shade of neon green. The wizard smiled jovially. "Last month, I somehow turned my entire beard brown while tending to an injury Bredo had sustained."

Steve stifled a laugh. He could still see a few traces of brown in the wizard's long beard. "I've been meaning to ask you. How long have you had your beard? You didn't have it the last time we saw you."

"I started growing it early spring of last year. I was told having a beard can make a person appear distinguished."

Sarah yawned and pretended to look the other way.

Dismissing his now polychromatic whiskers, Shardwyn motioned for them to join him at the table.

"I have found some information that will interest you. Have you heard of a sorceress by the name of Kylynne?"

"How in the world can you expect us to have heard of her?" Steve asked, exasperation evident in his tone.

Shardwyn nodded, his smile never faltering. "She was the most powerful sorceress of the time."

"Of what time?" Sarah wanted to know.

"Of the time when the amulet was broken."

Sarah nodded. "Got it."

"The king entrusted the sorceress with finding safekeepers for the amulet pieces. Kylynne trusted no one more than her own two daughters, so she gave one piece to each of them."

Steve nodded. "So, the daughters now had the pieces. With you so far."

"The eldest daughter had two daughters while the youngest daughter had none, so the pieces passed to the two girls. On and on the pieces passed through the generations, always bequeathed to the eldest sibling's children."

"Who had the pieces last?" Steve asked, turning to look down at the illegible scribbles on the page. "Does it say?"

Shardwyn frowned. "There are some missing pages. The last I see is that the pieces were bequeathed to sisters Lorinda and Lalonde. They were then passed to Lorinda's daughters Kaiya and Aurelia. Kaiya had two daughters but they were not named. Zinn made some effort to identify the sisters, but was unsuccessful."

"Caladonia and Celestia," Steve murmured. "They're sisters. They clearly have a piece each. Had a piece. Whatever. They must be Kaiya's daughters."

"Not necessarily," Sarah argued. "We don't know how many documented generations are missing. But yes, they could be."

"We should just assume Caladonia and her nutbag of a sister are the last two descendants of that Kylynne person and probably knew all about the amulet and what it was capable of doing." Steve looked at Shardwyn. "Would you agree?"

"I would, aye."

Sarah nodded as well. "I'll go along with that for now. Does it say anything else about the amulet in there?"

"One rule that was made abundantly clear is that the safekeepers were not allowed to use the amulet's power."

Sarah sighed. "They're clearly following those rules, don't you think?"

"It was broken," Steve pointed out. "Did the broken pieces still work?"

The wizard vigorously nodded his head. "Aye. Each piece was as strong as at least ten joriis. Joined together, multiplied a hundredfold."

"If Celestia has one of the amulet pieces, then we need to find out what happened to Caladonia's piece. What if Celestia has it?"

Shardwyn forced a laugh. "If Celestia had both pieces, then she would already have the prince."

"I wonder where Caladonia's piece is?" Steve wondered aloud.

"I wonder what Maelnar would say about this," Sarah countered.

Shardwyn jerked his head up and he stared at her. "What does *he* have to do with any of this?"

"Would you please get over your little spat with him? It's getting old. What does he have to do with this, you ask? Namely, he was alive when Caladonia was. He may know something."

"Are you gonna go get him?" Steve asked her.

Sarah nodded. "Yeah, I think I will. I should probably write him a—scratch that. We don't have time for this. Be right back." She closed her eyes and went still. She vanished moments later.

"I really don't like it when she does that," Steve muttered.

"That would make two of us, young sir."

"What if she got into trouble?"

Shardwyn abandoned his book and approached Steve. He laid a fatherly hand on Steve's shoulder.

"Fear not. If ever a woman could get herself out of a predicament, it would be her. It pains me to say this, but the dwarves are very honorable. They would not harm her."

"I know that. You know that. But what if something else happened? Say a rogue guur or something?"

"Those large insectoid creatures that were extinct?"

"Yeah. Those."

"They *are* extinct, Sir Steve. The dwarves eradicated the remaining guur a few years ago."

"Then what about —"

With an exasperated huff, Shardwyn gave Steve a gentle shake. "Would you please relax? She can take care of herself."

"I just don't like surprises."

"Who or what will surprise her, young sir? The dwarves? Surprising someone? Very unlikely."

As Shardwyn turned back to the tattered book, two short thick arms suddenly materialized on either side of him and then proceeded to jab the wizard in his back. Shardwyn yelped with surprise and dove under the closest table. Two black eyes sparkled with merriment as two human eyes peered angrily out from beneath the table.

"Greetings, wizard."

"Dwarf."

Maelnar rapped his knuckles on the table surface and grinned at the wizard squatting on all fours.

"Care to come out from under there or would you prefer to remain on the floor?"

Shardwyn muttered a string of curses under his breath as he crawled out from underneath the table.

Sarah's eyes were watering so badly she was constantly wiping them with the back of her arm. Steve's grin stretched from ear to ear.

"Good to see you again, pal!" Steve grasped the dwarf's arm and gave it a friendly shake.

"Likewise, Sir Steve."

"What has Sarah told you so far?"

"Only that Caladonia and Celestia were the last two holders of the Amulet of Aria."

"Why the blazes did you not tell us before, dwarf?" Shardwyn demanded.

Maelnar leaned to his right so he could see the fuming wizard. He shrugged.

"Will you be able to disclose anything now, or will you continue to be tongue-tied?"

"For a human, you certainly do know how to hold a grudge."

"Why you blathering little—"

"Anything pertinent?" Sarah interrupted.

"I always saw the sisters wearing chains. One silver and one gold. I never knew what they held."

Steve started sputtering.

"But—but you just said earlier that you knew the two of

them were holders of the amulet pieces!"

Maelnar smiled and nodded sympathetically.

"You asked me what I had been told. And I responded with what Lady Sarah had just told me. I did not know. Do you know how many little trinkets my ancestors have created? How am I supposed to know when one in particular is singled out and turned into a powerful talisman?"

Sarah held up a hand. "Wait. Your ancestor created this amulet?"

Maelnar nodded. "Every dwarven family takes great pride in the work they do. As such, detailed records are kept on each and every piece that is created."

"So how accurate is the info that Zinn wrote in that book?"

"Zinn? Zinn. Hmmm. Human scribe from several centuries back? Aye, I remember him."

Steve was incredulous. "You do? Wow."

"Who do you think told him about the amulet? Me."

"The reason we brought you here," Sarah interrupted, giving her husband a look that said it was her turn to ask the questions, "was to ask what you know about Caladonia and Celestia. Can you tell us anything that can help us?"

"They did not always see eye to eye," Maelnar began, tipping Shardwyn's chair down low so that the heaping piles of pillows tumbled to the floor. Once the chair was empty, he hopped up to take a seat. "Please remember that I did not call Caladonia 'friend' until her twentieth year. I was never a true confidant, as she only asked for advice on trivial matters."

"Did she ever mention the amulet to you?" Sarah asked.

Steve nodded. He had been curious about that as well.

"Not directly, no," the dwarf admitted with a sigh. "I knew Celestia had a penchant for mischief and malicious spells. I tried to tell Caladonia but she refused to believe her sister had, let's say, less than honorable intentions."

"For what?" Steve wanted to know.

"For anything. Caladonia told me once that they had been given the honor of devising a new method of lighting subterranean tunnels for one of the dwarf clans. The Chanus, I believe. Anyway, all the time Caladonia spent researching different ways to accomplish this, Celestia was busy learning how to identify hidden locations of gemstones."

"Well, all girls love gems, that's for sure."

"What'd she want them for?" Sarah asked, throwing her husband a dirty look.

"I suspect they were offered as payment to her informants. Caladonia informed me numerous times how she envied Celestia's ability to make friends."

"Which one of your ancestors created that amulet?" Steve asked.

"My grandfather's grandfather. Vorpal the Magnificent they called him. He was the only dwarf known to have openly vocalized his desire to ride a dragon."

Sarah caught sight of Shardwyn standing next to the table and noticed that he was pointedly looking over at Maelnar and then deliberately looking down at his book. The wizard tapped the sketch. Did he want Maelnar to confirm the sketch was accurate?

"Zinn sketched the amulet in that book over there. I actually saw a piece of it and it matched the sketch. Would you mind taking a look at it and tell us if it's the same one?"

Maelnar hopped out of the chair and landed nimbly on his feet.

"I would be delighted, Lady Sarah. Wizard, one side."

Shardwyn jammed his hands into his robe pockets and stepped aside with a scowl.

"Aye, that's it. Dragon and rider. There's no mistaking that."

"Any chance Celestia has both pieces of the amulet?"

"None whatsoever. If she had both pieces, then this discussion would be pointless."

"That's exactly what I told them," Shardwyn declared proudly, puffing out his chest.

Dwarf and wizard traded disdainful looks.

"So, what happened that caused the amulet to be broken?"

"It was stolen by the human king at the time."

Shardwyn gave a quick jerk as he snapped to attention and leaned back over the table to skim through his dilapidated book.

"You will not find any record of that in your book, wizard, so you can stop looking. I made sure to leave that part out. The human king abused the power and used the amulet to invade the surrounding kingdoms. He would have been successful had the amulet not been stolen back. Vorpal decreed then and there that if the amulet ever fell into his possession again he, or one of his progeny, would destroy it."

Having become completely enraptured by the history lesson he was hearing, Steve leaned forward. "So, what happened next?"

"The amulet was eventually recovered, but not until much later. I do not know who was responsible for the theft from the humans, or when it took place, only that my grandfather was the one who broke the amulet in two with a mighty blow from his hammer. The pieces were given to a trusted friend. A human sorceress."

"Kylynne."

"Aye. Kylynne. My grandfather told her he did not want to know what the fate of the amulet would be, only that it be protected from the likes of those who had stolen it before. I briefly saw the pieces as they were given to the sorceress."

Steve sat up. "You remember that? Seriously, man, how old are you??"

Maelnar chuckled. "I told you before and will tell you again: much older than you will ever be."

"You said that the amulet pieces act like joriis, right? Super strong joriis?"

Maelnar nodded. "Aye, Lady Sarah. Why do you ask?"

"Didn't I hear something about Celestia being able to affect the passage of time?" Sarah turned to her husband. "Didn't someone say that last time we were here?"

Steve nodded. "I remember hearing Celestia could take a kyte and prolong its life. Since she has a piece of the amulet, couldn't she use that to extend her own lifespan? That's gotta be how she's still alive. She's using her chunk of the amulet to amplify her jhorun."

"What would happen if we got the piece away from her?" Sarah asked, looking at Shardwyn, then at Maelnar.

"I would say if you remove the amulet piece, then she

would revert to her true age," Shardwyn hypothesized.

Maelnar nodded. "I concur."

Shardwyn turned to stare at the dwarf as though he had just announced he could transform lead into gold.

"Close your mouth, wizard."

"You agree with me?"

"Just this once, aye. Every few centuries I typically make a mistake. Hopefully this is not it."

Sarah sighed. "Getting back to the problem at hand, how can we face a power-hungry sorceress with an ancient jhorun-enhancing talisman? We would need … so that's why I was shown that vision! Caladonia was telling me we need to find her piece of the amulet. You said it yourself. Celestia doesn't have it or else she would have already won. We just need to find it."

"I am afraid it has been lost to time, Lady Sarah," Maelnar sadly informed her. "Caladonia never told me what she did with her piece, let alone acknowledging she even had it."

Steve turned to Sarah. "Can you do your visualization thing and see if you can locate it?"

Sarah crossed her arms over her chest.

"Go on. Say it. I *dare* you."

Shardwyn quizzically looked at Maelnar and raised an eyebrow. The dwarf shook his head. Together, wizard and dwarf watched the two humans.

In the most neutral tone of voice he could muster, Steve asked Sarah what she was referring to.

"I'm going to see if I can get an idea where we need to look. Go ahead. Infer I'm a witch and it'll be the last thing you do."

Steve smiled sheepishly and held up his hands in mock surrender.

"I would never, ever, in a million billion years infer that you, the love of my life, was a—"

"Hmmph. You'd better not or I will personally guarantee you that you'll smell like a little girl for the next five years. Now be quiet."

Maelnar motioned for Steve to squat down next to him, which he did.

"Smell like a girl?" the dwarf asked, puzzled.

"Sarah has some really nice fragrances that she likes to use," Steve whispered to him. "It makes her, uh, smell more feminine."

"Ah. You would prefer not to smell feminine?"

"Exactly."

Sarah closed her eyes and cleared her throat. "Hmmmm."

Afraid he had been talking too loudly and had been overheard, Steve hastily straightened and mentally started preparing an assortment of apologies and necessary bribes in order to avoid smelling like a bouquet of flowers for the foreseeable future.

Shardwyn approached.

"Do you see anything, Lady Sarah?"

"Actually, I do," Sarah answered, eyes still closed. "As soon as I started to think about the piece of amulet with that dragon head on it, I got an image. The problem is, I don't understand what I'm seeing."

"Tell us what you can see," Maelnar urged.

"Small stones, which have been scattered along the ground. It looks sandy. Like a beach maybe?"

"Are there any beaches in Lentari?" Steve asked Shardwyn. The wizard nodded.

"Most of our eastern coast borders the great sea."

"How long is the coast?" Steve wanted to know.

"Many, many leagues I'm afraid," Shardwyn answered.

"That really doesn't help us much."

"Do you see anything else, Lady Sarah?" Maelnar gently asked. "Do not force the vision. Do not think about what you are seeing. Let the images come to you."

Sarah took several breaths and relaxed. Instead of trying to figure out what the vision was showing her, she instead pretended she was watching a movie. What was she going to see next? Just a boring picture of some rocks sitting on an unknown stretch of sand? A narrow shadow suddenly zipped across her vision. Whatever it was, it had been moving very fast. However, nothing else happened. She was still looking at a pebble-strewn chunk of ground.

"Sorry, I'm not getting anything else. Just—oh!"

Steve was by her side in an instant.

"What is it? What did you see?"

"Shush! I'm trying to—"

Another shadow had appeared, and it hadn't moved off yet. Her vision started wavering. Ripples of distortion marred the image, like one would expect to find in a carnival house of mirrors. Ripples? That was it! She was looking at an underwater scene! That first shadow she had seen had been the passing of a fish. So, what was responsible for this larger shadow?

"It's underwater," Sarah reported, keeping her eyes closed and the vision firmly planted in her mind. "I don't know where, but it's definitely under the water. Something is standing nearby. Whatever it is hasn't moved off yet."

A curved orange object suddenly appeared in her vision. It almost looked like a—

"It's a griffin's beak! A griffin is drinking from the water!"

"She hid the piece at a griffin watering hole? Jeez, that could be just about anywhere."

Sarah grimaced. "I know. I'm sorry. That isn't very helpful."

Steve was instantly remorseful. "There has to be something that ... wait. Can you tell if anything is buried in the sand? A box, chest, anything?"

"If I could, then I would have said so."

"Do you think you can use your Jedi mind trick thing again and see if there's anything buried in the silt? The river bed, or lake bed for that matter, might be nothing but layers of dirt and sediment. You might be able to push that around a bit."

Sarah frowned. "I have to have a focal point. I need something to target. Besides, I don't even know if that'll work."

"Sir Steve has an excellent idea," Maelnar advised. "Caladonia gifted you with a very impressive jhorun, milady. Her jhorun was premonition. She must have foreseen your needing the amulet piece in the future. As such, she would have made certain that only the right person could retrieve it."

Sarah nodded. "I suppose it couldn't hurt to try. Here goes."

Reminding her jhorun that she was, indeed, looking at a live picture, Sarah selected a shiny blue stone in the lower right corner of her vision and instructed it to slide over to the left.

The stone shifted several inches to the left, leaving a shallow groove in the ivory sand.

"It worked! I just slid a rock a little to the left and I watched it move. How cool … I didn't know I could do that!"

"Pretend there's something under the surface," Steve suggested. "Imagine there's a chest under the sand. Can you push it upwards?"

"Let me see what I can do. Just a moment."

Concentrating on the image before her, Sarah imagined there was a small chest concealed in the depths of the sand and ordered her jhorun to raise it to the surface. The sand shifted as something beneath it changed position. The submerged ground bulged slightly as whatever had been buried started to rise to the surface. However, after a few seconds of watching the ground bulge outward, she felt, rather than saw, the object suddenly refuse to be lifted any further. Sarah doubled her efforts to raise the object out of the ground. However, the harder she pushed, the more the object resisted rising to the surface.

"It was working," Sarah reported, scowling. "However, the harder I push the more something pulls it back."

"Damn!" Steve started pacing around the closest table. "Any idea what it is?"

"None," Sarah answered.

Steve looked up at the wizard. "Shardwyn, can you do anything?"

"If the chest has been enchanted against removal, then I can only counteract the spell if I have a chance to examine the object."

Steve sighed. "Since we don't know where the piece is, then we can't remove it."

"Shardwyn." Sarah's voice sounded different. Anxious. Excited. "Do you have drains in here in case you spill something?"

"Of course, milady, of course. Why do you ask?"

"Good. I was just wondering."

Hundreds of gallons of water, complete with seaweed, shells, rocks, and a sizable chunk of sodden earth, suddenly splashed down directly in front of them. Waves of blue-green sea water threatened to pull everyone off their feet as the mass of water rapidly expanded to all four corners of Shardwyn's laboratory. Steve instantly grabbed Maelnar by one of his belts and hoisted him up onto the closest table while simultaneously hooking an arm around Sarah's waist.

Sarah's eyes had snapped open the moment the water appeared. Her mouth formed a surprised O as, clearly, she had underestimated the strength of her jhorun. She had simply ordered her power to teleport the object beneath the sands to her present location. She had expected some water, but never would have dreamed so much would have appeared.

The surging mass of water pushed through the main door and cascaded down the stairs to flow harmlessly out into the keep. Detaching herself from her husband's grip, she inspected the huge clump of earth that was sitting directly on Shardwyn's expensive-looking rug directly in front of the hearth.

"Shardwyn, I'm so sorry. I didn't think there'd be that much water."

The quirky wizard waved a hand dismissively in her direction. He walked over to one of his open bay windows and tapped a discoloration near the top of the frame, above his eye level.

"See this mark, milady? I flooded my workshop so badly I had water pouring out all the windows. Scared the guards half to death! Hoo, hoo, what a day that was!"

"How long ago?" Steve inquired.

"Hmmm? Oh, just last month."

Feeling much better, Sarah returned to inspecting the sopping mound of earth. Was something buried in there?

"So, what do we have here?" Shardwyn began invoking spells, cleaning much of the mud and water away from the object. When enough of the dirt had been removed, the object was revealed in its entirety: a box. A small one, no bigger than the chest they had seen during their first visit to Lentari, when the king had presented the crystal shield.

Several guards appeared in the doorway.

"Is all well in here?"

"Everything is fine. Just a little water," Shardwyn assured them, automatically dismissing the intruders.

Having been exposed to Shardwyn's infamous experiments, both guards shrugged and returned to their posts.

Gingerly picking up the muddy box, Shardwyn set it on one of his many tables. Pushing his sleeves up past his elbows, the wizard squatted down low and inspected the box up close without touching it.

"Well, perhaps if I—"

"Hang on a sec there, Shardwyn," Steve interrupted. "That decoration looks familiar."

"It has that same metal band around it," Sarah agreed.

"Indeed, Lady Sarah," Shardwyn told her. "It probably is—"

"It's a fire lock," Steve answered, interrupting the wizard for a second time.

"Leave it to Caladonia to use one of those again."

"You have seen this type of lock before?" Shardwyn asked, turning his incredulous eyes on the fire thrower. "How? When?"

"When we were searching for Caladonia's journal. Got it the last time we were here and it was kept in a larger version of that thing, complete with the same decorative metal band around it. I had to heat the entire band to a certain temp. Once it all hits the right temp, for the right amount of time, it'll open."

"Would you do the honors?"

"Gladly." Steve moved to the desk, picked up the small box, and strode outside.

"Where is he going?" Shardwyn asked.

"Do you wish to have your laboratory incinerated?" Maelnar asked, hopping down from the table. The dwarf hurried to catch up to Sarah as she exited Shardwyn's tower.

"I burned most of it down just three months ago," the

wizard harrumphed to himself. "Had the fires out in less than ten minutes."

Shardwyn joined the others outside just as Steve extinguished his fire rope. The decorative band of metal clicked loudly and dropped to the ground. The box lid slowly opened. Sarah leaned forward and gently reached a hand in, withdrawing it moments later, clutching a silver chain. Swinging gently on the end of the chain was Caladonia's piece of the amulet.

Husband and wife gave each other a high-five.

"Way to go, Sarah!"

# Chapter 10 - Broken Amulet of Aria

Sarah gently flicked the tip of the amulet and was silent a few moments as she watched the piece spin around and around on its thin silver chain. She gazed at the broken piece of jewelry and briefly wondered how many people had possessed it. How much trouble had this thing caused? Was it responsible for any deaths? Was she going to be tempted to use it like a certain hobbit and his magical ring of power?

Sarah's eyes widened. Had she just used an analogy from Middle Earth? She had never read the books and only watched the movies due to Steve's insistent yammering on how awesome they were. If her husband ever discovered she had used a Lord of the Rings analogy, he would never let her live it down. Therefore, he must never know.

"May I see the amulet, Lady Sarah?"

Sarah looked across at Shardwyn's outstretched hand. She walked around the table and was about ready to drop the amulet into the wizard's hand when Maelnar let out a shout and threw himself in between them.

"Absolutely not, Lady Sarah."

Shardwyn's bushy eyebrows shot up. "What are you on about now, dwarf? Think I was going to use it? I was not."

Maelnar actually appeared apologetic. "For once, Shardwyn, trust me. I believe you. That amulet, even just a part of it, is too powerful. It should not fall into any Lentarian's hands, no matter how pure their intentions are."

Sarah tapped Maelnar on the shoulder and spun him around to face her.

"What does that mean? I have to keep this thing? No way. I don't want it."

Sarah tried to hand it to her husband, but he threw up both his hands and backpedaled away from her.

"Don't give that thing to me. Are you kidding? Think about it. Fire thrower, plus a super powerful talisman, equals a very bad idea."

"You mean I have to keep this? That … that … sucks."

"If it has to go to a non-Lentarian," Steve said, pointing at the still spinning amulet, "then it's best if it was you. Your jhorun isn't as dangerous as mine is, and the last thing I want to see is my jhorun enhanced by any degree. Why do you think I won't let Mikal enhance it? It's strong enough as it is, thank you very much."

Sarah reluctantly draped the chain around her neck and tucked the amulet into her shirt.

"The last thing I want to worry about right now is this thing."

The king and queen appeared in the doorway, while half a dozen guards waited on the stairs. Shardwyn practically bowled the two of them over in his mad haste to greet the monarchs.

"Ah! Your Majesties! Come in, come in!"

"Good afternoon, Shardwyn." Kri'Entu turned to look down at the water still trickling out the door and down the stairs. "Water again?"

"It wasn't my fault this time," Shardwyn pointed out.

"Indeed."

Sarah meekly raised her hand. "I'm sorry. That was me."

"Is everyone safe?" Queen Callé asked, briefly looking around. "Everyone is unharmed?"

"We're good. Just a little waterlogged," Steve assured her. "Hey, guess what? Sarah found half of the Amulet of Aria."

Both of the Kri'yans gasped. "The Amulet of Aria? You found a piece of the amulet? How? When? Where was it?"

Sarah held up the silver chain she was wearing and gently pulled until her piece of the broken amulet appeared.

Kri'Entu stared at it, transfixed. He took several tentative steps toward Sarah when he paused.

"You are holding half of the most dangerous amulet in our history," the king told her. "The power that piece is said to possess makes a jorii pale in comparison. You should not give that to anyone, even me."

"I had a feeling you'd say that," Sarah muttered.

"I already advised her to do just that, Your Majesty," Maelnar added, pleased that the king had come to the same conclusion.

"Isn't there a secure vault, or a safe, or something we can store that thing in?" Steve protested, not happy that his wife would have to be the keeper of the piece.

"No Lentarian should ever be tempted with so much power," the queen added. "You both were given your jhoruns upon your first arrival here. They are both very powerful, and you respect that power. I do not believe you would ever abuse it."

"Nor do I," Kri'Entu added. "I cannot say with certainty that any other Lentarian would feel the same. As such, I formally request that you keep the amulet piece safe, Lady Sarah."

Resigned, Sarah dropped the piece back down her shirt. "I will, Your Majesty."

"May I make a recommendation?" Maelnar asked, turning to face the king and queen.

"Of course, master dwarf. Proceed."

"Since Lady Sarah is now the holder of the amulet piece, I would advise she become familiar with its power."

Sarah was incredulous. "Excuse me? The last thing I want to do is use this thing. Why in the world would I want to do that?"

Kri'Entu was nodding, as was Shardwyn.

"Excellent notion. Since Celestia is already using her piece of the amulet, it is logical to assume Lady Sarah's piece will become necessary if we are to have any chance of vanquishing the sorceress. It would behoove you, Lady Sarah, to become familiar with the amulet's properties."

"How exactly am I supposed to do that?"

"Practice, milady, practice," Maelnar advised. "I truly hope that you will never have to use it, but if you do, would it not be prudent to know what to expect?"

"Would Celestia be able to tell if I used the amulet?" Sarah asked, praying the answer would be anything but *yes*.

Shardwyn shook his head. "If the behavior of the jorii is any indicator, no. If the two of us were to possess a jorii each, and I used mine, the other holder would not be able to tell. Each jorii are independent from one another. I believe the amulet pieces will exhibit the same behavior."

Steve huffed out a breath. "You believe? So you don't know for certain?"

"Aye, I do not know for certain. It is only what I believe."

Sarah took her husband's hand. "It'll have to do. You're just going to have to protect me." She batted her eyes at her husband, who promptly rolled his.

"Just be on the lookout," Steve advised her. "If you see anything, hear anything, or even sense anything, you need to tell me, okay?"

Sarah nodded and drew an X over her heart. "I promise." She turned to the Kri'yans. "So what do you suggest I do?"

"Find a concealed location where you can practice undisturbed," Ny'Callé suggested. "We do not want it known that a piece has been found and is presently being used."

"What about the dragon cavern?" Steve asked, turning to the king to see if he agreed. "It's underground, away from the castle, and safe from prying eyes. It's a perfect place to see what it can do."

"Excellent notion, Sir Steve," the king agreed. "How many guards do you require? Enough of our reserve militia have been recalled, so if needs be, I can assign —"

"No guards."

"Are you certain? Celestia is out there somewhere. You might be attacked."

Steve pointed at the silver chain Sarah was wearing.

"Celestia is young and impetuous. You had better believe she's going to use her piece on us, but for now, we're pretty sure she doesn't know we have it."

"Then again," Sarah added, "we don't want to announce we have it, either. We want to be inconspicuous. We can't do that with a whole bunch of people following us."

Kri'Entu nodded. "Very well. If ever there are two people who can protect themselves, it would be the two of you."

Steve glanced through the window and noticed the setting sun. Shadows were slowly creeping along the wall, growing taller by the second. Sunset was only a few moments away.

"Tell you what. We'll get started on this first thing tomorrow."

"Agreed, Sir Steve."

"Do you think we could take Lia with us?" Sarah suddenly asked. "She loves castles and I know she's been itching to take a look around."

Kri'Entu nodded. "As long as she stays in your company, I do not see why she cannot accompany you tomorrow."

Sarah smiled. "Thank you. I know it will mean a lot to her. In the meantime, where is she now? We'll go let her know."

"Lady Lia is in the Antechamber."

Steve's eyebrows shot up.

"Still? Wow. She's gonna be ticked off. Maybe we should make her wait a little more."

Sarah playfully smacked her husband on the arm as they bade goodnight to the Kri'yans. Picking their way carefully down the dripping wet staircase to avoid slipping, Steve and Sarah emerged from the stone tower and headed back toward the castle.

"I really don't want to keep this thing," Sarah told her husband. "Who knows what it'll make my jhorun do."

"For once I have to say better you than me. Can you imagine what my jhorun would look like if it was enhanced by that much? I can't imagine what a single jorii would do to it let alone something that's as powerful as that amulet is supposed to be. Nuh uh, no thanks."

"That means I have to keep it," Sarah complained, crossing the moat and following her husband as he ducked into an entrance normally reserved for kitchen staff. The guards on either side of the door didn't bother questioning or even stopping them. Both nodded their heads as the famous Nohrin passed by.

"Which way to the Antechamber?"

With an exasperated sigh, Sarah pointed off to the left, past the numerous cooking hearths.

"How many times have we walked through here? Sooner or later you're bound to remember the way."

"What do I need to worry about directions for?" Steve countered. As he walked along the rows of hearths, each fire flared momentarily, as though a blast of oxygen had been directed at it. "I have you, so I'll never get lost."

"And if you're on your own?" Sarah asked, raising an eyebrow.

"I scream like a little girl until someone comes to rescue me."

Sarah giggled. "I thought you were trying to stop doing that."

"Yeah, well, it's in my blood."

They stopped before the heavily fortified door leading into the Antechamber, and two guards on either side of the door straightened. Both nodded.

"Nohrin. Do you prefer to enter?"

Sarah nodded. "Yes, please. Our friend is in there."

One guard's eyes widened. "You are acquaintances of the lady in there?"

Puzzled, Sarah eyed the guard. "Yes. Why do you ask?"

"The voice we heard coming out of there was female in nature, but the language was, umm …"

"Lia is a very spirited lady," Steve offered, doing his best to keep a straight face. "She has no problems speaking her mind."

"Steve?" a voice called out from behind the door. "Is that you? Get me the hell outta here!"

"Brace yourselves," the other guard muttered, releasing

the clasp holding the locking bar in place. Sliding the bar back and locking it into its open position, the guards pulled the door open.

There was Lia, hands on her hips, with a frown on her face.

"What the hell! I've been bored out of my mind! Where have you two been?"

"Over in Shardwyn's tower," Steve cheerfully told her. "We were telling him about Sarah's vision."

Lia looked at Sarah. "You had a vision? About what?"

"I saw Caladonia. She's a sorceress who lived several centuries ago. She's the sister of Celestia."

"The same Celestia that everyone is looking for?"

Sarah nodded. "That's right."

"How is that even possible?"

"Magic. That was the point of my vision. Caladonia wanted to tell me that Celestia has half of a powerful amulet. Without the second half, we wouldn't have a chance in defeating her. So, she showed me that her piece was going to be needed. I just found it. That's what we were doing."

"You found some magical trinket? Ooooo, I wanna see!"

"I don't think," Steve began, "that it's a good idea to—"

"Oh, don't be silly. Who's got it?"

"I do," Sarah answered. "It's been entrusted to me. You'll be able to see it tomorrow. I have to try and figure out how it works and what it'll do to my own jhorun."

Lia sighed. "That must be nice. I'm sure I'll be stuck in here the whole damn day tomorrow. Can you see if there's any chance they'll drop me off a magazine of some sort? Maybe a tabloid? Something. Anything!"

"Would you relax? You're coming with us."

Lia's frown disappeared in the blink of an eye. "I am? I get to leave this room? That's awesome! I so want to check out the castle!"

Steve smirked. "You'll be able to see whatever we see, as you're essentially in our custody."

The temperature dropped in the room. Lia's hands went back on her hips and she lifted her nose.

"Excuse me? Where is it written that I have to follow you around?" Lia looked at Sarah, her eyes pleading for a different answer. "Tell me it isn't so."

Sarah laughed. "I'm afraid it's the king's orders. Since you're still potentially a target, you have to stay with us so you'll be safe."

Lia's cheerful expression quickly melted into a frown as she turned back to Steve.

"Wipe that smile off your face or else I'll juggle your sorry butt right out the window."

Puzzled, Steve looked at Lia's impassive face.

"What's that supposed to mean? I didn't know you could juggle."

Lia said nothing as she crossed her arms over her chest.

Sarah and Steve eyed each other. What was she not telling them?

"Lia, what's the matter? Did something happen?"

"Little punk brat."

Sarah was confused. "Who are you talking about? Mikal? I don't get it. I thought you liked him."

"I *did* like him. Past tense."

"And you don't now?" Sarah asked. "What did he— omigod! Did he give you a jhorun?"

Lia was motionless, arms still crossed. Her eyes narrowed to slits as they darted between husband and wife.

"What jhorun did he give you? Come on," Steve insisted, "tell us!"

Sarah held up her hands. "Wait. Wait a minute. Didn't she just say that she'd juggle you out the window?"

"And I still don't know what she meant by that," Steve admitted.

Lia was still tight-lipped, saying nothing.

Sarah put on her best poker face and looked at her friend. "Lia, does your new jhorun have anything to do with juggling?"

Steve burst out laughing as Lia sent him a scathing look.

"Little punk. What did I ever do to him?"

"Oh man," Steve wheezed out between laughs, "that's priceless!"

"Bite me. Are your jhoruns really that strong?"

Steve walked over to his wife and proudly put an arm

around her shoulders. "She has the strongest teleportation jhorun that has ever been recorded."

"What about you?" Sarah turned to hug her husband. She looked back at Lia and hooked a thumb in Steve's direction. "He's classified as a fire elemental, but everyone calls it 'fire thrower'."

Lia shook her head. "Allow me to venture a guess. Strongest example of a fire thrower that's ever been recorded?"

Steve nodded his head. "As a matter of fact, yeah."

"And I'm a friggin' juggler."

Steve burst out laughing again. Sarah thumped him in his gut with her left elbow. "Hey, be nice."

"Why would Mikal give you the ability to juggle? I mean, that's pretty much levitation, isn't it? That's really cool …"

Lia beamed. "Thank —"

"… for a court jester."

"—you. Punk."

Steve walked over to a bowl of fruit on the king's desk and selected three jansas. Holding the fat purple pears, he walked over to Lia and presented them to her with a hopeful expression on his face.

"Absolutely not."

"Oh, come on! We wanna see what you can do!"

"Nuh uh. Forget it."

"We're in the Antechamber," Sarah reminded them. "Her jhorun won't work here."

Lia was instantly defensive.

"You don't know that."

"Actually, we do," Steve confirmed. "This room, in particular, is enchanted against magic. Only those with the strongest jhoruns can do magic in here."

"And I suppose yours works here?"

Steve held up a hand and ignited a chaser. Lia's eyes opened wide.

"Yep, it does. So does Sarah's." Steve's expression softened. "Lia, you have to understand that Mikal didn't give us our jhoruns. A sorceress did. Caladonia. That's why they're stronger than most."

"So, my magical jhorun thingamajig won't work in here?

That stinks."

"Give it a try," Sarah suggested.

Determined to prove them wrong, Lia glared at a bowl of purple fruit on the king's desk. Scrunching up her face, eyes almost closed, Lia glared at the fruit and willed it to rise up out of the bowl.

The jansa fruit sat motionless in the bowl.

"This is *sooo* not fair."

"How much do you know about your jhorun?" Sarah asked her. "Would you like some pointers? It took Steve and me a while to get the hang of it."

"I don't need pointers. I'm sure I can figure it out."

"You won't be here that long," Steve pointed out. "As soon as the coast is clear, you'll be going back home to Idaho. Your jhorun doesn't work there."

"Does anyone's jhorun work there?"

Steve gave her a smug smile. "Ours does."

"It does? Why won't mine?"

"Because Caladonia amplified our jhoruns to wizarding levels," Sarah explained. "She figured we'd need them in our world. Annie's doesn't work, either. Neither will Tristan's."

"Tristan has a jhorun, too? What does … He's from here, isn't he? That's why he talks so weird."

"Yep. He's Mikal's tutor."

"That explains a lot."

Steve held an arm out to the door. "Come on, if we're going to give Lia a few pointers about how jhoruns work, we need to get out of this room."

Guiding them down the long hallways, through the kitchen, back through the Great Hall, and finally up to the second floor where most of the residential quarters were located, they finally stopped outside their chambers.

"Is this your room? Wow. How big is it?"

"It has several rooms," Steve said, pointing to several doors on the far wall. "That door on the left leads to a sitting room. The one on the right has another bed in it. Why don't you take that one? We need to keep you close. Again, all joking aside, there's a nutbag sorceress out there who's just looking for ways to get us out of the picture. If she knows you're here, then she could go after you to get to us."

Lia said nothing and sank down into the closest chair.

Steve sat on the corner of the bed. Moments later Sarah joined him.

"I don't mean to freak you out. I just want you to understand the seriousness of this situation."

Now, in a much more somber mood, Lia nodded. "I appreciate it. I really do. No sight-seeing until the coast is clear, is that it?"

Sarah nodded. "Yes. Exactly."

"And this crazy sorceress wants to kill you two?"

Steve nodded. "Believe it or not, that's not her primary objective."

"Then what is?"

"Mikal. She wants Mikal."

"Why?"

"So she can marry him and rule Lentari."

"Isn't she kinda old for him?"

Steve grunted. "Yeah, she is. But, she hasn't aged. She can just wait until he's old enough and then marry him."

"She hasn't aged? How old is she?"

"No one knows for certain, but we do know she was around four centuries ago."

"How is that even possible? Does she have an anti-aging jhorun or something?"

"Actually, she does," Steve confirmed. "In a manner of speaking. Her jhorun allows her to slow down the effects of time. That, coupled with the amulet piece she has, she's been able to remain alive, living here in the castle, for centuries."

"Amulet piece?"

Sarah pulled on the silver chain she was wearing until her half of the amulet came into view. "The other half of this. That's what we're doing tomorrow. I need to learn how to use this. Just in case I have to use it, to help Mikal. So tomorrow morning, we're going out to the dragon cave and I'm going to experiment."

"And I get to go?"

"As long as you're with us," Steve reminded her, "yes. You may tag along."

"I *may* tag along? Oh, you're enjoying this, aren't you?"

"Like you wouldn't believe."

Lia punched him on his left arm at the same time Sarah punched him on his right.

* * *

"So, are there going to be dragons there? There better not be. I've seen enough dragons on this trip, thank you very much."

Steve followed Lia as she followed Sarah through a number of identical hallways, doors, rooms, etcetera, until they finally emerged into one of the main halls leading in and out of the castle. The massive arched hallway was leading them straight to the north gate. Past the gate and across the moat were hundreds of rows of fruit trees, all lined up with military precision.

Crossing the drawbridge, they turned right and walked along the water's edge. Steve explained to Lia that since the dragons were so massive, the king had thought it best to construct the cavern where there was plenty of room, had access to water, and was far enough away from the castle so the villagers wouldn't panic if they looked out the nearest window and saw one of the enormous wyverians using the cavern. It also meant, he told her, that it was a decent walk from the castle to the great subterranean cave.

As they walked, Lia looked over at the murky water and grinned. Steve smiled. He knew what she was thinking: a real-life castle with a real-life moat.

Lia stopped and hesitated. "Does anything—"

"Yes," Sarah automatically answered. "A large serpent lives in there. His name is Bredo."

"It has a name? Is it friendly?"

Steve laughed. "No. To tell the truth, we saw it up close and personal for the first time yesterday."

The waters stirred and the colossal snake's head rose out of the water. Lia screamed and ducked behind Steve, who instantly lit both hands, causing Lia to scream again.

"Would you knock that off? It's just—"

Up and down the scale she went, just like a siren from a fire truck. It was a wonder she hadn't passed out from a lack of oxygen.

"She's probably afraid of snakes," Sarah figured. She faced the snake, which had completely ignored the two of them. Bredo was zeroing in on Lia's hysterical shrieks and was moments away from striking.

Steve stepped in front of the large snake and shot two warning jets of fire in the air.

"Bredo, we don't have time for this. I warned you before. If you don't stop—"

Steve trailed off as the huge serpent was suddenly pulled up and out of the water by an invisible force. Thousands of gallons of water also rose up into the air, forming a gently pulsating blue mass just below where Bredo lay stretched out for all the world to see. The snake angrily twisted and turned in the air, trying to escape the force that held it in place. It caught sight of the water below it and doubled its efforts to break free.

Steve whistled in amazement. "Hon, are you doing this?"

When he didn't get an answer, he turned to look at his wife. Sarah's eyes were closed. At some point, she must have pulled up the amulet piece because she was now clutching it tightly in her left hand. She had extended her right arm in front of her, the index finger pointing straight at the obnoxious creature.

"Sarah? Still with me?"

Sarah's lips started to move. "Hmm? What's the matter?"

"Open your eyes and see for yourself."

Sarah's eyes opened and then her eyebrows shot up. "Ummm …"

"You can probably let him down now. The water, too."

Steve briefly leaned out over the moat's edge. The moat was rapidly filling back up as the overall level of water dropped to accommodate the missing volume of water.

"Watch out!" Sarah roughly yanked him backwards. She had released her grip of the amulet. She instantly felt the massive weight once the amulet's power had been removed. There was no way her own jhorun would be able to sustain that enormous mass of water, so she hadn't bothered to try.

The undulating mass of water directly below Bredo slammed back down into the moat, sending up spray everywhere. Unfortunately for the moat's enforcer, Bredo's mass was comfortably within Sarah's range of power and he stayed afloat.

Sarah rotated the snake around until it was facing her. Bredo struggled to find purchase with his coils so that he could make his way back into the moat. Without anything to latch onto, however, the only thing the snake accomplished was to appear as though someone had stuck its tail into a light socket.

"Are we going to have any more of these types of misunderstandings?"

The huge snake stared at her.

"Favor me with three flicks of your tongue, if you understand me."

"A snake is not going to be able to understand you," Steve argued.

Bredo's tongue flicked out of its mouth. Once. Twice. Three times. Sarah waited, but no more flicks were forthcoming.

"Excellent. I would advise you to learn my scent and my husband's. Even Lia there. If you ever attack any of us again, then I'm going to have a new ten-piece set of matching luggage, do you catch my drift?"

Steve suppressed a smile.

Bredo flicked his tongue three more times.

Sarah released her jhorun's grip on the snake. Bredo splashed back into the moat and vanished.

"I'd say that was a successful test of the amulet's power, dontcha think?"

Sarah nodded and looked at Lia, who had finally stopped screaming.

"You handled that well."

"It was a snake! A huge freakin' snake!"

"There's nothing to worry about. It won't bother—"

"Did you not hear me? That was a snake!"

"The big bad scary snake is gone," Steve said, in a

soothing, albeit mocking tone.

"It. Was. A. Snake."

"I didn't know you have such a deep-rooted fear of snakes," Sarah said to her.

"They creep the bejesus out of me."

Steve nodded, and extinguished his hands. "We noticed. Come on, we need to keep moving. The dragon cave is just past those trees."

Lia stared at his hands. "I knew what you guys had said, and I even saw your hand briefly lit earlier, but I think this was the first time I have ever seen you use your magical doohickey."

"How do you think I got you down from that pole in the dwarves' city?"

"Well, that explains the bursts of heat I felt. I thought you had cut me down."

Steve grinned. "I don't need no stinkin' knife."

"You can really control fire?"

"Yep." Steve ignited his right hand and held it up in front of her. "See?"

"I can feel the heat. How is it you're not getting burned?"

"Because it's my jhorun. I could actually be holding a book and if I didn't want it to burn, it wouldn't."

"That's amazing."

"You're calling me amazing?"

"No," Lia clarified, throwing Steve a dirty look, "I said your jhorun was amazing."

"Oh."

"So, this is supposed to be an orchard?"

"You see the trees, right?"

Lia stooped to pick up what looked like a long red banana. "What's this?"

Sarah glanced over. "That's a loken. Look over there. See those round yellow ones over there that look like pale oranges?"

Lia nodded.

"Those are sidah."

"And the purple ones?"

"Jansas."

Lia slowly turned in place to study the rows of neatly planted fruit trees. "How many are there?"

"I asked the queen once," Sarah responded. "She said that she didn't know, only that the orchard was responsible for providing fresh fruit for the entire castle. If that is the case, then there have to be hundreds of trees here."

Lia turned and pointed east. "What's that over there?"

"That's where we're going. See the glade? It's where we'll find the dragon cave."

A hundred square yards of open grassland was visible ahead of them, breaking the monotony of seeing nothing but row after row of fruit trees. Just off center of the clearing was an area where the ground bulged outward. The elevation dipped down on the eastern side of the swell, revealing an enormous tunnel curving down and to the north.

"You want me to go into that? No way."

"It's the dragon cave," Sarah pointed out. "It's where Kahvel comes to rest whenever he's here."

"Kahvel?"

"Dragon liaison to Rinbok Intherer. He was the gold dragon you saw earlier up in Verdayn."

"So, what's down there?"

Steve scratched the stubble on his face. "I think it's just a big cave."

"You think? You don't know?"

"We've never been down there."

"In that case, you first."

Steve strode past her and ignited both hands as he entered the tunnel. "Gladly."

Sarah snaked her arm through Lia's and gently guided her into the tunnel so they could follow Steve.

"Don't worry. The king told us he'd have some torches all set out so that we'd be able to see what we're doing. All Steve has to do is light them. And as soon as I see what it looks like, then I'll be able to teleport straight there in the future."

"Don't ever tell him that I said this," Lia whispered to Sarah, nodding her head toward Steve's flaming hands, "but his jhorun is very cool."

Sarah smiled and nodded.

"He really does inspire people to be on their best behavior whenever he's around. Hey, interesting tidbit. This is where a group of kidnappers hid when Steve and I first visited here."

"Kidnappers? Excuse me? No one said anything about kidnappers!"

"It was right after we learned we had become Mikal's bodyguards. Mikal was showing us around the castle, much like we're doing for you now. Four guys were hiding in this tunnel and as soon as we appeared, they tried to take him away from us."

"What happened?"

"That was the first time I teleported someone," Sarah recalled. "One moment I was trying to shield Mikal and the next I was collapsing on the floor in the throne room."

"Steve dealt with the kidnappers all by himself? What'd he do?"

"I gave them motivation to jump into the moat," Steve answered, with a grave tone.

"Steve's not fond of that particular memory," Sarah explained to Lia in a hushed tone. "He learned something unpleasant about himself that day. He had been responsible for the deaths of several men."

Lia gasped with surprise.

"He hadn't ever killed anyone before. It wasn't a pleasant feeling for him knowing that he had inadvertently taken a life. Sometime later, after things had settled down and we had made it back to Idaho, Steve told me that if someone ever tried to threaten me, or Mikal, or anyone else under his care, he was prepared to do it again."

"Yeah," Steve said, somberly. "Good times."

They were silent for a few moments when Sarah stopped walking, pulled Lia to a stop as well, and then targeted a small rock directly in her path. Within moments it had zipped forward to smack Steve on his right shoulder.

"What'd you do that for?" Steve called back. He rubbed his shoulder.

"You need to calm down!" Sarah told him from twenty feet away. Another small rock was floating next to her, waiting to be launched. "I know you can hear me and were thinking about that day we were attacked. Let it go. You're heating up the area."

"Hmm?" Steve looked at his hands. They were blazing brightly. The ambient temperature around him had also jumped by twenty degrees. "Sorry." Like shutting off the switch to a furnace, the temperature returned to normal and his hands returned to what Steve had started referring to as TTL, namely typical torch level.

The tunnel deposited them into a large pitch-black cavern that smelled of dank earth and musty air. Steve generated a large chaser, much to Lia's delight, and let it hang in the air long enough for Sarah to spot the torches lining the walls. With Sarah pointing out the locations, Steve guided the chaser along the perimeter walls, lighting the torches as it went by. Once the cavern had been properly illuminated, Steve extinguished the fireball and turned to face Sarah.

"You can't ask for a better place to practice," Steve commented. He turned in place as he studied the empty cave. "There's not much here."

Sarah laughed. "You were expecting a loveseat? Maybe a flat screen TV? I don't think dragons have the same misgivings humans do when it comes to creature comforts."

"Yeah, yeah, yeah. Okay, now that we're here, what are you going to do? You now know that the amulet definitely works. What should you try?"

"Well, I need to try teleporting something. I already know I can move objects now, thanks to Bredo. Hmmm. I think I should start small."

Sarah closed her eyes and wondered what she should try teleporting. She knew the jacket she had brought from home was sitting on the bed back in their quarters. Perhaps that?

Clasping the amulet piece tightly, Sarah closed her eyes and brought up an image from their room back in the castle. Yes, there was her jacket. It shouldn't be too difficult to teleport an article of clothing. She could have chosen something more difficult, but after witnessing what she was capable of doing with Bredo and the moat water, she had decided to be a little more cautious.

The jacket, bed, all the bedding, and three plush chairs

that had been in close proximity, appeared.

"Wow!" Lia exclaimed. "That was so cool!"

Sarah frowned. "I only wanted the jacket."

"So, send it back and try again," Steve suggested.

"Don't you understand? I just wanted the jacket. Look what else showed up!"

"Why don't you just send the jacket back and see if everything else goes with it?" Lia proposed.

"Everyone away from the bed," Sarah instructed. "Just in case."

Steve and Lia moved well away from the cave's new furniture.

Sarah closed her eyes and instructed her jhorun to return her jacket, and just her jacket, to the room. The jacket vanished. So did one chair and the mattress from the bed. The bedding dropped to the floor in a heap.

"Hmmm. Not what I had in mind." Sarah brought back the image from the castle and focused on the jacket sitting on the bare mattress. She really should teleport the jacket back first and then see about returning the blankets to the bed.

Sarah ordered her jhorun to return the jacket, but just the jacket. She opened her eyes to see the results. This time the mattress returned and the jacket was absent.

"Son of a biscuit eater."

"What's the problem? Is it hard to visualize what you're teleporting?"

Sarah shook her head. "Quite the contrary. I get a picture instantly. Think of it like this. When you were a kid, did you ever play one of those claw machines where you're trying to grab a toy you want? Do you know what I'm talking about?"

Steve nodded. "Yeah. Those stupid things are usually rigged where they won't hold on to anything. I remember once where I—"

"Don't lose focus. Now, imagine you have control of that claw and you're trying to pick up a thimble when there's a whole lot of stuff around it. Think you can just get the thimble?"

"Probably not," Steve admitted.

"The key here, I think, is to ignore everything else in the

image. If I can do that, I might be able to …"

The mattress and bedding disappeared, along with two of the chairs.

"Rats. I was close that time. Anyone see the jacket?"

"Sorry, no jacket," Lia told her. "Just a chair."

"Alright, I'm trying again."

Concentrating, Sarah again closed her eyes to re-examine her mental picture of their room. There on the bed, as though it was mocking her, was the infernal jacket.

"Just the jacket. Come on, mama wants just the jacket."

Steve snorted, slapping a hand over his mouth to stifle his laughter.

Her jacket appeared on the ground before her, along with the blankets on the bed. Also making an appearance were the dark green curtains from their room and a decorative duvet that had been draped over a sofa that had been visible in her vision. She was definitely going to have to keep her thoughts completely focused when she used the amulet.

Steve stared at the mishmash pile of blankets and curtains and jammed his hands into his pockets.

"Are those the curtains? What are they doing here?"

"Apparently anything I could see in my vision was fair game," Sarah explained, staring down at the piles of forest green fabric. "I kinda told myself that I might have been cold, hoping to encourage my jhorun into giving me just my jacket."

"But the curtains?"

"She could theoretically wrap them around her and she'd be warm," Lia offered, squatting to feel the luxuriously smooth velvet curtains. "Wow. That'd make a great sweater."

Sarah was smiling. While several other items made the journey with her jacket, clearly the extra incentive she had given her jhorun had played some part.

"There's no furniture this time, so I'll take it as an improvement."

Hoping she was coming closer to figuring out how her enhanced abilities were behaving, she told her jhorun she was now comfortable and would like her jacket to return to the room. She also informed her jhorun that she didn't need the curtains and blankets, either.

The jacket vanished. However, the other items remained on the ground.

Sarah forced a smile and tried again. She reiterated that she was perfectly fine now and didn't need anything else.

The curtains and bedding vanished.

"I think I have it," Sarah told the others. "It works like before, but now I have to be careful what I'm thinking at the time I teleport something. My jhorun is hyped up, like it took a bath in caffeine. But I think I can control it."

"You still have a chair here," Steve pointed out. "Can you send that back?"

Sarah looked at the chair. She didn't need to sit down in here. She didn't think anyone else wanted to sit, either. Therefore, it would be acceptable if the chair were to be returned.

The chair obligingly vanished. Steve stepped away from the empty space the chair had been occupying, presumably to avoid being accidentally teleported.

"That was awesome!" Lia exclaimed, smiling at Sarah. "To think that such cool jhoruns exist and I'm stuck with juggling."

Lia turned to see where Steve had wandered off to and swallowed a scream. Directly behind her, sitting motionless was a huge emerald green dragon. How long had it been watching them?

The dragon lowered its horned head down to her level and sniffed.

"You are *so* not having me for lunch," Lia angrily declared. "Absolutely not. Sarah! You have to get us out of here! Hurry!"

Sarah turned around and casually approached the dragon. She laid a friendly hand on the dragon's snout.

Lia's jaw dropped open. "Sarah, what the hell are you—"

Steve appeared from somewhere behind the massive serpentine form and looked at Lia as though she had just sprouted two heads.

"What's the matter? This is Pryllan. She's the one you saw in Idaho, remember?"

"Why didn't it make some noise? Is it trying to sneak up on us so it can eat us?"

"Look, I know you just recently turned forty, but I didn't think an additional year would make you paranoid as well."

Lia's fear vanished instantly as she glared at Steve.

"Why don't you take that—"

"This is the one."

Steve and Sarah turned to look up at Pryllan.

"What was that?"

"I scented this human before we left your world," the dragon explained. Pryllan's green slitted eyes shifted to Lia's. "You must be Lia. Steve mentioned your name earlier on our journey to his home."

"We really should make this official," Sarah said, walking over to Lia and gently pulling her toward the cave's newest arrival. Sarah looked up at the dragon. "Pryllan, this is Lia, a good friend of ours from our world. Lia, this is Pryllan, mate to Kahvel, dragon liaison to the humans."

Before Lia could muster up the courage to say hello, a gold dragon suddenly appeared in their midst. His scales were so lustrous and shiny that the flickering torches cast numerous spots all along the walls and ceiling.

The two dragons stared at each in shocked silence for a few moments before the gold dragon glared down at the humans.

"What is the meaning of this? Why was I brought here?" Kahvel hesitated a few moments. "*How* was I brought here?"

Sarah nervously coughed. "Sorry, Kahvel. That has to be my fault."

Kahvel's two golden eyes fixated on hers.

"Lady Sarah. I had been summoned by Rinbok Intherer. I was aiding in the creation and implementation of new strategies and tactics to be used against the human sorceress should the need arise."

"I'm sorry, Kahvel. I didn't mean to bring you here."

"An important meeting, Lady Sarah."

"I said I was sorry, Kahvel."

"A very important meeting, Lady Sarah."

Sarah smiled. "Are you asking me to return you?"

"As quickly as possible, aye."

Clutching the amulet tightly in her hand, Sarah politely ordered her jhorun to return the dragon to wherever he had been taken from.

Kahvel vanished.

Sarah, Steve, Lia, and Pryllan all inspected the cavern. Had anything else been teleported that shouldn't have been?

Sarah cleared her throat. "Husband?"

Steve nodded. "Check."

"Friend?"

Lia raised a hand. "Check."

"Green dragon?"

"Check." Pryllan responded. She deliberately twitched her tail so that it grated loudly along the stony floor.

Sarah smiled. "Gold dragon?"

"Absent," Pryllan told her.

"Good."

In the course of the next couple of hours, Sarah practiced teleporting her jacket, hair brush, Steve's boots, and anything else she could think of, just to make sure she could do it with the amulet hanging around her neck. She was not surprised to learn that the smaller the object, the more likely she'd teleport whatever the object was next to as well. Hopefully, if she was required to use her piece of the amulet against Celestia, the object requiring moving would be as large as possible.

"It's not perfect," Sarah told them, "but I think I have the nuances down."

"You sure?" Steve asked her.

In response, Sarah clasped the amulet one more time and teleported everyone, including Pryllan, to the surface.

"Way to go!" Steve congratulated her. "I can't wait to see the look on Celestia's face once she sees that you have the other half of her amulet."

"I just hope I won't have to use it," Sarah told him.

# Chapter 11 - Kidnapped Kid

The servant girl checked the corridor to assure herself she was alone. Approaching one of the dozens of unremarkable doors lining the hallway, she opened one and ducked inside, quickly closing the door behind her. As she chanted softly, a tiny globe of blue fire appeared in her palm, illuminating stacks of freshly laundered blankets and linens. She squeezed behind two large piles of blankets and ran her free hand along the stone wall, searching for the one circular stone nestled amongst a sea of naturally rectangular rocks. Once located, she pushed the rock and waited for the hidden door to open.

Slipping through the tiny entrance, she reached up to open the glass panel on the lamp hanging from the ceiling and placed the sphere of light into the compartment. The blue hues slowly melted away as the light strengthened, turning pale white. The girl began removing parts of her disguise. She unwrapped a white scarf from around her neck and tossed it into a large box in the corner. Her smock and apron followed shortly thereafter.

She passed by a large basin that, at one time, had been used for laundering garments, and hesitated long enough to glance down at the three inches of water that had collected at the bottom.

"Good morning," she said brightly to no one in particular. "I would ask if you slept well, but that would be silly of me."

Humming happily to herself, she began assembling the next disguise she would use. The prince had been moved again and she had yet to determine which part of the castle she'd have to search this time. To prevent suspicion, she always adopted different guises each time she ventured out to search. The problem was that it was becoming more and more difficult now that the entire castle had been alerted to her presence. She knew that the young prince's time was limited in the castle, so it was time to act. If he returned to his bodyguards' home world, then she didn't know when she'd be able to lure the boy back. Besides, she refused to let another opportunity slip by her.

For this next excursion, she would color her blond hair black. If she hunched her shoulders a bit, and refrained from standing upright for the next several hours, she would appear several inches shorter than her natural height of five and a half feet. She applied talcum to her face to lighten her skin tone.

Leaning over the basin to check her image, Celestia smiled. It was only a matter of time before the prince was hers, and together they would rule Lentari.

"I am so excited! This will be the day; I am certain of it! Wish me luck, sister."

Celestia waited a few moments and then huffed irritably as her own reflection continued to stare back at her.

"Come, come, you must be happy for me, Cal. I have waited so long. Why would you deny me my happiness? Have I not earned it?"

The surface of the water shimmered and Caladonia's sad eyes stared back at her sister. Slowly, Caladonia shook her head no.

"Why? Why must you always be so jealous? Why won't

you be happy for me?"

Caladonia locked her hands together and again shook her head.

"I do not care what you think," Celestia told her sister. "The prince and I are meant to be together."

*No,* Caladonia mouthed. *This is not meant to be.*

Celestia's sly smile returned.

"It is. We are destined for one another. Who else is suitable for the prince?" Celestia's smile melted into a frown. "You told me years before that it was impossible. You told me my destiny had already been written. Yet here I am, defying the sands of time!"

Caladonia's eyes flashed fire as she pointed to her own silver necklace and then to the gold chain her sister was wearing.

"Ah, very wise, sister. I must not forget to thank Mother for our gifts."

Caladonia shook her head angrily and vanished.

Dismissing her sister's less than enthusiastic demeanor, Celestia returned her attention to the disguise she had been assembling. Hair colored black and her garb changed to that of a member of the cleaning staff, she rummaged through her meager supply of potions. She scowled angrily as she again thought of all she had lost when her primary lair had been discovered. All those spell books! All her potions! She had painstakingly collected the nectar and pollen from practically every flower and plant she could find in the last two hundred years. There was no one in the kingdom who was more familiar than she with the local pontal. Now her precious vials were lost. All lost! How was she going to get to the prince now?

She slipped a worn white apron over her head. She reached for the straps to tie it behind her back when she froze. The boy's mother. She'd only attempted to impersonate the queen once, and it had almost led to her capture. The queen was simply too well guarded, too well known.

Thanks to the queen's unique jhorun, which forced anyone in her presence to speak only the truth, Celestia had avoided her as though she was infected with a contagious disease. The last thing she needed was to disclose her true intentions in front of the queen should she be asked any questions. Therefore, the queen had been off limits.

However, dire circumstances called for dire actions. Would she be able to get the queen, and only the queen, alone? She knew Mikal would leave the Antechamber if he thought he was in the presence of his mother. She just needed the mother out of the picture so that she didn't show up right when she was trying to sneak off with the prince.

Celestia sighed and paced around the tiny room. She had to do something. The longer she waited, the more likely the boy would be sent off world again. What could she do? There was only one thing she *could* do. Risk it.

Celestia checked her supplies again. Did she have all the ingredients necessary to brew a shifting potion? She hissed with frustration. She didn't. She didn't have anything she could use as an active transforming agent. She knew any one of four rare orchids would suffice. At one point in time, she had the nectar from each of them. As the years had passed, she had used all but one of them, the freia flower. She had stumbled across a small patch of them nearly fifty years ago and had harvested everything she could. The bright blue nectar had been stored safely away in her underground lair. Now it was presumably locked away.

Celestia hesitated. Locked away? Where? Who would have taken possession of them? She grimaced.

The wizard.

Shardwyn would have confiscated all of her things. Potions, rare plants and herbs, all of her spells and books. The infuriating wizard would have claimed them as his own. At least it meant she didn't have to track down another of the rare blue flowers. She would just have to reclaim what was rightfully hers, and that meant she had to infiltrate the wizard's tower.

Armed with a stack of fresh linen, Celestia exited the closet and headed toward the Great Hall. She knew Shardwyn resided in the large gate tower just north of the castle. After the fool had destroyed his workshop for the third time, he had taken up residence in the storage rooms in the tower.

Everyone was under the *false* impression that Shardwyn was a great and powerful wizard, so therefore, there would be few to no guards protecting him. All she had to do was slip in, get the nectar, and then slip out. She doubted he would even notice the freia nectar was missing, let alone that his laboratory had been infiltrated.

As she approached a patrol of guards, she slowed her step and hunched her shoulders even more, giving her a shuffling gait to make herself appear crippled. She had long ago learned that soldiers always tended to avoid anyone who appeared disfigured. Celestia kept her eyes down and smiled as the four soldiers all gave her a wide berth.

Passing under one of the castle's portcullises, she clutched her armful of linens tightly to her chest as she came within sight of the round tower. She almost slowed to a stop as she caught sight of another armed patrol, this one consisting of six guards. They had just appeared from behind the tower. Were these men now guarding the wizard? Celestia scowled. That would be a problem.

Fortunately, the men continued past Shardwyn's tower and moved off, across the bailey, angling west toward the vendors and their many carts full of wares.

She lurched forward, lightly dragging her right leg behind her, as though it was painful for her to bend her knee. The last time she had used this particular disguise was nearly thirty years ago, when she had spied on the former king to see if he bore the mark her sister had spoken of centuries ago. Several of the royal man servants had noticed her, however, and forced her to move off. That was the first time she had ever come face to face with Shardwyn. He had tipped his hat to her and completely ignored her, just like he'd done hundreds of subsequent times. He had been just as dimwitted then as he was now.

The guard waved her through to the tower's main entrance. As she slowly climbed the stone steps, she shifted her load of linens. She had to have a free hand ready to touch her amulet if things became too dangerous. She politely knocked on the door and waited, shifting her load to her right arm to give her tiring left arm a break.

The door creaked open and Celestia found herself staring straight at the smiling wizard.

"Yes?"

Celestia shuffled forward, coming uncomfortably close to the old man. From this distance she could easily distinguish three different potions the wizard had spilled on himself, and then could also see two others that had spilled onto one of his workbenches. The wooden table was sagging in the middle, as though a heavy anvil had been placed on top of it.

"I have fresh linens."

Shardwyn waved her in. "Of course, of course. The linen closet is just over there."

Celestia turned to look in the direction indicated and spotted a narrow door in the hall leading to the wizard's private chambers. She slowly navigated her way around tables, racks of drying herbs, and bookcases crammed full of huge tomes. There, stacked neatly in the farthest corner of the room, were crates of books. *Her* spell books. Were her herbs in one of those other crates or had the imbecile destroyed all her elixirs and potions?

"What are you waiting for?" Shardwyn scolded. "Put the bedding in the closet."

In an attempt to allay any lingering doubt the wizard might have about her hesitation, she stepped forward with her left leg and deliberately dragged her right leg behind her longer than she normally would have. Surely Shardwyn would notice she was crippled and would overlook her like everyone else.

"You remind me of someone, miss. What is your name?"

Celestia cursed to herself. She had exaggerated her disability and now she was paying the consequence. Could he really remember her from all those years ago? His mind was not that sharp. It was impossible!

"You bear an uncanny likeness to a chambermaid I saw many years ago."

Celestia's eyes widened. She frantically started to think of a spell which she could use that would incapacitate the wizard long enough for her to locate the missing potion ingredient she needed and then leave her enough time to make her escape. Unfortunately, nothing sprang to mind. She took a breath. While not ideal, a simple spell to temporarily obfuscate his mind would have to do. She inhaled and …

"Never mind, m' dear. I thought maybe you might be kin to her, but a physiological malady is not passed down from mother to daughter."

Celestia let out the breath she had been holding.

Shardwyn let out a short bark of laughter. "How silly of me. Right. Now, put those in the closet."

Celestia walked toward the closet door, all the while keeping an eye on the wizard. His attention had returned to one of his experiments and he was now completely engrossed by the spinning metal balls and whirring devices before him.

With Shardwyn preoccupied, Celestia crept toward the biggest rack of potions and elixirs she could see. She smiled victoriously. She had just spotted several vials that had previously belonged to her. Shardwyn had mixed all of her potions and ingredients in with his own. Thief. Well, one of the vials was just going to have to be reclaimed by its rightful owner. She just had to find it.

Careful not to touch any of the delicate glass vials, Celestia searched the large wooden rack. How would she find it in time? There were hundreds of colored liquids, powders, twigs, berries, and so on. The freia nectar would be a dense liquid the color of the bluest sky. She hadn't seen anything even remotely close to the shade of blue she was looking for, so she … wait! There it was! Nestled between a vial of bright yellow liquid and a small canister of a gray powder was the rare freia orchid nectar. She checked to make sure Shardwyn was continuing to ignore her. He was. She snatched the vial of blue liquid and safely tucked it into the bodice of her uniform.

Mission accomplished, she turned to head toward the door when Shardwyn appeared in front of her. Celestia blinked with surprise and she inadvertently brought up a hand to reach for her amulet. Sensing the non-threatening nature of Shardwyn's sudden appearance, she disguised her arm gesture as a natural female response to hold a hand over her heart.

"You startled me. I was just leaving."

"Excellent, excellent. Where are the soiled bedsheets?"

"Where are the *what*?"

"The soiled bedsheets. You were gone so long I assumed you changed the bedding. Where are they?"

Thinking fast, Celestia plastered her best, most effective charming smile on her face and batted her eyes. "I must have left them next to bed. Just a moment and I will retrieve them."

Celestia pivoted in place and scowled as she hurried back down the hall to the linen closet. She yanked out a fresh batch of linen and rushed into Shardwyn's private room. Rolling her eyes as she saw the extent of the cluttered room, she attacked the bed with renewed vigor, tearing off the dirty sheets and throwing them to the side. Expertly whipping the fresh linen over the lumpy mattress, Celestia had reassembled the bed in less than twenty seconds.

Nervously eyeing the hallway, she kicked the used bedding into a pile, took a deep breath so she would be unable to smell the pungent body odor the sheets stank of, and turned around. She gasped with surprise as again the quirky wizard was once more standing behind her.

"As long as you are collecting dirty linen, you can collect my things as well. There's an empty cart right over there, miss, which a previous chamber maid left here. I have been meaning to get it back to the castle. You may use that to take the laundry to the castle to be cleaned."

"A cart? But there are stairs! How did a cart make it up here?"

"It was quite a chore, if memory serves. Fear not. I will have one of the guards help you take it down. You may get started, there's a girl."

Celestia's mouth gaped open with shock. Not only did he want her to touch his filthy things, but he also expected her to return one of the castle's two wheeled carts? Full of dirty laundry? Shardwyn had already turned around and was moving toward his desk, presumably to notify the guard below that he had just received the honor of helping haul his dirty trousers down the stairs.

She bristled with annoyance. The sooner she collected

the dirty laundry, the sooner she could leave.

Fifteen minutes later, after making certain she had collected every piece of discarded clothing she could find, Celestia eyed the heavy cart. Somehow, somewhere, she would make Shardwyn pay for this outrage.

"You have done an admirable job," Shardwyn told her, smiling patronizingly at her. "If you would be so kind as to organize the rack of vials you see there, it would be greatly appreciated. My eyes aren't what they used to be, my dear girl. Powders on the top rack, sorted by colors if you please. From left to right is dark to light. Why, that rhymed! I will have to remember that for the next maid who sorts the racks. Moving on, the next two shelves are for liquids. Again, dark to light from left to right. You know, that would make a clever little song, would it not?" Shardwyn chuckled softly while Celestia glowered. "And finally, the bottom rack has everything else. Organics on the left and inorganics on the right."

Celestia was furious. This charade had gone on long enough! She had much more important things to do!

"I am sorry, but I must return. My superior will be missing me by—"

"Think nothing of it," Shardwyn assured her. "I will send a personal note with you that will see to it you remain in the good graces of your superior."

Celestia sighed as she looked over at the rack she had previously searched. There were hundreds of vials all scattered haphazardly about. It would take her hours to sort that properly! Damn that wizard! She sighed. Her ruse must be maintained.

"Very well, sir."

Two hours later, with no fewer than ten vials shoved down her dress, Celestia was finally able to exit Shardwyn's tower. With the burly guard guiding the cart full of malodorous garments in front of them, and making the loudest racket Celestia had witnessed in quite some time as the wooden wheels thumped down the stairs, they finally reached the bottom. Emerging into the waning daylight, Celestia took several deep breaths of fresh air.

"I do not know how you can suffer so long up there," the

guard told her, holding the cart's handle level while Celestia grudgingly took possession of it. "Most days it reeks in there. Makes me think Bredo slithered up there and regurgitated his dinner."

Celestia smiled in spite of herself. The guard waved her off as she strained to pull the heavy cart toward the castle.

Nearly an hour later Celestia dropped, exhausted, onto the thin straw mattress in her hidden utility room. She slowly untied her apron and tossed it into a second large crate tucked just behind the first. She carefully pulled the pilfered vials from her dress and reverently set them down on the tiny table where she conducted her work.

"What a rotten day," Celestia told the vials. "All for naught?" She picked up the tiny vial of nectar the color of the clearest sky. "I think not." Realizing she had just made a rhyme, she winced. "Wizard, if I take the time to make a rhyme, I will personally—"

Celestia snapped her mouth closed. She irritably shook her head and began to brew her potion. Unbeknownst to her, in the basin, Caladonia's image was laughing. Hysterically.

Three hours later it was done. Celestia poured the bubbling blue potion into an empty vial and sealed it closed with a bit of melted wax. Clutching the vial tightly, she went to slip it into a pocket when she hesitated. She already had some of her other spells there, but this one was too important to be confiscated. If she was discovered, then she knew her pockets would be searched first. Maybe she should slip the vial into a pouch and tie it to a belt? Or maybe…? She trailed off as she looked down at the front of her dress. She sighed. It was as good a hiding place as any. She placed the cold glass vial inside her bodice one more time and took several deep breaths.

This was her chance. This was her final chance to obtain the boy. If she failed now, then she was quite literally out of options. The boy would surely return to the Nohrin's home world. With her portal gone, she would be unable to track him as she did before.

The absence of her spell books had been a terrible blow. While not defeated, she had come very close to being rendered defenseless. She had to rebuild her spells. She had to have time to prepare. She had incorrectly assumed that she was invulnerable. She had underestimated the prince's bodyguards. How could two non-Lentarians be her biggest threat?

Celestia shook her head. She had to get Mikal and find a place to hide. Then the boy would come to trust her and fall in love with her. If he didn't, well, then she'd brew a potion that would accomplish just that. She was a sorceress. She could do anything.

Fifteen minutes later, sporting a head full of fiery red curls, Celestia left the closet and headed toward the Great Hall. Where would the Queen be? She would try the Great Hall first and see if the king and queen were there.

The first window she passed by forced her to change directions. It was already dark out. It was much later than she thought. The Kri'yans would not be attending to matters of the kingdom now. Maybe their personal quarters?

She took an immediate right and headed past the royal library and several large conference rooms. She ignored the armory and fell into step behind another girl bearing a tray full of steaming meat and vegetables. Perfect. She was on her way to the king and queen to deliver them their evening meal. Celestia hurried to catch up to the girl. She stretched her arms out and easily relieved the heavy platter from the young servant.

Surprised to learn that her tray had suddenly vanished, the girl turned to see what had happened to her delivery.

"Sleep," Celestia told the girl, invoking a small energy regeneration spell as she did.

The girl's head drooped and she stumbled forward. Shifting the weight of the tray to her right arm, Celestia caught the girl with her left and then spun her off into a passing closet. The girl landed with a soft thud amidst a pile of clean bedding. Celestia pulled the door closed and slid the bolt over, locking the door.

By the time she had incapacitated the third guard, Celestia was worried. She had never nullified that many soldiers before. The chances were too great that one would awaken and set off the alarm. She had definitely passed the point of no return. She *had* to get to the queen and get her out of the way long enough so she could impersonate her and abscond with the prince.

She deftly navigated her way through the many corridors. One advantage of living as long as she had was the many opportunities to explore the castle. There were only a few people who knew how to find the king and queen's personal chambers, and even fewer who knew the most direct route there. She was aware of two: Rhenyon, the insufferably loyal commander, and herself.

Ascending a nondescript flight of stairs to her left, she stepped onto a plush carpeted sitting area with a ring of blue chairs encircling the room. There was only one exit besides the stairs, and that was a long hallway that curved off to the left. Repositioning the heavy tray to rest on her other hip, she moved down the hallway and approached the private apartments of the king and queen. Just before she would have emerged from the shadows, she paused. Stationed in front of the massive arched door were ten guards. Five on either side. All were standing stiffly at attention.

Celestia remained in the corridor, just inside the dark shadows. She hadn't been spotted yet, thank goodness, but there were nearly a dozen soldiers standing guard. How was she supposed to—

"I just want to spend some private time with my son!" a female voice shouted. "Why can you not understand that?"

Shocked, Celestia stared at the guards. That was the queen's voice. Surely, they must have heard her outburst!

The guards fidgeted uncomfortably but did not break ranks.

Celestia backed deeper into the shadows, away from the door, and gently set the large tray of food to the ground. She stealthily approached the end of the hallway and stopped where she knew she wouldn't be seen. It sounded as though the queen was arguing about her son. What was going on? She had to know!

"It is not safe," the king's voice was saying.

"I have not been there to see him grow up, Entu! Our son

is being raised by someone else!"

"They are the Nohrin. You cannot ask for—"

"I know full well that they are trustworthy and we could not have found better bodyguards anywhere, but I have missed so much!"

"The Antechamber is more than—"

"The Antechamber? That has been Mikal's prison! Do not even think about suggesting that room."

Celestia heard the king huff out an exasperated breath.

"What do you suggest, my love?"

"Let us walk the halls as we once did. Let me take him out of the Antechamber. We will not leave the castle."

There was silence as the king thought about the request.

"Only if there are guards present."

"*Private* time, Entu. Private."

"Take the Nohrin then."

"They spend enough time with him. As much as I care for them, and would never wish them harm, I would like to spend time with my son without his foster parents nearby."

"You must take someone. On this, I will not bend. Take Rhenyon."

Celestia held her breath. Would the queen agree? This would be the perfect opportunity!

"Very well."

"Excellent. I will inform the commander. Then perhaps I will join you," the king suggested.

"Entu, I think that is a wonderful idea."

"As soon as we finish our supper, when it arrives, we will go see Mikal."

"Should we call for him to join us?"

"Mikal said he wanted to show Captain Pheron some new grappling techniques he has learned from Sir Steve. It will allow us some time."

"Where *is* our meal?" the queen asked. "Should it not have arrived by now?"

Cursing softly, Celestia rushed back down the hall to retrieve the tray. This was even better! The king and queen would enjoy their dinner while she could sneak Mikal out of the Antechamber , disguised as the queen. This was the opportunity she had been waiting for!

Ten pairs of eyes were trained on her as she approached. She bowed her head and remained motionless, saying nothing. One of the guards approached and began lifting various lids to inspect the contents. Once he was satisfied, he took the tray from her and then knocked on the door. One of the king's personal manservants answered and wordlessly took the tray from the guard. He disappeared into the room while the guard closed the door.

Celestia was already rushing back down the corridor, trying to get to the Antechamber just as quickly as she could. As she cut through one of the large empty meeting rooms, she hesitated. This room had a small alcove tucked away in a back corner. She smiled. It was perfect.

Fishing the tiny vial out of her dress, she downed the foul concoction and waited for the effects to take place. Within moments her features morphed into that of the queen's. Celestia removed her apron and the dull cream-colored dress she was wearing, revealing a much classier gown beneath it, something the queen would have worn. Actually, she knew the queen had worn it because she had stolen it from her wardrobe last year.

Making sure the long braid of brown hair was hanging straight down her back as she knew the queen wore hers, she stuffed her old dress and the apron under one of the chair cushions. By the time it was discovered, she'd be long gone.

Reminding herself that she was now the queen, and to look the part, she strode purposefully down the hall until she approached the Antechamber. The guards standing silently on patrol on either side of the door sprang to attention and bowed their heads. The guard closest to the door opened it and kept his eyes on the ground. Without so much as glancing in their direction, Celestia entered and scanned the room. Finally! There was the prince, sprawled out on one of the sofas, with his legs draped over the left arm. He sat up and swung his legs around to slap both his feet on the ground. The boy must have been asleep as there were sleep lines over his face.

"Mother!"

Mikal rose unsteadily to his feet and rushed over to embrace her. Surprised, Celestia awkwardly patted the prince on his back and waited, unsure what the socially accepted duration for a hug should be. Fortunately, Mikal released her after a few moments and then smiled warmly at her.

"I was hoping you would come for a visit. It is too quiet in here. Sarah says Steve is the same way. He does not care for silence."

"Why do you not like silence?"

Mikal eyed her suspiciously. "I told you last night. Were you not paying attention to me? I said that too much silence reminds me of a mausoleum."

"Of course, I remember."

"Are you sure? Why are you acting so peculiar?"

"I am sure I do not know what you are talking about," Celestia snapped. "It must be your imagination. Now, would you —"

"Why are you upset? Is it something I said?"

"No, it is nothing you said."

"So, someone else said something that upset you. Has father been acting unreasonable again?"

"Will you stop saying that I am upset?"

"But you sound like you are," Mikal insisted.

"Look, you need to …" Celestia bit her tongue and took a deep breath. Composing herself she looked at the prince and smiled. "Would you like to go for a walk?"

"Really? We can leave this wretched room?"

"We can, aye. Follow me."

Celestia turned and moved toward the closest door. She risked a glance behind her. There was the prince, following silently. It was working! He must be as anxious as she was to leave this dreaded room. She smiled. All she had to do was clear the castle walls and she would be able to activate one of her four teleportation spells she had tucked safely away inside her right pocket.

"Do you think we can find Captain Pheron? He wanted me to show him some more of my grappling moves I learned in Idaho. He was extremely interested to learn how—"

"Alright, fine, whatever you want. Let us be on our way."

"You still sound annoyed."

Realizing she needed the prince's cooperation in order to leave the castle unmolested, she plastered a smile on her face and turned to the boy. "Not to worry, my son, all is well."

Mollified, Mikal fell silent.

The door opened just before Celestia could grasp the handle. Her eyes widened in disbelief. Rhenyon stared back at her.

"Your Majesty. I did not expect to find you there."

The commander leaned around Celestia to see the prince behind her.

"Might I inquire where you are going?"

Celestia managed to curb her scowl. Then she smiled as she realized she had the perfect retort for the meddlesome soldier.

"I am going to spend some private time with my son."

"Where are you headed?"

"We are—"

"Going for a walk," Mikal finished for her, smiling at his mother.

Rhenyon's eyebrows shot up. "Alone? Unescorted?"

Celestia cursed to herself.

"Would you care to accompany us, Commander?"

Rhenyon smiled. "I believe a walk would do me good."

*Of course it would*, Celestia thought bitterly.

Rhenyon stepped aside and let the two of them pass, falling into step behind the prince.

They silently walked through the Great Hall. Soldiers, servants, and peasants alike all gave them a wide berth. No one questioned them, no one bothered them. Rhenyon, following closely behind Mikal, gently reached up and tapped him on his shoulder. He leaned forward to whisper in the prince's ear.

"Where are we going?"

"I am not certain," Mikal whispered back. "She wanted to go for a walk."

"Very well."

Celestia was lost in her thoughts. Thanks to the soldier following closely behind her, she was going to have to deal with him before she could hope to escape with the prince. What should she do? What *could* she do without drawing attention to herself?

Celestia slipped both hands into her pockets and took inventory of the assortment of bottles and charms she found there. Teleportation spells, another regeneration spell, and an illumination spell. Nothing she found would aid her in ridding herself of the pesky soldier following them like an obedient marjihn.

Her fingers closed around a small bottle with a rectangular neck. Her eyes widened, then her smile returned. She had forgotten about this one. It was her most prized spell: an air elemental. While nowhere near as powerful as a true air elemental, it should still be strong enough for a more than adequate diversion. She sighed. That spell had been in her possession for nearly two centuries. She almost had as much sentimental attachment to this spell as she did for the amulet she wore around her neck. The air elemental, amplified by the amulet's power, should wipe that smug smile off the commander's face. It would be a joy to watch.

They finally came within sight of one of the castle's main gates. The West Gate was protected, as all the castle gates were, with a massive iron portcullis, a gate house on either side of the immense arched doorway, and a heavy wooden drawbridge, which was presently down. However, she knew that in case of emergency, the counterweight could be chopped away by a single swing of the gatekeeper's axe, and that avenue would be sealed off from her faster than she could stretch up an arm to clasp her amulet.

"Surely you were not planning on going outside," Rhenyon began to protest from behind her. "The king would not grant you permission outside these walls without a full complement of—"

Celestia had had enough.

"Do not begin to lecture me where I can and cannot go, simpleton. If I wish to take my son outside, then I will do just that."

A commotion started somewhere behind them and grew in intensity. They could hear shouting and several crashes, as though fully loaded tables had been pushed over. Celestia cursed to herself. The noise grew steadily louder as what sounded like hundreds of footsteps headed their way.

Rhenyon caught the queen's arm and spun her back around so that they were facing the castle's interior.

"Your Majesty, we must go back inside. Something has happened. We need to get the prince back to the—"

Rhenyon grunted with surprise as a fierce blast of air slammed into his chest. The jet of air lifted him bodily off the ground and flung him straight backwards, smashing him into the closest stone wall.

Celestia grabbed Mikal's hand and pulled him forward, just as she had unleashed the full power of the air elemental. The prince turned to look back at Rhenyon as he collapsed to the ground in a heap.

"Mother, what has happened? Why have you—"

"Be silent! Quickly now! Hurry!"

Hand in hand, Celestia and Mikal ran across the open drawbridge. As soon as they stepped onto the cobbled street, she pulled Mikal to a stop and activated her regeneration spell, sending the boy straight into unconsciousness. Supporting the prince's weight with her left arm, she retrieved one of her teleportation spells with her right. Clenching the bottle in her teeth, she pulled her gold chain up and clasped the amulet tightly in her hand.

"No!!!"

Celestia looked back across the open drawbridge as the king, queen, and more soldiers than she had ever seen at one time appeared. She flashed the horrified Kri'yans a smile and vanished, taking Mikal with her.

# Chapter 12 - Nohrin to the Rescue

They had just bade Pryllan farewell when all hell broke loose. Steve, Sarah, and Lia were halfway across the drawbridge when the alarm bells started ringing. Steve grabbed Sarah's hand and they hurried across the wooden bridge. The soldiers gestured frantically at them to hurry across. The drawbridge trembled, indicating it was ready to be raised. Lia cursed silently and broke into a run to make sure she wasn't left behind.

"What's going on?" Steve asked one of the guards. He was ignored. He singled out another soldier and tried to catch his attention. "Think you can tell me what's—"

Several other guards appeared and together they ran into the castle, leaving only two guards at the gate. Getting irritated, Steve walked toward one of the gate keepers.

"What about you? What's going on?"

"Get inside!" the guard snapped. "Quickly! The drawbridge is being raised. The portcullis will be dropped in just a matter of moments."

"But—"

Sarah and Lia pulled him toward the castle's main keep.

"If we don't get out of the way, we're going end up trampled," Sarah told him.

Steve turned to his wife. "Don't you want to know what's going on? There's gotta be someone we can ask."

"For the love of Pete," Lia exclaimed, exasperated. "This is how you ask for help."

She stuck out her leg and waited for someone to trip over it. It only took a few moments. Lia helpfully pulled the soldier to his feet and held on to his hand.

"Hey there sexy, care to tell me what's going on?"

"Who are you? Release me at once!"

Lia snagged the soldier's other hand and pulled him over to where Steve and Sarah stood.

"Recognize them?" Lia asked the young guard, spinning him so that he was facing Sarah, then turning him again so that he was looking straight at Steve.

"Sir Steve! Lady Sarah! We have been looking for you!"

"What's going on?" Steve demanded, turning to look behind him as two squadrons of soldiers decked out in full armor clanked by.

"Kre'Mikal has been abducted."

"What?!" Steve instinctively reached out to take Sarah's hand while she and Lia gasped out loud. "Was it Celestia?"

The guard sadly nodded. "Aye. She managed to disguise herself as the queen and somehow lured the prince outside the castle."

"Damn! Damn, damn, damn!" Steve swore as he paced around. "How did she pull that off? Why didn't someone stop her?"

"If she looked like the queen, no one would have questioned her," Sarah pointed out.

The young guard, now free of Lia's powerful grip, started to edge away.

"Stay put," Steve snapped, his hands igniting in the process. He glanced down and gave them an irritated flick to put them out. "Where are the king and queen? Are they okay?"

"Their majesties were supping in their private chambers when the abduction took place."

"Where are they now?"

"They are both in the Antechamber."

"We have to go to them," Sarah announced, automatically moving off through the crowds of bustling people. "You coming?"

"Right behind you," Steve told her.

"You're not leaving me behind," Lia informed them. "I'm coming, too."

Steve turned to look behind him. "Try to keep up, old lady."

"You're gonna pay for that one, pal."

Steve and Lia followed Sarah as she ducked and weaved through several rooms and hallways until she eventually came to an abrupt stop.

"No one enters," a male voice said.

Steve peered around his wife and observed at least a dozen guards physically blocking the Antechamber's main entrance. He scowled. He stepped around his wife and physically pushed her behind him.

"Guys, we're going in there whether you like it or not."

Unimpressed, the soldiers didn't budge.

Steve reignited both hands and held them up in front of the skeptical soldiers.

"You know me," Steve pointed a flaming hand at Sarah. "You know her, too. We have to get inside to see what we can do to help."

"We know who you are, Sir Steve," one of the guards told him. "I am sorry, but I am under strict orders not to grant anyone passage."

Sarah scoffed. "We don't have time for this."

She hooked her arm through Lia's left and pulled her up so that she was level with Steve. Sarah then snaked her arm through her husband's and instantly teleported them to the other side of the door.

The first thing they all heard was sobbing. The queen was sitting on a large yellow and white sofa facing the hearth, while three young female servants did their best to console her. The king was sitting at his desk with his head in his hands.

When Kri'Entu finally noticed the three of them standing there, he jerked so violently that his crown flew off his head. The gold circlet spiraled noisily on his desk for several revolutions before finally coming to a stop.

"Sir Steve! Lady Sarah!"

Sarah's eyes filled. "I am so sorry, Your Majesty. We should never have left Mikal unprotected."

The queen's tear-streaked face finally lifted until her bleary eyes met Sarah's.

"Please. Is there anything you can do to find Mikal?"

Both Steve and Sarah nodded.

"You'd better believe it," Steve told the queen. He pointed at Sarah. "She's got the amulet. Hon, can you do that scrying thing and see if you can find him?"

Sarah pulled up the amulet and held it tightly.

"I can sure try. Everyone be quiet."

Callé rose from the couch and shooed the servants away. She met her husband as he had also risen, intent on approaching their son's bodyguards. The king's fallen crown sat ignored on the desk. The Kri'yans remained motionless, and looked at Sarah with all the hope they could muster.

"Everyone's staring at me. Stop it."

Steve smiled briefly. "How can you tell?"

"I can feel it. Give me a moment and let me see if I can picture anything."

Steve grabbed Lia's arm and pulled her with him as he walked over to join the two monarchs.

"That conniving b--"

Lia stomped on his foot.

"Ow! Wench, alright? That conniving wench must have been hiding somewhere in the castle." He shook his head and turned to look at the king then glanced around the room. "Where's Rhenyon?"

The queen sobbed again. "He has been severely injured. He was the only one who confronted Celestia and tried to save Mikal."

"What happened?" Lia asked, as gently as she could.

"She used an air elemental on him," the queen told her.

"He received terrible injuries as he was thrown against the outer wall."

"What are you worried about?" Steve protested, confused. "Magic exists here. Don't you guys have some sort of healing potion?"

"We did, aye, but someone sabotaged Shardwyn's rack of medicines and potions. All of his healing elixirs are missing."

Steve pointed at Sarah. "What about hers? She has that little vial of stuff in her medallion that can cure just about anything."

The queen's eyes widened. She quickly wiped her tear-streaked face with a silk handkerchief and looked over at Sarah, who had already removed her medallion and was holding it up. Her eyes remained closed.

"How did she know we were talking about her medallion?" the king whispered to Steve. "Did she hear us from across the room?"

Steve nodded. "Yep. Welcome to my world. Lia, could you grab that thing for me?"

"Umm, sure."

Lia hurried over to Sarah and took the medallion from her friend's outstretched hand. She studied the ugly pendant as she returned to Steve's side. It was an unremarkable thing. The metal might have been silver, but it was so tarnished that she couldn't tell. A cheap looking purple glass crystal sat in the center of the piece. She wouldn't have paid five bucks for it.

"What's so special about this thing?" Lia asked as she handed the medallion to Steve. "It's hideous."

"On purpose," he told her.

Steve pinched a spot near the bottom of the medallion and then mirrored the gesture at the top, gently twisting. A small panel popped loose, allowing Steve to expose a tiny compartment. Inside, he could see the vial of kaormac elixir.

"What's that?" Lia wanted to know, rising on her tiptoes so that she could see over Steve's shoulder.

"It's called kaormac juice. It'll cure just about anything." Steve resealed the tiny vial and handed it to the queen. "Help Rhenyon."

The queen nodded and rushed out of the room, taking her three servants with her.

The king breathed a sigh of relief and clapped a hand on Steve's shoulder. "At least we won't have to worry about the commander's recovery."

"One problem down, one to go," Steve told the king. "Don't worry, we're going to get your son back."

The king sighed and sank down into the closest chair. "I hope so. I do not like knowing I have failed him. As a father."

Steve took a seat next to the king. "The hell you have. We failed him, as bodyguards. We made a promise to you and your wife years ago to protect him. I sure as hell am not going to let it end like this. No way. We just have to —"

"Got something," Sarah called to them from the other side of the room.

Steve, Lia, and the king all rushed over.

"Whatcha got?" Steve asked her as he sat down next to her on the couch. "Can you see them?"

"I don't see Mikal or Celestia," Sarah began, frowning. "What I do see is rocks. I feel like something is blocking me. It's like … hmm. Okay, every time I think about Mikal, and a picture forms, someone snaps their fingers and breaks my concentration. And, this infernal thing gets warm." She held up the amulet. "Celestia *must* be using hers against mine and I don't think this one likes it one bit."

Steve cursed under his breath. "When I see her, I'm going to —"

Lia elbowed him in his gut. "Oh, cool your jets, Fireball."

Steve snorted. "Fireball?"

"I don't think Sarah was done talking."

Sarah nodded appreciatively at Lia. "I wasn't. Now, even though I can't get an image of the two of them, I can expand my search a little and look for anything in the area. Celestia is doing something to block me, but it only appears to be affecting the area she's in. All I had to do was keep searching until my vision didn't fuzz out. Then, I had to find something we could use to identify her location."

"You found something, did you not?" Kri'Entu hopefully asked.

Sarah nodded. "I found something, yeah, but I don't know what I'm looking at. I'll describe it and you can tell me if it sounds familiar. I'm hoping it does, or else I'll have to look for something else."

"Agreed. What do you see?"

Sarah fell silent as she inspected the image that had manifested.

"Okay, I see a lot of rocks. Big ones, like the boulders we saw in the dragons' valley up at Lake Raehón."

The king nodded. "Go on."

"The rocks remind me of the fake ones we've seen used at amusement parks, like Disneyland."

The king shook his head. "I am not familiar with —"

"They're red, like the rocks we saw in Sedona."

"I am not —"

"Exactly like Sedona?" Steve asked, looking at Lia, who shrugged. "Smooth formations or does it look like gunite?"

Sarah snapped her fingers and smiled. "That's the word. Yes, like gunite. The fake rocks."

Steve turned to the king. "Where's—"

"Wait," Sarah interrupted. "Griffins. I see what looks like a pair of griffins, posing for a picture. Reminds me of our safe."

"Reminds you of what?" Lia asked, confused. "What do griffins have to do with a safe?"

"Wait!"

This time, the king was excited. He turned to the stone wall behind his desk and activated the hidden wall, revealing his private safe with the griffin statue standing on top of it.

"Lady Sarah, do the stones look like this?"

Sarah cracked an eye and glanced over at the hidden compartment.

"Yes. A much larger version of that. I can see two of them."

"There are three in total. I know where they are."

Sarah's eyes snapped open. "You do? Where? We have to get going!"

The king spun around and walked to the large map of the kingdom pinned to the wall. He tapped a large island on the western coast. "You saw two of the Three Griffins. They are here, on Presages Island. Those rock formations can only be seen by sea."

"Why would she go there?" Steve asked the king. "The only thing I can see there, according to your map, is a lighthouse. Is there anything else? Why would she pick that spot?"

"I believe I can answer that, my dear boy," a new voice suddenly announced.

Everyone looked up to see Shardwyn stroll through the door. The wizard paused in mid-step and looked back through the door at the guards.

"Your ears will return to normal in a day or so. When I tell you I am on official business to the king, pay attention. Next time, you will have a tail to match."

Shardwyn closed the door in the guards' angry faces and turned to the king. He bowed.

"That island was once home to Katar, a small village that thrived hundreds of years ago."

"Back in Celestia's time," Sarah guessed.

Shardwyn's gray head nodded. "Aye. She and her sister were both born there. Why she has chosen to return to her home village I cannot fathom. There is nothing but ruins there now."

Surprising everyone, Lia raised her hand. "I have a question. You guys said she lost all of her stuff, right?

Steve nodded. "Right. Her lair was hidden down in the dungeon. We found it earlier and everything was confiscated. Why?"

"Well, I'd say she's probably looking for her old house. Maybe she thinks there's something there that she can use."

"Like what?" Steve demanded. "I don't think there'd be much of anything left after so many years have passed. But in case she *is* looking for something, we need to make sure she doesn't find it." Steve looked at Sarah. "How close can you get us?"

"I can drop us right in front of those statues. Anything closer and I lose the image."

"I'm coming, too," Lia announced.

"Vetoed," Steve told her.

"You don't have the right to tell me what to do." Lia accusingly told him. "If I want to help, then I'm going to —"

"Stay put," the king told her. "I will not place you in danger, Lady Lia. You are in no position to battle with a sorceress, whereas these two are. You will remain here."

"Aww, come on! I know the kid! I like him! Let me help. You can't send just the two of them!"

Kri'Entu was silent as he considered. "You may be right."

Lia's face took on her trademark smug smile.

"I will send Captain Pheron. Shardwyn, see to it."

Shardwyn nodded and left the room.

"Are you kidding me?"

Kri'Entu turned to see Lia with her hands on her hips. "I meant *me*. I wanted to be the one to help, not some strange guy."

"It's okay," Sarah told her. "Pheron is no stranger. He's a good choice. His jhorun is nocturnal vision."

Lia was impressed, but tried not to show it.

"So he can see in the dark. Big whoop."

"In case you hadn't noticed, it is dark outside," Steve pointed out. "He'll come in handy."

The doors to the Antechamber flew open and Pheron strode in. The captain was wearing dark leather armor and sported a baldric strapped across his back so that his sword hilt was just behind his right shoulder. A quiver full of arrows was strapped behind his left. Nestled in amongst the arrows was a de-stringed shortbow. The captain was clearly ready to travel.

Just before the Antechamber's heavy wooden door could swing closed, a red dual-headed axe was thrust in between the door and frame, stopping it. A loud metallic clang echoed loudly off the walls.

"Pardon the interruption," Breslin began as he pushed the door back open to allow Venk and Athos to join him inside. "We cannot help but notice that you are preparing for battle. We stand ready to assist."

"You are aware of the dangers involved should you encounter the sorceress?" Kri'Entu asked, already thinking of the ways in which he would be thanking the dwarves for their courage and bravery.

All three dwarves nodded. "We are."

"And you still wish to accompany the Nohrin?"

"We do."

"Permission granted, master dwarf."

The dwarves bowed again and joined Steve and Sarah.

"Glad to have you guys aboard," Steve whispered to the dwarves.

Breslin smiled at Sarah while the two dwarf brothers nodded their heads at Steve.

The door opened a third time and admitted a stream of servants, all holding various pieces of Steve and Sarah's leather armor. One male servant, no older than sixteen, approached Steve.

"If you will lift your arms, sir, I will attach the breastplate."

"Thanks, but I don't need anyone to put these on for me."

Sarah leaned close. "Ummm, we're in a rush here, so maybe you ought to consider it."

Steve sighed, lifted his arms, and waited while a complete stranger buckled the protective leather padding into place. He glanced over at his wife and saw that she was getting similar treatment. He had to admit that the servants were much more efficient than he was when it came to fastening the many pieces of leather in the correct places.

Steve cocked his head. How was it that their armor had been waiting for them? He shook his head. It didn't matter. A familiar sight caught his eye. His special enchanted gauntlets had also been retrieved and strapped to his forearms. He ignited his leather covered hands and watched as the flickering red flames completely enveloped the gauntlets. The young teenager who had been helping him with his armor leapt backwards with surprise.

"Sorry," Steve apologized. "Freaked me out the first time I did that, too."

He looked over at his wife and smiled. The young girl who had been helping her had just finished as well. Together he and his wife looked over at Pheron, who had stopped several feet before the king.

"Your Majesty."

The king nodded.

"Captain. I cannot help but notice the speed in which you arrived here. Prepared for battle, I might add. Accompanied by the Nohrin's armor."

"I was ready to depart the moment I learned the prince had been taken. Besides, everyone knows that the Nohrin will give chase."

"They will indeed. You will be accompanying them and will assist in whatever fashion you can to facilitate my son's return."

Pheron's six-and-a-half-foot frame bowed again.

"Most excellent, Your Majesty. When do we depart?"

"Right now," Steve told him.

"Will the sorceress be able to detect our presence?" Pheron asked, turning to look at Sarah. "If you possess the other half of the amulet, then will we be detected?"

Sarah shook her head. "I know she knows I have it. I don't know if she knows that I know that. So if she knows that I know —"

"Hold it." Steve interrupted. "It's going to take me too long to figure out what you just said. The longer Celestia runs around unchecked, the more likely it is that she'll disappear with Mikal and we'll never find her."

Pheron nodded. "Agreed."

Sarah slipped her arm through her husband's. With her free hand she motioned for Pheron to come over. Accustomed to Sarah's method of transportation, Pheron held out his left arm and waited for Sarah to hook her arm through his. The three dwarves all approached and laid their right hands over Sarah and Steve's. The six of them vanished moments later.

The king stared at the empty space where his son's rescuers just stood. "Do whatever it takes, my friends."

* * *

"What do you see?"

Pheron took several confident steps forward and peered

up at the twenty-foot-tall statues of the griffins.

"Nothing but stone. Remember, Sir Steve, do not use your jhorun unless we have to. If Celestia is out there hiding, we do not want to give away our position."

"Then you might want to take lead," Steve suggested. "I can't see enough to figure out where I'm going.'

"I was planning on doing the guiding," Pheron told them. He turned to study the three dwarves as they flanked their small group. "How well can the three of you see in darkness such as this?"

"Not as well as you can," Breslin told him, familiar with the captain's jhorun, "but better than an average human. We will be fine."

Sarah was clutching Steve's hand tightly. She could barely make out Pheron's still form and he was only a few feet ahead of her. How was she supposed to be able to move around like this? They were supposed to fight the sorceress in complete and utter darkness? How could they expect to survive if they weren't able to see who they were attacking?

In exasperation, Sarah closed her eyes and rubbed her temples. A tension headache was forming, and her bottle of aspirin was definitely out of reach. As soon as her eyes closed, however, an image appeared. She was once again looking at the griffin statues, only this time she was able to see all three of the stone statues. Sarah jerked slightly. The image wasn't showing her a dark scene but rather what the heavily treed island would look like during the day. What surprised her, though, was that she could see herself, Steve, Pheron, and the dwarves all peeking through the trees at the rock formations in the distance. She experimentally raised an arm into the air. She watched herself raise her left arm and wiggle her fingers. This was really weird!

Sarah opened her eyes to verify it was still pitch dark out. It was. She closed her eyes and the daytime image reappeared. She turned to face the other direction and the image's point-of-view swung around and stayed about thirty feet behind her and up ten feet or so into the air. Sarah faced a few other directions and watched as her "camera" kept rotating around, trying to find the best vantage point to observe herself.

"Ummm, there's something you guys need to know."

From her vantage point thirty feet away, she watched as her husband turned to her.

"What's the matter?"

"Believe it or not, I'm actually watching you right now," Sarah told him. She turned to Pheron, who had twisted around to watch her from where he was standing. She smiled at him. "Pheron, do you see that my eyes are closed?"

"Aye."

Sarah slowly approached him and tentatively reached out and took his hand. "I can see you."

"How?"

"I'm looking at one of my visions. It's showing us, right now, but in normal daylight."

"So, I'm the only dunce who can't see? That's just great. How long have you been able to do that?"

"It just happened," Sarah answered. "I think it's only because I'm wearing the amulet." She slowly turned in place so that she could inspect the surrounding areas. "It's really cool. I can see everything around us."

"What do you see?" Pheron asked her, dropping his voice as though he thought they could be overheard.

"Not much," Sarah admitted. "Just a lot of trees."

"Do you smell that?" Pheron suddenly asked, growing tense.

Both Steve and Sarah gently sniffed the air. Sarah's eyes widened. Steve cursed in disgust. A foul odor, reminiscent of rotting garbage, was wafting gently toward them, from the north. That could only mean…

"Trolls!"

"I see movement!" Sarah suddenly told them, spinning around to point north. "That way! I can see two trolls that are … No, better make that three, no four trolls … Uh, oh. That can't be good."

"Still want me to stay in the dark?" Steve asked Pheron. Not waiting for an answer, he ignited both hands. "You guys just need to tell me where to aim."

Half a dozen trolls emerged from the trees and roared their displeasure as they spied the humans and dwarves.

Three of the ugly hairy brutes ran straight toward them. Before Steve could even ignite a chaser, two of the trolls were yanked off their feet and forcibly slammed into each other, sending both monsters straight into unconsciousness. The third leapt over the inert forms of its companions and was headed straight for the three of them. A split second later, the troll screeched in terror as a wall of flames erupted out of thin air and rushed to intercept it. It was all over in less than five seconds.

Steve generated a huge chaser and flung it up into the air, instructing it to hover over the clearing. He gave the remaining trolls the one-fingered salute.

"Who's the next contestant on the Wheel of Pain?"

One troll ripped a huge stump out of the ground and hurled it at them. Sarah used her jhorun and caught the stump in midair. She held the stump in place for a moment or two before she smashed the huge block of wood back into the confused troll, knocking it senseless.

The remaining two trolls roared in unison and advanced. Both trolls slammed on the brakes as two chasers sprang into existence. The two fireballs wasted no time as they sped off after the trolls. The shaggy monsters roared their frustration as they turned and ran, ducking this way and that, shocked to discover they were unsuccessful in eluding the pursuing fireballs. The trolls decided to abandon the attack and retreat to the safety of the trees. True to their namesake, the chasers chased. A few moments later they all heard distant howls of pain, proof that the chasers had finally caught up with their targets.

Still using the light from the overhead chaser, Steve turned to his wife and gave her a high five.

"Nicely done! I loved how you smashed those two together!"

"What about you? You barely blinked and a huge wall of fire appeared and deep fried that one troll."

Realizing they weren't alone, the two of them turned to the other members of their group. Pheron was holding his unsheathed sword in his hand. Breslin, Venk, and Athos were holding their axes, but staring dumbfounded at the empty glade. Not one troll had made it past the husband and wife team.

Steve grinned. "Sorry. Should we have left some?"

Pheron slapped Steve on the back. "You just battled six trolls and you barely broke a sweat! That was incredible!"

The rancid smell returned, and stronger than before. Sarah's eyes snapped close and she quickly spun in place.

"There are more on the way!"

His smile gone, Steve looked at his wife. "How many?"

"At least a dozen."

"This whole battling-monsters-in-the-dark thing sucks." Steve turned to look up at his chaser still burning brightly up in the sky. "That thing isn't giving off nearly enough light. Why don't I just light something on fire so I can see what I'm doing?"

In response, five trolls appeared directly ahead of them.

Steve nudged Pheron in the ribs. "There's some for you. Don't ever say we don't do anything for you."

"Ha ha, Sir Steve. How do you—"

Apparently thinking she'd make an easy meal, one troll broke off from the others and sprinted toward Sarah. An axe whistled through the air, thrown with such precision that Steve instantly envied the thrower. It connected with the troll and knocked it off its feet. The troll slammed into a nearby tree and collapsed to the ground.

Another troll broke from the trees and sprinted toward them. Steve generated a chaser and cocked his arm, ready to throw the fireball. The shaggy monster was making its way toward them, but with so many shadows dancing in and around the trees, tracking the monster became difficult.

This troll, more cautious than the others, moved from tree to tree trying to get closer without making itself a target for the fireball.

"Thirty paces to your right," Pheron told him. "See those two stumps?"

Steve squinted at distant trees.

"No."

"What's it waiting for?" Venk wondered aloud. "They have never been afraid of humans before."

"Could be that," Steve suggested, pointing up at the hovering chaser. "As I'm learning, they really hate fire."

They spied the troll as it cautiously poked its head out from behind a tree thirty feet away. Now it was only twenty feet from Sarah. It was time to sic a chaser on it and hope he didn't light too many trees on fire. Just as he was ready to let the chaser fly, a piercing screech sounded from overhead. Dark blurry objects whooshed by him and attacked the troll. When the blurs finally retreated into the air, the troll was gone.

The other trolls emerged from the safety of the trees and ignored their adversaries on the ground, instead turning to look up at the sky. As soon as the trolls moved out into the open, the dark shapes returned and the other trolls disappeared.

"What happened to them? Where'd they go?" Steve looked at Pheron. "Come on Mr. Night Eyes, what'd you see?"

"Griffins! Dozens and dozens of griffins! They attacked the trolls and carried them off!"

Two thumps sounded behind them. Steve turned, expecting to see two troll pancakes. Instead, he saw two adult griffins standing before them. Griffins and humans stared at one another for a few moments before one of the griffins bowed.

"We meet again, fire thrower."

Steve stared hard at the griffin. "Pheris?"

"I am Phane. We met once before. I was younger then."

Steve whistled. "Wow. You've grown up! What are you guys doing here?"

"It is customary for male griffins to join another flock when they are old enough," Phane explained. "The flock I joined resides on this island."

"Then that's definitely good news for us," Steve commented.

Phane turned to look at the other two humans present.

"Lady Sarah. I remember you well. I am pleased to see you again."

Sarah smiled at the griffin. "It's good to see you, too,

Phane. How's your father?"

"Well, he continues to enjoy his duties as liaison to the humans."

Pheron approached the griffin and bowed. "While not formally acquainted, griffin, I do know of you. You aided the Nohrin while they rescued the queen several years ago, did you not?"

Phane nodded. "Aye."

"You will be pleased to hear your name is mentioned often by your sire. You will never find a griffin prouder of his offspring than Pheris."

At a loss for words, Phane stared at him. The griffin's head finally nodded.

"This is Breslin, son of Maelnar," Steve told the griffin, "and brothers Venk and Athos. They are here helping us."

The dwarves bowed while the griffins nodded back.

Pheron squatted next to Phane and lowered his voice. "You reside on this island? Then you must be familiar with the land. Was there once a former human settlement nearby?"

Phane nodded. He turned to his right and pointed a wing east. "There are remains of several stone dwellings that way."

"How far?"

"Less than a league."

"How long have the trolls been on this island?" Sarah wanted to know.

"This is the first I have seen any of their kind here. It will be the last, I assure you."

The second griffin standing to Phane's left squawked in agreement.

"There's a better than average chance there are more trolls out there," Steve warned. "There's also a human sorceress hiding around here, somewhere. Somehow, and I don't know how, she's found a way to control the trolls. You said what's left of the village is close by? That's probably where we'll find her."

"This sorceress is an enemy?"

Steve, Sarah, and Pheron all nodded.

"Then she is our enemy as well."

Steve squatted next to Pheron and addressed the griffin.

"I appreciate that Phane, I really do, but if you try to help us out, there's a chance you guys can get hurt. Perhaps we should deal with this on our own."

Both griffins squawked angrily. Phane shook his head no. "You warned us. We appreciate it. We will be careful."

Phane looked over at the other griffin and gave a short series of squawks and screeches. That griffin instantly took flight.

"What'd you tell him?" Steve asked.

"To have the cubs moved to a safer locale. And to summon the others. Observe, but do not engage. Besides the three of you, there should be no other humans on this island, correct?"

"Right. Just tell them to be careful," Sarah pleaded. "I don't want anyone to get hurt. Celestia has gone after the dragons before, so I know she won't hesitate to do the same with griffins."

"Your concern is appreciated." Phane leapt up into the air and was gone moments later.

Steve glanced up at the chaser still burning overhead. An instant later it poofed out, plunging the area back into total darkness. Sarah closed her eyes and again used her vision to help her see where she was going. Pheron strode confidently off to his right. The two griffins took off, acknowledging they'd be more help to everyone in the air.

"This really blows," Steve muttered, clutching his wife's arm tightly.

"Would you like a little bit of cheese with your whine?"

"Bite me. I can't see—"

"Watch what you say, potty mouth."

"Squat," Steve finished. "I was going to say squat! Jeez!"

Sarah playfully smacked him on his stomach.

Walking through complete darkness, eyes open as wide as he could get them, Steve scowled to himself. He couldn't bring himself to walk at his normal pace no matter how hard he tried. He knew Sarah would do everything she could to make sure he didn't walk into a tree, but he could tell she was still getting used to the constantly changing perspective of having to watch herself walk from afar. She typically stumbled as soon as she faced another direction, as her vantage point also shifted. It was akin to suddenly walking sideways on a moving treadmill.

"Phane's coming," Sarah announced.

She pulled her husband to a stop. Pheron and the dwarves came to a stop, too. Sure enough, Phane effortlessly glided down to them and landed on the grass.

"Success. We have spotted a human woman and a boy. They are in the ruins of what must have been a large stone structure."

"What were they doing?" Steve asked.

"Was the man resisting?" Pheron asked.

"The woman was seen moving stones around while the man did nothing."

"Did nothing?" Sarah glanced at the captain before returning her gaze to Phane. "Was he moving at all?"

"He was sitting against a wall," Phane told her. "We thought he was unconscious until the woman moved to another room. The sitting man then moved to be with her and proceeded to sit back down."

"She's got him under some type of spell," Steve observed. "Otherwise, he'd be trying to fight her off."

Pheron tapped Phane on his wing to get his attention. "Take us to them. As quickly as you can."

* * *

Celestia let out an exasperated sigh. Why couldn't she find it? Wasn't this the correct house? Wasn't this where she and her sister were born? If so, then their shared room should have been right about … an enormous pile of rubble met her eyes, the result of several walls collapsing inwards. Her eyes narrowed. Their room had been much bigger than this. Celestia's eyes followed the traces of what was left of the walls. This wasn't her old house.

Scowling, she stormed by the prince, but not before she commanded him to follow.

"It must be here. This should have been it."

Celestia thought back to her childhood, however many

centuries ago that was, to when Katar was a thriving village. This section of land had four dwellings. Her parents had their house, there was the former soldier and his mistress, the rich spice merchant from Capily, and the old man who always wore black. Four houses.

Celestia's eyes moved from house to house. They lingered, however, on the last house. She didn't remember that dwelling being quite so large. The ruins were easily twice as large as the rest of the ...

With a smile, Celestia realized her mistake. There weren't four houses, but five. She had forgotten that next to the spice merchant lived a little old lady who had baked fresh bread every day. That meant she was indeed looking at the wrong house. Her parents' house was the third house, which would be—

She spun to her left. There, sitting a few feet away, were the remains of a dwelling she had previously ignored. In her mind's eye, she could still imagine the large two-story structure in its prime. There had been bright colorful flowers decorating the second story windows. The windows and doors were always open. Her mother had never hesitated to open her home to a stranger should the need arise.

Celestia called for Mikal to follow as she entered what was left of her childhood home. Pushing feelings of nostalgia aside, she moved with purpose as she sought out the room she had shared with her sister as a girl. Tucked safely away in her old room, she hoped to find her collection of spell books. She had never bothered to collect them as no one knew of their existence, not even her sister. Once she had them, she could disappear with the prince and wait until he was old enough to marry. By that time, he should be completely infatuated with her. Then, he would be hers to do with as she saw fit.

Her amulet suddenly grew warm. She paled. The Nohrin were getting close! Not now! She hadn't found her books yet!

Desperate to stall the prince's bodyguards while she searched, she summoned the last of the trolls she had under her power. She had brought three dozen of the brutes with her, in case the Nohrin found some way to track her here. She knew the trolls would be no match for the fire thrower and the teleporter, but she didn't care. She just needed more time.

A fireball slammed into her and knocked her off her feet. She would have been horribly burned had it not been for the protective shield, which sprang into existence a split second before the impact. Getting to her feet, she let out a very unladylike curse as she spied the all too familiar Nohrin, followed closely by a third person and three dwarves. Where were those infernal trolls?

Right on cue, trolls began appearing out of the trees. Most had been roused from their slumber and were anxious to find where they could focus their anger. Eager for a nighttime snack, the trolls lurched toward the humans and dwarves, who were slowly backing away.

Bright jets of flame lit up the surrounding area as the Nohrin and their companions attacked the trolls. Howls of pain assaulted her ears, but she ignored them. Verifying the prince was still safely ensconced in her spell, she resumed her search.

Moving assuredly through the ruins, she located her old room and slid several stones away from the farthest corner adjacent to the exterior wall. She carefully lifted up a large flat stone and smiled. Her secret compartment had remained untouched, even after all these years. She reached in and withdrew three books, the first spell books she had ever written. Most of the spells they contained were gibberish, based on the whims of a silly girl and her sister. However, there were a few spells that could, she knew, be modified to become useful. But for that she would also need her journal; it contained the first ever mention of her sister's premonition about the one who could give jhorun: the Bakkian. She was anxious to re-read Caladonia's earliest premonition. Perhaps there was something in there that she could use to her advantage now.

A quick inspection of the dusty compartment revealed the worst: the journal was missing!

Celestia was furious. Who had known about her journal? No one! No one, except maybe…? She rushed through the rest of the ruins, looking for some water. In what was once the kitchen, Celestia found a small pool of rainwater, which had collected in a shallow depression of an enormous stone. She angrily peered into the water.

Her sister was already waiting for her.

Caladonia was smiling. She reached for something that was on her lap and held it up so that Celestia could see it. The journal.

Celestia screamed in frustration.

Mikal stirred. The brief moment in which Celestia had vented her anger had weakened her control over the prince. He was starting to awaken! Celestia hurried over to the boy's still form and invoked the sleep spell once more, hoping to send the boy back to a dreamless state.

Mikal stirred again. He was resisting the effects of the spell. He was fighting her!

Cursing, she yanked up her amulet and clasped it tightly. She chanted the words to return the prince back to a barely conscious state, but again she felt the resistance. The prince was fighting harder!

Before she could summon the full power of the amulet, another fireball spiraled by her and slammed into what was left of the wall directly behind her. Pieces of mortar and rocks rained down. Without thinking, she took a few steps back.

"The prince is mine!" Celestia screamed at the Nohrin as they came into view. "We are destined to be together!"

In response, the fire thrower held up his right arm, palm facing up. A large fireball appeared and instantly streaked toward her.

Still clutching her piece of the amulet, Celestia channeled her amplified jhorun into her protective shield. The hurtling ball of fire collided with the shield and split in two, with both halves continuing past her to smash into the already smoldering stone wall. What was left toppled over into the next room.

Celestia sneered. "Is that the best you can do, fire thrower? You will never—"

The sorceress's rant was cut off in mid-sentence as Mikal appeared next to her, looking very much awake, and slammed his fist into her midsection, causing her breath to whoosh out of her. Celestia doubled over as she now found it difficult to breathe.

Mikal regained his feet. His eyes were clear, but Celestia's enchantment was still strong. It would take some time for the effects of the sleeping spell to wear off. He shuffled forward, intent on joining his bodyguards when a small hand clamped down on his right shoulder. More than anything, the shock of her touch kick-started his senses. Mikal's eyes narrowed. He looked down at his right shoulder and saw her hand.

Without thinking, he grabbed her right hand with his left and pulled her forward, catching her off guard. Off balance, Celestia stumbled forward just as Mikal rammed his elbow backwards into her already sore abdomen. The spell Celestia had been chanting became lost in her wheezes as she once more doubled over.

Mikal dropped to one knee, reached backwards to hook his right hand behind her neck, and bent the sorceress forward, taking her full weight on his shoulder. Just as her weight registered on his back, he lurched forward, sending the sorceress flying through the air to crash heavily on the rock-strewn floor.

Mikal regained his feet and hurried over to Steve and Sarah. Pheron promptly grabbed the prince's arm and shoved him behind all three of them. Clashes and howls sounded nearby as Breslin, Venk, and Athos continued to finish off the last of the trolls outside the ruins.

Celestia rolled painfully to her feet, her face a mask of sheer hatred. Her lips were moving. She had started another chant.

*I need an explosion*, Steve told his jhorun. *Impress me. I need something that'll shut her up! Make it quick!*

He instantly felt his body start to tingle as his jhorun gained in strength. He grabbed his wife's hand and yanked her down. He cast a quick glance backwards at Pheron and Mikal.

"Get down! Quick! Breslin, if you can hear me, look out!"

Sarah, Pheron, and Mikal all dropped like stones and made themselves as flat as possible on the floor.

The tingling Steve felt suddenly turned to biting stings,

causing him to yelp in pain. Knowing what was coming, he cringed and screwed his eyes shut.

The force of the detonation took them all by surprise. Sarah was sure she had lost her hearing. Pheron figured he had broken a rib or two as several large stones bounced off his chest. The three dwarves fortunately heard Steve's warning and dropped instantly to the ground. Mikal was whooping aloud.

"That was so cool!"

Steve opened his eyes and inspected the carnage his blast had created. Where was Celestia? Maybe buried under rubble, like what had happened to the guur queen several years ago? Steve sighed. Unlikely. There was nothing left of the house, not that there had been much to begin with. There had simply not been enough material to conceal anyone. Now there were definitely no more walls. Most of the piles of rubble had also been swept away by the powerful blast. No traces of Celestia could be found.

"There she is," Sarah told him as she regained her feet.

Celestia's protective shield had saved her from being incinerated, but it didn't prevent her from being thrown into the air like a paper doll. She had collapsed to her knees as spasms of pain ripped through her. The sorceress held a hand to her injured side and looked down; it was covered in blood.

She snarled in anger at them. Reaching into her robes to retrieve the amulet, she breathed a sigh of relief as the pendant replenished her jhorun. Her many cuts and bruises slowly disappeared.

"What's going on?" Sarah asked. She didn't know why the sorceress was still kneeling in the soft grass, and she certainly didn't like the way Celestia had started to smirk at them.

Steve cursed. A chaser formed in each hand. "She's using her amulet! She's healing herself! Hurry, we have to end this once and for all!"

Celestia locked eyes with Sarah. The sorceress gave her a knowing smile and vanished just moments before Steve's two chasers went soaring through the space she had just vacated, followed shortly thereafter by the three axes.

Sarah worriedly looked at her husband. "She's going back

to the castle!"

"What? How can you tell?"

"Trust me, woman's intuition! She's going after the king and queen!"

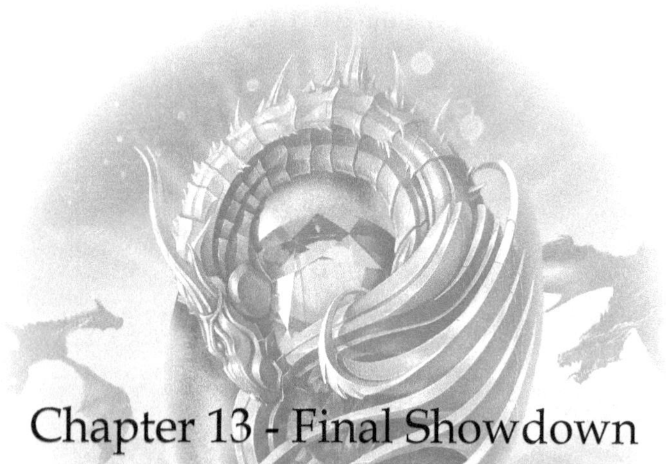

# Chapter 13 - Final Showdown

Sarah grabbed her husband's hand before he could wander off. She cast a quick glance behind her to verify Mikal and Pheron were close. The prince was still trying to shake off the aftereffects of Celestia's spell and was sitting on the ground while the captain hovered nearby.

"Guys! We have to go!"

Pheron pulled Mikal to his feet.

"Can you walk, Your Highness?"

Mikal curled his fingers and rubbed his eyes. "Aye, I can walk."

The teenager spun on his heel and made it about three steps before falling face first onto the grass. Before Pheron could reach his side, Venk and Athos each grabbed the prince by an arm and pulled him to his feet.

"Here, I will carry him," Pheron told the dwarves, slipping his sword back into its scabbard. He took Mikal's right arm and swung the boy over his shoulder.

Sarah hurried over to inspect the boy for injuries. "He's

out cold."

"He's probably sleeping," Steve told her. "Let's just get out of here."

Sarah placed her hand over her husband's and looked up at Pheron. The captain moved his hand, still holding on to Mikal's, over on to Sarah's. Breslin, Venk, and Athos approached and slapped their hands over Pheron's. In the blink of an eye, they were all back standing in the Antechamber.

"Mikal!" The king rushed to Pheron's side but was promptly pushed aside when the queen beat him to it.

"My son! What has she done to him?"

"I think she hit him with some type of sleeping spell," Steve explained. "When he was awake, he was super groggy. He didn't say much."

Kri'Entu placed both hands on his wife's shoulders and steered her to the side. The king checked his son's vitals to verify he was, indeed, sleeping. Relieved, the king looked at the captain.

"Would you please take him to the healers?" Kri'Entu nodded at his wife. "Just to be sure."

"I will stay by his side," the queen assured her husband.

Once his son had been carried out, followed closely by the queen, Kri'Entu turned back to his son's bodyguards. "I cannot thank you enough. Once more you have—"

"Your Majesty?" Steve interrupted. "I'm sorry, but I think we need to save the congratulations for later. We believe Celestia is on her way here!"

The king's gaze swiveled from Steve to Sarah. "How certain?"

"Very," Sarah confirmed. "There was something about the way she looked at me when she realized she lost Mikal. Her expression pretty much said she'd have him again, and that it'd only be a matter of time."

"Not in my lifetime," Kri'Entu angrily vowed.

Sarah shuddered. "You didn't see her face."

"Are you sure?" Steve asked.

"I could see it in her eyes. She already knows how she's going to get him back."

"All that from one glance?"

Sarah shrugged. "What can I say? Women have more expressive body language than men."

The king thoughtfully nodded, unable to argue the point. He looked at the soldiers standing guard inside and singled one of them out.

"Send word to every village constable. They must be prepared. Activate the village militias. In case she has something planned for the villages, I want them protected. Is that clear?"

The guard nodded. "Perfectly, Your Majesty. I will see to it personally."

The king laid a comforting hand on Sarah's shoulder and gently pushed her into a nearby chair as he walked beside her.

"She looks exhausted, Sir Steve. Let her rest."

Bemused, Steve nodded. "You got it. Where's Lia?"

"Much to her chagrin, I sent her to your quarters so that she could rest. She was very reluctant to leave."

"I'll bet."

"I can no longer afford to have any men watch over her," the king informed him.

"Bring her back here," Steve suggested. "We'll keep an eye on her."

"Agreed." Kri'Entu glanced briefly at one of the guards. The young soldier nodded and left.

"He got you, no doubt about it."

Alarmed, Steve turned to observe the dwarves. The three of them were in the midst of an inspection of their armor. Venk was looking at a large dent in Athos' armor.

"Are you injured?"

"No," Athos assured him. "I need new spaulders."

Steve approached.

"Did someone say jhat they're hurt?"

Breslin shook his head. "No, Sir Steve. Athos had his armor dented during the attack. Give him a hammer and he can fix it himself."

"True," Athos confirmed. He looked at his brother. "You might want to look for some tools yourself. You took several blows as well."

Surprised, Venk looked down at his cuirass. His chest

plate could use some touch-up, too.

"Breslin, how is it your armor looks just as pristine now as it did when we departed Borahgg?" Venk wanted to know. "You fought the trolls just as we did. I saw them rain blows upon you! How did your armor remain undamaged?"

Breslin shrugged. "Just lucky. This armor has been in my family for years."

Sarah sighed heavily as she leaned back into the plush chair. She closed her eyes. A vision instantly formed. This time she was looking at the castle through the West Gate.

"Oh, great," Sarah muttered, keeping her eyes closed. "Here we go again. I'm looking at another vision."

"What do you see?" Steve asked her, sinking down into the chair next to hers.

"This castle, but from outside, as if I'm looking through the West Gate."

"Normal vision or is it showing you the daytime version again?"

"It's another daytime vision. If this is going to happen every time I close my eyes then—"

Sarah gasped with surprise as her vision suddenly zoomed north. She watched, mesmerized, as the image deftly skimmed along the treetops and even swerved to the left to avoid several griffins who were trying to outperform one another with daring feats of aerial acrobatics. Sarah found herself leaning to the left, in time with her vision, as she *sped* by the frolicking griffins.

Steve knelt down in front of her and put a hand over hers. "What's going on? What do you see?"

"This is new. My vision is moving. At the moment I'm skimming over a sea of treetops, heading north."

Just as suddenly as it started, the vision came to a stop. Unsurprisingly, she was looking at more trees.

"What's with all the trees?" Sarah wondered aloud. "What's the point of—"

In her vision, several trees had started swaying back and forth, as though something was shaking the trunks. Sarah gasped with alarm as she caught sight of trolls. Hundreds of them. They were pushing through the trees as though it was too inconvenient to walk around them. They were all marching south. Straight toward them.

"Trolls!"

The king had been busy giving orders to various people as they started arriving for their orders. At the mention of trolls, the king paused in mid-sentence and glanced over at her.

"How many? Can you tell where they are?"

"There are hundreds of them," Sarah told him, her eyes still closed. "And I don't know exactly where I am, only that I'm north of the castle. If I were guessing, I'd say at least five miles away, maybe ten. At the rate the trolls are moving, I'd say they'll be here in a few hours."

The door opened and Lia was escorted in. She smiled at her friends and instantly joined Steve at Sarah's side.

Sarah gasped as her vision was yanked away again, this time heading east. Several miles from the trolls, also moving south, were creatures so vile and disgusting that she opened her eyes and practically jumped out of her chair. Since Steve was standing in front of her, the only thing she accomplished was to nearly knock him over. Steve gently lowered her back down.

"Whoa, it's okay. What happened? What did you see?"

Sarah shuddered. "Something big. Something scary. Taller than us. It reminded me of that demon thing from when the queen was kidnapped, only it was a different color. It was horrible!"

"The thing Pryllan smashed into goo?" Steve asked.

Sarah nodded.

"Was the creature taller than a man?" Kri'Entu asked her, already knowing the answer. "Heavily muscled, white matted fur, two tusks in its lower jaw, and a single horn on its skull?"

Wordlessly, Sarah nodded.

"What is it?" Steve asked, turning to the king. "What'd she see?"

"A theron. An ancient creature that typically dwells deep beneath the earth. They usually band together and live in tribes consisting of ten to twelve females, and one male."

Steve nodded. "Reminds me of lions."

Sarah's eyes snapped open and she turned to give her husband a derisive glare. "Really? Really? These are *nothing* like lions."

"How many?" the king asked, hoping the numbers would be low.

"At least a hundred," Sarah told the king, closing her eyes again. "Probably more."

"Course?"

"South. They're heading straight here."

Steve shook his head. "Figures."

"I can see—no wait, here we go again. Now I'm heading west. This is really getting old. I want to … okay, I've stopped. I'd say I'm about ten miles or so from where those malwerns are."

"The first time you stopped you saw trolls," Steve recalled. "The second was those theron things. Do I want to know what you see this time?"

Sarah was silent as she watched the image. She hadn't seen anything notable yet. The only thing she could tell was that she was watching an empty glade. A small creek was visible, snaking its way through the tall grass, before it disappeared into the trees.

"Nothing. Everything is quiet. I'm looking at a clearing. There's a little stream going through the middle of it, but aside from that there's—" Sarah trailed off as she saw a creature sitting in one of the trees ringing the clearing. A careful inspection of the trees revealed that the creatures were everywhere. As for what they were, Sarah unfortunately knew with absolute certainty that it wasn't good: she and her husband had been attacked by them in her world. She was looking at malwerns.

The ugly gray winged monkeys were sitting in every available branch of every tree she could see. Sarah thanked her lucky stars the vision didn't include the audio portion of the program, as she saw several of the creatures opening their mouths, presumably to start their ear-shattering shrieks.

The clearing exploded with movement as hundreds of the unpleasant creatures took flight. High overhead, the writhing mass of winged monsters hesitated a few moments before moving off. South.

About ready to open her eyes in the hopes that the vision would leave her alone, something happened that caused Sarah to leap back out of her chair in alarm. For the first time ever, Sarah heard a voice. A female voice.

*Prepare thyself, Nohrin. Protect the prince.*

It was Caladonia. Sarah was sure of it. She wasn't sure how a sorceress who had been dead for centuries would be able to project her voice hundreds of years into the future, but then again, if Caladonia could observe them by looking through a reflection in the water, anything was possible. The vision faded, leaving Sarah feeling alone and empty.

"It was Caladonia," Sarah told them as she opened her eyes and then looked down. Steve was flat on his back staring up at her. Why was her husband on the floor?

"What are you doing down there?"

"Excuse me? You're the one who jumped up and bowled me over!"

"Hmmph. Thought it would take more than that to knock you over. My mistake."

Lia grinned and gave Sarah a high-five. "That's what I'm talking about!" Suffering an uncharacteristic moment of remorse, Lia pulled Steve to his feet.

"You okay?" she quietly asked him.

Steve nodded. "Yeah, thanks." He turned to his wife, confused. "Sarcastic comment aside, you said you saw Caladonia in the clearing? What was she doing there?"

Sarah laughed. "No, you goof, I mean Caladonia was the one who showed me what's heading this way. Jeez. Really?"

Steve shrugged, as if to say stranger things could happen.

"There are malwerns in the clearing. *Were* malwerns in the clearing," Sarah hastily corrected. "They are all in the air now and headed this way."

"Of course they are," Steve muttered. "Why not? The more the merrier, right?"

"I heard her."

"Who?"

"Caladonia. I *heard* her. She spoke to me. She told me to prepare myself and to protect the prince. Then the image faded out."

"If you have a chance to communicate with Caladonia again," Kri'Entu said, rising to his feet, "then please express my gratitude for her warning. She is right. The castle must be ready for their arrival."

The king motioned for the guards to come over.

"I want your commanding officer to report to me at once. Commander Rhenyon is indisposed, so find out who—"

The Antechamber's doors opened and three more soldiers appeared. One had a very familiar face. Steve was on his feet in a flash.

"Rhenyon! We were just wondering how you were doing. How the hell are ya, buddy?"

"Better. You have my thanks. Here, I was told to give this to you."

The commander returned the tiny vial of healing elixir to Steve, who in turn handed it to his wife. After it was safely stowed back in Sarah's medallion, Rhenyon turned to the king.

"Reporting for duty, Your Majesty."

"Fortuitous timing, Commander. Alert your men. Unspeakable dangers are headed this way. Trolls, malwerns, even therons. You must protect the people. Have all non-essential personnel evacuated to the castle. The catacombs below are extensive. Guide the people there. Go door to door if you must. You must account for everyone."

Rhenyon nodded. "Aye, sire." He turned and beckoned to one of the men who had arrived with him. The commander relayed the orders and then watched the young guard rush off.

"Three different species, all headed south." The king turned to look at the commander. "How long will it take to evacuate R'Tal?"

"Less than an hour to get the townspeople inside and perhaps an additional hour for the villagers living outside the city. To verify everyone has been accounted for could take another two to three hours. Less, if we hurry."

"See to it personally, Commander," Kri'Entu told him. "Homes can be rebuilt. Crops can be replaced. Our people cannot."

"Have you guys fought therons before?" Steve asked Rhenyon. "How do you fight something so much bigger than you are?"

"With care, Sir Steve," Rhenyon answered. "Believe it or not, that's not what concerns me. It's the malwerns. They will pose a much greater challenge."

"How do you fight those things?" Steve wanted to know. "With earplugs?"

"In a matter of speaking, aye," Rhenyon admitted. "Shardwyn will have to administer something to our ears before we can hope to face the malwerns. The problem I'm foreseeing is, in order to address the malwerns, we will—in essence—be deaf. That is, until an antidote is applied."

"You're gonna be in trouble if you need to tell someone what to do," Steve pointed out. "How will you communicate?"

"With hand signals."

"You do know that malwerns are highly flammable, don't you?"

Rhenyon nodded. "Of course."

"So, I assume the best defense is the most effective offense? What do you use, flaming arrows?"

Rhenyon shook his head. "Flaming arrows are only used out in the open. There are houses all around us, Sir Steve. We cannot run the risk of setting any dwellings on fire."

"But the malwerns will burn up before they hit the ground!" Steve protested, not understanding why the soldiers would choose to not utilize a very effective method of neutralizing the paralysis-inducing monsters. "As long as you hit them, you should be fine, right?"

"And if someone misses? What if a flaming arrow lands on a roof?"

"Okay, okay, I can see your point. It's just too bad that—"

Steve trailed off as he spotted Lia quietly admiring one of the many tapestries hanging in the Antechamber.

"Lia!"

Lia's head whipped around. "What? I wasn't doing anything."

"Didn't say that you were. Wow. Take it down a notch. I have a question for you."

Surprised, Lia wandered over.

"What can I do for you fine gents?"

Steve raised an eyebrow.

"Don't ruin the moment. What's your question?"

"You can juggle, right?"

Lia scowled. "Just had to bring that up again, didn't you?"

"No, that's not what I mean. You can juggle, which means you can raise objects into the air. How high?"

"How high?" Lia repeated, puzzled. "You know what? I really don't know. That's a good question. Why?"

Steve pointed to the ever-present bowl of fruit on the king's desk. "If you had something the size of one of those fruits over there, and it was on fire, do you think you could hit something flying through the air?"

"Are you referring to whatever it is that's headed this way?"

"One group of them, yes. The malwerns. They really should be renamed *shriekers*, but that's neither here nor there. If you could hear them, then you'd know what I mean by that."

Sensing an opportunity to make herself useful, Lia cracked her knuckles.

"Betcha I could."

Rhenyon looked at her. "Are you certain, milady? If we were to provide you with a supply of burning embers, does your jhorun provide enough accuracy to hit a moving target?"

"There's only one way to find out," Lia told him.

A thought occurred. Steve turned back to Lia. "The better question would be, if you saw something falling toward the ground, and it was burning, could you either stop it or else cause it to land somewhere else?"

Rhenyon nodded. "Excellent question. If you saw a flaming arrow miss its target, then could you prevent it from setting a roof on fire?"

"Jeez, no pressure guys. I can't believe I'm going to say this, but I *just* learned how to juggle, alright? To tell you the truth, I don't know. However, I will tell you this. Give me a chance to help out and I'll do my best."

Rhenyon turned to Steve. "You have a very courageous

friend, Sir Steve. She honors your world with her bravery."

Beaming, Lia batted her eyes at Rhenyon while Steve rolled his.

"Puh-lease."

Sarah raised her hand. "I have a question. Wouldn't it be safer if Lia and Mikal were just sent back through the portal to our world?"

Lia's smile vanished as she stared accusingly at her friend. "Sarah! What the hell!"

Sarah swatted her husband on the arm to silence his laughing.

"It'd be for your own safety," she explained to Lia, who now had her hands on her hips.

"I finally get a chance to help out and you want to take that away from me? I don't think so!"

"If I may intervene?"

Lia and Sarah turned to the king.

"As much as I would like to send my son back to the Nohrin's home world," Kri'Entu told them, "I cannot. Our portals are off limits until we can verify they have not been tampered with. With regret, Mikal remains here. As such, Lady Lia as well."

Lia pumped her fist in the air. "Woo-hoo! I get to stay!"

"Just promise me you'll be careful," Sarah told her.

Lia drew an X over her heart. "Cross my heart!"

She gave a victorious thumbs-up to her friends as she followed Rhenyon out of the Antechamber.

"So, what can we do?" Steve asked the king. He jammed his hands in his pockets. "There's gotta be something that we can lend a hand with."

The king nodded. "There is. If the two of you would kindly assume your duties, I would be forever in your debt."

"Assume our duties?" Steve repeated, frowning. "What do you mean by that?"

Sarah smiled. "He wants us to stay with Mikal."

Kri'Entu nodded. "I do not think anything will happen to my son if he stays in your presence."

Steve opened his mouth, about to protest, when Sarah deliberately stepped in front of him. She addressed the king.

"It's no problem. We'll stay put."

"My thanks. I have to see to—"

The king trailed off as he cocked his head. They all heard it: shouting. Lots of it.

Two arms appeared on either side of Sarah and physically picked her up. Steve spun in place and deposited Sarah directly behind him. Both of his hands had turned dark red.

"Does anyone else hear that?" Steve asked, looking at his wife. "I hear a ringing in my ears."

"Me, too," Sarah admitted, her eyes opening wide. "It's those creepy monkey things. They're already here, aren't they?"

"How'd they get here so damn quick?" Steve demanded. "You just saw them in the vision a little bit ago, right?"

Sarah nodded. "Apparently they can fly faster than I gave them credit for."

Kri'Entu beckoned to one of the two remaining guards. "Find my son and the queen. Escort both here immediately. Carry him here if he cannot walk."

The guard bowed and departed instantly.

The king pulled a small gold device resembling a pocket watch from within his robes. He tapped the surface three times.

There was a light popping sound, like the first tentative pops from a bag of microwave popcorn. Seconds later, Shardwyn appeared in the room with them.

"The malwerns have arrived," the king told him. "If ever there was a time to impress me, Shardwyn, this is it. Our people have not had adequate time to evacuate to the castle. Facilitate the evacuation using whatever means necessary."

"I will, Your Majesty." Shardwyn vanished just as quickly as he had appeared.

Four soldiers arrived, followed closely by the queen, the prince, and four more soldiers. Mikal was on his feet and definitely looking more alert than the last time they'd seen him.

"Entu, what is happening?" Ny'Callé released Mikal's arm and covered both of her ears. "Are we under attack?"

Mikal covered his ears, too.

"Are your ears ringing?" Steve asked him, rubbing his own ears.

Mikal nodded yes.

"Mine, too. Remember the Grand Canyon? Remember the shrieks and screams? Those things that made them are getting closer. You're going to need to stay in here, sport."

Sarah cleared her throat. "Um, that's for his parents to decide."

"Oh, yeah, sorry. Your call, Your Majesty."

Kri'Entu smiled. "I agree with your call, Sir Steve. Mikal, you will remain here with your mother."

"Still want me to stay in here?" Steve asked as he ignited both hands. A chaser formed and then was tossed from hand to hand, like a baseball.

The king's gaze fell back on Steve, his face hardening. Steve's smile faded.

"Without a doubt. Protect them."

Steve's chaser poofed out. Dejected, he sank down into the nearest seat. The king departed, taking the soldiers with him. Steve let out a sigh.

"Welcome to my world," Mikal smirked.

Sarah giggled and tried to disguise it as a series of coughs. The queen smiled and looked away.

Irked, Steve leaned back in his chair. Within moments he was scowling. "Let me get this straight. The castle is under attack by a group of those ugly malwerns. The archers are unable to hit them with any amount of accuracy and the—"

"Not true," Sarah corrected him, waggling her finger. "They can hit them, but since flaming arrows work the best, and they won't risk burning the town down, that's not a feasible option."

"Right. Whatever. And the *one* guy who'd be perfect for taking them out is stuck here, sitting on his butt. Does that about sum it up?"

"You forgot to mention Lia is out there battling the malwerns," Sarah helpfully added.

"Don't remind me."

Thirty minutes later, the door to the room burst open and three soldiers hurried in, completely out of breath.

"What is it?" the queen worriedly asked, rising to her feet. "What has happened? Has something happened to the king?"

In an overly loud voice, the first soldier to enter the room addressed the queen. "YOUR MAJESTY! TROLLS HAVE BEEN SIGHTED IN THE CITY! YOU MUST NOT LEAVE THIS ROOM FOR ANY REASON! KING'S ORDERS! WE ARE HERE TO SEE TO YOUR SAFETY!"

Steve got to his feet. "There's no need to shout. We heard you just fine."

"Shardwyn's probably taken his hearing," Sarah pointed out.

"MIKAL!" The queen's sharp exclamation caused everyone to jump, except those who were auditorily impaired. "What are you doing? Sit back down here this instant!"

Mikal shook his head. "No. I'm going to help."

"You are most certainly not! I forbid it!"

Mikal squatted down and took his mother's hands in his own.

"This is all happening because of me. Celestia wants me and will not let the matter drop until she gets her way. Hundreds of lives are at stake, Mother. Hundreds! How can you not expect me to fight alongside my countrymen?"

Recognizing the determination in her son's eyes, Callé turned to the husband and wife team. "Please," she implored, her eyes filling. "Talk him out of this. Do not let him go outside!"

Sarah squatted down next to the queen and laid a comforting hand on her arm.

"I don't think he'd stay in here even if we told him to stay put, either. I think he'd find a way to sneak out."

"I would," Mikal agreed.

"Look at it this way," Steve reasoned as he squatted down next to his wife. "If the outcome is that Mikal's going to go outside with or without permission, then at least in this manner we can accompany him to make sure he stays safe."

Mikal smiled victoriously and was instantly met with frowns from all three of them. Steve's face was grim.

"Wipe that look off your face, pal. No one here agrees with this. But, you're old enough to start making these kinds of decisions yourself. I just hope you've thought this through."

Mikal's smile faded away. Solemnly he nodded. "I have. I want to fight."

"Then we need to get Shardwyn in here."

Composing herself, the queen rose from her seat and smoothed out her dress. She walked over to the king's desk and opened a side drawer. Shifting a pile of papers out of the way she pulled out a black velvet pouch. She handed it to Steve.

"Use this. It is a twin to the one my husband carries. It will summon Shardwyn."

Steve opened the pouch and held it upside down over his hand. A replica of the king's device tumbled into his hand. Mimicking the gesture he had seen the king do, he tapped the gold-colored gizmo three times. Shardwyn appeared instantly.

"You called? I still think that I can—"

The wizard trailed off as he noticed the king wasn't present. Confused, he turned to Steve, who was still holding the wizard summoner.

"What are you doing with that? That charm belongs to the king."

"He's preoccupied. Listen, we have to go outside, but before we do, I need you to—"

"Go outside?" Shardwyn interrupted, frowning. "You cannot face those abominations until I apply my salve."

Steve rolled his eyes. "You don't say? Well, do your thing."

Shardwyn reached into his robes and withdrew a small blue jar with a black lid. Removing the lid, he dipped a finger into the gelatinous white goop and without preamble, poked his finger into Steve's ear. A dollop the size of a pea was deposited just inside his ear. Shardwyn repeated the process with Sarah and Mikal before he finally sealed his jar and it disappeared back into his robes.

"NOW WHAT?" Steve practically shouted as he looked at the wizard. "HOW LONG BEFORE IT STARTS TO WORK?"

The queen winced and covered her ears.

Surprised, and in a much quieter voice, Steve addressed

Shardwyn. "It's already working, isn't it?"

The wizard nodded.

"This is so weird. I can't hear myself talk. No wonder the guard was shouting."

Sarah looked at him. "WHAT?"

Steve shook his head. It wasn't important.

"Everyone deaf?"

Sarah and Mikal looked at him with blank expressions.

"I'll take that as a yes. Okay then. Let's see. Jhorun charged? Check. More mimets in case I need 'em?" Steve patted Mythrin's scabbard, assured by the presence of at least ten fully charged power crystals. "Check. Hearing gone? Totally."

Mikal's bodyguards watched as the prince kissed his mother goodbye and then together, they ran for the door. They had just made it past the kitchens when Steve stumbled for the third time. Sarah looked over at him and gave him a worried look.

Steve shook his head. He was okay. Scowling down at his feet, as though they alone were responsible for tripping him up, he broke into a run. Trying to run when you couldn't hear your own footfalls was proving to be more difficult than he imagined. His mind felt fuddled, almost like he was experiencing one of those dreams where he couldn't talk or move.

As they exited the castle, Steve looked up just in time to see two malwerns fly overhead. One of the ugly gray monsters caught sight of the three of them and swooped down low to investigate. Its mouth opened, revealing pointed needle-sharp teeth.

He heard a faint buzzing in his ears. Apparently the malwern's screech was powerful enough to penetrate his deafened ears. A quick glance at his wife and Mikal verified that they, too, could hear the buzzing noise.

He ignited his right hand and blasted a jet of fire at the screeching monster. Not expecting a plume of flames to materialize out of thin air, the malwern's black eyes opened wide with surprise before it got hit square in the chest. Only a few specks of ash made it to the ground before blowing away in the wind.

Another malwern appeared. This one landed on the roof of a nearby building. It looked straight at him and opened its mouth. Sure enough, the buzzing returned. Steve glared at the ugly winged monkey. It was within range of a fire jet, but now that it was staring at him, it would more than likely fly away before the jet could reach it.

He pulled the Nohrstaf free from its harness on Mythrin's scabbard and handed the shapeshifting weapon to Mikal. The teen's eyes lit up with surprise. Delighted to be trusted with such a powerful weapon, Mikal nodded his thanks.

Steve tapped Mikal's chest and then pointed at the malwern sitting fifty feet away. He then tapped the Nohrstaf. Nodding, Mikal looked down at the ugly little club and waited. Sure enough, the club changed into a short bow sans bowstring. Confused, Mikal looked at Steve for guidance. Steve drew back on an imaginary bow, like he was ready to fire an arrow. More confused than ever, Mikal repeated the movements, pretending that the bow had been strung. A shimmering line appeared, right where the bowstring should be. As soon as he pulled back on the string, an arrow composed of silver light appeared.

Mikal grinned. All those video games he had played with Steve and Tristan suddenly came back to him. He sighted along the arrow and targeted the screeching malwern. He released the string and watched, mesmerized, as the malwern disappeared into a poof of silver light.

Grinning, Steve gave Mikal a congratulatory slap on the back. Mikal targeted the next malwern he could see and brought it down in a puff of light. Encouraged, he scanned the skies, looking for his next target.

Steve nodded. Good. No more buzzing. That had to mean there weren't any more of the little buggars anywhere close, so they should really start looking for—

The buzzing returned and within moments, a headache formed. What was going on? Why wasn't Shardwyn's goop working? Steve sighed. It probably was. That's how strong the malwern's screeches were.

Wanting more light, Steve ignited a large chaser and flung

it upwards. There had to be more in the area. All he needed was to see enough to know where to shoot. The enormous fireball flew upwards and hovered twenty feet in the air.

Properly illuminated, Steve scanned the surrounding rooftops. Well, that explained the buzzing and headaches they were plaguing them. Steve grunted with annoyance.

At least a dozen malwerns were squatting on the rooftops of nearby buildings. There were several others clinging precariously to the sides of the soldier barracks. There were even three or four spiraling overhead. All were looking straight at them and all had their mouths open. One of the malwerns disappeared in a flash of silver light.

Mikal pulled back on the string and another arrow appeared. He sighted the next malwern and fired. He managed two more shots before the winged monsters took to the air. However, a split second later, two empty carts, the type vendors would use to display their wares, smashed into a group of the winged gray monkeys, silencing them all instantly. The broken carts then moved several feet to the right and smashed into the next group. All in all, Sarah was able to smash close to a dozen of the malwerns before they fled the scene. Steve ignited the remains in the air so that no one was grossed out by the falling goo that just moments ago had been recognizable as malwerns. Three of the creatures stayed behind to try their luck with their screams, but ended up being taken out by Mikal and the Nohrstaf.

Steve's eyes were drawn to one of the rooftops. One set of remains he had ignited had fallen onto a thatched roof and within moments, the fire was spreading rapidly along the dry roof. Steve extended his jhorun to the spreading flames and pulled the energy inwards. The flames poofed out within seconds. Steve continued to absorb the energy until nothing remained. No fire, no embers, no problem!

Sarah tapped his shoulder and pointed over at the barracks. There was a group of soldiers slowly getting to their feet. Steve and Sarah trotted over while Mikal continued to search the skies for potential targets.

"You guys okay? Crap. I forgot, you can't hear me, either."

Steve pulled the last soldier to his feet. It was Darius!

He and the soldier clasped forearms. Steve gave him the questioning thumbs up signal. Darius nodded.

Three of the gray winged monkeys flew by overhead. Steve threw two chasers the same time Mikal released an arrow. The malwerns vanished in twin bursts of fire as well as a pulse of silver light.

Sarah pointed at a young soldier. Steve took an arrow from his quiver, lit it on fire, and gave it back to the soldier. He pointed up at the sky. The soldier nodded. Others saw what they were doing and immediately copied him. Within moments, dozens of malwerns were lighting up the sky as they disappeared into the flames.

For the next twenty minutes Steve and Sarah watched as many of the nasty, shrieking monsters were turned into ash. The small group of soldiers they were with had incredible archery skills, no doubt about it. However, trying to hit a moving target in the dark of night meant Steve had his hands full torching errant arrows while Sarah redirected hers at stone buildings, the cobbled streets, and even suspended several in the air until Steve could extinguish them. Several of the flaming projectiles managed to find their way to a couple of rooftops which promptly went up in flames. Thankfully the fires were spotted and extinguished long before they could spread to the neighboring buildings.

A flash of light caught Sarah's attention. Had someone else managed to take out one of the malwerns? How'd they do it? Who was responsible? Two more bursts of light appeared briefly and then vanished just as suddenly as two more malwerns vanished.

Sarah caught her husband's attention and pointed west. Steve looked just in time to see three more rapid flashes. He tapped Darius on his shoulder and pointed left.

With flaming arrows drawn, the soldiers slowly followed the Nohrin and the prince as they hurried across the courtyard toward the flashes that kept appearing every couple of seconds.

Something slammed into Steve's back and drove him face first into the hard ground. It felt like a four-hundred-pound sumo wrestler had just tackled him from behind. Grunting painfully, Steve rolled onto his back and took a couple of deep breaths. Sensing movement nearby, Steve glanced to his left and saw that Darius and several of the soldiers had drawn their swords and were trying to drive off three malwerns who were flying circles around Sarah. Concerned and angry, Steve readied a blast that he figured should eliminate all three malwerns simultaneously. However, before he could, Sarah had grabbed her amulet and waved her arm in a large circular motion. The three malwerns were forcefully smashed together and then were flung far out into town.

Darius' concerned face appeared and stared down at him. He offered Steve an arm up. The lieutenant's mouth was moving incredibly fast, no doubt cursing out the winged monsters. Darius tapped his chest then tapped Steve's, concern still evident on his face.

Steve held up his hands. *What? Don't worry about it. I'm okay.*

Darius shook his head and again tapped his own chest, and then he unsheathed his sword.

Steve raised an eyebrow. *So?*

Sarah approached and mouthed two words to him: *YOUR SWORD!*

Alarmed, Steve glanced down at his chest. His baldric! It was missing! Those nasty malwerns had ripped Mythrin right off his chest! A quick glance at his companions verified his was the only sword missing. Why was his weapon the only one targeted? He fervently hoped the baldric had simply broken and it had fallen to the ground.

Concerned that he wouldn't be able to replenish his tiring jhorun, Steve dropped his eyes to the ground and started searching for his weapon. Of all the rotten luck!

Sarah tugged on his arm. Once he finally glanced up, she turned and pointed up at the sky. Steve's eyes widened. The malwerns had taken his sword?

Watching Steve's face closely, Sarah nodded.

Steve paled. If Mythrin had indeed been taken, that meant his supply of mimets had also been taken, which meant … Steve angrily shook his head. It meant Celestia knew about his mimets and wanted to be certain once he depleted his jhorun, it would stay that way.

The soldiers formed a protective ring around the Nohrin and Mikal as they carefully traversed the large courtyard. They came to an abrupt halt as the origin of the other flashes of light was revealed: Lia. The manager of the Cookbook Nook was crouched next to a makeshift fire while four or five soldiers frantically searched for small pieces of wood, coal, essentially anything that would burn. One of the guards gave her the signal. Lia flung her arms up into the air just as the malwerns zipped by overhead. The embers flew, inevitably making contact with one—or more—of the foul creatures, and then they'd be rewarded with more bursts of light overhead.

Lia gave the soldier closest to her a high five. More chunks of wood were shoveled into the hearth. Several more flaming objects were selected and Lia waited for the next signal. It was then that she looked up and spotted Steve and Sarah.

As the next group streaked by, Lia repeated the arm gesture from before and the three burning embers sped straight up, again colliding with three unsuspecting malwerns. Three more bright flares appeared and moments later they were all dusting off the remains of the creatures.

Lia looked back at Steve and smiled smugly.

*Top that*, her eyes challenged.

Steve shook his head no. He had to conserve what little jhorun he had left.

Dismayed, they watched as more and more of the malwerns appeared in the skies. Dozens of them. Hundreds. They were landing on buildings and ripping out large chunks of thatched roofing. They were picking up anything they could carry and flinging it at nearby buildings: windows were broken, doors were smashed, and holes were punched through roofs.

The lack of suitable victims to terrorize was driving the malwerns into a frenzy. What good was it to have the ability to paralyze when there were no living creatures to torment? From house to house they flew, ripping, shredding, and destroying whatever they found. Since the denizens of the city were now hiding in the caves beneath the castle, no townsfolk could be found. So the monsters did the next best thing they could: take their anger out on any inanimate object they could get their hands on.

Complicating matters, an official messenger appeared, clutching a handful of sealed envelopes. One was handed to Darius.

*Trolls have been sighted. Use whatever means necessary.*

The young lieutenant handed Steve the order and worriedly looked west, through the gate, at the houses lining the streets. His face grim, Darius turned to one of the soldiers and pointed up at the portcullis above their heads. He slid a finger across his neck. The soldier nodded and ducked into the doorway just to their left. Moments later the heavy iron grate came crashing down, sealing off access to the town outside.

Steve and Sarah both jumped with surprise as a bright flash of light appeared behind them and then streaked past, soaring high over their heads. Tracing the object back to its starting point, Steve spotted a trebuchet. He watched as a team of three men adjusted the aim and reloaded. Four more stone hurlers were rapidly assembled, complete with squadrons of archers to protect them. Each one targeted a different direction. The last trebuchet to be assembled had wheels on its base and was therefore able to be repositioned much easier than the others.

Steve suddenly smiled. An idea had just come to him. He turned to Lia and beckoned her closer.

*You stay with them,* he mouthed to her, pointing at the soldiers. He then pointed at the trebuchet on wheels. *Meet us there. Five minutes, got it?*

Lia crossed her arms over her chest. *Seriously?*

Steve vigorously nodded and motioned for Sarah and Mikal to follow him. Together they ran toward the castle. Running as fast as they could, they sprinted by the guards protecting the main entrance and wove around the many peasants running through the halls. A dozen knights in full armor appeared directly in his path. Sarah and Mikal slid to a stop and watched as Steve went into a slide as he tried to do the same. His only saving grace was that the three knights he managed to take down didn't fall on him.

One of the knights grabbed Steve by his left arm and pulled him to his feet. The knight clearly retained his hearing as he turned to his companion and said something. The second knight straightened as he looked hard at Steve. Then they spotted Mikal and both knights bowed.

Realizing he could use more hands for what he was preparing to do, Steve looked at the three knights and motioned them to follow along. The knights hesitated as they looked at one another. Steve reached out and tapped a knuckle on each of their breast plates and again indicated they should follow. The knight who had helped Steve to his feet said something to the others and they turned to follow them to the kitchens.

The king's personal chef was still present, along with several serving girls. The girls were cowering behind stacks of empty cauldrons while the cook bravely wielded the biggest knife he could find. Recognizing the knights for who they were, the cook visually relaxed. He approached one of the knights and said something, presumably asking him what he needed.

Hoping that his voice still worked, even though he couldn't hear it, Steve relayed to the knight exactly what he was looking for. Baffled, the knight turned back to the chef and repeated his request. Incredulous, the chef hurried over to one of the storerooms and pointed at a large number of heavy sacks. Steve nodded. Perfect. Sarah tapped him on the shoulder. She gave him a questioning look. *You sure about this?*

Steve nodded. He ran over to the pile and slung a sack over his shoulder. He motioned for the soldiers to grab as much as they could and to follow him. Mikal went to grab a sack when Sarah shook her head no. She tapped the Nohrstaf, which was still in 'bow' form. Mikal nodded. He would continue to provide cover.

Doing as they were bid, the first knight leaned down to grab a sack. He instructed the others to follow his lead. Sarah watched as each knight picked up a sack of flour. She tapped

Steve's shoulder and pointed at the rest of the two dozen sacks still stacked neatly in a pile.

*Do you want all of them?*

Steve nodded. Sarah then pulled up her amulet piece and held it in her hand. All twenty- four sacks silently rose into the air. Nodding his head appreciatively, Steve led the procession back outside where Darius and the soldiers were waiting by the trebuchet.

Steve approached the large wooden contraption and looked at the huge jug of pitch sitting in the sling, ready to be lit. He shook his head no and pointed to one of the sacks. Skeptical, one of the soldiers removed the jug and replaced it with a sack. Two soldiers nocked arrows and waited for Steve to light the tips. Steve shook his head no and pointed at a nearby torch. When everyone was ready, he pointed at a section of town several hundred feet away that had malwerns and trolls alike rampaging through the streets.

Darius gave the signal. *Fire!*

The soldiers shrugged. The release handle was pulled and the counterweight dropped. The arm whipped out, hurling the sack at the distant street. Unable to hear the impact, or see exactly where the sack had hit, Steve had to assume there was now an airborne cloud of flour particles somewhere in that direction. He looked at the archers. *Fire!*

The men looked at their lieutenant. Darius cuffed one soldier on the back of his head and angrily indicated they were to do as they were bid.

Two flaming arrows were released. Twin fire trails streaked across town and disappeared as the arrows shattered upon impacting several stone walls.

Steve angrily pointed back toward town. *Fire again!*

As soon as the second set of arrows smacked into the cobbled street, only a few feet away from where the sack had burst open, several sparks finally introduced themselves to the highly explosive cloud of flour dust. The street lit up as though several sticks of dynamite had been detonated. Windows were shattered, trees were snapped off at the trunks, and more importantly, dozens of malwerns went up in flames. The howls of the trolls were heard by everyone in the kingdom who hadn't been rendered deaf.

Lia smiled and gave Steve a high-five. She turned to the closest soldier within reach, smacked him on the shoulder to get his attention, and pointed at the next sack.

The soldier looked at Darius for confirmation, worry evident on his face. Darius nodded and urged his men to hurry. The next sack was loaded. The lieutenant pointed at another section of the same street but farther away. The trebuchet was rotated a few degrees and the counterweight was raised a little higher to accommodate the greater distance. Two archers lit their arrows and signaled they were ready.

Darius raised his arm and looked back at Steve, who nodded. The signal was given and the sack was flung several hundred feet away. The arrows followed seconds later.

The explosion effectively cleared the street of all abandoned vendor carts, signs, low lying shrubs, and the like. It also eliminated another dozen or so malwerns both on the ground and in the air. Steve couldn't tell if they had managed to take out any trolls.

He nudged Darius and pointed northwest. A dark pulsating mass of creatures was moving their way. Malwerns, at least a hundred of them.

Two sacks suddenly rose unassisted into the air and were flung at the writhing horde of malwerns. Just before the sacks disappeared into the darkness, they burst open as though they had been slit down the middle. A streak of silver light flashed by and the entire night sky lit up in the massive explosion. When the flames eventually tapered off, there was nothing left to even indicate that over a hundred malwerns had previously been swarming about in the air. The townsfolk were going to wonder why, on the following day, it looked as though someone had scattered ashes all over the ground.

Steve twisted around to look at his wife. Sarah nodded, as if to say *yes sir, that's how it's done.*

For the next half an hour, Sarah kept the skies free of malwerns as Darius and his men did their best to keep the trolls away from the castle. Catching on to what the small group of soldiers was accomplishing, the men manning the other trebuchets stopped using pitch and began using flour.

The next fifteen minutes put a serious dent in the castle's supply of flour as explosion after explosion sounded throughout the city. Unfortunately, as long as the flour bombs continued to drop around the city, buildings continued to catch on fire. Repeating the trick he had learned during his battle with Thaden several years ago, Steve absorbed the energy from the accidental fires and kept his jhorun levels full all while torching any and all of the trolls he could see.

It still wasn't enough. Their adversaries were too numerous. No matter how many times the trolls were scared away, they kept coming back in greater and greater numbers. Sooner or later, they were going to get bold enough to attempt a run on the West Gate. To make matters worse, they were down to three bags of flour.

The sentry positioned at the top of the battlement waved a torch, attracting their attention. The trolls were massing on the other side of the gate; a direct assault was inevitable.

One of the guards, a terrified young boy, suddenly grabbed one of the last bags of flour and sprinted toward the gate. Lia, catching sight of what the guard was doing, momentarily forgot that both of them were deaf and screamed a warning at Steve. When he naturally didn't respond, Lia instructed her tiring jhorun to pick up a piece of torn sod and fling it at his head.

Lia would later swear, on her mother's life, that she didn't remember the rain that had fallen earlier in the day.

A small clump of grass, sodden earth still attached to the roots, thumped into the back of Steve's head. Before he could reach behind and grab whatever it was that had struck him, the muddy soil detached itself from its grass counterparts and fell down the back of his shirt.

Shockingly cold, the wet clump slid down his back, leaving a muddy streak across his skin. Steve whipped off his tunic and was able to twist around to grab the muddy mess before it had a chance to fall any lower. His shocked eyes landed on Lia's, who was laughing so hard she had tears streaming down her face.

He reacted on pure instinct. Clutching the handful of mud, he flung his arm toward her, much like he would if he had been throwing a frisbee. The mud landed with a wet plop right below her chin and instantly slid down the front of her shirt.

Lia gasped with shock as the mud found a very convenient resting place and settled there. Cool, calculating eyes found his and suddenly, despite the seriousness of the situation they were all in, Steve burst out laughing.

Several guards snickered.

By this time, the young guard appeared at the top of the battlement. He propped the sack up against the wall and prepared to drop it over. Steve cursed as he noticed what was about to happen.

"BAD IDEA! UBER BAD! ROYALLY BAD! DON'T DO IT!"

The terrified young soldier looked down at the rapidly approaching trolls and heaved the bag of flour over the side. The heavy bag smacked into the ground with a thud and split open, coating half a dozen trolls in a fine coating of flour dust. The soldier yanked a nearby torch from its holder. Steve sprinted the ten feet separating him from his wife and tackled Sarah and Mikal to the ground and held them down. Lia and the soldiers were already face-down on the ground.

The detonation ripped a twenty-foot hole through the wall, next to the closed gate. Oddly enough, the gate managed to remain upright. The young soldier, however, was given the ride of his life as he was blasted off the wall and thrown thirty feet from the perimeter wall.

Darius made it to the boy first. A quick look at his legs confirmed both were broken. Steve was slowly picking himself up off the ground when Sarah sat up and pointed at the jagged hole in the wall. Trolls were nimbly leaping through the opening and running straight for them.

Steve ignited both hands and was ready to send a wall of flames at them when he noticed the flour flying off the trolls' pelts. He raised a hand and aimed a short blast at the closest troll.

The troll running for him never had a chance. The flour ignited instantly and flared as the troll howled and fled the scene. Several other trolls were ignited in the process.

Half a dozen of them eyed him angrily while more of the brutes clambered through the wall to join the rest of their kind. Within moments, three dozen trolls, with more still arriving, stared hungrily at the small group of humans.

Darius pointed at Lia and two of the guards then pointed down at the wounded man. The soldiers nodded and hooked their arms under their injured companion and pulled him to the safety of the castle.

Steve looked at Lia and also pointed at the castle. For once, Lia didn't argue. She turned and sprinted across the courtyard, intent on catching up to the three soldiers.

The trolls suddenly halted their advances and sniffed the air. One began to howl. Then another. Soon all of the trolls were howling. What would make them all howl at the same time?

Curiosity getting the better of them, Steve and Sarah both checked the sky. Thankfully, they couldn't see any more malwerns. He then caught sight of movement coming up the cobbled street. Looking through the torn wall, he could see. Either something was on fire as it approached or else it might be a wagon of some type with several lit torches on it. He couldn't hear the clip-clop of a horse's hooves, but he could feel the tremors of something large that was approaching. Unless they had Clydesdales here, it had to be something bigger. He sincerely hoped it was horses.

It wasn't.

What came into view had everyone gasping with shock, Steve included. He, Sarah, and the rest of the soldiers took several tentative steps back.

The therons had arrived. Huge muscled creatures averaging nine to ten feet tall, they had dirty white fur, huge hands with three claws each, and a lower jaw which sported two-foot-long curved tusks. Protruding at least a foot and a half out from its forehead was a single curved horn. Steve briefly thought the creature could have been a cross between a unicorn and a yeti.

The procession rounded the last turn in the street and made for the Western Gate. Four therons led the pack; two were holding the front of an enormous wooden carrying chair while two more brought up the rear.

Steve and the others looked through the broken wall and stared, aghast, as the hulking monstrosities loomed closer. A single one of those things looked as though it could easily bash its way through the stone garrison. Shuffling along behind the huge chair were dozens more of the horned yetis.

Ignoring the gaping hole in the wall, the dimwitted beasts of burden lumbered up to the closed gate and waited while several more of the huge brutes approached the gate. One after the other, the therons began beating on the heavy metal grating.

WHAM! WHAM! WHAM!

Already weakened by the flour bomb, the stone ramparts finally crumbled apart and the huge metal grating was pushed over. Two dozen of the hairy nightmares stepped over the fallen gate and caught sight of the small band of humans.

Prompted by hunger, several therons lowered their heads and charged forward.

Steve shook his head in disbelief. Monsters that were capable of ripping them from limb to limb were choosing to try and run them through with their horns? How stupid was that?

A twenty-foot-long wooden beam, three times the thickness of a railroad tie, dropped in front of them and hung suspended several feet above the ground. Steve looked at his wife. Sure enough, she was clutching her amulet. Curious as to where she found the wood, Steve risked a quick glance around and spotted a pile of lumber that had to have contained spare parts for the trebuchets should one of them become damaged.

As the therons neared, one end of the large beam dropped low, forming a 45° angle with the ground. The top of the beam waggled back and forth, dropped low enough to smack the ground a few times, then rose back up. If Steve didn't know any better, he'd say the large beam was being gripped by a giant baseball player.

"Batter up," Sarah murmured.

The first theron chose to ignore the piece of lumber, costing it dearly. The beam swung back a few feet and then powered forward. The theron was forcefully knocked backwards and eventually slammed into the perimeter wall, rendering it senseless. The second theron was too stupid to realize that the wooden beam should have been treated as an adversary and approached it with the curiosity of a kitten checking out a ball of yarn.

The bat swung again. This time the theron went airborne and cleared the wall, disappearing from sight.

The trolls surged forward, eager to try their luck.

Sarah's eyes narrowed and she nodded. Her baseball game had just been preempted for a game of whack-a-troll. The wooden beam changed angles and now was held like a hammer. It began smashing the trolls into the ground much like the dragons had done to Thaden's minions during their battle with the Ylanian wizard.

Wave after wave of trolls kept surging forward, like a relentless tide. The wooden beam kept pounding away. There were so many creatures rushing her at the same time, therons and trolls alike, that it was just a matter of time before some slipped by her. Fortunately for Sarah, her husband was waiting.

With his jhorun tiring rapidly, Steve served up orders of deep-fried troll and barbecued theron, garnished with a sprinkling of malwern. However, he wasn't going to be able to keep this up too much longer.

As if sensing his thoughts, and having a very uncharacteristic change of heart, the therons ceased their attack and trudged back to the fallen gate. What trolls were left wisely chose to join their brethren still wreaking havoc through the town.

Husband and wife nervously eyed each other. Something was up. Sarah reached out to hook a finger in Mikal's tunic and yanked him over to where they stood. The teenager glanced down at the bow he had been holding. It was back to its default form of a small club.

Celestia, who had been reclining daintily on her chair while twirling a stalk of larkspur in her hand, finally stepped down to the ground. Her hand remained on the gold chain around her neck.

She surveyed the carnage. She smiled sweetly at the small

group of soldiers until she locked eyes on Steve. For a brief second her smug facade slipped and a scowl appeared. The sorceress blinked and her smile returned. Her mouth opened, but he couldn't hear what was said.

Steve touched the drop of salve inside his ear and hit it with a blast of fire. The salve disintegrated. He repeated the process for Sarah and Mikal.

"What will it be, fire thrower?" a dulcet voice asked him.

"What will *what* be?" Steve asked, looking at the woman before him.

Celestia was resting a hip on one of the massive stones that had been blasted out of the perimeter wall. She studied her adversary closely. She smiled and sadly shook her head.

"Clearly, you should not try and match wits with me, simpleton." Celestia rose to her feet. "I said that *if* the prince voluntarily comes with me now, no one else will be hurt. Should he refuse, you will deal with them."

The sorceress flicked her hand, as though she was shooing away a bothersome fly. Twenty of the horned yetis that had been waiting just outside the West Gate trudged off. Sounds of wood splintering and stones breaking drifted back to them moments later.

"My therons will level this town, and have fun doing so, until the king obeys. I will give the prince an hour to say his goodbyes. Just remember, my therons will cause a lot of damage in that time, so the sooner he surrenders, the more of the town will survive."

"Mikal will never go with you," Steve told her with a sneer on his face. "Nor will I let him, even if he wanted to."

"Spare me, fire thrower. I know you are almost out of jhorun. Powerful as you might be, you are no match for my therons."

Steve's eyes widened. How had she known that?

In response, Celestia strutted back to her litter and reached inside. Smiling triumphantly, she turned to show Steve his treasured broadsword, still in its scabbard. The jhorun replenishing crystals were presumably in their pouches as well.

"Without this, you cannot —"

Celestia abruptly cut off as an unknown force tried to rip the sword out of her hands. Belying her stature, Celestia gripped the sword tightly with both of her hands and was physically dragged along the ground until she slammed into the closest theron. In fact, her head came dangerously close to making contact with the theron's rear.

The theron turned briefly to see what the commotion was. Finding nothing significant, it returned its attention back to the small group of humans.

Hastily straightening her robe, she returned to the side of her litter and slipped the baldric over her shoulder. She glared at Steve, who twisted around to stare at the castle's main gate. There, standing just inside the gate, but watching intently, was Lia. She waved.

"Sorry!" she called out to him. "You never know until you try!"

Steve stifled a laugh and returned his attention to the sorceress.

"So, you have my sword. I got news for you, lady," he snapped out, not bothering to hide the hatred he felt for her, "I've got other ways to recharge. Observe."

A jet of fire blasted out of his right hand and streaked toward the sorceress. Celestia's amulet, swinging freely on its gold chain, sent out a pulse of blue light and her protective shield appeared just before the flames could touch her.

"Of course, there are other ways to replenish a jhorun," Celestia said dismissively, waving her hand. "Who do you think told my sister how to do it? Do not try to be clever with me. Your jhorun is almost depleted."

Steve scowled. Yes, his jhorun was fatigued. At the moment he was no match for Celestia and her amulet. The problem was, she knew it.

There was a commotion behind him. Steve turned to see the king, Rhenyon, and several people he didn't know stride purposefully toward them in full armor. Flanking the king were at least three squadrons of men. He didn't know where they had been, but the king's armor was dented, dirty, and there were trickles of blood dripping down the side of this left leg. Rhenyon looked even worse.

"Be gone, sorceress," the king curtly told her. "You have no claim on my son, nor will I give him up. Take your minions and go."

Celestia bristled with annoyance. "*I* have control over the malwerns. *I* tamed the therons. You will do as *I* say. Tell your son to step forward and we can end this."

Rhenyon had his hand on his sword. He looked ready to tear into the closest yeti. The commander hesitated and cocked his head. Keeping his eyes on the sorceress, Rhenyon addressed the king.

"Your Majesty, do you hear that?"

Kri'Entu turned irritably to Rhenyon.

"Do I hear *what*, Commander?"

"The shriek of the malwerns has disappeared."

Surprised, Kri'Entu cocked his head and listened for the telltale screeching of the winged monsters. He could hear the grunting and smashing of the therons as they rampaged through the town, but no traces of the malwerns could be heard. Even his headache was gone.

Shocked and embarrassed, Celestia jerked her hand up to grab her amulet. She silently chanted, frowning as she did so. After a few minutes, she looked up.

"What did you do? Why are there so few malwerns?"

**There would be none left if we could find them all. They are quite adept at hiding when they are afraid for their lives.**

Steve snorted and automatically looked up.

*Pryllan? What's going on? Did you guys do something to those nasty suckers?*

**Let us just say that they are quite tasty.**

*Ewww! You guys ate them??*

**Do not mock us until you give one a try.**

*Not a chance in hell, my friend. How do you feel about trolls?*

**Disgusting creatures. No dragon would ever eat a troll.**

*No, I mean if any of you see any in town, take them out.*

**Gladly. Most have already fled. Mountain trolls fear dragons above all things. Did you know there are therons about?**

*Therons, you say? Hmm, we might've noticed. Can you do anything about them?*

**They are much larger than the trolls and are harder to eliminate. I have already informed Rinbok Intherer of their presence. More dragons have been summoned.**

*How many?*

**Thirty more will be here in a quarter of an hour.**

*There are still a dozen or so therons here in the courtyard. Can you help us with them?*

**There are ten of us here now. we have already eliminated a dozen of the white creatures. several dozen more continue to roam unchecked. I would advise you to wait for the others to arrive.**

*Acknowledged. Do what you can out there. We'll deal with these guys in here.*

**Agreed.**

Steve smirked as he looked back at the sorceress. She was still chanting as she desperately searched for her winged allies. Abandoning her search, she checked on her trolls. They, too, were mysteriously absent.

Celestia's smile faded as she realized she was losing her advantage. Furious and desperate, she looked at her therons.

The huge brutes surged into action. Roaring, they brushed aside the humans in their path and thundered toward Mikal.

"Protect the prince!" Rhenyon shouted from across the courtyard. "And close the gate! Seal the castle!"

The portcullis came crashing down as the guards all drew their swords and rushed to protect the prince. The more men that flung themselves in front of the prince, the angrier the therons became. Soldiers screamed in pain as they were swatted aside like flies. Mikal, kneeling on the ground and firing arrow after arrow at the therons bearing down on him, refused to move. It took twelve shots before the theron he was shooting at stumbled to the ground. Hoping to choose more effective targets, Mikal focused on the theron's head. He sent his next arrow through the monster's eye. Enraged, the theron began thrashing about, making it more dangerous. Resigned, Mikal kept shooting arrows.

"Lady Sarah!" Rhenyon called as he dealt blow after blow

to the theron he was facing. "Get Kre'Mikal out of here! Now!"

Sarah, however, was presently preoccupied. Celestia had finally noticed her sister's amulet swinging from the neck of the female Nohrin and was throwing everything she had at the teleporter.

Celestia produced a small pouch, untied the string, and threw it at Sarah. A swarm of black beetles erupted from the tiny leather pouch and swarmed toward her.

Sarah yanked two huge stones from the broken courtyard wall and smashed them together, crushing the swarm as one would swat a fly with a flyswatter. Sarah let the stones drop.

Celestia brought up another spell from memory and chanted it into existence. Several hundred gallons of water from the moat suddenly rose into the air and sped toward Sarah.

Catching sight of an old nemesis, Sarah pulled Bredo from the moat and tossed him toward the sorceress.

Bredo's mouth was open and he hissed with delight as he watched himself soar toward a free snack. Celestia let out a high-pitched shriek of terror when she saw the half-ton serpent sailing toward her. She fortified her shield but was still slammed to the ground as Bredo did his best to wrap his coils about her. The serpent suddenly dropped to the ground.

Sarah lifted Bredo back to the moat and scanned the area, only to discover Celestia had disappeared.

She noticed that a fierce battle raged on as the castle militia engaged the therons. Darius and his team were standing over the body of a theron, its body pierced by many sword thrusts and its fur stained black from its own blood.

The king was fighting back-to-back with Rhenyon as, along with his guards, they prevented the remaining therons from entering the castle. Shardwyn had appeared and was casting spell after spell, summoning lightning, funnel clouds, earth elementals, anything he could think of to stymie the sorceress long enough to gain the upper hand.

It suddenly got eerily quiet. Too quiet. Confused, Sarah hurriedly scanned the area. Where was Steve?

"Come on, lady, take your best shot."

Sarah's head jerked around as she searched for her

husband. She'd heard him, but she still didn't see—

There he was. Standing directly in front of Celestia.

"I have had my fill of you, fire thrower. Be gone!"

An unseen force lifted Steve bodily from the ground and flung him across the courtyard. Sarah screamed a warning, but to no avail. Luckily Steve had curled into a fetal position by the time he struck the ground. Groaning painfully, he slowly regained his feet. Turning so he faced the sorceress, Steve slowly walked back to her.

Sarah rushed across the courtyard, oblivious to several therons reaching for her. Rhenyon pulled her to a stop before one of the yetis could grab her.

"Let me GO!" Sarah yelled at Rhenyon, beating her fists against his chest. "She'll kill him!"

Steve was again flung across the keep. He took even longer to get to his feet and this time, when he started to walk back to the sorceress, he had a limp.

"I can do this all day, lady. You're not getting Mikal, and that's final."

"ENOUGH OF THIS!" Mikal bellowed as loud as he could.

The raging therons paused; Celestia gloated victoriously.

"No more blood will be spilled on my behalf!"

Kri'Entu pushed through several rows of motionless guards and approached his son.

"Mikal, go inside. I will deal with—"

In his haste to reach his son, Kri'Entu came dangerously close to one of the therons. It growled threateningly and raised a mighty forearm, ready to strike.

Rhenyon yanked the king out of harm's way. On the other side of the courtyard, Steve hastily adjusted his course to veer toward Mikal.

"What the hell are you doing?" Steve snapped at him. "You need to get someplace safe and you need to do it *now*."

"There *is* no safe place for me," Mikal argued. "Whether I am here, or in your world, I am always at risk. I am tired of this. No more bloodshed. I will go with Celestia."

The king cried out in fear while Celestia smiled triumphantly.

"You can't give up now, Mikal," Steve softly told him. "There's too much at risk here. If she gets her hands on you again, then who knows what will happen to Lentari? We can't let that happen."

As their small procession neared Celestia, Steve was startled to see her rapidly glance around at the remaining therons. Nearly a dozen of the monsters remained in the courtyard. Steve paled. What was she doing?

"I think that's been long enough, fire thrower," Celestia calmly told him. She addressed her therons. "I don't trust him. Eliminate him. Now. Bring me the prince."

Three therons leapt past Celestia and rushed toward the two humans, intent on ripping Steve limb from limb. Mikal cried out a warning and lunged forward to pull Steve away. At the same time, Steve raised both hands and blasted them with everything he had left.

The instant Mikal touched Steve, time seemed to stand still.

What came out of Steve's hands looked—and felt—like it belonged on a launch pad for NASA. Flames, brighter and hotter than any Steve had ever witnessed, incinerated everything in his path. Monsters, trees, greenery, everything instantly turned to ash. The flames struck the courtyard's perimeter wall and punched through it as though it had been made of paper.

Celestia was also in the line of fire. Literally. However, her amulet flashed and the protective shield once more saved her.

Channeling all his anger and frustration into his hands, Steve torched everything in his path. Hoping against hope that the infernal sorceress would at long last be eliminated, he eased up on his fire jets and finally let them extinguish. Once his vision adjusted to the absence of light, his eyes opened wide. He watched, horrified, as an entire section of the city went up in flames.

"Watch it burn, fire thrower," Celestia gloated, flicking bits of ash from her hair. "Is that the best you can do? You cannot—"

The sorceress suddenly cried out in pain and pawed at

her throat. The amulet's protective capabilities apparently had not included its chain. The thin gold necklace had melted in the intense heat of the blast. The molten gold trickled down Celestia's neck, and her piece of the amulet, held securely in place by the gold chain for more than four centuries, started to tumble to the ground.

A look of sheer terror crossed Celestia's face and she screamed. Forgetting about the searing pain on her throat and chest, she desperately slapped at herself in a vain attempt to catch the amulet before it could fall. There. She managed to catch it just as it fell past her waist. Relief flooded through her as she straightened and looked lovingly at her amulet. If she had lost that, then she would have—

The amulet piece zipped out of her hand and landed squarely in Sarah's, who instantly tossed it to Steve.

Celestia gasped with alarm. Her body was already stiffening up. Without the power of the amulet to keep her young, she was rapidly reverting to her true age.

Everyone watched, transfixed, as Celestia aged in front of their eyes. Her skin wrinkled, turned white as snow, and then became dust. Her hair rapidly turned gray, then white, and then disappeared. Celestia literally crumpled to dust right before her eyes, and her clothes collapsed to the ground. Dust poured out of the neck and sleeves of her gown. Sarah watched as Steve leaned down to retrieve Mythrin. He gave his sword a shake to remove the dust and buckled his baldric over his shoulder.

Mikal, eyes open wide, approached his bodyguard and stared at the pile of clothes once worn by his former captor.

"What happened? Is she gone?"

"She's dust in the wind, dude."

Kri'Entu arrived and pulled his son into a hug. Feeling someone tapping his shoulder, Steve turned to see Rhenyon.

"What did you say happened to the sorceress?"

"She's turned to dust. I have her piece of the amulet, and I don't want it. I have the strongest urge to torch something. Here, you take it."

"Absolutely not," Rhenyon protested. "You need to keep it."

"Hell no. Didn't you see what happened when Mikal touched me? There's no way I want to hold on to something stronger than that."

The queen arrived, Lia hot on her heels.

"What has happened? Where is Mikal? Is he safe?"

Mikal detached himself from his father and embraced his mother.

"I am fine, Mother. The sorceress has been destroyed."

"What? How? When?"

"The chain holding her amulet melted," Steve explained, holding up the piece of amulet responsible for keeping Celestia alive. "Without it, Celestia's age caught up with her."

Sarah embraced her husband. "So it's over?"

"Yeah, but if y'all will excuse me, I need to put out one mother of a fire."

# Epilogue

"The repairs are coming along nicely."

Rhenyon nodded. "With so much of the city damaged or destroyed, it gave us the opportunity to make a few changes. Notice the West Gate? It now has an inner and an outer gate."

"Nice," Steve observed.

"It was also decided," Rhenyon continued, leading the group past carpenters and stone masons, "that the street parallel to the gate will house the new barracks. Twin barracks, on either side of the street, will run several hundred feet toward the town square. If you look toward the—"

A baby squalled, drawing the commander up short. Rhenyon turned to see Sarah's sister, Annie, pull a bottle of milk from her bag and offer it to her baby. Tristan approached and offered to hold the diaper bag, but Annie said she was okay. She then tried unsuccessfully to sling the heavy bag back over her shoulder when her hands were batted away. The strap was slid off her shoulder and the bag removed from her possession. Annie gratefully looked over at Lia and smiled.

Lia then handed the bag to her husband, Adam, whom she had brought along for this trip. Adam glanced down at the diaper bag and sighed.

Continuing the tour, Rhenyon led the group through town, pointing out repairs, new additions, and the like. As they passed through the town square, they noticed the king had chosen not to replace an entire block of burnt and damaged buildings. Instead, taking some advice from the queen, Kri'Entu had turned the land into a large park where people could sit, have lunch together, or even find a quiet place to read a book.

Deciding to leave the dog in her home world had been tough, but Mikal had decided that since there were so few dogs in the kingdom, and not wanting to risk Peanut catching some unknown disease, she would stay with Steve and Sarah. Mikal, however, had insisted on visiting every other weekend, which his foster parents were more than happy to grant.

"It's so very pretty here," Bonnie Miller observed. She turned to smile at her husband who hadn't said more than five words since stepping through the portal. "Don't you think so, Stan?"

Steve's father nodded, still too overwhelmed to speak.

As they came to the edge of the park, they saw three brand new half-timbered cottages lining the street. The first two were smaller single-story dwellings that were roughly a thousand feet square. A single gable stretched from one end of each cottage to the other. The third was styled the exact same way, only it was two stories instead of one.

"Oh, those houses are adorable!"

Rhenyon smiled and said nothing.

"For a human habitat, it is not so bad."

Stan gasped. Bonnie screamed. Adam dropped the diaper bag and took a few steps back. Standing directly behind them, watching intently, was Pryllan. Steve immediately stepped between their group and the dragon, with his hands up in a non-threatening manner.

"Everyone, this is Pryllan. As you can probably figure out, she's a dragon. She's saved our lives countless times. Whether she's rescuing me when I get lost, or taking on trolls, or even taking out therons, she's been there for us." Steve turned to the dragon. "Okay, let me make some introductions. These are my parents, Stan and Bonnie. And standing over there next to Lia is her husband, Adam."

Pryllan nodded at the three humans. She companionably joined their group as Rhenyon steered them toward the area of town Sarah had referred to as "downtown." Shopkeepers appeared, all offering their wares as the procession made their way by. One shopkeeper, selling roasted meat, stared up at the passing dragon in awe. Pulling a roasted haunch of meat from the fire, he shyly offered it to the dragon.

Pryllan hesitated as she passed the shop and stared down at the tiny morsel of meat. She lowered her head and opened her jaws, curious to see if the human would place the meat anywhere near her fangs.

Committed now to giving the dragon the meat, the shopkeeper glanced nervously around at his peers and cautiously approached. Tossing the meat up and over the dragon's lower jaw, the shopkeeper gave Pryllan a friendly smile and hustled back into his shop.

While everyone was walking back to the castle, Rhenyon slowed his pace until he drew up alongside Steve.

"Can I ask you a question?"

"Sure."

Rhenyon leaned in a little closer and dropped his voice to a whisper. "What happened to the Amulet of Aria?"

"It's safe and sound in our world," Steve answered.

Rhenyon nodded. "Excellent. No one here should ever be tempted by its power."

"That's exactly what the king said."

"Both pieces?"

Steve nodded. "Both pieces."

"Good."

When their procession finally returned to the castle, Steve and Sarah were shocked to see that everyone, including the king and queen, were waiting for them in the courtyard. Brightly decorated banners adorned the walls, fresh flowers had been planted, and everyone was in their finest attire.

"We just left the castle on this tour thirty minutes ago,"

Annie whispered to Tristan. "How did they do all this so quickly?"

Sarah shrugged, seemingly unaffected by the drastic change in appearance.

"I would say Shardwyn had a hand in it."

Introductions were made for those who hadn't been acquainted yet. Humans, dwarves, griffins, and dragons all mingled together peacefully as a sumptuous meal was served. Roast meat, raw meat, seafood, steamed vegetables, essentially every manner of food available was present for virtually every palate.

After everyone had eaten their fill, the king rose from his table and clinked his goblet several times. Everyone in the courtyard fell silent.

"We are thankful to our friends, new and old alike, for joining us today to celebrate the completion of repairs to the city. We felt there was no better way to express our thanks to the people than by having a feast. And, we must not forget to express our thanks to the Nohrin, responsible for the downfall of Celestia and thereby freeing my son from her clutches."

People Steve didn't know started clapping him on the back. He waved to the crowd and blasted several jets of fire high into the air. The crowd roared its approval.

"We also thank Lady Lia for her bravery and courage in assisting Lieutenant Darius during the malwern attack."

Lia smiled and raised her arms victoriously up into the air. Her husband rolled his eyes and grinned at his attention-loving wife.

The queen cleared her throat. She turned to a table next to her chair and picked up a small pewter box. She gave it to the king. Kri'Entu smiled as he opened the box and withdrew three keys.

"Lady Lia, if you please."

Surprised, Lia made her way to the king's podium.

"The kingdom of Idaho must be a truly amazing place," the king began, smiling as he studied the woman before him, "since friendship is valued so strongly that one friend would follow the other into the throes of war. You have shown that your compassion and loyalty to your friends is only surpassed by the size of your heart. I applaud your bravery."

Lia was, for once, speechless.

"Tristan, Lady Annie, if you please."

Annie handed Zachary to her sister and joined Tristan.

"Lady Annie." Kri'Entu smiled when he saw her. "We will never forget the kindness you have shown Mikal. You followed my son when he foolishly activated the Nohrin's portal. You stayed by his side when he was in danger. And Tristan, you have demonstrated time and time again that there was no other person suitable to be Mikal's tutor. With your expert guidance, Mikal will become a very wise king. To the both of you, we are eternally thankful."

Tristan bowed while Annie blushed.

"Sir Steve, Lady Sarah, if you please."

Sarah handed Zachary to Steve's mother. Sarah took her husband's hand and they approached the king. The queen joined her husband at the podium. Mikal appeared moments later and joined his parents.

"There is nothing we can give you," the queen began, "that adequately expresses our gratitude for loving and caring for our son all these years. You have done a remarkable job. He has grown into a fine young man." She dabbed her eyes with a handkerchief and continued on. "Thanks to the two of you, my son can finally return home."

Sarah's eyes filled. She held out her hand, open palm up, and teleported a tissue from her purse. She dabbed her own eyes and sent the tissue back.

"It has been our pleasure to help raise Mikal. He's a wonderful boy. I'm so very thankful my husband goaded me into going through the portal back when we first got the house. If it wasn't for that, we wouldn't be standing here."

Sensing that things were about to go mushy, Steve jammed his hands into his pockets.

"I've never been one to get all emotional on anyone," he began. All eyes were fixated on him. "But what I will say is that I am honored you two trusted your only son to our care. We were more than happy to help out. I'm truly going to miss him."

"Miss him?" the king repeated, frowning as he turned to his wife. "Have you not told them?"

"Told us what?" Sarah wanted to know.

"No. Be my guest, my love."

The king smiled as he turned to face his guests.

"You have no doubt noticed the three cottages adjacent to our new park, have you not?"

Everyone nodded.

"Then you have no doubt deduced who the owners are?"

Sarah squealed with delight and clapped her hands together. A little slower on the uptake, Steve looked at her. His eyes widened.

"Are you guys giving us those houses?"

"One will go to Lady Lia and her husband. Another will go to the two of you, Sir Steve. And the final house, with the extra room, will go to Tristan, Lady Annie, and their two fine children."

"Entu," the queen scolded, "you have not told them the best part yet."

"Of course, I was just coming to that. You should also know that I have made you all honorary citizens of Lentari."

Mikal leapt across the podium and hugged Sarah.

"It means you can come to visit whenever you want!"

Steve put his arm around his wife and gave her and Mikal a hug. "We just became snowbirds, didn't we?"

# Author's Note

Unbelievable. The third and final installment of the Bakkian Chronicles is officially wrapped. I've been asked over and over if there will be a fourth. It's really strange to say this, since I've been working on this series for so long, but Mikal's story is done.

Now, that being said, I should point out a few things. First, there were no plans on extending the trilogy. I thought that I'd bring the story to a close and that'd be it for Lentari. After all, Bakkian Chronicles was supposed to be a trilogy.

However … :)

Response from the fans has been overwhelming. More and more people kept asking if there will be a fourth book. So, my official answer is … No. Not in the Bakkian trilogy. But set in Lentari? Yes. There's another book in the works. As a matter of fact, I've already got the plot sketched out and I've started working on it. The Tales of Lentari was born, and now has nine books, with a tenth in the works. I should also mention to the fans of the Bakkian Chronicles that a short story does exist that takes place right between book II and book III. It's called Bakkian Chronicles — the Disneyland Debacle. I was given the honor of submitting a short story to help benefit a woman dying of cancer, and I decided to try my luck at writing a short story. It's not that long, but I will say that it was inspired by true events that happened to my wife and I during one of our visits to the Magic Kingdom. It can be found in Sweet Dreams — The Lyndsey Roughton anthology. I will also be releasing it as a free short story soon.

So. Will the fourth story feature new faces or old? The answer is … a little of both.

I started thinking about other possibilities. Surprisingly, four different possibilities leapt to mind. All would make great stories. As before, if you'd like to see what I'm working on, or else ask a question or two, I encourage you to do so! Nothing makes my day more when a fan stops by my blog to say hello.

Here's where you can find my blog: AuthorJMPoole.com. I was dragged kicking and screaming into social networking, so if you're on Facebook, feel free to add me as a friend! facebook.com/BakkianChronicles

And if you haven't heard of Goodreads, I encourage you to check it out. It's a great way for authors and readers to interact with one another and it is also a great place to find your next book! Some of my favorite books are from independent (indie) authors just like myself. Two book titles which were on Steve's bookshelf, Demon Gates and Hemlock and the Wizard Tower, are real books that I've personally read and would recommend to any fan of fantasy.

Some of my favorites are:

*Demon Gates*, by Robert Day

*Ashar'an Rising*, by Robert Day (the sequel!)

*Hemlock and the Wizard Tower*, by B Throwsnaill

*Hemlock and the Dead God Legacy*, by B Throwsnaill (the sequel!)

*The Blue Moon Detectives Collection*, by JH Sked

*Klondaeg the Monster Hunter*, by Steve Thomas

*Wind Scarred*, by Sky Luke Corbelli

*Firecracker*, by Charles R. Verhey

I've read each and every one of these books and can say that they are fantastic. Give them a try and help support an indie author!

Speaking of which, I want to thank each and every one of my fans. You guys mean the world to me. Every time someone leaves a review, whether good or bad, it helps me become a better writer and by offering more publicity. Liked the book? Didn't like it? Feel free to let others know what you think.

Stay tuned! Our favorite dwarf brothers gear up to search for the fabled lost dwarven city of Nar!

J.M. Poole

August, 2012

# Fan Submissions

Several months back I posted a request for help on my blog. The one thing I find very difficult to do, when writing, was coming up with unique names for the various characters in my stories. So, I put it to the fans. I asked for submissions. Here's what was used!

Lukas & Madisonia (dwarf children) — Vicki Willis
Venk & Tobin (dwarf brothers) — Emil
Sarkan (dragon) — Emil
Kaiya (human sorceress) — Emil & Kaiya Keefe (warriorcats)
Ehren (dwarf) — Emil
Sautin (dwarf) — Sautin
Arealin (dragon) — Sautin
Lorcan (dragon) — Sautin
Zinna became Zinn (human historian) — anonymous
Caradoc (dragon) — Bob Lee
Zabbe (dragon) — Dwayne (Lucky7)
Kylynne (human sorceress) — Dwayne (Lucky7)
Lolande (human sorceress) — Dwayne (Lucky7)
Lorinda (human sorceress) — Kaiya Keefe (warriorcats)
Aurelia (human sorceress) — Kaiya Keefe (warriorcats)

Thanks, guys! I appreciate all the suggestions! Whereas not all made it in, the vast majority did, so I truly appreciate it!!

Craving more Lentari? Breslin, Athos, and Venk return, in *Lost City* (Tales of Lentari #1). Husband and wife team, Steve and Sarah, return in *Something Wyverian This Way Comes* (Tales of Lentari #2). Don't forget to sign up for the newsletter so you'll never miss another contest, giveaway, or book release!

# ABOUT THE AUTHOR

Jeffrey M. Poole is a professional writer who writes in both the fantasy and mystery genres. His series are listed below. Jeffrey lives in picturesque Southern Oregon, with his wife, Giliane, and their Welsh Corgi, Kinsey. His interests include archery, astronomy, archaeology, scuba diving, collecting movies, collecting swords, and tinkering with any electronic gadget he can get his hands on.

In March, 2015, Jeffrey became a proud member of SFWA, the Science Fiction & Fantasy Writers of America! Jeffrey encourages readers to connect with him on Facebook (facebook.com/bakkianchronicles). Fans can also follow him online at: www.AuthorJMPoole.com. Sign up for his newsletter here.


# BOOKS BY JEFFREY POOLE
*Epic Fantasy*
## BAKKIAN CHRONICLES
*The Prophecy*
*Insurrection*
*Amulet of Aria*
Disneyland Debacle (short story)
Winter Wonderland (short story)


*Epic Fantasy*
## TALES OF LENTARI
**(Coming soon in newly edited editions!)**
Lost City
Something Wyverian This Way Comes
A Portal for Your Thoughts
Thoughts for a Portal
Wizard in the Woods
Close Encounters of the Magical Kind
The Hunt for Red Oskorlisk (short story)
May the Fang be With You (Pirates trilogy #1)
The Hammer is Strong with This One (Pirates #2)
These are Not the Stones You're Looking For (Pirates #3)
Blast from the Past

www.ingramcontent.com/pod-product-compliance
Lightning Source LLC
Chambersburg PA
CBHW032000130726

47903CB00012B/210